D1141481

A Child of Her Time

Also by Maggie Bennett

A Child's Voice Calling
A Child at the Door
A Carriage for the Midwife

A Child of Her Time

MAGGIE BENNETT

BCA

This edition published 2004
by BCA
by arrangement with Century
a division of The Random House Group Limited

CN 129234

Typeset by SX Composing DTP, Rayleigh, Essex
Printed and bound in Germany by
GGP Media Pößneck

Acknowledgements

My thanks
– to my sister Jenny Taylor for her reading, and my friend Maureen Delaney Hotham for her listening at every stage of this story.

– to Judith Murdoch, literary agent, for her constant help, encouragement and support.

– to Jane Baxter, Local Studies Librarian at the Old Town Hall, Richmond upon Thames, for her friendly helpfulness in dealing with my enquiries.

– to Terry Reagan, who was so willing to share his intimate knowledge and memories of Lambeth, including the old Hospital and the Cinema Museum.

Author's Note

The child character Claud Berridge in this story shows all the symptoms of severe autism, though this condition was not described or named until 1944 by Leo Kanner, an American doctor. Until then, such children were not distinguished from other children with severe mental handicaps, or they were mis-diagnosed as schizophrenic. Claud's symptoms are typical of severe autism, which varies enormously in degree between affected individuals, and in the 1920s his condition would have been unexplained.

Part I

A Goodly Prospect

Heavens! What a goodly prospect spreads around . . .

– James Thomson, poet, on his first sight of
Richmond in 1727

Chapter 1

All their friends and neighbours in North Camp said the same. It was the what-d'you-call-it, the cinema thing, that turned Miss Phyllis Bird away from the path of duty and on to the road to ruin. As if her poor parents hadn't suffered enough already, losing both their sons in the war.

North Camp, named for a Roman settlement on the site, had been a quiet farming district on the Hampshire–Surrey border at the turn of the century, but after the war it began to expand and learn modern manners. The old coach-works in Union Street was converted into a dark, stuffy cave where, for a penny on a Saturday afternoon, stable-lads and kitchen-maids crowded together on wooden forms to watch the moving photographs on a white-painted wall and get up to heaven-only-knew-what behaviour. And it wasn't only the lower elements: young sons and daughters of the better classes also flocked to the 'pictures', and for threepence could take a seat further back from the flickering screen, where they clapped, cheered and carried on as foolishly as the rabble at the front.

Well, perhaps not quite all of them. Rosie Lansdowne might squeal and giggle, but Phyllis Bird and Betty Goddard sat in rapt silence, seeing themselves as Mary Pickford or the new British actress, Maud Ling, in her latest picture, *On Wings of Love* – which meant that they too could surrender to the arms of Rudolph Valentino or the gorgeous Reginald Thane, lean and sardonic, one black eyebrow raised as his lips closed over the lovely Maud's . . .

And Phyllis had been such a model daughter up until then. At eighteen she had become the one and only assistant at Miss Daniells' Infants' School, next to the church, and by playing the piano, marshalling the little ones to and from the outside lavatory and generally comforting and encouraging them, she had taken a lot of work and worry off Miss Daniells' ageing shoulders. After the war she'd stayed on, living at home with her bereaved parents, taking a Sunday School class, serving on stalls at the church summer fête and the hospital garden party, playing tennis on Saturday with Rosie Lansdowne, who worked in her father's dairy shop, or cycling with Betty Goddard, who served in Thomas and Gibson's, the haberdashers. Such wholesome recreations were permissible enough, but the cinema was considered no place for a respectable young lady.

At twenty-five Phyllis Bird often wondered if her friends felt the same despairing emptiness in their lives as she did. At church on Sundays the girls would glance in the direction of the rector's son, once a golden youth but now a one-legged cripple, brooding over his memories of the Somme battle-fields where Tom and Ted Bird had fallen. At the bakehouse they would joke kindly with Silly Billy Hickory, who'd been severely shell-shocked and had a terrible stammer; he had also been permanently deafened, and you could hear his mother shouting to him all the way down Highfield Road. These had been healthy young men that the girls might have married, but were now damaged survivors of a lost

4

generation – and North Camp had fared no worse than countless other towns and villages.

Some of the bereaved families had recovered sufficiently to get on with their lives, but not Mrs Ethel Bird. At forty-six she was settling into a premature decline towards old age, as if she looked for death, though she still had her monthly inconveniences – 'the other', as she'd always called it – and its depressing regularity was a constant reminder of the happy past, the agony and the joy of bearing her two lost sons. She kissed their photographs when she lit the oil-lamps at evening, for this was a house of perpetual mourning, where the war poet's words were literally true: 'and each slow dusk a drawing-down of blinds'.

And Miss Phyllis Bird sometimes wondered how she was going to get through the next twenty or thirty years.

Miss Daniells spoke with well-meaning, if chilling, candour. 'A girl of your age is not likely to marry, Miss Bird,' she said one day during the dinner break when the children were playing outside. 'So you had better fill the life that God has given you by serving Him through good and useful work. You should go to college and get your teacher's certificate. The Board of Education would certainly offer you a grant on my recommendation. I'd miss you, of course, but you'd be coming back here as a certificated teacher.'

Miss Bird did not know what to say because becoming a certificated teacher was not what she wanted out of life. Miss Daniells looked at the clock.

'Goodness, it's half-past one. Time to call them in again.'

Morning and afternoon school each began with a hymn, and Phyllis sat herself down at the piano as

5

the children filed back into their places. She could have played the opening bars with her eyes shut.

'Jesus wants me for a sunbeam, to shine for Him each day,
In ev'ry way try to please Him, at home, at school, at play.'

The little voices rose in chorus.

'A sunbeam, a sunbeam, Jesus wants me for a sunbeam,
A sunbeam, a sunbeam, I'll be a sunbeam for Him!'

As she strummed the cheerful tune, Miss Bird felt that she simply could not stand the emptiness of her life for much longer. Yet how could she escape?

'Look, girls, here's this magazine I found at my gran's. It's called *Family Doctor*,' said Rosie Lansdowne with a giggle. 'It's got a page where you can write in and ask questions about illnesses and things – here, look!'

They pored over the section on women's matters, and then turned to the page where readers' letters were answered. The general tone was extremely severe, and some letters were considered unfit to print, so only the answers were given.

'A young man such as yourself should break this dangerous habit at once,' thundered the medical expert. 'Otherwise you will pay the price in future years.'

'What d'you think they're on about?' asked Betty, but Phyllis kept her sudden unease to herself.

'And look at this one,' said Rosie. '"We will not answer your question, as we do not discuss such distasteful matters in *Family Doctor*."'

'This one's even worse,' said Betty, and read on: '"What you are suggesting is a criminal offence, and your letter ought to be put into the hands of the police. We have destroyed it."'

'Oooh, I think I know what that might mean,' said Rosie, unusually serious. 'D'you remember Clara Hemmings, who was sent away all those months, and then came back ever so pale and quiet? My gran said it was 'cause she'd had a *baby*, though I don't know what happened to it. D'you think she might have tried to –' Rosie lowered her voice to a sepulchral whisper – '*get rid of it*? It's against the law, and you can be sent to prison.'

While the other two girls ooh'd and aah'd, Phyllis was seized with nameless anxiety. It was not only young men who were subject to worrying habits. In a life of dutifully observing the conventions she had a secret consolation that she could never talk about to a soul. *Not ever*. She did not indulge in it very often, but sometimes the craving became irresistible, and when she had to give way to it, she locked her bedroom door and lay down on the bed. And then . . .

And then it would happen, a glorious daydream, in which Reginald Thane came and lay down beside her. No longer a moving photograph on the cinema wall, he began to caress her, touching her body all over, until at last there was a wave of physical release that made her gasp and moan aloud. Only as the sensation subsided did regret and anxiety return to trouble her. Her young body, so healthy and vigorous, her womb ready to ripen and swell with a

7

child that her breasts would suckle – oh, would she ever fulfil her natural destiny, or would she grow old and wrinkled and dry without knowing the joy of marriage and motherhood? How many years would pass before she gave up hope? How would she bear it?

One Sunday after church Mr Bird took his daughter aside in the front parlour while Mrs Bird was in the kitchen preparing dinner.

'Miss Daniells came into the shop yesterday and wanted to talk to me about you, Phyllis,' he began awkwardly, for they seldom talked seriously together.

'Yes, Dad?' For some reason she felt herself blushing.

'Well, your mother's going to need you here at home, that's something we all know, but you might as well get on as far as you can with your teaching, and I agree with Miss Daniells that you ought to go to college and study for your certificate. She seems to think that you'll be able to take over from her one of these days, and of course you'll need to be able to keep yourself.' He paused for a moment and glanced at her tense expression. 'She says you'd have no trouble getting a grant from the Board of Education, and of course I'd – er, help you out, gladly, while you were at college, so . . .'

His voice trailed off, and Phyllis suddenly wanted to cry. She closed her eyes and ran her tongue over her bottom lip.

'What you're saying, Dad, is that I'd better go to college sooner rather than later, and then come back here for the rest of my life.'

'Well, I don't know about that, Phyllis, but you can

8

see that your mother's never going to be really right again, and . . .' He looked at his daughter with a kind of sympathy whilst pleading for her understanding. 'It's what you can do for your brothers now, Phyllis – in fact it's the only thing you can do for them, to look after their mother.'

'Yes, I can see what you mean, Dad.'

'Good girl.' Again there was that look of pity. 'I mean, you're twenty-five now, and time goes by, so you'd better start thinking about your future.'

What future? It almost frightened her with its blankness.

'You'll want to be independent, though you've always got a home here, and it will be yours when –' Mr Bird cleared his throat. 'You know, Phyllis, just because we lost our boys doesn't mean that we think any the less of you. In fact, I don't know what your mother would have done without you. Nor what I'd have done – you're all we've got.'

'All right, Dad, don't say any more. I'll think about what you've said. I'd better go and help Mum. She'll soon be ready to dish up.'

She thankfully made her escape, and Ernest Bird was left looking out of the window on to the quiet road, empty on a Sunday afternoon. The words had cost him an effort. With no son to take over the gentlemen's outfitters he had built up over the years, and his position as churchwarden to maintain, though his wife no longer accompanied him to church, it was not in his nature to drop his guard, to hug his remaining child and weep with her over their bitter loss. Not for him the relief of breaking down and raging against a cruel fate, of howling his grief aloud. Instead of drawing them together, the absence of Tom and Ted had separated husband and wife,

9

parents and daughter: they could not bear to talk about it.

And then the unforeseen happened. Or Phyllis made it happen, whichever way you look at it. In the post office, which was also the general store and newsagent, Phyllis saw a copy of *The Lady*, and bought it on impulse, or so she told her parents later.

'Lookin' at them posh adverts, are you, Miss Bird?' asked the postmistress with a smile. Phyllis smiled back and tucked the magazine into her shopping basket. In the privacy of her room she opened it and turned to the Situations Vacant section. The advertisement sprang immediately from the page, as if it had been waiting for her alone.

Kind and capable nursemaid required to assist Nanny with girl aged 6 and boy aged 4 in writer's West London household. Must be over 25 and have experience with young children. Good references essential. Generous terms for successful applicant.

There was a box number, and Phyllis wrote off as soon as she had secured the references of the rector and a disappointed Miss Daniells, who frankly said she hoped Miss Bird would not get the post. Within a week Phyllis was summoned to an interview at a West London employment agency, along with four other applicants, and in another week she received a letter to inform her that she had been appointed as nursery assistant at the home of the playwright Harold Berridge at Number 3 Travis Walk, Richmond. She was to commence her duties on

1 September, a Thursday, and was asked to present herself by four p.m. on the Wednesday.

She clasped the letter against her heart as her spirits soared. Miss Bird was about to spread her wings at last!

Chapter 2

Phyllis settled herself into a corner seat by the window. There was nobody else in the compartment, and she gave a long-drawn-out sigh of relief that was almost a groan. Her trunk was in the guard's van, and she closed her eyes as the train pulled out of North Camp Station; she was on her way at last.

Nobody had come with her to the station. Her father was at the shop, and her friends were also at work. Her mother had offered to see her off, but Phyllis knew that it would be painful for her, a reminder of seeing off Tom and Ted, who had never returned.

'I shall be thinking about you, Phyllis, and hoping that you . . .' Ethel Bird had hesitated behind her barrier of habitual sadness. 'It'll be very different from here.'

It had better be, Phyllis had thought grimly, but aloud she'd said, 'I'll think about you too, Mum, and I'll write to let you know how I get on. Don't worry about me, there's really no need.'

'Your father and I will miss you.'

'And I'll miss *you*, but I honestly think it will be good for me to have a change. If you ever need me, you've only to send word, and I'd come home at once.'

'Home.' Ethel Bird had sounded utterly lost. 'Home isn't the same any more, not like it was. Nothing's like it was,' she'd added, half to herself.

'Dad needs you,' Phyllis had said, feeling that she should be a little firmer with her mother. 'And without me being here, he'll need you all the more.'

'I don't know, Phyllis, we aren't the same as we were. Not any more.'

'Don't forget that he's lonely too, and he *does* need you. You really ought to try, Mum – I mean, I know it's terribly sad for you, but –'

Ethel Bird had raised her head and looked straight into her daughter's eyes. 'You *don't* know, Phyllis,' she'd said with sudden sternness. '*Nobody* knows. Nobody but a mother can possibly know. Can you cure a broken heart?'

Not for the first time Phyllis had turned away in pity and a kind of shame at this naked grief. There was nothing more that she could say; nothing that could possibly help.

Talking with her father had been somewhat easier, because he had come straight to the point and spoken his mind. 'Frankly I'm disappointed in you, Phyllis, especially after what we – what you said about looking after your mother. I never expected this.'

'I'm sorry to disappoint you, Dad, but it was after we talked that I realised I simply have to get away for a while, to have a *bit* of a life of my own before I get too . . . before it's too late. Just for a year or two. I'm not running away from my duty to Mother, I just want to see something of the world before I settle down here for good.'

'You won't see much of the world as a servant in this man's house. You were far more useful to Miss Daniells and the school than you'll be waiting on two pampered children. What on earth do they want two nurses for, anyway? Your mother brought up the three of you without any help from a nursemaid.'

Phyllis had wondered about this herself, but was not prepared to admit as much.

'It's to get some experience of a different kind of life, Dad, that's why I'm going. I *know* I'll only be a domestic servant, but it will be interesting to live in – to see –'

'How the other half lives, I dare say,' her father had broken in. 'I don't like to think of you being at their beck and call just because this man's made a little money from writing for the stage. You'll just be wasting your talents as a teacher.'

Phyllis had rolled her eyes heavenward and made an effort to be patient. 'I'll be back, Dad, maybe sooner, maybe later, but I *must* have a year or two away from – from North Camp. And you never know, Mum might even be better without me for a while. She's not fifty yet, for heaven's sake; she shouldn't live like an old woman, it's not right.'

'All right, Phyllis, let it rest, we won't argue.' He'd cleared his throat and given her a small reluctant smile. 'I dare say you'll need a few new things, so you can have twenty pounds to get yourself fitted out.'

'*Dad!* That's too good of you. I don't know what to say.' The generous gift was so at variance with his words. 'Are you sure?'

'Of course. No need to stint on my own daughter. Excuse me, I'd better go and water the tomatoes. They're looking a bit droopy.'

He had not only been as good as his word, but he had made her up a stylish dress in serviceable olive-green worsted, with a matching jacket to wear on her entry into the wider world. She wanted to thank him properly, to hug him and say she was sorry, and that she loved him, but it was impossible: neither parent would let her get too near.

14

And now, thank heaven, she was leaving it all behind her. She looked down at the smooth lines of the olive-green outfit, the fashionably low waist, deep V-neck and long jacket, all hand-stitched at Bird's Outfitters. She had spent some of the money on tan leather shoes with little Louis heels and T-bar straps, and a matching handbag with ivory handles. A long necklace of green beads and a high-crowned straw hat with a drooping brim completed the picture, and Phyllis smiled at the memory of Rosie's squeaks of admiration and Betty's round-eyed awe at such elegance. Miss Daniells had said the skirt was too short, but could not fault the general effect. Phyllis's mother had silently approved and handed over a prayer book in which her father had inscribed, 'To our daughter Phyllis, entrusted to God's care and protection, September 1921.' It was now packed in her trunk and, thinking of it, her eyes filled with tears, which she resolutely blinked away. I must look forward now, not back, she told herself. She might even surprise her parents and make them proud of her!

The train drew into Waterloo Station and came to a halt with a final blast of steam. Phyllis pulled back the sliding partition into the corridor. Two young men were alighting, leaving the door open for her to step down gingerly, holding her skirt closely round her legs.

'Need any help, miss?' asked one of the men in a friendly tone, and Phyllis thought of her trunk in the guard's van; but she was wary of accepting assistance from strangers, especially men, though this one seemed respectable enough. He was about twenty, and wore a sharp, smartly cut suit and a trilby hat over his wavy brown hair. He sported a

15

neat moustache and a cheery smile. His companion looked on with an amused air.

'Well, thank you, er . . .' faltered Phyllis, trying to maintain her self-assurance as a cool-headed modern girl. 'I do need a porter for my trunk.'

The young gentleman beckoned to a man with a luggage carrier. 'Over here, the lady needs some help. Is this the trunk, m'dear? Right, mate, take it up to the concourse.' He turned back to Phyllis. 'Where d'you want it, miss? Gettin' a taxi?'

'Oh, no, I'm travelling down to Richmond,' Phyllis explained, quite bewildered by this unexpected attention.

The young man nodded to the porter. 'Take it over to the Hounslow platform, mate, and we'll follow.' He smiled at Phyllis. 'Come on, m'dear, you're in luck today. Me and Sonny here are goin' in the same direction.'

He chuckled and led her across the concourse, which thronged with travellers all going different ways. She found herself walking between the two of them, and when they reached the platform from which the suburban trains departed, the helpful young man checked that her trunk was safely stowed on board, tipped the porter and opened the door with a flourish.

'In you get. It don't take longer'n twenty minutes. Go on, Sonny, you can sit back to the engine.' He guided Phyllis to a window seat and sat down beside her, opposite the oddly named Sonny, whose pale eyes roved over her appraisingly. It was a new sensation for her, and she knew that she ought to be offended by it, so looked away.

'It's time I introduced myself,' said her rescuer. 'Edward Ling, at your service. And Mr Stott here works with me, only everybody calls him Sonny. So may I ask what brings you to Richmond, Miss – er?'

'Bird,' she replied with a shy smile. 'And I'm going to Richmond to start a new – to work as a nursemaid.'

'Oh, very nice. Private, is it?'

'It's at the home of Mr Berridge, actually,' she said with a certain pride.

Edward Ling's dark brown eyes widened. 'What, Harold Berridge the playwright? Did yer hear that, Sonny? Very grand! Me sister knows him well. And where are yer from?'

'North Camp – that's in Hampshire, just a little place.'

'I thought yer must be a country girl with that lovely complexion. An English rose!'

A snort of laughter from Mr Stott had the effect of spoiling the compliment, and Phyllis looked demurely out of the window. To accept assistance from a stranger was one thing, but this amounted to flirting and should not be encouraged. And these two were very young, scarcely more than boys, a new generation that had missed the war.

They passed through Queenstown Road, Battersea and Clapham Junction – thickly populated streets with patches of green here and there, many churches and other big buildings; everything she saw was new and exciting. As the train rattled its way between Putney and Barnes, Mortlake and North Sheen, the views became much more rural. Phyllis surreptitiously pushed up her hat brim to get a better view of wooded hills with splendid houses set upon them. She could hardly believe that it was so close to London.

'It's like a town in the country!' she breathed, and Mr Ling nodded.

17

'Yeah, me and me sister wouldn't live anywhere else. Er – would yer pardon me, a mere male personage, if I was to offer a small suggestion, Miss Bird?' He leaned closer to her as he was speaking, and with both hands he carefully pulled her hat forward over her forehead.

'But I can't see!' she protested, laughing and blushing.

'Then yer can turn the brim up a bit at the side like this, see – only keep it down on the other side. It's the very latest look.'

After this adjustment Phyllis could see out of one eye, the other being obscured by the curving brim.

'Take me word for it, Miss Bird, that's the way they're worn now. I wish yer could see how fetchin' yer look. Just right – isn't she, Sonny?'

Mr Stott grinned, and Phyllis turned back to the window to find that they were arriving at Richmond. Even from the railway it impressed her as a beautiful riverside town.

'Come on, Miss Bird, I'll help yer down and then sort out yer trunk and get a taxi.'

In next to no time the trunk was stowed in the boot of a large cab, and Mr Ling saw Phyllis comfortably installed in the back seat. He passed some coins to the driver.

'Number three Travis Walk for the young lady,' he said to Phyllis's astonishment. 'An' take her round the top way for her to see the view. Goodbye, Miss Bird, it's been a pleasure!'

He waved his hat to her as the taxi drew away and she called out her thanks. Meeting an acquaintance of Mr Berridge had been a most auspicious start to her new life, and her sense of elation continued as the cab took her along a busy High Street, full of shops displaying quality clothes, shoes and household furnishings of all descriptions. There were high-class grocers and tempting tea-shops, all on a much grander scale than anything North Camp had to offer, and her head whirled as the cab ascended out of the town and up a steep hill, affording a wide view of the curving Thames flowing between green banks and under a finely designed bridge. Phyllis caught her breath at this first sight of the prospect from Richmond Hill in the late summer sunshine, the trees reflected in the gently moving water. Already she felt as if she were at the beginning of an adventure as yet unrevealed.

She was still enraptured when the cab drew up at Number 3 Travis Walk, and she stepped out in front of a tall Victorian terraced house with shallow steps leading up to a porticoed front entrance; other steps descended to a basement. Four storeys stretched above, crowned with an ornate stone coping.

The taxi driver had got her trunk out on to the pavement, and Phyllis was wondering if she should go to the front door, which at that moment opened and a slim woman appeared, dressed in grey.

'Miss Bird?' she called.

'Yes, er, madam,' replied Phyllis, walking up the steps, putting on a smile. The driver followed her, heaving the trunk on his shoulder.

'Good afternoon,' said the woman coolly. She let the driver lug the trunk inside the door and deposit it in the hall, which smelled fruitily of warm spice and vinegar, not unpleasant but rather unexpected.

'Leave it there,' she told him, and Phyllis gave him sixpence from her purse. Closing the door, the woman turned to Phyllis. She was pale-skinned, with fine features and greenish eyes; her auburn hair was drawn softly back into a bun at the nape of her white neck. Phyllis thought she was probably only a year or two older than herself.

'I'm Nanny Wiseman. Mrs Berridge is not at home, but I'll show you your room and introduce you to the children. Wait here while I call for Gannon.'

She went a little way ahead to a passage from which stairs led down to the basement. Phyllis stared around the panelled hall; a small table and an umbrella-stand stood on each side of the black-and-white tiled floor, and a row of hooks for coats was surmounted by a shelf piled with hats, scarves and gloves. A large mirror was placed conveniently opposite.

'Gannon! Gannon, are you there?' called Nanny Wiseman. A muffled reply came from below. 'Will you take Bird's trunk up to her room?'

The *Miss* had been dropped, Phyllis noticed; she was now an untitled nurserymaid. The nanny beckoned her to follow, and they went up two flights of stairs.

It was a beautiful house. A half-life-size reproduction of the *Venus de Milo* stood in a niche at the corner of the first landing, and the walls were covered with pictures, prints and such objects as a mounted stag's head and a shelf of silver rowing trophies. From an open door a whiff of cigar smoke added to the rich mixture of aromas in the house, and a man's voice softly called, 'Is that the Wise-Woman I hear passing?'

Phyllis saw Nanny Wiseman stiffen slightly and glance over her shoulder, though she made no reply and continued up the second flight of stairs. At the top a landing rail had been extended to a height of almost six feet and a tall gate placed across the stairs, fastened with a padlock. The nanny took out a key, opened the gate to let them through, and relocked it behind them.

'These are the day and night nurseries, and our living quarters,' she said. 'And here are Edith and Claud Berridge.' She opened a door into a large, airy room where a little girl and boy sat at a table with an aproned housemaid.

'Thank you, Williams, you may go back to Cook and her chutney making,' said the nanny with a nod, and the girl – or rather woman, for she must have been in her thirties – rose from her chair.

'Thank yer, Nanny. They been all right while yer was away.'

'Good. This is Bird, who'll be assisting me.'

The maid gave Phyllis a curious look, and left the room just as a man appeared at the top of the stairs with the trunk. Nanny Wiseman went to unlock the gate for him, saw him put the trunk into a small bedroom, then locked up behind him and the maid.

Meanwhile six-year-old Edith Berridge was taking stock of the new nurserymaid.

'Mummy says I can call you Phyllis,' she said pertly, presenting a bright little face framed in straight brown hair cut in a square bob with a fringe.

Her brother was absorbed with coloured building bricks and did not look up. Phyllis smiled at Edith and put her face down close to Claud's. He was a beautiful child with large, light blue eyes and golden hair.

'Are you going to call me Phyllis too, Claud?'

He totally ignored her. Ah well, he was only four, she thought, and turned to Edith who was drawing on a slate. Then, without warning, Claud swept all

21

the bricks off the table with a shout of, 'Piccadilly Circus!'

'Don't pick them up, he'll only do it again,' said the nanny. 'In fact, the less said to him the better until he's had a chance to get to know you.'

Phyllis nodded. 'It's all right, I'm used to young children,' she said, although the boy's reaction had caught her off guard. 'May I see my room?'

'Yes, it's the next door along. We shall take it in turns to sleep in the night nursery with the children, but your room will be private to you and must be kept locked at all times. Here's your key – have you got a key-ring?'

Phyllis opened her handbag, and immediately Claud lunged towards it, grabbed it from her hands, and ran with it out of the door and threw it with all his might over the high rail where it tumbled down the stairs, emptying its contents on the way.

'Piccadilly Circus!' he roared again, shaking the stair-rails like a caged animal. It all happened so quickly that Phyllis could hardly take it in. Nanny Wiseman shot after him, seized his hand and dragged him back to the nursery.

'Isn't he a naughty boy!' said Edith, apparently unperturbed.

'Yes, he is,' answered Phyllis at once. 'May I have my bag back as soon as possible, Nanny? It's got money in it.'

'I'll open the gate and get it for you, but first you'd better go to your room and unpack. I have to get the children's tea and settle Claud down before Mrs Berridge comes up to see them.' The nanny spoke as if nothing untoward had happened, though Phyllis felt that Claud should not be allowed to get away with such naughty behaviour. She went into her

22

room and removed her hat and jacket, running a comb through her short dark hair.

When Nanny Wiseman came in with the handbag, Phyllis nodded towards the white overall and folded cap at the foot of the bed.

'Shall I put on my uniform?' she asked. 'I don't actually start until tomorrow.'

'Yes, if you're going to help with the children's tea,' replied the woman shortly, and Phyllis thought how unfriendly she was. Never mind, the sooner she got started, the better – and if Mrs Berridge was coming up, she might as well be found at her post.

The children's tea was taken at a small table by the window. There was bread and butter with honey, an apple cut into small pieces, and fairy cakes, all served on thick enamel plates. Nanny Wiseman poured milk into mugs and tied a large towelling bib around Claud's neck; she nodded to Edith, who put her hands together and closed her eyes to say grace.

'Thank you for the world so sweet, thank you for
   the food we eat,
Thank you for the birds that sing, thank you,
   God, for everything.'

'Amen,' replied Phyllis, but before grace was finished Claud was reaching out for the bread and honey.

'Aaah! Aaah!' he yelled, stretching out his hands across the table, scraping his little chair along the linoleum floor. When Nanny handed him a quarter-sized honey sandwich he stuffed it into his mouth and reached out for more. Some milk was spilt while he gulped from the mug held by Nanny, and in a short time his bib was wet and sticky, and the floor

23

strewn with bits of apple and fairy cake. Edith chattered away as she ate her tea, but Nanny had to give all her attention to Claud, and Phyllis began to see why a nursery assistant was required.

'Careful, now, Claud, here's another piece – well done, all gone,' said Nanny, brushing away the crumbs on her apron, and wiping her hands and Claud's face on a clean tea-towel.

'You've got a streak of honey in your hair at the front, Nanny Wiseman,' Phyllis pointed out, and at that moment they heard the sound of the stair-gate being opened, followed by light footsteps across the landing.

A smiling lady appeared at the door, a picture of elegance in a peach-coloured silk dress with the fashionable low waist and wavy hemline; her light brown hair was carefully arranged in kiss curls on her forehead and cheeks, and her age might have been anything between twenty-five and thirty-five.

'Ah, what a pretty sight!' she trilled, clasping her hands together and advancing in a cloud of expensive perfume. 'And I see that our new nurserymaid has arrived – Bird, isn't it? How was your journey up from – where is it, Woking or somewhere? You really shouldn't be working already, but I see you've made yourself at home. That's good! And I'm sure that Nanny's showing you what a happy little family we have here.'

'Good afternoon, Mrs Berridge,' said Phyllis, presuming that this lady must be no other.

'Have they been good, Nanny? Has Claud eaten his tea nicely? Ah, I see that Cook has been busy baking his favourite little cakes again – lucky boy! And, Edith darling, have you got a kiss for Mummy?'

Edith held her face up for a fond kiss from her

24

mother, but Mrs Berridge did not attempt to kiss Claud, who completely ignored her. She chattered away practically non-stop, asking questions but not seeming to expect any answers. Nanny Wiseman said almost nothing at all as she whisked away Claud's bib and nodded to Phyllis to clear the table.

Edith sat beside her mother at the big table, showing her what she had drawn on the slate and written in an exercise book. Claud began to build a house with his bricks, laying the blocks one upon another, and dovetailing them at the corners. Mrs Berridge saw Phyllis watching him.

'Yes, he's a *very* intelligent little boy for his age,' she enthused. 'Only he needs very careful handling, poor darling, because his brain's ahead of his tongue, as it were, and he gets *so* frustrated when he can't express himself as he wishes.'

'He can say "Piccadilly Circus" well enough,' ventured Phyllis with a smile.

'Oh, yes, he knows any number of long, difficult words, but he has a problem in finding the right ones to exchange his thoughts with the rest of us.' Mrs Berridge smiled fondly at the little boy, who was clearly lost in a world of his own, and Phyllis was unconvinced about his extraordinary intelligence. She politely withdrew to wash the tea things at the nursery sink in a corner of the room, and after about fifteen minutes Mrs Berridge rose to take her leave.

'I'm *so* pleased that you've come to join our happy little household, er, Bird. Mr Berridge and I agreed that Claud was getting a little too much for Nanny Wiseman to cope with all on her own, especially at night when he's inclined to be restless,' she said confidingly, her long earrings shaking and sparkling. 'I'm sure you'll enjoy it here, and you'll find that there's no standing on ceremony in this house. We call the young maids by their Christian names, Cook is Cook, and the manservant is Gannon. You will be – let me see, what's your first name? – and we all call Nanny Wiseman Nanny!'

Except for Claud, thought Phyllis, who didn't seem to acknowledge anybody, not even his own mother, who continued to chatter until the very moment she left the nursery.

'If you start work tomorrow, er –'

'Phyllis, Mrs Berridge.'

'Phyllis, of course. Let me see, you'll be working with Nanny tomorrow, Friday and Saturday morning – and then you'll be in charge on Saturday afternoon while Nanny takes a few hours off – and *you* may take the afternoon off on Sunday. It will give you a chance to have a look around Richmond – only you *will* be back in time for the children's tea, won't you? Oh, and Nanny, before I forget, we're having a dinner party on Monday – nothing formal, just the Cassons and a couple of Harold's friends from the theatre, but we must be sure to have the children ready to come down and meet the guests before dinner.'

'Very well, Mrs Berridge.' Nanny's brief, unsmiling reply somehow managed to convey her complete indifference, but the lady gave a last radiant smile as she took her leave, unlocking and relocking the gate at the top of the stairs.

Phyllis was puzzled. She was not particularly impressed by Mrs Berridge, who struck her as a pretty but rather silly woman, but why was Nanny Wiseman so cold and aloof? Could it be that she resented the arrival of an assistant in her special domain? But if today had been a sample of Claud's usual behaviour, some kind of help was certainly needed. Even if the household was as friendly and easy-going as Mrs Berridge had said, it was clear that the nursery was a separate world where locks and keys were the order of the day.

By six o'clock the children were bathed, their teeth cleaned and nightwear on. Edith was easy to manage, and Claud seemed happy enough while he was in the bath, though he rebelled against being towelled down and put into his pyjamas under which he wore a folded napkin and rubber pants. Nanny Wiseman took sole charge of him.

'He knows me, so it's less trouble,' she said. 'You'll get your turn on Saturday. Besides, we want to be ready for Mr Berridge. He always comes up to say good night.'

Phyllis gave a start. 'Mr Berridge? Will he come up tonight?'

'Any minute now.'

And as if on cue, there he was, a handsome man in his late thirties, as genial and easy-going as a successful playwright and family man might be expected to be. He took a chair and Edith rushed to sit on his knee. He kissed her and looked around approvingly.

'Ah, my favourite moment of the day, even though the Wise-Woman won't let me have a cigar on her territory. Now then, has everybody been good? What's happened today, Edie?'

'We've got a new nurse, and her name's Phyllis, and she thinks Claud's a naughty boy,' said Edith with childish candour.

Phyllis blushed, and Berridge turned to look at her as if he had only just become aware of her presence.

'So! Phyllis is passing judgement on us already.

27

We shall all have to mind our ps and qs then, won't we?'

Phyllis's cheek burned an even deeper scarlet, and she tried to protest. 'But I didn't mean it quite as it sounds, sir. I'd only just met Claud, and he – he was probably upset –'

Then she saw that he was laughing silently. He was teasing her. Harold Berridge the author of *Circle of Time* and *Design for a Living Room* was teasing her, Phyllis Bird of North Camp, and enjoying her discomposure, though not unkindly. He nodded towards Claud.

'You'll observe how little notice he takes of me, his own father. If I were to stand on my head, Phyllis, how d'you think he would react?'

'Oh, Daddy, are you going to stand on your head *now*?' asked Edith, looking up at him in anticipation. 'Shall I get off your knee?'

'No, no, darling, we mustn't frighten Miss Bird, or she might fly away, and we don't want her to leave us so soon, do we?' His smile faded, and he bit his bottom lip. 'You know, Wise-Woman, I'm inclined to ask Godley to see him again, and maybe recommend one of these child specialists to give an opinion. Mrs Berridge doesn't seem to think there's any need for concern, but I'm not so sure.'

'It would do no harm to ask Dr Godley, I suppose,' replied the nanny in a non-committal way, and Berridge turned back to Phyllis.

'And what does our Arcadian shepherdess think?' he asked with twinkling eyes. 'Doesn't take much notice of anybody, does he?'

Phyllis smiled shyly. 'I really haven't had time to get to know Claud yet, sir.'

'But you must have had lots of experience with

young children at the dame school you were at. Don't tell me there weren't any oddities there!'

Phyllis thought of the many children she had encountered in seven years at Miss Daniells'. There had been the slow ones, the squints, the boy who had fits and the thin little girl whose movements were oddly uncoordinated, though she had learned to read and do sums as well as the others. Miss Daniells had coped with most of the country children who came to the school, but there had been one boy whose uncontrolled behaviour had upset the others so much that she had reluctantly asked his parents to take him away. Later he had set fire to a chicken-house and had been sent to some kind of reformatory. But this little boy was only four.

'I'd like to be a friend to Claud, sir, if I could get him to trust me. I certainly intend to try.' She glanced towards Nanny Wiseman, whose face was expressionless. 'I'll do my best, sir.'

'Well said! I shall follow your progress with the greatest interest, Phyllis.' He smiled quizzically, and put his head on one side as he regarded her. 'I see you as Phyllis the shepherdess leading your flock of sheep – no, your little lambs – over the green hills of Arcadia. Yes, that fits you very well. What did the poet say? "*Et in Arcadia ego.*" Ah, yes.'

Once again she blushed and lowered her eyes. Never before had anybody spoken like this to her – or about her. An Arcadian shepherdess! And this from *Harold Berridge*, the brilliant playwright: she was here in his house, and he was asking for her help. His pretty, shallow wife obviously didn't share his concern over Claud, and Nanny Wiseman was coldly unforthcoming – but she, Phyllis Bird, would use all her knowledge and patience to gain this little boy's trust and obedience, so that his father would thank her. For here was a man she could admire and respect, a man she could personally serve by helping his son.

Happiness swept over her in a warm wave, filling her lonely heart. She was determined to succeed. She had found her destiny: it was for *this* that she had come to Richmond!

Chapter 3

Having escaped from the restrictions of life at North Camp, Phyllis was determined to meet the challenges of Number 3 Travis Walk, not only with enthusiasm but also with enjoyment. She had no intention of being dismayed by Claud's unpredictable behaviour, nor by Nanny Wiseman's initial reluctance to let her supervise him.

'I know him, and he's used to me, Bird,' she said again in her coolly superior way. 'It's because he was taking up so much of my time that you were engaged as an assistant.'

Her management of Claud seemed to consist mainly in doing battle with him, overcoming his resistance by using force when necessary, though she never raised her voice or slapped him, even when his yells must have been heard down through the house. However, when Saturday came and Nanny got ready for her afternoon off, Phyllis had her first chance with the boy.

'Williams will be coming up to assist, but you'll be in charge of the children,' said Nanny, putting on her hat and gloves. 'Let Claud play quietly with his bricks, and don't take them out walking. They may play in the walled garden at the back of the house, but no further afield, and you must not leave them alone for a moment, do you understand?'

'Perfectly well,' Phyllis replied with equal coolness. 'I shan't take my eyes off Claud, but I want to get to know Edith as well. I hope you enjoy your afternoon, Nanny.'

A bright-eyed young housemaid called Jenny came running up the stairs to the padlocked gate as the nanny let herself out.

'Mrs Berridge sent me 'stead o' Williams, 'cause she can't stand the little perisher, Nurse Bird,' she said cheerfully. 'An' I don't mind 'im, as long as there's somebody to see to 'im.'

'Oh, call me Phyllis, and I'm so glad to have you,' said Phyllis with real warmth. 'You see, I'm determined to get to know this little boy, and make him trust me. Mr Berridge says he –'

'Oh, Mr Berridge!' exclaimed Jenny, closing her eyes as if to swoon. 'I'n't 'e *lovely*, Phyllis? We're all smitten with 'im, an' I can see *you* are an' all!'

Phyllis was a little disconcerted by this, but smiled and said yes, Mr Berridge seemed very nice, and she was sure he would be pleased if Claud could learn to say 'Daddy'.

'Now, Jenny, will you clear the children's dinner table, and keep an eye on Edith for me, because I'm going to sit down with Claud and try out some ideas of my own.'

Jenny watched with interest while Phyllis talked quietly to the boy as he played with the building bricks on the big nursery table. She asked him questions and tried to place a brick here and there, which made him give a warning growl. She smiled, she cajoled, she called Edith over to play 'Pat-a-cake, pat-a-cake, baker's man', and tried to make Claud hold up his hands and play it with her, but it was all to no avail. He pushed away her hands, and met her smiles with a long, hard stare in the opposite direction. He absolutely resisted meeting her eyes,

32

and twisted his head and his whole body away from her to avoid it; and there, she thought, might lie the key to opening up his solitary little heart.

'At least 'e's bein' *good*,' commented Jenny revealingly. 'Yer want to see 'im when 'e gets in a paddy!'

But Phyllis already had. The previous evening when Nanny Wiseman had interrupted his brick-building to say it was time to get undressed for bed, he had resisted with all his strength, kicking and clawing, howling like a terrified animal; he had even sunk his teeth into Nanny's wrist, and she had abruptly shaken him off with a frown, though she had not said anything either to him or to Phyllis, who was watching in perplexity.

'He's just like a cornered rat, Nanny,' she had said. 'Whatever does he think you're going to *do* to him?'

'He'll calm down when he gets in the bath,' replied Nanny, and sure enough, when he lay back in the warm water and could splash his legs up and down, it was as if the tantrum had never been.

'Come on, Jenny, we'll take them out in the garden for an hour. It's a lovely day, and the fresh air will do us all good,' said Phyllis, giving up the attempt for the time being. She would have to bide her time, she told herself, and use her influence with Claud whenever the opportunity arose.

Sunday morning offered her just that. The Berridge household trooped off to St Matthias' Church at the end of Friars Stile Road – except for Mr Berridge, who was working in his study; Cook, who was getting the dinner ready; and Nanny Wiseman, who was busy doing some last-minute sewing in preparation for Edith's return to school the following day. Mrs Berridge was 'dressed up to the nines', as Jenny

33

whispered to Phyllis, and smiled around at everybody as she took her place in her usual pew. Edith was next to her, then Claud with Phyllis on the end. Gannon, Williams and Jenny sat separately, nearer the back.

The service was the usual matins, and the church was full of Sunday worshippers. Claud was reasonably docile while the choir and congregation were singing, but he started to get restive during the prayers, and when the vicar got up into the pulpit for the sermon, he became seriously fidgety. Phyllis tried to shush him, and tightened her hold on the reins he always wore when outdoors, when, to her utter dismay, he let out a shout: 'F'r ever and ever, Amen!' She glanced at Mrs Berridge, who continued to gaze raptly at the vicar, apparently oblivious of anything else but his words. Heads turned in their direction, and Phyllis tried to sit Claud on her knee. He began to struggle furiously, and the next thing she knew was that a smiling man in a well-cut dark suit and bow tie had come from across the aisle and was bending over her and the boy.

'Take the little monster out, my dear!' he whispered, and Phyllis had the impression that he was trying not to laugh. Without further ado she led Claud out of the west door, followed by the gentleman.

'You'd better take him home,' he said kindly, 'and don't worry, I'll tell Mrs Berridge. Now then, young Master Claud, you've caused enough of a stir for one morning, so behave yourself. Do keep a firm hand on those restrainers, my dear. Off you go!'

'Thank you very much, er – sir,' said Phyllis, wondering if he was a churchwarden, though his jaunty tie did not really go with that office; he obviously knew the family.

When the others returned from church, nobody said a word about the disturbance, at least not to Phyllis. It was as if they all pretended that Claud was not really naughty at all, and she found it puzzling. Still, she had her afternoon off to enjoy, and as soon as Sunday dinner was cleared away she eagerly changed into her olive-green dress and jacket, setting her hat at the fashionable angle recommended by the helpful Mr Ling.

'Do I leave by the front door?' she asked, and Nanny shook her head.

'We only use the front door when we're with the children. You'll have to go down to the kitchen and come up the basement steps to the entrance. And make sure you're back by five.'

Once out on to Richmond Hill, Phyllis's spirits rose. To her left the road continued to climb towards the summit, where a huge building project was in progress; directly below her lay the Thames, half hidden by trees and riverside mansions, and to her right at the bottom of the hill the centre of Richmond beckoned. Phyllis inhaled deeply as she made her way down towards it. The very air was good to breathe, and she filled her lungs, a butterfly emerging from its half-life as a grub.

Being Sunday, the shops were closed, as were the innumerable tea-shops throughout the town, but there were plenty of afternoon strollers, young couples, pairs of girls and families out for an airing with their children. In Hill Street Phyllis caught sight of a cinema, a proper one with steps leading up to a foyer and an auditorium built behind it. She smiled, remembering Union Street and the flickering screen she had watched with Rosie Lansdowne and Betty Goddard: what would they make of a grand place like this, the New Royalty Kinema? And wouldn't it be fun to go to the pictures with a friend? Perhaps young Jenny would come with her one day if they could both get the same time off.

In George Street she gazed at the displays in the windows of Gosling's department store, and the expensive shoes in Lilley and Skinner's. What would her mother say to such luxury and variety, compared with the little row of mainly family-owned shops in North Camp Parade? At the thought of her sad, black-coated mother, Phyllis felt a pang of unease – not quite regret, and certainly not guilt, for she had no desire to return; it was more like a stab of pain at the cruel pity of it all. Surely Richmond too had been touched by the war, yet on this sunny Sunday afternoon, apart from a one-legged ex-serviceman selling ice cream on Bridge Street, there seemed to be little sign of it. All around her were ladies dressed in the same stylish fashions as in the shop windows, their pointed toes tapping daintily on the pavement, their red lips smiling as they greeted each other: it was a different world.

She turned off down King Street and through a narrow paved court at the end, and found herself facing a broad, open green expanse, surrounded by gracious eighteenth-century houses. A little further on she came to a smaller adjoining green, and there before her was the Richmond Theatre, a beautifully proportioned building with an elaborately carved archway over the entrance. Although closed for today, it seemed to be a meeting place for a group of ladies and gentlemen, who were chatting and smoking around a bill-poster advertising autumn productions and the pre-West End premiere of *Key to Tomorrow*, the latest play by Harold Berridge. Phyllis caught the name of her employer, and somebody made a remark about him being the new Shaw; her heart beat a little faster because she actually *knew* Mr Berridge and his children. She imagined herself smiling and telling these people (with a slightly superior air) what a lively, amusing man he was to talk to. The bit about the Arcadian shepherdess she would keep to herself, of course, a warm, glowing sensation that nobody else could share. Nanny Wiseman had heard him say it, but she hardly counted.

It was time to start retracing her steps, and she left the Green by Friars Lane, which took her down to the waterfront. Here all was bustling activity, with ladies in their Sunday finery parading up and down the riverside walk, and half the population seemed to be out on the sun-dappled water in small boats. Phyllis stood and drank in the scene, knowing herself to be a part of it, for she lived here now. If it were possible to fall in love with a place, she thought, Richmond had her heart.

A group of Salvation Army musicians were standing in front of the Assembly Rooms, and when they struck up with 'Amazing Grace', Phyllis noticed a little cluster of sedately dressed ladies standing nearby; they were giving out tracts with an air of dedication. As she watched, one of them came over to speak to her.

'Good afternoon, madam – please excuse me, but you look like the sort of lady we are trying to recruit to help us with our work,' she said pleasantly. 'May I tell you about the sort of things we do?'

'Er, yes, by all means, though I'm afraid I haven't much time,' Phyllis replied. 'Are you with the Salvation Army?'

'Oh, no, though we're taking advantage of their music to attract attention,' smiled the young woman, who had a sweet face and was about the same age as Phyllis. 'We're the Ladies' League of Christian Befrienders, though we usually just call ourselves the Befrienders. We work with young girls, you see, mainly from the servant class, and especially those brought up in orphanages. They've never known a mother's love and care, and it's all too easy for them to be – well, tempted by a certain type of man. Even those employed in the houses of the well-to-do can be in moral danger, and we try to offer them friendship and guidance.'

'Oh,' said Phyllis. 'Oh, I see.' In fact she saw that thanks to her father's high-class tailoring the young woman had mistaken her for a lady of means, with time on her hands to spare for good works. She supposed that she should feel flattered, but in fact she was distinctly embarrassed. The young woman was still talking.

'Of course, some of them have already fallen into disgrace, and we have members of the Befrienders who go to visit mother-and-baby homes and give what comfort we can, and sometimes a little practical help with getting a new place.' She paused, cleared her throat and went on earnestly, 'Our aim is not to condemn these unfortunate girls, you see, but to bring the love of the Lord Jesus into their lives – to show them that they can be forgiven and make a new start. We meet on Monday evenings at Mrs Wright's home on Queen's Road, and we'd be very happy to welcome you. Our meetings start at seven thirty.'

Phyllis could not help seeing a comical side to this encounter. 'Thank you. I haven't really got the time to give to your, er, your league of ladies at present, but I'll bear it in mind for the future,' she said with what she hoped was the right balance of dignity and goodwill. 'I'll take one of your leaflets.'

And putting the tract in her bag, she hurried away up Richmond Hill, back to her humble service in the house of a well-to-do employer. And she was more than content to be a servant *here*, in the home of the famous playwright, hearing his voice and laughter drifting up the stairs like the delicious aroma of his cigars.

Phyllis's duties involved the sweeping and dusting, mopping and polishing of the third floor, a self-contained apartment comprising the day and night nurseries, two small but comfortable bedrooms for Nanny and herself, a bathroom, a linen store and a broom cupboard, all of which were kept locked against Claud's marauding invasions. She also had the care of the children's clothing, the ironing and mending. She became better acquainted with the two housemaids, Williams, who was a dour-faced war widow, and Jenny, who brought up the nursery meals in covered dishes and made no secret of her feelings for the master of the house.

'I reckon 'e's lovely, Phyllis, don't you? 'E calls me little Jenny Wren an' says ever such nice fings abaht me eyes an' me 'air. Nearly made me drop me tray on the stairs, 'e did!'

When Edith commenced the new term in the infants' class at Holy Trinity School for Girls in Princes Road, Phyllis accompanied and fetched her, which made a pleasing break in each day. Edith was a rather self-consciously 'good' little girl, who liked to show off her achievements and did not seem to resent the attention given to Claud. 'He's a naughty boy, isn't he, Phyllis?' she would remark with a certain satisfaction, though Phyllis kept her own counsel and watched him. He seemed totally unable to direct his energy into the usual children's games and activities. As well as his fascination with his building bricks and his periods of staring blankly at nothing, he would suddenly climb all over the nursery furniture, swing on the curtains, turn taps on and desperately search for an opportunity to escape, to climb up to a window or scale the locked stairgate. He usually allowed himself to be dressed and washed, have his hair combed and his teeth cleaned, but sometimes he would unaccountably resist, struggling violently and shouting meaningless words. He would sweep the bricks and any other objects off the table, and at meal times the crockery would go flying if he was not securely restrained in his chair. Some nights he would roam around, refusing to settle or stay in bed, so either Nanny or Phyllis had to sleep in the night nursery.

Mrs Berridge appeared to be completely blind to her son's behavioural problems, and gave the nursery staff little or no help with him. Her time was spent fluttering and twittering around the house like some exotic bird, holding afternoon 'At Homes' in her drawing room, where she would entertain friends with her piano playing and singing. Phyllis thought her completely idiotic, unworthy of such a distinguished husband, but she kept these thoughts to herself, and behaved towards the lady with the same cool politeness she showed to Nanny Wiseman.

And she had her reward in Mr Berridge's evening visits to the nursery.

'Well, how's he doing, Wise-Woman? Has the shepherdess had any luck yet?' he asked, kicking off his shoes and putting his socked feet up on a nursery stool.

Nanny did not answer, so Phyllis replied shyly, 'I think the secret is to make Claud look into your eyes, sir. And I do try to hug him, even when he resists it.'

Berridge turned his full attention on her at once. '*Really?* And is that what you've been doing, Phyllis? Well, go on, then, show me, show me!'

Phyllis approached Claud, who was sitting at the table with his bricks as usual.

'Look at me, Claud,' she said. He ignored her.

'I said *look* at me, Claud. Are you going to be a good boy for Phyllis?'

Again he showed not the slightest response, and she bent down, putting her arms around him. He began to whine and struggle. For a four-year-old he was quite strong, but Phyllis, conscious of Berridge's eyes upon her, pinned his arms to his side and spoke firmly.

'Look at me, Claud – no, this way, *look at me*. LOOK AT ME!'

Holding the back of his head, she forced him to look straight at her, eye to eye. Berridge held his breath. Nanny's face was expressionless. After a long, long minute in which Phyllis did not relax her grip on the boy, he looked at her at last and seemed to give up the fight. It was recognition of a kind.

'Good boy,' she said breathlessly, releasing him but keeping a firm hold on his hand. 'Now go to your daddy over there. Your *daddy*.'

She led him towards his father, who had got up from his chair and was holding out his arms. 'Well done, Claud! Come and give your daddy a kiss. Good boy – my good boy.'

Without actually responding, the boy allowed

himself to be hugged and did not try to break free. Suddenly he looked up and shouted, 'Go by the Piccadilly Lion! The Piccadilly Lion!'

Phyllis saw that Mr Berridge's eyes were full of tears. 'If only he could be taught to show some human affection, just a little interest in us, his parents, I'd be so grateful,' he said in a low voice. 'The eyes are supposed to be the windows of the soul – what do you think, Wise-Woman?'

'I'm not sure that it's wise to use force,' murmured the nanny.

'But if it gets results –' He broke off and gave Phyllis a look of sheer gratitude; she smiled back with joy in her eyes. It was a telling moment between them, after which he quickly left the nursery.

Phyllis would have liked to share her thoughts about Claud with Nanny Wiseman, but the woman's face was closed and unsmiling. What on earth was the matter with her, Phyllis wondered; what possible reason could she have for being so unforthcoming, so downright unfriendly? Did her disdainful silence reflect her contempt for them all – Mr and Mrs Berridge and no doubt Phyllis too? If that was how she felt, why did she stay?

Refusing to show that she minded – for why should she care about Nanny's opinion after seeing the open gratefulness in Harold Berridge's eyes for her and her alone? – Phyllis turned her attention to getting the children ready for bed, and was soon listening to Edith gaily chattering in her bath.

'You're smiling, Phyllis,' said the little girl. 'Is it because you're happy?'

'Yes, dear, I think it must be,' she answered, hugging the exultation in her heart.

And when at last she fell asleep that night, it was

the master's face she saw in her mind's eye, and his voice she heard in her dreams.

Over the next few weeks Nanny Wiseman gradually let Phyllis take on more of Claud's care and supervision. At times she thought that he was possibly becoming more aware of her, but it was difficult to be sure. Occasionally he would join in tunelessly with her singing of 'Over the Hills and Far Away' or 'Pop Goes the Weasel', though Nanny frowned and covered her ears with her hands in protest at what she called the noise; but without any support or encouragement apart from Mr Berridge's smiles and compliments on his nursery visits, Phyllis found the little boy distinctly unrewarding as a charge. He showed no affection, and the daily struggle to gain his attention, let alone his obedience, was uphill work.

'Me an' Williams don't know 'ow yer stick it,' declared Jenny. 'What wiv that little 'orror, and that ovver one – 'er wiv a face to turn milk sour. Don't yer get lonely sometimes, Phyllis?'

'No, not really. It's more interesting than what I was doing before,' Phyllis insisted, though she had to admit to herself that if it were not for Harold Berridge and her determination to win his son's heart, she was sometimes discouraged by her lack of progress with the boy.

And then towards the end of September something happened that raised her spirits considerably. A surprise meeting opened a gateway to yet more new horizons, though it began inauspiciously enough.

'You haven't forgotten that we're entertaining the Twickenham people on Friday evening, have you, Nanny?' trilled Mrs Berridge. 'So *very* amusing –

though it's as well that the films are silent, when you hear that dreadful accent of hers! But she's devoted to Harold, and *loves* to see the children, so make sure they're ready to come down to the drawing room at seven.'

Nanny was tight-lipped as she gave Phyllis her instructions. 'They can go down in their dressing gowns and slippers. It means that their tea and everything will be an hour later than usual, and Claud will be tired and irritable. However, those are the orders.'

'Couldn't they have their tea at the usual time and rest for an hour before bathtime?' suggested Phyllis. 'Or afterwards?'

'No, I don't want them to fall asleep and then have to be woken up to go on parade,' replied the nanny shortly. 'Tomorrow's Saturday, and they can sleep late – that's if Claud ever gets to sleep tonight after all the excitement.'

Phyllis wondered if Mr Berridge would make his usual visit to the nursery, but Jenny told her that he was having a bath and shaving before receiving his guests.

' 'E don't 'alf look a toff in 'is evenin' get-up, Phyllis – an' *she'll* be all done up in frills an' fevvers – cor! All right, Nanny, I'm jus' goin',' she added quickly, picking up the tea-tray and heading for the stair-gate.

As seven o'clock approached Nanny Wiseman seemed unsettled, and finally told Phyllis that she had a headache and would go to lie down for a while.

'*You* can take the children down, Bird. It means keeping a firm hold on Claud. Now's your chance to show them all how clever you are with him.'

'Very well, Nanny,' replied Phyllis, ignoring the shaft of sarcasm and inwardly delighted at the prospect of seeing the Berridges in full evening regalia and meeting their amusing guests at close range.

They heard the clock on the first-floor landing strike seven.

'Right, children, who's coming downstairs with me to see Mummy and Daddy and their friends?' asked Phyllis, who had put on a clean starched apron and adjusted her cap.

'Me!' cried Edith, jumping up from her chair, while Phyllis took hold of Claud's left hand and led them through the unlocked gate and down the stairs to the drawing room. The door was open, and half a dozen people stood around with glasses in hand, laughing and chattering. Phyllis paused on the threshold with a child on each side of her.

Mrs Berridge stood close by, talking to a large middle-aged lady with three rows of pearls and a haughty expression, but Phyllis's eyes searched for the master, and found him beside a slim and extremely attractive young woman dressed in a diaphanous gown that seemed to float around her, all pink and mauve and blue. A wisp of gold-threaded gauze encircled her fair hair, the ends hanging down on her bare shoulders. Huge outlined eyes looked out of a porcelain-pale face, and her red mouth was painted in a perfect Cupid's bow. Phyllis caught her breath, for this vision was none other than Maud Ling, the film actress and star of *On Wings of Love*!

'Oh!' Phyllis did not realise that she had exclaimed aloud, and heads now turned to look at her and the children.

'*There* they are, the darlings!' cried Mrs Berridge, holding out her arms to Edith, who ran towards her.

45

'The moment we've been waiting for – my most prized possessions!'

And then it all happened. In her astonishment at seeing her idol in the flesh, Phyllis relaxed her grip on Mrs Berridge's other prized possession, and off he flew, straight for the actress, grabbing at the thin, silky material of her gown and bunching it in his hands.

'Over the hills and far away!' he roared, while Miss Ling tried to fend him off and a horrified Phyllis rushed after him, tugging at his dressing gown.

'Claud, let go *at once*,' she pleaded, and as usual he took no notice.

'Hey, stop that, young man!' shouted his father. 'Stop it, d'you hear me?'

'Where's Nanny? Why isn't she here?' demanded Mrs Berridge.

In the middle of the clamour there was an awful tearing sound, and a whole panel of Miss Ling's gown was ripped away from the skirt. Claud waved the piece of material, and Phyllis thought she must be in the grip of a nightmare; she was on the verge of tears as Mr Berridge frantically apologised to the actress.

'My dear Maud, I'm so terribly sorry. If it's possible to have it mended professionally –' he began, but his wife broke in with a mother's pathetic plea.

'He gets *so* excitable, and the new nurserymaid isn't quite – she doesn't yet understand –' she wailed, while the other guests exchanged glances, raised their eyebrows or tactfully looked away to hide their amusement.

'Oh, I'm so sorry, Miss Ling,' muttered Phyllis, hanging on to Claud's arm as he squirmed in her

46

grasp. 'It was my fault for letting go of him.'

Miss Ling smoothed her hands down over her depleted gown, and made a little grimace.

'All right, don't worry, duck, plenty worse troubles at sea,' she said, and, turning to Mr Berridge, she cut his apologies short. ''Nuff said, 'Arold. Me 'ousekeeper'll soon sew it back in – she's a wizard wiv the ol' Singer. Can I 'ave anuvver drink? I went an' spilt the first one.'

Mr Berridge hurried to refill her glass, and if Phyllis hadn't been so shaken by the social disaster, she might have been taken aback by the rich cockney vowels from such an elegant creature, followed by a broad, unladylike wink in her direction.

'Orf yer go, duck, take 'im upstairs 'fore 'e does any more damage, an' leave the little gal dahn 'ere to charm us all. Least said, soonest mended, eh?'

Phyllis managed a whispered 'Thank you', and made her exit with a subdued Claud, who had been prevailed on to yield up the piece of torn silk. Dreading Nanny Wiseman's questions, she was relieved to find her still resting in her room, and when she later reappeared, pale and silent, nothing was said. Tomorrow would be soon enough to recount what had happened, and Edith could be relied on to fill in the details. Phyllis sighed, suspecting that Nanny would not be entirely sorry to hear about the fiasco – in fact, not sorry at all.

But that was not the end of the matter. Shortly before ten there was the familiar scraping of a key in the lock, and Williams stood at the nursery door.

'Phyllis is to go dahn an' see Miss Ling,' she announced.

Phyllis, about to get ready for bed, looked at her in alarm. 'Heavens, Williams, what's the matter now?'

47

'I dunno.' The woman shrugged. 'The missus jus' sent me up to fetch yer to see Miss Ling,' she repeated in the same flat tone.

What new ordeal was this? Was she to be seriously reprimanded, or – heaven forbid – dismissed? She braced her shoulders and descended to where the guests were putting on coats and making their farewells. Maud Ling was half listening to the well-built lady with the pearls, and a young man was doing his best to speak to her, but she turned away from them to give Phyllis all her friendly attention.

'I 'ope I ain't got yer into trouble, duck, 'cos of all the upset earlier on.' She took Phyllis's arm and led her aside from the others. 'I 'eard the Berridges 'ad got a new nursemaid, an' I felt sorry for 'ooever it was – now I'm even sorrier. 'As 'e settled dahn, the little devil?'

'Yes, thank you, Miss Ling, he's fine,' Phyllis said gratefully.

'Fank Gawd for that. Nah, listen, d'yer go to the pictures?'

'Oh, Miss Ling – I love them, and I've seen every one of yours,' answered Phyllis, hardly able to believe her ears.

'Good, I 'ad a feelin' yer might. Can yer get time orf one Sunday afternoon, to come over to tea an' a little film show? I live in Montpelier Row, orf Richmond Road, ovver side o' the river. It's a nice place; the 'ouse is called Florizel.'

Phyllis's brain whirled, and again she had the sensation of dreaming, except that this was no nightmare. 'Thank you, Miss Ling, I'd love that. I – I'll ask Mrs Berridge about a Sunday half-day,' she stammered.

'I'll speak to Cynfia Berridge meself if yer like, duck. Make a nice change for yer, I dare say. Just let me know when, an' I'll get me bruvver to fix up a show. So long!' She turned back to the lady whose flow of words had been interrupted. 'Sorry abaht that, Mrs Steynes – an' George. What was that yer was sayin'?'

Tired as she was, Phyllis found it difficult to settle that night, and her wakefulness was not due to her mismanagement of Claud, because look where it had led her! She, Phyllis Bird of North Camp, was invited to tea with Harold Berridge's friend *Maud Ling*, the glamorous star of the cinema screen! And what was more, she instinctively liked the actress, a girl probably from a humble background who had made good and was not ashamed of her origins.

Yes, this was a new opening indeed, an undreamed-of opportunity to see more of the world. For how could Phyllis foresee that it was another step closer on the road to ruin?

As soon as Dr Godley appeared in the nursery with Mr Berridge, Phyllis recognised him as the man who had come to her rescue in St Matthias' Church. Edith was at school and Mrs Berridge out shopping when he made his morning call, and Mr Berridge clearly regarded him as a family friend.

'I'll tell Cynthia that you just dropped in to see how he was doing, Charles,' said the playwright in front of the nanny and nurserymaid, and Phyllis saw this as a deliberate move to avoid his wife's barrage of silly chatter, and that he also expected them to back him up in his little white lie.

Sharp, humorous eyes twinkled behind the doctor's spectacles as he nodded to Phyllis.

'I hear that you're well experienced with young children, my dear. And how are you enjoying life in the home of the illustrious Harold Berridge?'

'Very much, thank you, Doctor.'

'Good! I've heard excellent reports of your handling of Young Master over there with his building bricks. Now, then, I want you to pretend that you're alone with him. Don't mind us, we'll just watch from the sidelines. Come and sit down with us, Nanny, and we'll argue for and against this Gandhi fellow, who wants to turn us out of India. Or shall we stay nearer home, with Mr Michael Collins, who wants to turn us out of Ireland? What should we do, get out or stay put? All right, Miss Phyllis, you just carry on.'

Phyllis spoke quietly to Claud, asking him what he was building and lightly laying a hand on his shoulder. At first he took no notice, but all of a sudden he jumped up, taking her by surprise as he had in the drawing room; too late she put out a hand to seize him, only to be shaken off as he shot over to where the other three were sitting. He hurled himself at the doctor and took a swipe at his glasses, which flew across the floor.

'Hey, steady on, young man!' protested Godley, but Claud leaped on to his lap, shouting something unintelligible while beating at the doctor with his fists and kicking with his feet. Nanny Wiseman jumped up to intervene, but Godley held the child tightly, raising his voice above the uproar.

'Now, now, that's enough! Stop that, d'you hear me, *stop it*! Be quiet! I shall hold on to you until you do, so you might as well do as I say.'

The shouting and hammering with hands and feet went on for another ten seconds or so, and then the child's body went limp, as if he had given up the fight.

'That's better. And you'll stay here on my knee while we all take a big breath and calm down. Dear me!' The doctor's hair was awry, his bow tie askew and his silver watch dangled from its chain. 'Just as well my other patients can't see me, or they'd say I'd been indulging in your excellent port, Harold. Can somebody retrieve my glasses? I can't see a thing.'

Phyllis shamefacedly picked up the spectacles, one side of which had been shattered. Godley replaced them on his nose.

'Thank you, my dear. I'll have to make do with one eye for now. Yes, Harold, we shall have to talk. A referral will certainly have to be made. It can't be put off any longer. There's a specialist at Great Ormond Street . . .'

Berridge looked stricken. 'Of course, Charles, we'll go down to the study. I'm so sorry about the . . . perhaps a glass of port would actually be a . . .'

'A very good idea, certainly. Right, young man, back you go to Miss Phyllis.' The doctor rose from his chair, smiled and thanked the nanny and nursemaid for their co-operation, and followed Mr Berridge out of the door.

Phyllis's heart ached for her master as she thought of the decisions that lay ahead; the unwelcome news to be broken to Cynthia Berridge. It was impossible to teach their son to behave like a normal child. He lived in a world of his own, unable to understand or to be understood, and totally without love for anyone.

And she longed – oh, how she longed to comfort his father.

Chapter 4

Not until the third Sunday of October was Phyllis able to accept Maud Ling's invitation and escape from the strained atmosphere of Number 3 Travis Walk. It had taken Cynthia Berridge a long time to forgive her husband for going behind her back, as she saw it, in the matter of Claud. He did not tell her of Godley's visit until an appointment had been made with an eminent child specialist at the Hospital for Sick Children in Great Ormond Street, to which Nanny Wiseman accompanied the boy and his parents.

Mr Berridge's face was grave on their return, and although the nanny said little or nothing, he talked freely to her and Phyllis on a late evening visit to the nursery after the children were in bed. In a private interview he'd had with the specialist, the great man had not been hopeful; he had encountered a small number of other children with this strange inability to relate to people, he said, even those closest to them, and they became more difficult to deal with as they grew older and bigger. There was no known cause or cure, and the majority of such children ended up in institutions for imbeciles, though he added that they were not necessarily unintelligent, and often showed an unusual aptitude for subjects like music, drawing or mathematics; but they seldom learned to communicate by speech, and by no standards of behaviour could they be called normal.

Dr Godley was advised to prescribe a sedative, syrup of chloral, to be given as necessary, and especially at night when Claud would not settle to sleep, and the suggestion was made that the boy might attend for two or three days a week at the Agincourt School in Twickenham, which took backward boys from the age of four.

Mrs Berridge hysterically dismissed the specialist's gloomy prognosis as nonsense, but her husband insisted that the sedative be given at Nanny Wiseman's discretion, and that Claud be enrolled at the Agincourt School forthwith, attending two days a week. Phyllis was detailed to escort him in the Berridge car, driven by Gannon, and she was finding it difficult, to say the least; only her secret devotion to Harold Berridge enabled her to cope with a situation that showed no signs of improving. If only there were somebody she could talk to, a friend's listening ear to share her thoughts! Nanny remained annoyingly remote, and Phyllis felt that she should not discuss the Berridges' private business with Williams or Jenny, though they were full of sympathetic curiosity.

But never mind, today she was on her way to Maud Ling's home at last, and Nanny had said she need not return until ten. Sweet freedom for a few blessed hours!

Crossing the bridge, Phyllis turned into Richmond Road and soon came to a wide green expanse stretching off to the left, with a stately white mansion in the distance; another quarter of a mile brought her to Montpelier Row and a terrace of fine Georgian houses, one of which had the word 'Florizel' worked into the metal of its wrought-iron gate. This was it! Phyllis reminded herself that she had been invited, and rang the doorbell.

She was confronted by a large, rather formidable lady of about fifty, dressed in lavender-coloured silk. Her dark, heavy-lidded eyes took in the visitor, and she nodded.

'Ah, you are this Miss Phyllis, yes? Miss Ling waits for you,' she said in a deep voice with a strong foreign accent. 'Come this way, if you please.'

Phyllis followed her into a spacious, high-ceilinged room with a French-casement door open on to a garden with a distant view of the riverbank. On a chaise longue heaped with bright cushions sat Maud Ling, lovelier than ever in a simple flower-patterned tea gown. Phyllis had so often gaped at her screen image, a black-and-white moving picture, a silent shadow; but here was the real, breathing woman, smiling to welcome her. And presenting her with a surprise!

'I b'lieve ye've already met me little bruvver, Phyllis,' she said slyly, and right on cue Mr Edward Ling stepped through the casement door. He gave a sweeping bow. 'At yer service, Miss Bird!'

Of course – *of course*! His name was Ling, he lived at Richmond, he had spoken of his sister and her acquaintance with Harold Berridge: he was Maud Ling's brother!

'Oh – yes,' she said aloud, smiling and shaking her head at her lack of perception. 'I can see the resemblance now. It just didn't occur to me when you helped me with my luggage that you might actually be –'

'No, yer was worried in case me an' Sonny wasn't to be trusted with an innocent young lady up from the country – that's right, i'n't it, Miss Bird?'

Phyllis felt herself blushing, and Maud laughed. 'Don't take no notice of 'im, duck. Come an' sit dahn an' tell me what's bin goin' on.' She patted the chaise

54

longue. 'Make yerself useful, Teddy, an' get us a drink. Nah, then – 'ow's poor ol' 'Arold? Sounds as if that nipper's bin playin' up worse'n ever. Charles says 'e's goin' to the Agincourt School. Is it doin' 'im any good?'

Phyllis accepted a sweet sherry from Teddy, as Mr Ling seemed to be known, and breathed a thankful sigh at such frank and open understanding.

'It's a nightmare, Miss Ling,' she said simply. 'On his very first day he screamed at the top of his voice, on and on, and fought like a little fury. The infants' class is run by a nice motherly soul called Mrs Parker, and most of the little boys are fairly docile – one or two of them are mongols, they're not much trouble – but after half an hour of non-stop yelling from Claud everybody was upset, and poor Mrs Parker was at her wits' end, so they put him in a room on his own, which meant that he had to have somebody in there with him.'

'Go on!' said Maud, all ears. 'What 'appened then? Did 'e settle dahn?'

'No! The headmaster asked if I could stay with him until he settles in, so that's how I spend Mondays and Thursdays – an extra member of the staff – and Claud really isn't any better for having me there to feed him his dinner and take him to the lavatory. I read Beatrix Potter books to him while he's playing with those building bricks, but if he's never going to mix with the other boys, he might as well stay at home.' She gave a rueful smile. 'When Gannon comes to collect us at half-past three, you can almost hear the sigh of relief that goes up from the whole school!'

Teddy chortled, but Maud made a face. 'Ain't it a shame, eh? Poor ol' 'Arold. Finks the world o' them kids, 'e does.'

'Yes, I'm very sorry for Mr Berridge too,' admitted Phyllis, her eyes softening. 'And to be honest, Miss Ling, he doesn't get a lot of understanding from Mrs Berridge. She thinks that Claud is an unusually intelligent child, but *she* doesn't look after him at all.'

'Don't talk to me about 'er – the woman's a fool,' said Maud. 'Warblin' away at that piano as if she 'ad nuffin' better to do.' She put on a shrill, affected singing voice and gave a very passable imitation of Mrs Berridge at one of her afternoon At Homes.

'Come down to Kew in lilac time, in lilac time, in lilac time,
Come down to Kew in lilac time, it's oh, *so* near to *Lon*-don!

'Cor, talk abaht a caterwaul!'

Phyllis couldn't help chuckling in agreement. Maud obviously knew the family well, and sympathised with Mr Berridge. It was a comfort to confide in her.

'An' what abaht that nanny? 'Ow d'yer get on wiv '*er*?' asked the actress curiously.

'She hardly says a word,' Phyllis answered. 'I have no idea what she's thinking, though I'm sure she resents me being there, she's so cold and unapproachable. Things would be so much easier if we *talked* to each other about Claud – or anything else, for that matter. She's the same with everybody, though.'

'Don't be too 'ard on 'er, duck,' said Maud unexpectedly. 'She's one of 'undreds o' fousands o' lonely women left over from the war. Same as meself – an' same as yerself too, duck, I dare say. A lot of us lorst the men we was married or engaged to, but a lot of 'em lorst their men before they even met 'em, if yer

56

see what I mean. There ain't many left over from that bloody war for us to marry. Not that I'd find anuvver like the one I lorst. Nuffin's the same as it was. Can't ever be the same.'

It might have been Phyllis's mother speaking. *Nothing's the same as it was.* Maud's smile had faded, and a deep sorrow shadowed the large eyes; for a brief moment Phyllis saw a woman looking much older, lost and alone. Somebody else saw, too: the large lady was at Maud's side in an instant.

'It is time you take a rest from much talking, *cara mia*. Remember what Dr Godley said. I will pour a glass of tonic water. Teddy, you forget your duties – take Miss Phyllis to see the garden before we have tea.'

'C'mon, Miss Bird, we got to obey the signora, an' I'm not objectin',' said Mr Ling, who really seemed a most delightful young man, Phyllis had to admit. She wondered how much younger he was than his sister. Maud had clearly been touched by the war and the loss of the man she had loved, whereas her brother must have escaped by being too young for the last call-up. A year, or even half a year could make all the difference: a North Camp boy who was eighteen in 1918 had been called up for active service, and was dead by Armistice Day, while the boy next door to him had not been eighteen until December that year, and so was spared.

Stifling a sigh, Phyllis rose and followed Teddy through the casement door, leaving the signora fussing over Maud with cushions and shawls.

The afternoon sunshine was beginning to fade, and the air held that indefinable tang of autumn that precedes the first winds and whirling leaves. It had been a lingering summer, and the trees were still a blaze of colour; Teddy pointed out Marble Hill Park, the green expanse that Phyllis had passed.

'We could stroll down to the river if yer like,' he said, taking her arm in his. 'Though we mustn't be late for tea, or Belle goes mad.'

Phyllis guessed he meant the Italian lady. 'Is she Miss Ling's housekeeper?' she asked.

'I s'pose she is, sort of. She was an opera singer, the great Bella Capogna. Sang at La Scala and all over the place, so she says – till her voice packed up an' the love of her life ran off with a younger model an' all Belle's money. Nobody wanted her any more, and Maud came across her at a seaside hotel at Margate, singin' with a couple o' musicians down on their luck. They got talkin', an' Maudie asked her to come an' stay. Which she did, only she forgot to go away again, an' now she rules us all with a rod of iron.' His grin belied his words. 'Devoted to Maudie, she is – an' keeps the hangers-on at bay.'

Teddy's London accent was not as pronounced as his sister's, and he brimmed over with self-confidence. He told Phyllis that he'd gone straight from school to the offices of the *Daily Chronicle*, and in a couple of years had become their youngest reporter; his interest in photography had brought him to the new studios at Twickenham to learn about cinematography, and Maud had followed him there at the end of the war, hoping to get work as a messenger, tea-maker and general factotum.

'But with her looks, an' bein' early days, she got a part in a picture they was makin', an' the next thing was she had a leadin' role in *Downfall of a Nobleman*, a big success.'

'Oh, yes, I saw it three times,' replied Phyllis, smiling at the recollection of sitting with Rosie and

Betty in the old North Camp cinema, drooling over the wicked Lady Blanche who had seemed so aristocratic. Little did they guess how she sounded when she opened her mouth!

'Yeah, that's where the future is, in films,' said Teddy, his dark eyes shining. 'Would yer be interested in takin' a look round the studios some time, Phyllis? The Alliance Company's spendin' a fortune doin' 'em up, extendin' 'em back from the railway station, puttin' in a new lightin' system – it'll be the biggest centre for film-makin' in the country.'

Phyllis would have liked to accept, but wondered when she would have the free time from her unremitting schedule with Claud. Harold Berridge's need of her outweighed all other considerations.

'Perhaps we'd better go back indoors now,' she said. 'We don't want to upset the signora!'

On their return she found that another visitor had arrived, a tall, middle-aged man with a long, thin face and observant grey eyes. He was sitting beside Maud with an air of easy familiarity, and Phyllis felt sure that she had seen him before – but where? Suddenly his name flashed into her head, and her face flamed: this was *Reginald Thane*, Maud's leading man and one-time object of Phyllis's lonely fantasies! In an instant those secret dreams evaporated into thin air, and she thanked heaven that this stranger could not read her thoughts. These days she had a real man to adore, a man who talked with her and told her of his concern for his son; a man who needed her help and relied on her loyal service. But – Reginald Thane! And she hadn't even recognised him at once. He was older than he appeared in his pictures, and not at all masterful; when Maud introduced him he smiled diffidently and said he

59

was delighted to meet such a charming young lady, such a refreshing change from would-be film actresses who only wanted to talk about themselves.

'Though *he's* the biggest bore o' the lot for goin' on about what he played at the Ol' Vic, an' his new career in films,' whispered Teddy. 'An' just watch him knock back the Scotch. Hello, Reg! Keepin' yerself pure these days?'

'Shut up an' be'ave yerself, Teddy,' said Maud sharply. 'It's gettin' nippy – close the casement door, an' go an' 'elp Belle wiv the tea trolley.'

Phyllis remembered that Thane's name had been romantically linked with Maud's, though as they sat exchanging studio gossip, they seemed more like good pals than lovers. There was something rather nice about him, Phyllis felt, though he was more like a kindly uncle than the irresistible hero of *On Wings of Love*, full of smouldering passion. Even so, she averted her eyes, embarrassed by her private memories.

Over smoked salmon sandwiches, pastries and cake, Maud recalled the dinner party at the Berridges' when Claud had ripped her gown.

'Yer'll never credit what we talked abaht that night over the soup an' fish! At first I fought I couldn't't've 'eard right, but it was a fact – they was on abaht *birf control*, of all fings!'

Teddy nodded. 'Yeah, that's right, it's this clinic they've opened up in Holloway, an' now there's goin' to be another in south London, not far from the Elephant and Castle, so Georgie Steynes says. He wrote a bit about it for the *Chronicle*, but they wouldn't print it 'cause he said he was in favour of it, an' that i'n't allowed in polite circles.'

'Ah, I s'pose that's why the *Hon* Mrs Agatha

Steynes was puttin' in a word for it, then,' said Maud, carefully aspirating the H in *Hon*. 'I fought she'd be dead agin it, but she's got to support 'im, ain't she, 'cause she finks the sun shines aht o' 'is backside. I'm all for 'elpin' poor women, them wiv the least money an' the most kids, but I never reckoned I'd be listenin' to that sort o' stuff over a dinner table! An' in mixed comp'ny an' all!'

'I can't see it taking on,' remarked Reginald Thane. 'You underestimate the enormous amount of prejudice there is against these clinics, Maudie dear. The Church, the medical profession, the newspapers – you've just heard what your brother said about the *Daily Chronicle*. And the sort of women who most need the advice are the least likely to defy public opinion and ask for it.'

'I ain't so sure, Reggie. If my parents –' She paused. 'I was the eldest o' seven, Phyllis, an' Ted was the youngest. All the ovvers died. Mind yer, 'im an' 'er bofe drank like fishes, an' wouldn't've known what they was doin' 'alf the time, Gawd 'elp 'em.'

Teddy shot his sister a cautionary look. 'All right, Maudie ol' girl, leave it there. 'Sall ancient history, i'n't it? An' we ain't done too badly, neither – better'n plenty who had a better start. Cor, these sandwiches are a bit of all right, Belle! D'yer want another cup o' tea, Phyllis?' And he deftly steered the conversation into safer channels, though Phyllis would have liked to pursue the subject of birth control. She was not even sure what it meant, though there might have been some mention of it in the women's pages of Betty Goddard's gran's copy of *Family Doctor*. She didn't like to ask, especially as Maud had hinted that it was vaguely improper, and by now Teddy was talking about the studios and forthcoming films. The

61

Alliance Company was planning an ambitious hour-long version of the life of Queen Elizabeth, and a couple of American actors from the new studios in California were being approached to take part in it, bringing American money with them to augment the cash-strapped post-war British film industry.

After tea had been cleared away the evening entertainment began. A white screen was set up against a wall, the curtains were drawn and the lights turned out. Teddy had a selection of bits and pieces of film brought back from the cutting room, rejected scenes of *On Wings of Love* and other films, also informal shots he had taken in and around the studios. The projector began to whirr, and Phyllis sat enthralled as the pictures appeared on the screen. With Teddy as operator and commentator, assisted by asides from Miss Ling and Mr Thane, it was just like going to the pictures at home, she thought.

'Now there's one of our finest Shakespearean actors today,' said Thane, nodding at the screen where a velvet-clad figure writhed in apparent agony after drinking from a poisoned cup.

'Ain't 'e the ol' geezer 'oo played the mad professor in *The Quadrangle Murders*?'

'My dear Maud, come on! He's only about five years older than I am.'

'That's what I mean, sixty's a bit long in the toof to play 'Amlet, ain't it?'

A guffaw from the projectionist was almost too much for Phyllis, who had to stifle a giggle, imagining Thane's pained expression hidden by the darkness. Favourite discarded scenes followed in quick succession: false beards coming adrift, wigs askew and skirts getting caught in doors. When a menacing villain opened his mouth and swallowed half his moustache, the company were in hysterics, though Maud's peals of laughter turned into a prolonged bout of coughing that left her panting for breath.

'That is enough! You go to bed at once,' ordered Signora Capogna, and Maud could only gesture apologetically at Phyllis.

'It's all right, Maudie, I'll walk Phyllis home,' volunteered Teddy, but Maud shook her head.

'No – too far – an' too cold. Reggie'll take yer, Phyllis – in 'is Chevrolay,' she gasped, and the actor rose at once. Phyllis said she didn't want to put Mr Thane to such trouble, but she was overruled by Maud's insistence, and found herself seated in Thane's magnificent saloon, all polished woodwork and soft leather upholstery. He gave her a tartan blanket to wrap round her legs for the short journey, and in no time at all, it seemed, they were at Number 3 Travis Walk. It was half-past nine.

'Thank you very much, Mr Thane, it's most kind of you,' Phyllis said as he got out and came round to open the passenger door for her. He gave a little cough, and seemed to make up his mind to say something.

'Er – young Teddy Ling has never been able to resist a pretty face, my dear – and all too soon he falls for another one. I shouldn't like to see you disappointed as others have been.'

Phyllis was both surprised and offended at what she saw as a most uncalled-for caution.

'I beg your pardon, Mr Thane, but I can assure you that there is no need for you to worry on that score,' she said with dignity. 'Thank you again for the lift, and good night.'

And not waiting to hear his murmured apology,

63

she turned away and descended the basement steps. No doubt he meant to be kind, but he was not to know how deeply her heart was involved with another man.

Cook answered her quiet tap at the kitchen door, and let her in; she and Gannon had been sitting by the dying fire in the range, a picture of cosy domesticity.

'Thank you, Cook. Good night. Good night, Gannon.'

She did not see the look the pair gave each other as she climbed the stairs from the kitchen to the entrance hall, and continued up to the first and second floors. The house was in silence. At the third floor she took out her key and silently turned it in the padlock, relocking it carefully behind her so as not to disturb the children.

There was a light beneath the door of the day nursery, so Nanny Wiseman must still be up. Was she having trouble with Claud? Without a moment's hesitation Phyllis pushed open the door.

And stopped dead in her tracks, for there before her were Harold Berridge and Nanny Wiseman, standing together in the firelight. He was wearing a dressing gown and his feet were bare. He put his hand up to his face.

'Oh, no. Oh, my God, no,' he said. 'No.'

But Nanny Wiseman clung to him and looked straight at Phyllis with defiance, even triumph in her glittering green eyes.

She was completely naked.

Chapter 5

It changed everything.

For the second time that day Phyllis had to face the end of a dream. Encountering the real Reginald Thane had been merely a private embarrassment, but in that one shocking moment of revelation at the nursery door all her fond, foolish illusions about Harold Berridge were shattered. To her it seemed that he and Nanny Wiseman had used her for their own ends, and by treating her as a fool had turned her into one; in a curious way she seemed to have lost her own innocence, and now had to face the reality of her infatuation with the man she had regarded as her master.

All that night she tossed and turned upon her bed, remembering his evening visits to the nursery, his geniality, his compliments and commendations, his tender teasing, calling her the Arcadian shepherdess leading her flock of lambs through summer fields – oh, how she had revelled in those smiles, those glances that had won her devotion and made her determined to train Claud into becoming a normal child, something she now knew to be impossible, but how she had longed to succeed! Now all those sweet exchanges were lost, gone at a stroke and rendered meaningless, even insulting, because all along he had been conducting an illicit affair with that woman. How they must have laughed about her behind her back! When she recalled the adoring looks she had given him in front of the nanny, she raged while she grieved. It was not to be borne.

And in a fresh wave of misery she thought of how she had joined in Maud Ling's mockery of Mrs Berridge. Without any sense of disloyalty she had confided to Maud that the playwright got little or no understanding from his wife, and they had dismissed her as a fool. Now that Phyllis knew of his infidelity with the *Wise-Woman*, it was as if she herself had also been betrayed, as much deceived as the wife who had no idea what was going on.

What would she do now? What *should* she do?

Get away, her instincts told her. Leave Travis Walk and find another situation in Richmond. There must be opportunities for nursery staff, and she could study the advertisements in the weekly *Richmond & Twickenham Times*. She simply could not go on living under the same roof, seeing him every day, hearing his voice, his laugh, inhaling the aroma of his cigars, while knowing all the time that he and that nanny – oh, she simply could not endure it. She wept until she fell into an exhausted doze from which she awoke and remembered, and wept afresh. Over and over again she saw the pair of them standing there in the firelight, he with his hand over his eyes, she in her proud nakedness. The image of them was imprinted on her mind's eye, and she thought it would never fade.

How should she face the woman in the morning? Nothing could be said in front of the children, and she would be spending the morning and afternoon with Claud at the Agincourt School. Not until after the children were in bed that evening would she be alone with Nanny Wiseman, and she resolved to maintain a dignified silence. At an early opportunity

66

she would hand in her notice, but what reason would she give for leaving? Might she say that Claud was too difficult for her to cope with? Following the specialist's gloomy forecast, it was obvious that the boy was not going to get any easier and, in any case, everything was changed now; she no longer had the incentive to give up hours and hours of her time to a child who would never be able to respond. She had done it all for Harold Berridge, while all the time he had been making love to Nanny Wiseman: she was his *mistress*. In her heart of hearts Phyllis knew herself to be jealous, and so she grieved while she raged.

Morning came and she washed her face, dressed, lit the nursery fire and laid the breakfast table for the children. Edith woke at half-past seven and chattered happily while Claud submitted to being dressed. At a quarter to eight the nanny appeared, and one brief glance showed that she too had passed a sleepless night. Her proud defiance had given way to silent evasion, and she did not meet Phyllis's eyes.

She's wondering if I'll go to Mrs Berridge and tell her, thought Phyllis. She could lose her place, disgraced and dismissed without a reference, and *he* would have to beg forgiveness of his wife. Or would he leave with the nanny? Somehow Phyllis could not envisage him leaving his children, yet what did she truly know about him? In any case, there was no point in speculating what might happen because Phyllis had no intention of using her knowledge. Deep down in her injured heart she knew that the family should be preserved, and for the sake of the children she would not betray the lovers. But neither would she continue to be treated like a fool. They could manage without her!

'Did you have a nice time with your friends, Phyllis?' asked Edith in her artless way, porridge spoon in hand.

'Yes, thank you, dear, a very nice time,' Phyllis answered with a smile. Nanny was leaning over Claud, encouraging him to feed himself, and Phyllis could sense the tension in her every movement. She seemed to be holding her breath.

'Did you come home very, *very* late, Phyllis?' asked the little girl, her head on one side.

'Yes, dear, it was quite late when I came back. Come on now, eat up your porridge and then you can have some bread and butter.'

'Was everybody fast asleep when you came up the stairs, Phyllis?'

'Yes, dear, everybody was in bed and asleep,' she answered, and thought she saw the nanny slowly exhale. It was a message given and received. Nothing else was said.

As was usual on Mondays and Thursdays, Gannon drove both children to school with Phyllis. After dropping Edith off at Princes Road, Claud was taken to the Agincourt School where Phyllis prepared for another day of battling with his resistance to communication of any kind. Another attempt was made to include him in Mrs Parker's class, but after half an hour of unremitting screaming and struggling it was abandoned, and the headmaster looked grave when Phyllis and Claud returned to their solitary room where the boy quietened.

'I'm afraid that this child must be numbered among our very few failures,' he said heavily. 'It is most unfortunate, but I shall have to make a reluctant request that he be withdrawn –'

'I'm sorry, Headmaster, but I'm only the nursery-maid employed by his parents, and you will have to contact them. It's no concern of mine,' Phyllis interrupted, to the man's surprise, and when Gannon arrived to take them home the school secretary handed her a letter addressed to Mr Berridge. They collected Edith from Holy Trinity School, and outside Number 3 Travis Walk Phyllis thanked Gannon as she always did, and walked with the children up to the front entrance.

Harold Berridge was waiting for her, though he tried to make it look as if he had just come down the stairs. His face was a picture of guilty apprehension – like a naughty schoolboy threatened with a caning, Phyllis thought. Edith at once ran to her father's side, and Claud stamped his feet in frustration, trying to pull off his coat but restricted by the reins strapped over it. Without a word Phyllis handed Berridge the letter; he glanced at the envelope and put it in his pocket.

'Phyllis –' he began.

'Daddy, Daddy, we had music today, and I played the triangle, and Miss de Witt said I ought to learn to play the piano!' cried Edith, jumping up and down. Her father patted her head, but his eyes were on Phyllis, who busied herself with the boy's reins.

Berridge stepped forward and spoke quickly in a low tone. 'Forgive me, Phyllis, but I must say this. I hope – er – I trust that for the sake of faith – I beg that you'll forget about – you know, last night.'

Faith? Was he talking about the faith his wife had in him, which he had betrayed? Phyllis did not look up as she wrestled with the buckles of the reins.

'You can hardly expect me to forget, sir, but if you

are asking me not to speak of it, I shall certainly not do so,' she replied coldly.

'Thank God. I mean, thank you, Phyllis. I'm very grateful, and –'

'But I shall look for other employment,' she added. 'Now, children, come along. Hold my hand, Claud, there's a good boy.'

Berridge opened his mouth to speak further, but at that moment Jenny appeared on the stairs leading up from the kitchen.

'Good aft'noon, Mr Berridge, good aft'noon, Phyllis!' she said brightly, smiling up at the master. 'Cook says d'yer want nurs'ry tea at five or are they comin' dahn to the drawin' room?'

'I haven't the slightest idea, Jenny. You'll have to consult with Nanny Wiseman,' replied Phyllis, disappearing off up the stairs with the children. The housemaid gaped after her.

'Cor, what's up wiv 'er, then?' Jenny turned a questioning look on Berridge, but got no answering smile, only a shrug as he strode away down the passage.

It was nearly eight o'clock. The children were in bed and the two women were at last alone, neither parent having visited the nursery that evening. Phyllis sat darning socks and stockings by the light of the incandescent gas-mantle, and Nanny Wiseman hovered near, her crocheting bag unopened in her hand.

If she thinks I'm going to speak, she's mistaken, thought Phyllis grimly. I've put up with her silences night after night, week after week, and now it's my turn.

But when Nanny Wiseman eventually broke the silence, her words were unexpected.

'Please don't leave, Bird.'

So he had somehow managed to tell her already. Phyllis was angry with herself for blushing. Why should *she* be shamed, *she* had done nothing wrong? Yet her heart beat faster as she carried on darning furiously, not looking up.

'You can hardly expect me to stay on here, after last night.'

'No, Bird, please let me try to explain. You've been such a great help, especially with Claud, and very much appreciated, please believe me.'

'Really? I've been made a complete fool of, it seems to me,' retorted Phyllis, digging the needle in and out of the heel of Edith's sock.

'No, you're wrong there, Bird – listen! You've been wonderful with that boy, and I'm sorry I haven't said so before, but there's been a conspiracy of silence where he's concerned. His father and I have known for some time that there was something seriously wrong, but his mother's always refused to see it, and Harold – Mr Berridge – has played along with her to spare her feelings, mistakenly in my view. We've *all* had to pretend, servants and everybody. But now they've got to face the facts. You heard what the specialist said – the boy's never going to be any good. I know *she* doesn't appreciate all that we do, but *he* does. In fact he says you've been a godsend – Phyllis.'

It was the first time she had used Phyllis's Christian name.

'That may be so, but I don't see what Claud's got to do with you and – and *him*,' she muttered, as if referring to something highly distasteful. 'You've taken me for a fool, and you'd have gone on doing so if I hadn't come in early and found you out. I can't

71

possibly stay here under the same roof with *that* going on, for God's sake.'

Tears of angry disillusionment rose to her eyes once again, and she could say no more. She swallowed hard to stifle a sob, and found Nanny Wiseman standing close to her.

'I'm so sorry, Phyllis. I know it must be very difficult for you, but please hear me out. You must understand that Harold Berridge is no ordinary man. He's a genius, the successor to George Bernard Shaw in the eyes of many critics. His wife doesn't realise this; she doesn't understand that his work will be valued and performed a hundred years from now, long after we've all gone. *I'm* the one who gives him the help and support he needs. In fact this latest play, *Key to Tomorrow*, is based on us. Do try to understand my position, Phyllis. I'm the one person in the world he can turn to. He needs me, so how can I refuse him? How else do I put up with that stupid woman? How else do I cope with that hopelessly mental child? I bear it all for Harold, you see. It's all for *him* – oh, yes, it's *all* for him.'

Her voice had risen in mounting agitation, but she made an effort to bring herself under control. Phyllis lowered her head, admitting to herself that she understood only too well where Claud was concerned: all her own time and energy expended on the boy had been for the sake of his father.

'And now he's been asked to remove Claud from Agincourt School,' went on the nanny. 'The head-master says to try him again in a year's time, but you know and I know that he'll never be any different, just more difficult to handle as he gets bigger. He'll grow to be a man in size, a monster to be kept hidden away out of sight. It's a tragedy for Harold, and she's no help, just a silly, self-deceiving woman, no use at all. But *I'm* here for him, oh yes, he knows he can count on his Wise-Woman in the shadows. I'll always be here.'

Phyllis hardly knew what to make of this new and unexpected side to Nanny Wiseman, who had been so coldly silent up until now, never once showing a glimmer of friendliness. Still reeling from her own disappointment, she was not inclined to sympathise.

'I thought you resented me,' she muttered. 'You've never once asked about my family or why I applied for this situation or – or anything about me.'

'But that would have meant talking about myself, and how could I do *that* in the circumstances?' countered the nanny. 'God knows, there's not much to tell. I lost my only brother in the war, along with his closest friend, the man who would have become my husband if he had survived. My mother died and my father remarried. I've got an older married sister, otherwise nobody in the world – only Harold.' She went over to the window and looked out into the dark. 'He's all I live for, because he needs me.'

'Good grief, anybody would think that you were the only one to lose somebody in the war!' exclaimed Phyllis with a surge of bitterness. 'There was hardly a family that *didn't* in our road at North Camp. My own two brothers were killed at the Somme, and it broke my mother's heart. She's turned into an old woman who lives in the past and hasn't any love left for me or my father. She might as well be dead, like yours! My father says that the war changed every-thing, and the world will never be the same again. I just had to get away from that miserable house – that's why I came to Richmond. My father thinks I'm selfish, and I suppose I am. Perhaps I ought to go back – oh, I don't know!' And with a gesture of despair she threw aside the mending basket.

For a moment there was silence, and then Nanny Wiseman turned back from the window and faced her. 'I'm sorry, Phyllis. Perhaps we're both selfish. You're right, that hideous war took away a whole generation of men, the best we had, and left behind a whole generation of women to live out the rest of our lives as well as we can. Please, Phyllis, don't go, at least not straight away. Stay to help us over Christmas – that's never an easy time. Harold would be so grateful – and so would I.'

Phyllis hesitated, knowing that she was in no state to make an important decision. She felt utterly drained of energy and emotion after the turmoil of the past twenty-four hours.

'I'll make cocoa for us both,' she said at last in a flat, tired voice, and the nanny visibly brightened, as if the words had indicated that she would stay.

'That's very good of you. And please call me Faith.'

'I beg your pardon?'

'Call me Faith. It's my name.'

'What? Oh – oh, I *see*,' said Phyllis, remembering Berridge's plea, *for the sake of faith*. So it was Faith with a capital F, then.

'Better than Hope or Charity, anyway,' said the nanny with a wry smile.

Phyllis made the cocoa in two mugs, and they sat and drank it together. If not exactly friendship, it was the beginning of a better understanding and on a more equal footing.

To her surprise, Phyllis felt her grief and rage lessening, and her thoughts now turned in a completely different direction – towards Maud Ling and her circle at Twickenham. She recalled that Teddy

74

Ling had offered to show her over the film studios, and she had not given him a proper answer. Was it now too late to accept and enjoy a glimpse into the magic world of the cinema? Would she be invited to Florizel again, or had she lost the chance?

The days grew shorter and colder; November came in with mists drifting up from the river, now more visible through the leafless trees, and Gosling's window displays glowed in the early dusk, reminding shoppers that Christmas was only a few weeks away. Now that Claud no longer attended school, Phyllis took him for walks at all times of the day; it was the easiest way of dissipating his undirected energy, to tire him out before the evening routine of tea-time, bath-time and bedtime. He seemed to enjoy stomping along, his eyes on the ground, sometimes singing tunelessly to himself, and fidgeting with impatience if Phyllis stopped to look at a shop window or speak to somebody.

As when Dr Godley stopped his car beside them at the top of Nightingale Lane.

'Good morning, Miss Phyllis! It's a cold day to be out walking with Young Master, isn't it? Hello, Claud – don't worry, I won't come too close, you might knock my new spectacles flying. So, my dear, how are you keeping these days?'

Phyllis warmed to his friendly interest, and explained that walking was a useful form of exercise for both Claud and herself.

'And keeps him suitably occupied, ah yes,' nodded the doctor. 'My dear, I was so sorry when the specialist confirmed all that I feared,' he went on, lowering his voice. 'Disheartening for you after all the hard work you put in, and very sad for the family.

His parents will have a hard decision to make sooner or later.'

He spoke seriously, and Phyllis waited in some surprise. Why should he stop to discuss the problem of Claud with the nurserymaid? He soon made himself clear.

'Miss Phyllis Bird, you're a sensible, intelligent young woman, and your talents are wasted here,' he told her bluntly. 'I believe you were an assistant teacher of infants for several years, so your best course would be to study for your teaching certificate and make sure of a lifelong income. Or have you considered becoming a qualified nurse, perhaps specialising in sick children? My daughter, Pamela, has just started training at St George's Hospital at Hyde Park Corner where I studied medicine, and she loves it, though a probationer's life is hard. It's the best way to learn, caring for patients at the bedside. Think about it, my dear, and don't look so surprised!'

For Phyllis's jaw had literally dropped at hearing this unsolicited advice from the Berridges' family doctor. Was he actually telling her to *leave* them for a career in teaching or nursing? Was he reminding her of her single status and the unlikelihood of marriage for her generation? What business was it of his? She stared back at him while Claud tugged fretfully on his reins and, as if reading her thoughts, the doctor continued with the same directness.

'The truth is, Miss Bird, that you could stay where you are for years, and have nothing to show at the end of it. As long as this young man's parents can rely on you to do everything for him, using up your own precious years in the process – they will let you go on doing so.'

'Nanny Wiseman does her share,' said Phyllis, to be fair.

'Ah, but Miss Wiseman is a rather different case. She's been in the household for some time – she's part of the furnishings, you could say – and incidentally has a much easier time now that you've come to be OC Claud. If you left to better yourself, she would have her own decision to make – but I'm talking about *you*, not her. Think over what I've said, and don't dismiss me as an old know-all. The family doctor has a unique viewpoint, remember.'

It was impossible to be offended by the kindliness in his sharp grey eyes, the genuine concern he felt for her best interests.

'I'll think about what you've said, Doctor,' she said with as much dignity as she could muster, with Claud pulling away from her with all his strength.

'Very well, Miss Bird, I'll leave you to your charge. Oh, and by the way, Miss Ling has been asking about you. It's very clear that she likes you! Why don't you go to see her again on your next half-day?'

This was more like it! Phyllis gave the doctor a brilliant smile as Claud jerked the reins and almost pulled her off balance.

'Thank you, Dr Godley, I'll remember what you said!' she called after him as he let in the clutch and drove off down the steep slope to the Petersham Road.

Yes! She would send Miss Ling a note that very day.

Phyllis had no objection to taking Claud for winter walks, for it was often a relief to get away from the atmosphere in the house. Everything had changed since her fatal discovery: there was a subtle shift in

77

the balance of relationships in the household. Although Mr Berridge's manner remained genial on his evening visits, Phyllis now kept out of his way, finding herself jobs to do while he sat toasting his socked feet at the fireguard and listening to Edith's prattle. Faith Wiseman gave no sign of their secret intimacy, and yet of course it was always there, whether acknowledged or not, a palpable force that filled the air. Phyllis no longer felt free to chat with Jenny and smile at her ravings over the master's attractions, and Williams gave her a suspicious look when they met on the stairs, which made her feel uncomfortable. Number 3 Travis Walk had become a house of whispers, and Faith Wiseman's eyes showed the strain of it, though when the two of them settled down for the winter evenings in the nursery she relaxed and even sometimes laughed over the day's events – things that Edith had said, and people's different reactions to Claud on his walks.

When Phyllis asked if she might take a half-day off on the first Wednesday in December to visit the Twickenham circle, Faith told her to go, even though the children would be taking tea with their mother in the drawing room on that day.

'Oh, but you'll need some help then,' said Phyllis with a grimace.

'No, I'll be all right. You'd rather go and see your Twickenham friends than take tea with Mother, I dare say,' remarked Faith drily.

'Well, if you're sure . . .'

'Yes, Phyllis, I'm quite sure. Go and enjoy yourself.'

It suddenly occurred to Phyllis that the lovers might want her out of the way, so she said no more. It was impossible to ignore their liaison, and although she refused to be a go-between, she could not avoid feeling like a fellow conspirator, breathing the same air.

Chapter 6

Phyllis's behind-the-scenes tour of the Twickenham Film Studios was made doubly enjoyable by her guide, an eager and attentive Teddy Ling. His exalted status as a cameraman was shown in the smiles and nods of the technicians, some considerably older than he, and he left her in no doubt of his innovative flair.

'Bein' Maud's brother i'n't exactly a handicap,' he admitted with a grin, 'but I've always been interested in photography, an' this lot was just waitin' for me to come along. Soon's I saw it, I knew I'd come home.'

They stood in front of an extended stage on which had been built a row of shop fronts, representing a street.

'See this camera trolley that runs from one side o' the stage to the other? That was my idea, an' there's a lot more I'm goin' to do with it, like raisin' an' lowerin' the seat, an' swivellin' it round so's to take in a scene slowly, one bit at a time, like.'

He laid a hand casually on her shoulder as they looked up at the newly installed lighting system, which he told her was absolutely essential to good cinema-photography. She saw the enthusiasm sparkling in his dark eyes.

'An' to think this was a skatin' rink before the war, Phyllis! I'm tellin' yer, the Alliance Comp'ny's turnin' these studios into the best in the country – you just wait an' see!'

Gazing up at the stage, which could be a busy street one week and a group of gypsy caravans the next, Phyllis was suitably amazed, and by the time she had seen the carpenters' and painters' workshops, the two wardrobes full of exotic costumes and the chaotic office, she was as full of admiration as he could wish.

He took her arm as they walked back to Florizel, where they found Maud entertaining two young men. One of them Phyllis recognised as Sonny Stott, who had been with Teddy on her first meeting with him, and the other was clearly an admirer of the actress, following her with his eyes and hanging on her every word. He was introduced to Phyllis as Mr George Steynes of the *Daily Chronicle*, a serious youth with an intense expression and slicked-down straight hair.

'Georgie's got two passions in life,' whispered Teddy in Phyllis's ear. 'One of 'em's Maudie, an' the other's to make a name for himself. He'll either be editor o' the *Chronicle* one o' these days, or the head o' some big comp'ny or other. Ambitious, that's our little Lord Georgie.'

'Is he really a lord?' asked Phyllis, who now remembered seeing him with his mother at the Berridges' dinner party.

'Nah! His grandfather was one, though, on his mother's side – that's why she's a *Hon*.' He jokingly aspirated the H as Maud had done. 'Right now he's on this birth-control wagon, but next year he'll go for something else, I bet, whatever's in the news.'

Teddy laughed, but Phyllis felt a little awkward at the mention of birth control again. She had enquired at the Richmond Library whether there were any books on the subject, and a tight-lipped lady had informed her that they didn't keep those sort of books, although she'd added grudgingly that a Dr Marie Stopes had written one called *Wise Parenthood*, which could be ordered from a bookseller. Her disapproving tone had stopped Phyllis from enquiring further, and a medical dictionary had failed to yield any information. And yet here were two young men who did not mind referring to it openly and commending it as a good thing.

At half-past six Belle Capogna served dinner. Phyllis sat next to Maud, with Teddy on her other side, and listened with fascination to their talk of the film planned for the New Year, *The Virgin Queen*.

'When will you start – er – shooting it?' asked Phyllis, remembering the terms Teddy had used about film-making.

'Soon's we can, duck, an' it ain't 'alf goin' to be a good 'un, the best I've ever done,' said Maud, smiling in anticipation.

'And you'll be Queen Elizabeth, Miss Ling – Maud?'

'None ovver. I'm 'Er Majesty. We got Denver Towers comin' over from them 'Ollywood studios in California to play opposite me. 'E'll be Lord Robert Dudley, the Earl o' Leicester.'

'What, not Reggie Thane?' asked Sonny Stott with a grin.

'No, Reggie'll be playin' Sir Somebody Garland, one o' me courtiers.'

'But won't he be in love with Her Majesty as well?' Stott winked at nobody in particular as he spoke, and Phyllis thought him an unpleasant young man, though she could not have explained quite why.

'Yeah, but they can't bofe 'ave me, an' in any case I'm a virgin queen, don't forget, married to England,

82

me country. Reggie'll get the Lady Rosamund as a consolation prize – she's one o' me ladies-in-waitin'. Ooh, there won't be a dry eye in the 'ouse – I mean the pictures, wherever it's on.'

'We haven't got an actress to play Rosamund yet,' Teddy told Phyllis. 'Our director, Fred Paul, had his eye on Gladys Cooper, but she's in Harold Berridge's new play at the Richmond Theatre – which means she'll go on to the West End in it. Lovely woman, she is, but there aren't many stage actors who can see the potential of films, not yet. Soon as we've got the cast together, we can start rollin'.'

'Er – what does Mr Stott do?' Phyllis asked him in an undertone.

'Sonny? Oh, he's a jack-of-all-trades at the studios, turns his hand to anythin'. He'll be the assistant cameraman, carpenter, electrician, whatever yer care to name. He'll climb up to the ceiling like a monkey 'cause he's small – and not only that, he'll be playin' a pageboy in *The Virgin Queen*.'

'Will he? He only looks about fifteen, but I suppose he must be older,' she remarked.

'Blimey, he's twenty-five, even though he don't look it,' said Teddy. 'He always gets roped in to play a kid if we need one. Boy or girl, he does both!'

Phyllis was astounded. Stott was the same age as herself. And so how old was Teddy? His sister Maud must be nearing thirty, and there had been five others between her and Teddy, so he couldn't be as old as Stott. And she could hardly ask him his age.

After dinner, when Maud wanted to hear the latest news about Claud, Phyllis carefully confined herself to the facts – that the boy had been taken away from the Agincourt School and that it was her daily duty to take him on walks to use up his surplus energy. They also spoke of Dr Godley, who was Maud's GP – like Berridge she referred to him as Charles – and much admired by Signora Capogna, who was always quoting him as she dosed Maud with cough linctus, warning her against catching cold and endlessly nagging at her for smoking, which brought on coughing fits.

''E's got a nice place on the Petersham Road. Tudor 'Ouse it's called, goes dahn to the river at the back,' said Maud. 'Wife keeps 'erself to 'erself, bit of an invalid ever since she 'ad Pamela, that's their daughter 'oo's trainin' to be a nurse. Belle worships the ground 'e walks on!' She smiled indulgently at the signora, who shrugged and declared that Maud would be wise to heed the good doctor's advice and take better care of her chest.

Phyllis could only agree that Dr Godley was a good GP and a likeable man, but she did not repeat his personal advice to her in case it led to questions about the Berridge household, and once again she had the disagreeable sensation of being a conspirator with the master and the nanny.

Further talk with Maud was cut short by George Steynes, who monopolised his idol for the rest of the evening, but this was no problem for Phyllis, comfortably settled with Teddy on the chaise longue, listening to his amusing observations and whispered asides. There was no doubt about his interest in her on this their third meeting; he was clearly putting himself out to be charming. Annoyed with herself for blushing and not knowing what to say, she had no idea how much her bashfulness added to her attraction for him. Her eyes, brown like his but not so dark, shone with her pleasure in his company, transforming a passable young woman into a very pretty girl.

'Are yer goin' to let me take yer back to Berridge's tonight, Phyllis?' he asked, and she nodded and replied that it would be most kind of him, meaning that it would be too wonderful for words, and hoping that she would not be hopelessly tongue-tied.

Maud ordered her brother to see both Phyllis and George Steynes on to the nine forty-five bus that ran from St Margaret's Station to Richmond, where Phyllis could alight at Bridge Street and Mr Steynes could go on to get the Waterloo train. Mr Ling had other ideas, however, and having seen George on to the bus, he walked arm-in-arm with Phyllis the whole way, ending with the steep climb up Richmond Hill. Outside Number 3 Travis Walk he gently pulled her into the patch of blackness between the steps leading up to the front entrance and those descending to the basement.

'When can I see you again, Phyllis?' (Oh, the intoxication of those seven little words!)

'I – I really don't know, Teddy. Our half-days are different each week. I could send a note to Florizel when I know.'

Her breath caught in her throat as he took her gloved hand in his. She felt his warm breath on her face, and even in the dark knew that he was smiling down at her.

'It was a lucky day for me when Maudie noticed yer at the Berridges' and asked yer over,' he said quietly. 'I think yer're the sweetest girl I've ever met, Phyllis.'

She felt herself trembling, and he put an arm around her; the other kept hold of her hand.

'Phyllis –'

She knew that he was going to kiss her, and all of a sudden she drew back. 'Teddy, you do realise that I – I'm several years older than you?'

'What does that matter? How old d'yer think I am?'

'About twenty?' she gasped, for this was what she had been wondering about all the evening.

'Soon be twenty-one! An' I'm too much of a gentleman to ask a lady her age. Besides, I don't care. All I know is that you're a lovely girl. Ah, Phyllis . . .'

And he kissed her gently, softly, his lips upon her flushed cheek and then for a brief moment on her lips. It was the most incredible sensation that she had ever experienced, for it was her first kiss.

'Good night, Phyllis, my sweet girl,' he whispered. 'Good night. See yer in me dreams.'

'Good night, Teddy.'

She went down the basement steps, her head in a whirl, her heart soaring. She had been kissed by a real young man who thought her a sweet girl and wanted to see her again. And why should she worry about the five-year age-gap between them if it didn't worry him? Was this love at last?

In the day nursery Faith Wiseman sat beside the dying fire, a dreamy half-smile on her face that Phyllis felt must reflect her own. Their eyes met.

'Have you had a good evening with your friends, Phyllis?'

'Oh yes, very good, thank you, Faith. What about you? How was tea with Mrs Berridge?'

'He was there too,' came the low reply. 'A frightfully jolly little family tea-party.'

'Oh. And – were you there?' asked Phyllis cautiously.

'Of course I was. She couldn't possibly cope with

that child otherwise. I put on my usual stony face and kept quiet. She did all the talking.'

Phyllis could imagine. 'And how did Claud behave?'

'Abominably. You know how he hates anything out of the usual. In fact we had to move back up here as soon as tea was finished, to let the maids clear up the mess on the carpet.'

There was a slight flicker at the corner of her mouth, and Phyllis dissolved into giggles.

'Oh, I'm sorry to laugh, but I can just picture it – sorry!'

'Don't be.' And they laughed quietly together. As Faith turned her face towards Phyllis, the firelight caught glints in her uncovered auburn hair, and her green eyes shone softly. Phyllis had the feeling that she was seeing this woman for the first time.

'You're so beautiful, Faith,' she said on an impulse. 'I can understand why any man would –' She checked herself, and then spoke again, emboldened by the joy of her first kiss. 'It's such a *waste*, you being shut away up here, living a secret life, not being able to – oh, Faith, have you never thought about getting out of here, training to be a sick children's nurse or something like that?' She found herself repeating the advice that Dr Godley had given her, simply because it was good advice, as applicable to Faith Wiseman as to herself, perhaps more so. 'Think about it: you've got a life of your own to lead, so why don't you –'

She drew back quickly as the nanny stared at her. Her face had paled, and was completely changed: it was as hard as stone.

'Good God, haven't you understood *anything*? Didn't you hear a word of what I told you? My life is

totally fulfilled by him who loves me and needs me –
and not only for writing his plays. I keep this
marriage going, if only that silly woman realised it –
or rather, I keep the illusion of it going, because in
truth it's no marriage at all, just a hollow sham. He
gets *nothing* from her, they haven't had – what shall I
say, conjugal union – since that wretched boy was
born. *I'm* his real wife, his wife in all but name. *I* give
him the love and fulfilment he needs and doesn't get
from that stupid creature. I'm absolutely essential to
Harold Berridge, don't you understand? And I'm
perfectly content to accept that, knowing that I have
his love. So don't come telling *me* what to do, Phyllis
Bird. You're wasting your time.'

Something about the defiant superiority in her
tone stung Phyllis into putting into words the
question that had sprung to her mind.

'So let me ask you, Faith Wiseman, aren't *you*
risking having a baby?'

As soon as it was out of her mouth she wondered
how she could have asked such a question. Would
Faith say, 'How dare you!' or even slap her face?
Would she turn away shocked and mortally
offended?

In fact, she answered the question. 'No, certainly
not. Harold loves me far too much. He wouldn't
dream of taking such a risk. Have you never heard of
birth control?'

There it was again, the mysterious forbidden
subject, but by now Phyllis was beginning to
understand.

'I know that there are birth-control clinics,' she said
with an air of knowing more than she actually did.

'Clinics!' Faith's tone was contemptuous. 'Those
places are for poor, downtrodden women with

selfish husbands who give them babies year after year. People of a better class use protective sheaths worn by the man and obtained from a doctor. Fortunately Harold and Dr Godley are friends, so there's no difficulty.'

Phyllis's head spun. 'You mean that *Dr Godley* supplies these – things that men use?'

'These safeguards, yes, to prevent conception. Why shouldn't he? Who more appropriate than the family doctor who's also a family friend?' Faith's eyes flashed, but then she frowned and seemed to regret having confided so much. 'Look, we'll say no more about this, Phyllis. It is, after all, a very personal matter. I'm very tired, and I'm going to bed now. I shan't want any cocoa tonight. I'm glad you enjoyed your evening. Good night.'

'All right, Faith. Good night.'

But the nanny had already left the room, leaving Phyllis to ponder on what she was finding out about life. It was as if she had been led through a gateway and on to an unknown road along which she had to travel, whether she wanted to or not.

She suddenly thought of Dr Godley supplying the necessary 'safeguards'. Did he think that they were for Mr Berridge and his wife? Or did he know about the nanny?

With a little shiver she banished such bizarre pictures from her mind and let her thoughts turn back to Teddy Ling and the scene of their farewell less than half an hour ago, sealed with a loving kiss. What bliss, what happiness! No need there for *birth control*, thank goodness.

Mrs Berridge was becoming more irritable and unreasonable with every day that passed. She informed all her staff that they could each take a two-night break to visit their families either before or after Christmas, even though such absences would cause her great inconvenience at a busy time when she was feeling far from well. Phyllis was told that she could have the nights of December the fifteenth and sixteenth, a Thursday and Friday, and Nanny Wiseman would take the nineteenth and twentieth.

It was over three months since Phyllis had left North Camp, and she had mixed feelings about seeing her parents again. How much would she tell them of her life at Richmond? Would she mention Teddy Ling? She had met him twice since that evening of the first kiss: once when he had taken her to the Castle Tea-Rooms and they had talked and danced a few steps together; and on another afternoon they had gone to the New Royalty Kinema to see Charlie Chaplin's first full-length film, *The Kid*, much praised for the touching scenes with little Jackie Coogan, though Phyllis had been so deliciously overwhelmed with nervousness that she'd found it hard to concentrate. Afterwards they'd gone back to Florizel for tea, and Maud had beckoned her upstairs to what she called her 'bood-wah', all scent sprays and powder puffs.

'Me little bruvver's a good boy, but 'e's got a lot to learn 'fore 'e settles dahn, if yer get me meanin', duck,' she said in a friendly, confidential way, which Phyllis interpreted as the same kind of caution that Reginald Thane had felt obliged to give her. Feeling rather uncomfortable, she said she quite understood that Teddy's career in cinema-photography would keep him occupied for some time.

'That's right, duck, I tell 'im 'e ought to go to

America for a couple o' years, to see 'ow they do it in California. Widen 'is 'orizons, like.'

Phyllis's heart plummeted at the mention of America, but she smiled brightly and said that Teddy had told her of his plans.

'Yeah, but don't take it all as gospel trufe, Phyllis, an' while we're on the subject o' Teddy, I might tell yer 'e's got a bit of a rovin' eye – an' there's plenty to see on a film set, all them beautiful gals – an' some of 'em'll do anyfing to get into films. If I was you, duck, I wouldn't get too serious. After all, 'e's only a kid really, i'n't 'e?'

And I'm twenty-five and you think I'm too old for him, thought Phyllis with a tiny flicker of resentment. Because by now she knew she adored him and would wait until he was older, say twenty-five or six. But would he still be interested in her when she was over thirty? Phyllis was willing to wait and see.

North Camp had not changed: it was as drab and depressing as ever. The silent house in Rectory Road that had once rung to the sound of children's voices was now unwelcoming to Phyllis, who shivered in the dark passageway through to the kitchen, or climbed the stairs to her icy-cold bedroom.

'I'm so pleased to see you again, Mum!' she made herself say to the sad-eyed woman. 'I've missed you all the time I've been away. Have you seen anything of the Lansdownes? I've got lots to tell Rosie about the film studios at Twickenham!'

'You're looking well, anyway, Phyllis. What are the children like to look after?' Mrs Bird was making an effort to show some interest in her daughter's life, and Phyllis told her parents that Edith Berridge was a nice little girl, but that poor Claud had serious

91

mental problems and might one day have to go into a special home.

'That's the reason they need to have two nursery staff,' she explained. 'Claud will probably never be able to speak, so the specialist said.'

'That's very sad for the family,' said Mr Bird, though his wife observed that the Berridges had at least still got their son. 'And they know he won't ever be killed in a dreadful, wicked war,' she sighed.

Ernest Bird swiftly changed the subject. He had read a review in *The Times* of Harold Berridge's play *Key to Tomorrow*, and was interested to know more about the man.

'Not that you'll see much of him, I suppose,' he said to his daughter. 'You'll have more to do with the mother. She must be upset about the boy – it stands to reason.'

Phyllis nodded in agreement, not wanting to say anything remotely controversial, and added that Mr Berridge came up to the nursery most evenings to spend time with his children.

When her friends Rosie Lansdowne and Betty Goddard came to tea on the Friday, she enthralled them – and bewildered her parents – with the story of how she'd met Maud Ling at the Berridges', and her subsequent invitation to the actress's home in Twickenham. When she said she'd also met Reginald Thane they were struck dumb at first, and then squealed with excited envy. It was difficult to answer their eager questions without causing a degree of disillusionment at the contrast between the middle-aged, mild-mannered man and his screen image, and her parents were astounded. They had never once gone to the pictures, so did not even know the names of the idols who were on such familiar terms with their daughter.

Phyllis decided not to mention her friendship with Maud Ling's brother, but simply told them that he was a very clever young cameraman who was interesting to talk to. Rosie and Betty were highly impressed, and Mr Bird privately feared that they would repeat these stories all over North Camp to the further disapproval of the neighbours. Nothing had changed.

'Well, it's good to know that you're seeing a bit of life, Phyllis,' he conceded when he saw her off on the train. 'It isn't as if there's much for you here. We miss you – I miss you a lot. The house is quiet now you're not there at the end of each day. But I can see that the life suits you.' He gave her a brief, awkward hug and kissed her cheek. 'But I wouldn't spend too much time at those film studios, Phyllis. You stay with the family; they need you for that poor boy.'

'Don't worry, Dad, I don't get that much time off!'

'All right, then, here's your train. Take care of yourself, my girl.'

'You too, Dad. Goodbye. I'll be thinking about you and Mum at Christmas.'

She waved to him from the window until he was out of sight, then she settled herself in a corner seat with a guilty sigh of relief. Just suppose – just *imagine* what her parents would say if they knew the truth about Harold Berridge's liaison with his children's nanny. It was a measure of how far she had grown away from them.

'Cor, talk abaht a little perisher! If I 'as to put up wiv anuvver two days of 'im while Nanny's away, I'll give me notice in, an' that's a fact!'

93

Williams was well and truly fed up, as she put it. Jenny had a cold, so had been kept away from the nursery, and Williams had been sent to assist Nanny while Phyllis was away.

'Anybody can see 'e ain't right in the 'ead. It don't need no specialist chargin' umpteen guineas to tell 'em that,' she grumbled. 'And what wiv *er* airs an' graces . . .' She lowered her voice and nodded towards Nanny Wiseman, who had been equally exasperated with the surly housemaid.

'Thank goodness you're back, Phyllis. That woman's no use at all. She won't even take Claud out walking with his reins on. I've had to do everything. D'you think you'll be able to cope while I'm away visiting my sister at Watford?'

'Yes, I'm sure I can, Faith,' said Phyllis, though Mrs Berridge seemed to have her doubts.

'It really is *most* inconvenient, having first one and then the other away just now, with Edith on school holidays and so many demands on my time – not to mention losing your services downstairs, Williams, just when I need you most.'

'Don't worry, Mrs Berridge, I shall be entirely responsible for Claud while Mrs Williams acts as nursery housekeeper,' said Phyllis tactfully in the housemaid's hearing, at which Williams brightened up considerably, delighted by this advancement of her position and the title of 'Mrs', befitting her status as a war widow.

'That's right, an' I'll look after Edith, ma'am. She's a good little soul, no trouble at all.'

'Very well,' sighed the lady. 'We shall just have to manage without Nanny as well as we can, but it's a lot of extra worry for me, of course.'

Mrs Williams was as good as her word, sweeping

and dusting, ironing and mending, fetching their meals up from the kitchen and clearing them away while Phyllis took the children out walking or made Christmas decorations with Edith; Claud took no notice, but went on building houses with his bricks as usual.

'It's a jolly sight easier wiv you than it is wiv '*er*,' remarked Mrs Williams when she and Phyllis had a rare chance to talk. 'It's a shame we're all stuck 'ere for Chris'muss.'

Phyllis learned that Mrs Williams' mother, also a widow, lived in Lambeth. 'Seems all wrong, me slavin' away 'ere, an' poor ol' Ma all on 'er own, but the money's better in Richmond. One o' these days I'll 'ave to go an' look after 'er, an' Gawd knows 'ow we'll manage. S'pose I ought to be grateful me baby died.'

Phyllis stared in horror. 'Oh, Mrs Williams, how dreadful – and losing your husband too. I'm so sorry, I had no idea.'

'No, well, there y'are, not many know, 'cause I don't say much abaht it. Only I always remember at Chris'muss.'

Phyllis said no more then, because Mrs Williams seemed to regret letting slip this other loss in her life; but from then on Phyllis regarded the plain, blunt-featured woman with both pity and respect.

Faith Wiseman returned on 21 December, obviously glad to be back, and Phyllis was overjoyed to receive a Christmas card from Teddy Ling, quite separate from the one that arrived 'from all at Florizel', and accompanied by a little basket of crystallised fruit, with the message, 'To the sweetest girl I know'. She kept it on her bedside table, and felt that she could never eat the contents, but would gaze upon it and touch it reverently every morning and night. In no time at all Christmas was upon them, a frenetic whirl of present-giving, games in the drawing room and a surfeit of festive fare. Claud, who hated any deviation from his usual routine, was particularly fractious, and Edith became overexcited, overtired, and was sick on the Axminster carpet. Faith Wiseman was moody and absolutely refused to go to church on Christmas morning.

'I'm not a believer, not any more,' she declared. 'Not after that terrible war that robbed us of our future.' Phyllis had to take the children to St Matthias on her own because neither parent attended and Mrs Williams and Jenny had to stay to help Cook in the kitchen with the dinner.

Mrs Berridge's nervous, unpredictable behaviour showed no sign of improvement, and she found fault with her husband and every member of the staff in turn. Harold Berridge wore a harassed look, and by the end of Boxing Day he had shut himself in his study while his wife could be heard sobbing in the bedroom; she went on and on, until at last he rushed out of the study, slamming the door, and they all heard him remonstrating with her.

'I'm going to ask Charles Godley to call and see you tomorrow, Cynthia. You can't just go on like this, it's driving us all mad. There must be something the matter, and we need to find out what it is, for God's sake.'

Dr Godley duly called the following day, and was closeted with Mrs Berridge in her room for twenty minutes. Then he emerged and announced to her husband that it was happy news: another child was to be born to them at about the end of June.

Phyllis never forgot the stricken look on Faith Wiseman's face, like that of a mortally wounded animal.

Chapter 7

With Christmas over and the New Year not yet begun, the last days of December were for Phyllis a time of apprehension and uncertainty. While a part of her was inclined to go looking for other employment in Richmond, her instincts warned her that now was not the time; Dr Godley's announcement had somehow changed everything, and Faith Wiseman's unhappiness hung over the nursery like a storm cloud, erupting in sudden squalls of impatience and sharp words followed by brooding silences. Phyllis found herself virtually in charge of the daily routine and, with the children needing to be kept occupied and the weather cold and wet, she felt cut off from the rest of the household, and unable to make contact with the young man she adored.

It was on the Thursday that the tension reached a climax. Phyllis had written Teddy a note to explain her position, and took the children out with her to post it in spite of the rain. They had lingered a while in the town while Edith gazed into shop windows, and returned as it was getting dark, mackintoshes glistening and the children's little waxed sou'westers dripping down their backs and forming pools on the tiled floor of the entrance hall. She hurried them up to the nursery to get them towelled dry, and found Mrs Williams putting more coal on the fire. She gave Phyllis a look that warned of trouble ahead.

'It'd nearly gorn out.'

'Where's Nanny?' asked Edith, voicing Phyllis's own question.

'She ain't 'ere. Went orf wivout so much as a word soon after you left wiv the kids, an' ain't bin seen since.'

'Did she say –'

'I jus' told you, Miss Phyllis, not a word. An' if she don't turn up by the kids' tea-time –' she nodded towards Edith, who was all ears – 'I reckon somebody ought to be told.'

Phyllis was mystified. 'Is Mrs Berridge . . .?'

'Taken to 'er bed for the day.'

'And Mr . . .?'

'In 'is study. Saw 'im in there meself,' answered Mrs Williams, precluding any doubt as to the master's whereabouts. ''Ad 'is lunch wiv the missus, an' then went back to 'is desk.'

Phyllis was aware of the first stirrings of alarm. A part of her mind was alerted to heaven knew what possibilities, and her first thought was to report the nanny's absence to Mr Berridge. Yet if Faith turned up again within the next half-hour, safe and sound, Phyllis would look foolish and might even be blamed for causing an unnecessary panic.

'If she's not back by six I'll let Mr Berridge know,' she said with deliberate calm, while fighting off visions of policemen taking notes and asking why she had not reported Miss Wiseman's absence earlier.

Mrs Williams went downstairs with the face of one who could say more if she had a mind to, and Jenny was sent up to help with the tea.

'Nanny's bin a bit funny lately, ain't she?' she said, agog with curiosity. 'Where d'yer fink she might've gorn, Phyllis?'

Phyllis frowned and shook her head, concentrating her attention on restraining Claud from stuffing food into his mouth before swallowing what he had already got. Jenny shrugged.

Just after five thirty they heard the stair-gate being unlocked, and Phyllis gave a sigh of relief. But it was Harold Berridge who strode into the nursery, all smiles.

'Ah, there you are, Phyllis – and little Jenny Wren! Have we all been good today, Edie?' He sat down by the fire, and Edith at once went to his side for a kiss.

'Nanny isn't here, Daddy, and nobody knows where she is.'

'What?' He looked up sharply at Phyllis.

'That's right, sir, she's gone out. She's been out for about two hours, so Mrs Williams says.'

'Oh, my God.' He rose at once, gently pushing Edith aside. 'Have you any idea where she went, either of you?'

'No, sir, she didn't say, apparently,' said Phyllis, wishing she had told him earlier. 'I'd been out walking with the children, and when we came home she wasn't here.'

'Never said nothin' to nobody, Mr Berridge,' Jenny broke in. 'Just upped an' went.'

'Why wasn't I told before? Now I shall have to go and look for her,' he said, and Phyllis saw the unmistakable fear in his eyes. 'Look, I'll have to say that I've been called to the theatre to see the director. For God's sake don't mention anything to anybody else, will you? Don't tell Cynthia. She's not well; we don't want to worry her. Hell, I must go straight away.'

And he was gone, leaving the nurserymaid and housemaid staring at each other.

'Blimey, Phyllis, there's summat goin' on between 'em, ain't there?'

'Ssh, Jenny, I won't have gossip, and especially not in front of . . .' Phyllis nodded towards the children, but Jenny insisted on having her say.

'Williams an' Cook said it was 'er, but I fought it was *you*, Phyllis. Sorry!'

'That will be all, Jenny. You may go downstairs at once,' said Phyllis, her face flaming.

She bathed the children and put them to bed, giving Claud a dose of his syrup of chloral, and somehow managing to fend off Edith's questions with smiles and reassurances. Then she turned off their light and sat down by the fire in the day nursery to wait for she knew not what. By now she was thoroughly frightened, though she told herself that the responsibility now lay with Harold Berridge and not herself.

It was nearly eight when she heard the key in the lock, and jumped up in hope and fear but as soon as she heard the two voices, she sat down again with an almost audible groan of relief. The door was ajar, and she heard most of what was said.

'Now you will be all right, won't you? You won't ever put me through this sort of caper again?'

'No, Harold, I won't, now that I know you still love me,' came the low reply. 'Only you should have told me straight away, instead of avoiding me – torturing me like that.'

'I know, Faith, I know. I was a coward, I didn't know how to face you. Ssh, the door's open, and Phyllis is waiting for you in the nursery. The poor girl's been frantic.'

'Kiss me, darling, please.'

'Ssh, ssh. There now, no more silliness, eh? Be a

101

good girl for me.' There was the sound of another kiss, and then Phyllis heard his footsteps going down the stairs.

Faith Wiseman came into the nursery. She was wet and chilled to the bone, but had a look of unmistakable triumph in her green eyes as she unbuttoned her coat.

'I'm sorry if you've been worried, Phyllis, but I needed to go for a good long walk in Richmond Park. Thank you for holding the fort.' She put her hat and gloves on the fireguard to dry, and sat down to take off her wet shoes. 'Poor Harold, I shouldn't have given him such a scare, but at least I understand now how it happened. That stupid woman's a hundred times more demanding than I could ever be, and now look at where it has landed her – another child that neither of them wants.' She held out her hands to the fire. 'It's so *unfair* that a man of his intellect should be chained to an idiot like her!'

She closed her eyes momentarily, and then looked up at Phyllis as if nothing untoward had happened. 'Could you make a pot of tea, Phyllis? And perhaps some toast? I haven't eaten since lunch, and I'm rather hungry.'

There was no real apology for the worry she had caused, and Phyllis suspected that there was no real regret: she had achieved her object in scaring Berridge half out of his mind. Whatever he had said to her had apparently restored her trust in him, but all Phyllis could feel was an overwhelming relief, as if some awful, unnameable disaster had been averted.

The matter of Nanny Wiseman was now openly talked about below stairs; whatever whispers there

102

might have been about the master's preferences before, the events of that fateful Thursday had banished all doubt, and the truth was known by everybody except Mrs Berridge.

Faith regained something of her former composure, but not her confidence. The news of Cynthia Berridge's condition had shaken her badly, and every mention of it was a reminder that she, the nanny, did not and could not ever share the status of the wife of the distinguished playwright and mother of his two children, soon to be three. Phyllis, who had once imagined herself in love with the master – and how unreal that seemed now! – could not but feel the nanny's humiliating position in the household, and for the time being she made no enquiries about employment in Richmond or Twickenham. Her consolation was her love for Teddy Ling, which transformed every part of her life, and though she was by no means sure that he loved her in the same way, their snatched meetings and her constant thoughts of him enabled her to survive the stressful months of Mrs Berridge's pregnancy, which was proving far more difficult than either of her previous ones, or so she said. Nausea, lack of appetite, nervousness and fatigue all combined to make her querulous: she was full of complaints, and Mrs Williams muttered darkly about needing a full-time nurse on the staff.

Whenever Phyllis could escape for an hour or two, Teddy Ling usually managed to arrange an absence from the studios, and on one occasion she met him there – and also met with the amused glance of Sonny Stott, who always seemed to be around on the set. If she had only an hour to spare, Teddy waited for her at the Rose Cottage Tea-Rooms at the bottom of Hill Rise, but on a free half-day she called at Florizel, where Maud always wanted to hear the latest from Travis Walk. The expected event in June gave rise to a great deal of comment and speculation. A midwife, Mrs Chaney, had been booked to attend the confinement and would move into the Berridges' home about mid-June.

'That's if her engagement with Lady Seale of Guildford House has ended by then,' Phyllis explained. 'It seems she only books with ladies of quality!'

'Well, did you ever!' laughed Maud. 'When's 'er ladyship due, then?'

'About six weeks before Mrs Berridge, so she should be free in time. She came on a first visit last week, and made it quite clear that she only deals with the mother and newborn baby, and isn't a nursery assistant!'

'Little does she know what she's in for, duck!'

Phyllis did not add that Nanny Wiseman had muttered that she would keep well out of Mrs Chaney's way, and in fact Phyllis had been quite intrigued by her glimpse of the tall lady in navy blue who carried a large Gladstone bag like a doctor's; it must be very gratifying to be a midwife to the gentry, she thought, recommended by family doctors and satisfied patients.

But all these matters, like the continuing problems with Claud, faded into the background when Phyllis was with Teddy. She listened with rapt attention when he told her about the secrets of filming interior and exterior scenes, close-ups and long shots, and the qualities necessary for successful cinema-photography. His dark eyes would sparkle, and when she and he were alone together in the wintry garden of Florizel or in Marble Hill Park, those eyes would soften as they looked into hers, and his arm would slip around her waist. His hand cunningly found its way inside her coat, between the second and third buttons, and she closed her eyes in sheer bliss, the pride a woman feels in knowing that she is desired by the man she loves. His mouth closed upon her softly opening lips in kisses that took her breath away.

'Oh, Teddy, Teddy . . .'

But alone in her room at Number 3 Travis Walk she sometimes wondered how long this happiness would last. Could she compete with his ambitions in the world of the cinema? Would she ever be able to share his life and career? And how many years must pass before he was ready to marry?

Meanwhile Maud's next and much-anticipated picture, *The Virgin Queen*, had been delayed. Denver Towers, who was to have come over from Hollywood in the New Year, had been engaged to play the lead in a film about the American Civil War, and rather than lose such a star performer the British film had been put on hold. And there was still no Lady Rosamund. Teddy was philosophical.

'We'll need better weather, anyway, for the outdoor shootin'. Just think of it, Phyllis, Hampton Court in the spring – the Queen an' her ladies frolickin' in their costumes an' veils, playin' hide-an'-seek among the trees!'

She listened entranced while Love gave colour to his words and all his imagined scenes.

And then all of a sudden calamity struck. Teddy reported that Maud had gone down with influenza, and the next news was that pneumonia had set in and she was critically ill. Signora Capogna kept all visitors away, nursing the actress night and day, sleeping in her room and praying to the Blessed Virgin that her dearest friend might recover. Dr Godley called daily, sometimes twice, and looked very worried. Cards, letters and gifts of flowers arrived from all over the country, and Mr George Steynes telephoned every day to enquire about her and send his heartfelt good wishes, much to the signora's irritation.

Teddy was desperate. 'I can't think about life without her,' he confessed to Phyllis as they sat at a table in the tea-rooms. 'She's always been there for me. Our parents were drunks, an' she looked after me when I was a kid, else I'd've gone the same way as the others. She used to beg in the streets, an' got caught pinchin' food from some toff's kitchen – that's when we were sent to the Waifs an' Strays home in Dulwich, where I was brought up. I left when I was fifteen and she took me into her lodgin's an' helped me find work, first as a newsboy an' then a messenger at the *Daily Chronicle*. An' in the war she – oh, she's had a terrible life, an' I owe her everythin'. I couldn't bear to lose her, Phyllis.'

His voice broke, and she put her hand over his on the table, deeply touched by his concern for his sister, and for confessing to her this somewhat different version of their shared past. In normal circumstances she knew that pride would have stopped him from revealing so much. She said they could only pray for Maud, and pointed out that she was getting the very best of care, but she felt helpless to be of any real use.

But then the tide turned, and by mid-February Dr Godley pronounced his patient to be out of danger, though for several weeks after the crisis had passed Maud remained weak and listless. Everybody privately agreed that *The Virgin Queen* could not have been filmed on schedule, and so the delay had turned out to be fortuitous.

By mid-March, when Teddy felt that it was safe to leave his sister in Belle's care, he told Phyllis that he had decided to spend some time at the Isleworth Studios as assistant cameraman on some of the two-reelers they were turning out there.

'I might as well take advantage of a lull while we're waitin' for Maudie to perk up an' for Towers to get himself over here,' he said. 'Bertie Samuelson's formin' a new comp'ny at Isleworth, an' they've bought this magnificent house, Worton Hall, a real old mansion with umpteen rooms an' acres o' gardens, lawns, terraces, wooded glades – talk about opportunities for exteriors!'

'You mean it could pretend to be Hampton Court?' asked Phyllis with a smile that hid her sinking heart.

'Precisely! Or Greenwich Palace or Nonesuch or any grand place yer care to name. Anyway, I'm goin' to see how the land lies with Samuelson.'

Always optimistic where films were concerned, Teddy quickly found a place for himself at Isleworth, but it meant an end to quick meetings with Phyllis. She was usually able to see him at Florizel when she had a half-day, but their visits did not always coincide, and Maud, of course, wanted to talk to her brother now that she too saw less of him; remembering how nearly he had lost her, she had to be indulged, and Phyllis had to agree.

Worton Hall lived up to his expectations, and he declared that nowhere else would do as background to *The Virgin Queen*. Some sort of a deal would have to be made with Samuelson, but Maud warned him not to be too cocky.

'That'll be up to the Board o' Directors o' the Alliance Comp'ny, an' they won't thank yer for tellin' 'em 'ow to spend their money,' she said severely. 'An' I dunno as I want to go over to Isleworf an' a lot o' people I don't know. I'm at 'ome 'ere at Twickenham.'

She lay back on the chaise longue and closed her eyes, her face still gaunt and grey beneath the powder. Belle at once suggested that Mr Teddy should take Miss Phyllis out to see the daffodils in the park.

'Better 'n that, we'll get the bus to Kew,' he replied, 'an' get a breath o' spring if the wind i'n't too strong for yer, Phyllis. How about it?'

Phyllis needed no second bidding.

As she was setting out with Claud on a fine spring morning, Dr Godley too was just leaving the house in Travis Walk.

'Miss Phyllis – and Young Master – which way are you going, up the hill? I'll walk with you, if I may?'

'Why, of course, Doctor,' said Phyllis in some surprise. 'Are you going to advise me again about my future?'

'My dear Miss Bird, I beg your pardon, it was unforgivable of me, and now that circumstances have changed, I want to ask if in fact you'll be staying on for a while. I heard that you might be leaving.'

Phyllis gave him a sidelong glance. 'So I'm to forget about training to be a teacher or a nurse, then – is that what you're saying now, Dr Godley?'

'I can see you're not going to let me off easily, Miss Bird. I apologise for what I said to you earlier, but I don't retract it, I merely postpone it. You see, I've just told Harold that I'm concerned about his good lady.

She needs plenty of rest, and no emotional upsets. Her blood pressure's rather high.'

Phyllis nodded, assuming that he was telling her not to dismiss Mrs Berridge as a silly woman who was making a lot of fuss over a natural process.

'That housemaid who came in with her breakfast – is she a capable sort of woman, would you say?' he asked.

'Certainly. Mrs Williams is most reliable.'

'Good. I'll suggest to Harold that another maid be taken on to free the excellent Mrs Williams to care for the invalid.'

Invalid. So he must be really worried.

'You've got your hands full with Young Master here, or I'd suggest *you* took over Mrs Berridge,' he went on. 'And another thing I'd like to ask you is, er – how is poor Miss Wiseman these days?'

Phyllis hesitated, wondering what he meant, how much he knew. 'I try to give her all the help I can, Doctor, but it isn't always easy,' she said carefully.

'No, it can't be. It's a difficult time for her, and thank goodness you're there, my dear. You'll move on eventually, and other arrangements will have to be made for –' he nodded towards Claud – 'but first we must get this baby safely born.'

Their climb had brought them in sight of the extensive building works at the top of the hill, and Godley pointed to the site.

'I see they're getting on well with the Star and Garter, though it'll probably be another two years before it's completed – and God knows there are enough damaged ex-servicemen to fill it when it opens its doors, and plenty of opportunities for dedicated single nurses for years to come.' He lowered his voice and she heard him mutter, 'Terrible, terrible.'

Was he remembering his own wartime experiences, she wondered.

'Right, I'd better let you go, Miss Bird. We'll keep this little chat to ourselves, shall we?'

'Of course, Doctor.'

'Good girl.' He smiled and retreated back down the hill, turning into Nightingale Lane towards the Petersham Road. He knows everything, thought Phyllis uneasily. Once again she had been made a fellow conspirator.

'Phyllis! Miss Phyllis! 'Ave yer seen the *Standard* this evenin'?' asked Jenny. Phyllis had just come in with Edith, whose school had broken up for the Easter holidays.

'No, why? What's in it?'

'Ain't yer young man told yer? Them two actors over from America – look, 'ere, read it!' Under a headline, 'British Film Studio Welcomes USA Actors', Phyllis read the news item.

Mr Denver Towers, well known in Hollywood for his adventurous film roles, arrived at Southampton Docks yesterday, and travelled by railway to the film studios at Twickenham, to be welcomed by the Alliance Company film directors. He was accompanied by Miss Georgia Kift, who is to appear with him in a film about the life of the Tudor Queen Elizabeth, to be made at Twickenham and Isleworth studios. Also taking part in this prestigious venture will be Britain's own much-loved actress Miss Maud Ling, now happily recovered from her recent illness, and Mr Reginald Thane.

'Didn't 'e tell yer, Phyllis?' It was generally known at Travis Walk that Phyllis was walking out with Miss Ling's brother.

'Oh, I've known for weeks that Denver Towers was coming over,' she replied lightly. 'But Miss Ling's illness caused a delay, and Mr Ling's been very busy travelling between the two studios. Come on, Edith, let's get you out of that uniform.'

The fact that she had not seen Teddy for over a week, and had known nothing of Towers' imminent arrival was a shock to her, and on her next free half-day she made the familiar journey to Twickenham on foot, arriving just after three. Maud and Reginald Thane were talking in the cluttered living room, and glanced at each other quickly when she joined them.

'There's only Reg an' me 'ere, duck. Teddy's taken the ovvers up to Waterloo to see the 'Ouses o' Parli'ment, an' maybe go dahn as far as the Tower. Americans like all that sort o' stuff. They won't be late back, 'cause we're startin' shootin' tomorrer. Y'ought to see what I got to wear – a great stiff skirt stickin' aht all rahnd me like a shelf. They 'as to put a little wooden stool underneaf it so's I can sit dahn!'

Phyllis smiled and took a seat, hiding her disappointment; Thane seemed glum, and she suspected that she had interrupted a private talk between the two of them. When Belle came bustling in to advise Maud to take an hour's rest because of her early start the following day, Phyllis thankfully rose and said she would walk in the park.

Once out in the bright April sunshine she took no pleasure in the signs of spring all around her: she was full of doubts and anxieties. Teddy had treated her with less than common courtesy, and she felt that Maud and Thane were aware of this, though they

111

had not put it into words. After all, both of them had warned her . . .

She stayed in the park until just after five, returning to Florizel to find that Teddy and his guests had also returned. As soon as she set eyes on Miss Georgia Kift she recognised a deadly rival, even though Teddy came straight to her side and kissed her in front of them all.

'Oh, Phyllis, I'm sorry – I should've let yer know. It's been pandemonium around here,' he muttered, but then smiled, raised his voice and announced, 'Miss Phyllis Bird!'

Denver Towers strolled over at once, tall, golden-haired and tanned by Californian sunshine. His blue eyes travelled over her.

'Very happy to meet you, Miss Bird,' he drawled in deep, caressing tones. 'Y'know, Teddy, this is my idea of an English rose. Is it the climate that produces such flawless complexions?'

Phyllis blushed, which he found enchanting, but she soon realised that no English rose could compete with Georgia, a sleepy-eyed southern beauty with a lazy charm that ensnared men on sight. She moved around the room, acknowledging the admiring looks as no more than her due, bestowing her smiles upon Teddy, on Thane and on Sonny Stott who had joined the party, but she had few glances to spare for her own sex.

She is a man-eater, that one, thought Belle Capogna.

Teddy's a dead man, thought Maud. Poor Phyllis – but maybe it's better now than later.

Reginald Thane thanked God that he was not as other men, but he sighed, nevertheless.

'What d'yer think of our Lady Rosamund, Phyllis?

112

I'n't she an eyeful, eh?' whispered Teddy. 'What *is* it about these American girls?'

Phyllis didn't know, but whatever it was, Georgia had it in abundance, and knew how to use it.

Over drinks and a buffet, Phyllis found Denver Towers again at her side. 'No doubt about it, you British win hands down on historicals,' he told her. 'I've got the best part of my career as Sir Roger Garland.'

'Sir Roger – I thought that was Mr Thane's part,' she replied, looking across the room to where Teddy was standing beside Georgia. He's trying to think of something to say to her, she thought; he's as tongue-tied as I was with him at first.

'We've made a few changes to the story,' Denver was saying. 'Thane's the wicked Earl of Leicester who gets me sent to the Tower of London because the Queen's in love with me – but I'm in love with the Lady Rosamund, though I have to hide my feelings because of the Queen's jealousy.' Towers had in fact rewritten and recast *The Virgin Queen*, and told the director that he hadn't crossed the Atlantic just to lose out to *that* old pansy.

Phyllis was confused by the changes. 'So does Sir Roger get beheaded in the Tower?'

'Bless yer, no, duck, we can't go cuttin' orf the 'ero's 'ead!' laughed Maud, coming up to them at that moment. 'No, 'im an' the Lady Rosamund escape an' stow away on a ship goin' to the New World.'

'Where they start up a rival studio in the Californian desert,' murmured Thane, at which Sonny Stott choked on his Valpolicella, and Maud wagged a reproving finger at them both.

'Now, you two, be'ave yerselves, an' don't give a

bad impression to our guests. This is goin' to be a big drama!'

'On the contrary, it's the most God-awful balderdash, Maudie, a waste of your talents and mine,' interjected Thane loudly, filling up his glass. 'In fact you're the only good thing in it, my darling.'

There was an awkward silence, and Phyllis wished she knew Teddy's opinion of the rearranged plot. And she longed to be reassured that she was still the sweetest girl he knew.

But it was not to be. Teddy got deeply involved in a discussion with Towers and Miss Kift, and Reginald Thane got very drunk. The party broke up early and Maud insisted that a taxi-cab be called for Phyllis. Teddy saw her into it, and gave her a quick good-night kiss, promising that he would get in touch as soon as the busy film schedule permitted.

She returned to Travis Walk with her face set like flint, resolving to see Teddy through this emotional crisis. Georgia Kift had come over from America, and in the course of time she would go back there. Phyllis would wait, patiently and calmly, until Teddy had got over her.

Yes! She would wait for as long as it took, and let nobody guess at her aching heart.

Chapter 8

As the time for Mrs Berridge's delivery drew nearer, the atmosphere at 3 Travis Walk became increasingly oppressive. Faith Wiseman's unhappiness was reflected in her moody silences, and Claud's unpredictable behaviour taxed Phyllis's patience to the limit; even Edith's childish chatter got on her nerves. Below stairs Mrs Williams could seldom escape from her mistress's petulant demands, while Dr Godley grew more worried about the lady's swollen ankles and blotched, puffy face. He ordered complete bed-rest with the curtains drawn, so the servants had to tiptoe past her room and speak in whispers on the second floor.

There being no accommodation for another housemaid, extra assistance was provided by a grimy charwoman who came in daily to do 'the rough' – an unsatisfactory arrangement – and the whole household looked forward to the day when Mrs Chaney would move in and take over the care of Mrs Berridge – and the new baby, when it arrived – for the traditional month of nursing.

And once that happy event had taken place, Phyllis promised herself that she would leave the Berridges and find useful work elsewhere, perhaps nearer to the Twickenham studios. She had heard virtually nothing about the progress of *The Virgin Queen*, but kept telling herself that when it was completed Georgia Kift would go back to where she had come from, and Teddy would turn again to his faithful sweetheart who would receive him without any reproaches.

Meanwhile she braced herself for Ascension Day which fell on 25 May and was a school holiday. Mr Berridge had planned a treat, a picnic in Richmond Park, beside the two Pen Ponds. Gannon was to make two trips, first with the picnic hamper, groundsheets, folding deck chairs and the 'Catering Corps', a reluctant Cook and eager Jenny; then he would return for Nanny, Phyllis and the children. Williams, of course, had to stay behind with Mrs Berridge, who was resentful at not being included, but Dr Godley absolutely forbade it.

'Won't you be joining us?' Faith asked Mr Berridge, her eyes fixed on his face with barely concealed desire.

'I'll stay to lunch with Cynthia, and walk up in the afternoon,' he told her. 'To see if you're all being good!' he added to Edith, who as usual was jumping up and down in her excitement.

Phyllis foresaw a day of struggling single-handed with Claud and having to look as if she were enjoying herself.

Ascension Day was bright and sunny. Gannon duly made his two trips, and by eleven o'clock the four picnickers had climbed the grassy slope to the tree-crowned summit south of Sawyer's Hill, and descended to where the sunlight dazzled on the expanse of the two Pen Ponds. The deck chairs had been set up near to where Cook and Jenny were spreading out the contents of the hamper on a large sheet, and Phyllis would have been glad to rest for a while, but Edith at once ran down to the water's edge and Claud impatiently strained on his reins to follow her. Men were fishing in the Great Pond, but the children were only allowed to paddle and play beside the little one. Claud had a toy boat with a red sail, which Phyllis set forth on the water, and she made a paper boat for Edith; both ended up in the reeds on the other side. Faith Wiseman walked slowly back and forth along the broad bank between the two ponds, her head down and apparently oblivious to the activity around her. When luncheon was served, she only picked at the cold ham and boiled beetroot, and gave Phyllis no help with Claud; the birds had a feast with his messily crumbled sandwiches and seedcake. Cook brewed tea over a spirit-kettle, and there was home-made lemonade for the children.

As Phyllis had expected, Faith came to life as soon as Harold Berridge appeared, his face flushed beneath a straw boater and his jacket undone, having walked up from the house.

'Phew, it's turned out warm!' he smiled as Edith ran up to tell him about the fate of the two boats, but Faith seized his arm.

'Do let's go for a stroll around the Great Pond,' she begged, her green eyes imploring. 'It's such a beautiful day, a perfect afternoon – ah, do, do!'

He looked around at the others, who were all ears and eyes. 'But what about Phyllis? She'll be tied to Claud all day,' he protested, adding in an undertone, 'We mustn't be selfish. This is a family treat.'

Tired and perspiring as Phyllis was, her hands chafed by the constant tugging of the leather rein, she would have preferred to be left in charge of the children rather than play the part of unwanted chaperone, but it was difficult to put this tactfully. As it was, she had no need, for it was Edith who effectually prevented the pair from strolling away on their own.

'Daddy, Daddy, come and see what I've found!' she cried, attracted by the teeming wildlife of the pond – the frogspawn and the tiddlers. Again and again she took hold of his hand and dragged him towards the water's edge, even persuading him to take off his shoes and socks, roll up his trousers and join her in a muddy paddle. When he had dried his feet and put his shoes back on, he offered to take Claud off Phyllis's hands for a while, but she declined, knowing how it would infuriate Faith to have to drag the boy along with them. The nanny was already in a state of barely controlled exasperation, a volcano threatening any minute to erupt, and the last two hours dragged by with only Edith enjoying herself. Phyllis heaved a huge sigh of relief when Gannon appeared again to take them home.

'Hasn't it been a nice day, Phyllis?' said the little girl, clambering on to her father's lap as they all bundled into the car.

'Yes, dear, a lovely treat for Ascension Day,' Phyllis replied, avoiding the eyes of both Mr Berridge and the woman whose miserable frustration was almost palpable as the car drove up Sawyer's Hill and out of the park.

The sound of clanking metal and hurried footsteps broke in on Phyllis's sleep, and she heard a voice calling urgently to her.

'Phyllis! Miss Phyllis, are yer awake? The master wants yer to 'elp wiv the missus.'

'What? Who – what time is it?' mumbled Phyllis, shaking off the fragments of a dream of being held in

Teddy's arms. Claud gave a fretful mutter, reminding her that she was sleeping in the night nursery. Faint light filtered through the curtains, and her little bedside clock said twenty past three.

Knock, knock. 'Miss Phyllis!' said Mrs Williams, and Phyllis started up, now fully awake. She leaped out of bed, pulled her dressing gown off its hook and wrapped it around her. Merciful heavens, was Mrs Berridge having the baby five or six weeks early?

'All right, Mrs Williams, I'm coming.'

Out in the corridor Nanny Wiseman had appeared. 'What's the matter, Williams?'

'The master wants Miss Phyllis to 'elp 'im wiv the missus.'

'Why, does she think she's in labour?' asked the nanny, but Phyllis cut her short.

'I'm sorry, Faith, but you'll have to keep an eye on Claud. He's awake and might start wandering around.' And without another word she hurried down the stairs after the maid, praying that she would be able to cope with whatever awaited her.

In the Berridges' bedroom Harold was completely distraught. 'Oh, Phyllis, she's having the most terrible *fit* – bitten her tongue half through – blue in the face – foaming at the mouth,' he babbled. 'I've telephoned Godley to come at once, but she needs help *now*, and I can't ask Faith. Oh, is there *anything* we can do in the meantime?'

On the bed Cynthia Berridge was a frightening sight. Her whole body twitched in a series of convulsions, and flecks of bloodstained saliva bubbled at her blue lips; her eyes were open and staring sightlessly, the lids fluttering.

Phyllis forced her memory back to Miss Daniells' school where one of the boys had had epilepsy and

119

was sometimes seized with fits in the classroom or playground. She thought quickly, trying to remember what Miss Daniells had done for the child.

'Get something between her teeth to stop her biting her tongue – a wooden spoon, something that won't break,' she said, and Williams rushed off to fetch one from the kitchen. 'And can we get her over on to her side, and put a towel under her head to catch the dribbles?'

She and Berridge between them rolled the rigid body over on to the left side. 'Pull her left arm back underneath her, so she can't roll back again,' she said, and as soon as the wooden spoon was produced, she wound a handkerchief round the handle and, squeezing Cynthia's jaw to make her open her mouth slightly, she slipped it in between her teeth so that it protruded on either side of her mouth. The woman gagged on it with choking sounds, but she could no longer injure her tongue.

They heard the doorbell ring and the sound of footsteps in the hall. The door had been left unlocked, and Dr Godley dashed up the stairs. When he saw Mrs Berridge he struck his fist against his forehead.

'Eclampsia, and in a fit, by God! It's not good, Harold. Not good at all.'

'Then for God's sake do what you can for her, Charles,' groaned the husband. 'Save her for me – oh, help her, Charles!' The door was open, and his words could be heard on the staircases.

The doctor quickly opened his bag and took out a rubber apron, which he put on. 'Now, Phyllis, I'm going to need your help. Harold, you'd better wait outside. Get yourself dressed and take a glass of something.' Turning back to Phyllis, he spoke quietly. 'She needs urgent sedation, and the only way

I can give it to her in these circumstances is by the back passage.'

'Yes, Doctor,' Phyllis heard herself speaking calmly as he took from his bag a length of red rubber tubing and a glass funnel.

'I need half a pint of warm water, not too hot, with a pinch of salt in it.'

'I'll fetch a jug from the kitchen, Phyllis,' said Mrs Williams at once. 'You stay 'ere wiv the missus.'

Godley attached the funnel to one end of the tube. 'She's on her side already, that's good. Is there something to grease the end of this rectal tube? Face cream? Good, that'll do. And we'll need a couple of towels.'

The lubricated tube was passed gently but firmly into the rectum, and when Mrs Williams returned with a jug of tepid salt water, the doctor took a small brown glass bottle from his bag. 'An ounce of this must be added to the saline solution – there we go. Now hold the funnel, Phyllis, and I'll pour it in. Hold it up high for me – good girl.'

Phyllis grasped the funnel with one hand, and with the other prevented the tube from coming out. A little of the solution leaked back around it, and the room was filled with the overwhelming odour of paraldehyde. Ounce by ounce the solution ran into Cynthia Berridge's body, and began to have its effect on every nerve and muscle. She gradually relaxed and ceased twitching; her eyelids closed and she breathed deeply. Her face flushed pink. Godley felt the pulse, and nodded.

'That's better. Leave the tube in for the time being,' he muttered. 'Stay with her while I go and have a word with Harold. She should go to hospital if she can stand the journey by ambulance.'

'What about the baby, Dr Godley?' Phyllis ventured to ask.

He shook his head, turning down the corners of his mouth. 'This is a very dangerous condition, my dear, and the child is probably dead after that prolonged fit. We must concentrate all our efforts on saving the mother.'

It was now four o'clock and beginning to get light. Mrs Berridge lay deeply asleep while the doctor spoke to her husband outside the room and asked to use the telephone. Jenny hovered on the stairs, and Mrs Berridge's serious condition was known throughout the house.

Phyllis wondered how Faith Wiseman must be feeling: was she hoping for the death of the woman she so despised? It was not a pleasant thought.

And then, all in the space of less than a minute, the situation completely changed. Cynthia woke up with a loud, muffled cry. She turned over on to her back, and the rectal tube shot out with a sudden emptying of the bowel into the bed. She screamed, clutching her abdomen and drawing up her knees.

Dr Godley rushed into the room. 'Oh, my God, she's bearing down, I think. Just hold on to her, Phyllis, and let me see.' Phyllis held her arms firmly around the woman's shoulders while he separated the thighs and saw the crown of the child's head advancing.

'All right, Mrs Berridge, my dear, I'm here, Dr Godley – you're all right, Cynthia – just give a little push down for me if you can.'

Phyllis supported the groaning woman as with another contraction a tiny baby was expelled into Godley's hands. Williams was doing her best to scoop up the semi-solid matter that seemed to be smeared everywhere, all over the mother's legs and the bedlinen. The combined smell of that and the paraldehyde was terrible, but the three attendants scarcely noticed it in their efforts for the newly born child.

'A clean towel to wrap it in, please!' demanded Godley. 'And can you get me a pair of scissors and a piece of string or something to tie this off?'

Williams produced nail scissors from the dressing-table drawer and a length of narrow pink ribbon. The umbilical cord was tied and cut, and the placenta slithered out within the next half-minute.

'What have we got here, then?' said Godley. 'A little boy, and alive, by some miracle. Hello, young man. You've taken us by surprise, haven't you?'

And to the wonder of them all, the scrawny little creature answered him with a mewing cry, a high-pitched squeak that proclaimed him to be a living, breathing, new human being.

'It must have been the rectal infusion that stimulated the contractions,' said Godley, wiping the back of his hand across his forehead where damp strands of hair clung. 'But in any case old Mother Nature had decided to intervene and get the baby out of danger – she sometimes knows best. All right, Harold, come in and see what we've got here for you. A little boy!'

Harold Berridge came into the room, bursting into sobs of joy and relief. 'A son! Oh, she's given me another son, another chance – oh, let this one be a normal child!'

'I'll try to get in touch with Mrs Chaney, but I believe she's still waiting for Lady Seale's confine-ment,' said the doctor. 'Phyllis, you take the baby for the time being, wrap him up well and weigh him on the kitchen scales – I'll guess about four to five pounds, and lucky to be alive. Is there a feeding-bottle in the house? He'll need fattening up, and his mother won't be in any state to feed him. You could try him on a little boiled cow's milk and water, half and half.'

Cynthia Berridge suddenly sat up. 'Where am I? What's happened?' she asked, staring at the group around the bed. 'Harold, tell me what's happened – and what on earth is that *dreadful* smell? It's given me the most awful headache.'

Her husband leaned over and embraced her with tears and kisses. 'Dearest Cynthia, you've given me another son,' he said brokenly. 'Thank you, oh, thank you, my darling. I love you.'

In the middle of this emotional scene the door opened and Edith appeared in her nightie, followed by a completely naked Claud.

'Phyllis, what are you doing?' she asked. 'What's that you're holding? We haven't had any breakfast and Claud's got nobody to dress him. Where's Nanny?'

Silence. Harold Berridge straightened up and looked enquiringly at Phyllis, who shook her head. He turned to Mrs Williams and the doctor, but neither of them could give him an answer. His face turned deathly pale.

'I shall have to let the police know this time, Charles,' he said, moistening his lips.

'Yes, Harold, you will,' the doctor replied.

An early angler casting out his line saw the body floating in the shallows at the southern edge of the Great Pond.

Chapter 9

The whole household was thrown into a state of shock as the news spread like wildfire, and not only in Travis Walk. By the end of that fatal Friday, long before the evening newspaper's version of events, it seemed that the whole of Richmond knew that the playwright had become father to another son, Michael, and that the Berridge children's nanny was dead, drowned by her own deliberate action.

Phyllis's first response to the news was shocked disbelief, a numbing of her emotions; then came bitter regret that she had not tried harder to understand Faith; and as the initial shock gave way to realisation of the tragedy that had taken place, a deep rage took hold of her, a burning resentment of the way Harold had used Faith Wiseman as long as it suited his purpose, but when he felt his marriage and family life threatened by her passion for him, his coolness had broken her heart.

It was almost a relief to have her usual duties to attend to. Edith had to be hastily got ready for school and taken there by Gannon; Claud had to be washed, dressed, fed and toileted; he still had to be constantly watched. Yet now for the first time ever, Phyllis found him the easier one to cope with, simply because Edith was a normal, inquisitive child who asked questions.

'But where has Nanny *gone*, Phyllis?'

'She's gone a very long way, dear, to a place where

'– where she'll be happy, and – and she'll stay there.' Phyllis did not meet the little girl's eyes, for she felt unable to embark on a confusing explanation about death, and how Nanny had gone to be with Jesus.

'But when will she come *back*, Phyllis?'

'Not for a very long time, dear – in fact she won't be coming back again, not ever,' Phyllis blurted out in a kind of desperation. 'Please, Edith, don't ask me any more questions now. Gannon's ready to take you to school. We've all got to be very good – and brave.'

Which she herself was conspicuously failing to be, she thought miserably. Her head ached, a constant dull pain behind her eyes that would not go away. She did not want to eat, and cups of tea were tasteless and unreviving. Wherever she looked she saw images of Faith, the defiant green eyes proclaiming her love for Harold Berridge and her belief in his need of her: Faith returning from her wanderings in Richmond Park on a cold, wet winter's night; Faith walking restlessly up and down the bank between the two Pen Ponds – was that only yesterday? – and she saw in imagination that final hour of anguish in the grey dawn, Faith plunging fully clothed into the dark water, going in deeper and deeper, colder and colder until her head disappeared beneath the surface. Had her body protested against its fate, struggling and lashing out before succumbing to the death wish of her mind? Phyllis could not banish the picture, and thought she would see it for ever.

And yet when it was her turn to be questioned by the grave-faced police inspector in the drawing room, she carefully concealed her knowledge.

'Were you aware that Miss Wiseman was worried or upset about some personal matter, Miss Bird? Some – er – relationship in her life, perhaps?'

126

'No, Inspector, none that I know of.'

'Did she ever say anything about taking her own life? Did she ever mention the subject of suicide at all?'

'No, she didn't.' That at least was true.

'She didn't confide in you, even though you spent so much time together in the nursery?'

'No, Inspector, she was usually quiet and didn't say a lot.'

'Would you say that she was sometimes moody and unpredictable in her behaviour?'

'Perhaps a little bit, sometimes – but she kept her feelings to herself,' faltered Phyllis. 'She was an excellent children's nanny.' Tears welled up in her eyes, and the inspector thanked her and said that would be all.

There seemed to be nobody she could turn to. Mrs Williams was much too busy to talk, and Jenny had to assist with the cleaning and laundering following the messy childbirth. Dr Godley was kept constantly occupied throughout that Friday morning.

A consultant obstetrician came to see Mrs Berridge and gave his opinion that she would probably make a good recovery now that the baby was born, and the likelihood of further fits would diminish with every hour that passed; already the puffiness of her face and legs was lessening. He felt that she would make better progress at home under the care of a trained nurse than in hospital. He also advised that she be told that Nanny Wiseman had been called away on account of family illness; there would be time enough later to tell the shocking truth.

Mrs Chaney, the midwife, arrived, saying that she could stay for a week only, as she was due to move into Guildford House on 1 June in preparation for

127

Lady Seale's confinement. Another monthly nurse would then have to be engaged, and both Dr Godley and Mrs Chaney knew of private nurses that could be called upon, there being now no need for a midwife, but a nurse well-trained in the care of small babies was essential.

'And what will happen to my poor darling little Claud, Dr Godley, now that we've lost the nanny who understands him almost as well as I do myself?' wailed Mrs Berridge, who insisted on trying to sit up and talk. 'The nurserymaid we engaged to help her last year is really quite good, and she'll have to take over until Nanny comes back. So inconvenient!'

Godley made no reply, knowing that he would have to talk very seriously with Harold Berridge about Claud's future.

'What a relief to have Mrs Chaney here!' sighed the lady. 'Williams is such a dull, plain, plodding creature who can't possibly understand a mother's sensitivities, and that young housemaid is hopeless, an empty-headed chatterbox – but now I shall be properly cared for.'

The doctor's usually humorous mouth was set in a very straight line as he answered. 'There was no midwife present at your delivery, Cynthia, and heaven only knows how I would have managed without the combined efforts of Phyllis Bird and Mrs Williams.'

'Really?' She stared in surprise. 'Actually I can remember very little about the birth. It was the pregnancy that was the worst ordeal, and that went on for months. I'll see that Williams and Bird are paid an extra ten shillings at the end of the month. Dear me, little Michael cries a great deal! Mrs Chaney only fed him half an hour ago, and there he is crying again already. Do you think he may have colic?'

That afternoon Dr Godley climbed the nursery stairs to speak to Phyllis before Edith was due home from school.

'My dear girl, how can I ever thank you for what you did in the early hours of this morning? The Berridges will be forever in your debt, whether they realise it or not. Sit down, Phyllis. You can keep an eye on Young Master while we have a talk. How are you feeling now?'

She felt her eyes welling up again, and began to tremble; she could not speak.

'My dear, this has been a great shock to us all, but perhaps to you more than anybody, as you were closest to Faith Wiseman. The sooner you get away from here, the better it will be.'

At hearing the kind concern in his voice, she looked up, her lips quivering. 'I just can't get her out of my mind, Doctor. It was *awful* being asked all those questions by the policeman, and not telling the truth, just to save *that man*.'

'Ah.' He was alerted by the bitterness of her tone. 'I'm glad that you were discreet, Phyllis, and I'll have to watch my own words at the inquest. Remember that we're sparing her reputation as well, poor girl. Nothing you might have said about, er, Harold Berridge could bring her back to us, and might have caused a great deal of trouble for the family. Please don't reproach yourself on that score.'

'But I should have been a better friend to her, Dr Godley,' said Phyllis wretchedly. 'I didn't show her any sympathy. And now when I think of what she went through yesterday at that ghastly picnic –

129

she looked so dreadful, so despairing. Oh, poor Faith!'

She burst into tears, seeing again the lonely figure walking up and down the bank with her terrible thoughts. She pictured her on the nursery stairs, hearing Berridge's plea to the doctor. *For God's sake do what you can for her, Charles. Save her for me . . .* How the words must have pierced her, their unequivocal message ringing in her ears . . .

'I'll never forgive Mr Berridge, never,' Phyllis sobbed. 'Pretending that he loved her when he hadn't got the faintest intention of giving up his wife and his family life. *That's* why she drowned herself – she realised that he was finding her a nuisance and not worth the risk of a scandal. I can see it all now – he must have dreaded that Mrs Berridge would find out. He didn't love poor Faith at all!'

Godley put a firm hand over hers. 'Hush, Phyllis, ssh, ssh. I'm sorry, but that's the way of the world, especially now, when so many young women are surp—' He checked himself, and continued, 'Try not to blame Harold too much. He's only a man, and the poor girl made herself available. I know he should have been stronger, but there you are, he's married to Cynthia and was very worried about her – so was I! – and he panicked when he thought he might lose her. But that was no fault of yours, Phyllis, so you must not go on blaming yourself.'

When she had calmed a little, he spoke seriously about what she should do next. 'Now, listen to me. The Berridges are going to have to face facts at last, and shoulder their responsibilities towards this poor boy.' He lowered his voice, though Claud had shown no reaction whatever to their conversation. 'He'll have to go into a special institution to be cared for, and you must get away from here, Phyllis.'

'Yes, Doctor, I know. I couldn't bear to stay on without Faith. But what about poor little Edith? She's going to lose both of us, and she'll feel so let down.'

He sighed. 'Yes, it's hard on that little girl, but you must remember that she is the Berridges' child and not yours. Her father is extremely fond of her, and she of him – in fact they'll help each other to survive the upheaval, I'm pretty sure of that. And another nanny will be found for her and the new baby, but *this* young man is the big problem. His parents will never find another treasure like you, willing to act as nurse and gaoler for twenty-four hours a day, and with precious little appreciation. I have a suggestion, Phyllis: how would you like to work as a nursing assistant at a private maternity home for a while? I know where there is a vacancy, and as you're just the sort of sensible, practical young woman that's needed, I'd be happy to recommend you. It would tide you over until you decide what you want to do in the long term. How do you feel about it?'

Phyllis wiped her eyes. 'It might be a good idea, Dr Godley,' she replied, having no immediate wish to enter another family home as a domestic servant. Also, she did not want to commit herself too deeply at present, for she still dreamed of Teddy turning to her again when the glamorous Miss Kift had gone back to Hollywood.

'Right!' said the doctor, slapping his knee and getting up. 'I'll have a talk with Berridge, and tell the matron of Oakleigh House that I've filled the vacancy! I'd like to see you out of here by the end of the month.'

Phyllis opened her eyes wide. 'As soon as that, Doctor? But Mrs Chaney will also be leaving then, won't she?'

'Humph.' He gave a grunt, remembering Mrs Berridge's remarks about her domestic staff. 'There'll be a replacement for her, but the time has come for some changes here.'

And serve them right, he added silently to himself.

The tragedy of the Berridges' nanny was reported briefly in national newspapers over the weekend, and Phyllis wondered if her parents would read of it, or have it pointed out to them by neighbours agog with curiosity. The household was still in turmoil, and when Jenny came up to the nursery to help, she reported that Mrs Chaney got very little rest, 'what wiv the missus wantin' somefin' all the time, an' the baby always 'ollerin'.' Phyllis's own nights were disturbed by Claud's restlessness and the baby's distant high-pitched crying that marked the hours of the night and brought back troubled images to her mind.

At some point on the Saturday she knew that Dr Godley had been closeted with Berridge in the study, and there had been a long discussion at which a decision was reached. With great reluctance the playwright agreed that Claud, now five years old, should be sent within the next week to Tall Pines, a private home for mentally defective children near Epsom. Dr Godley had already been in touch with the medical supervisor to make arrangements for the boy's admission.

'Get it done, Harold, and don't say anything to Cynthia for the time being, not until she's recovered. As for Phyllis Bird, the girl's on the verge of a complete breakdown from nervous exhaustion, and I'm recommending her to the matron of Oakleigh House as a nursing assistant. She's been overburdened for long enough.'

Berridge groaned aloud, but had no choice but to acquiesce. He knew that he depended on Godley's discretion to avoid an all-out scandal, which would be disastrous. His wife's life had been saved and he had another son, but these blessings had to be paid for; he would always be haunted by Faith's reproachful eyes, and now he had to part with his elder son, a different kind of lifelong burden.

'I'll tell Cynthia it's just a temporary measure, until we've all settled down again into a normal routine,' he compromised.

'I'd advise you to say nothing at all to her until she's up and about again, Harold – and then tell her the truth, which is that it has to be permanent,' replied Godley bleakly. 'I blame myself, you know, for not being more forthright with you on this – and other – matters. We all turned a blind eye, with the exception of Miss Wiseman. She always knew how it was with Claud.' He sighed and shook his head. 'But this girl Bird deserves a better fate, and I'm not prepared to stand by and watch her trying to tackle that boy single-handed for the foreseeable future, totally unappreciated.'

'Of course not, Charles,' said Berridge unhappily. 'I've been abominably selfish, I know.'

'Well, it hasn't only been you, Harold.' Godley was about to mention Cynthia Berridge's infinite capacity for self-deception, but decided that he had said enough for one day. He pitied this man who had become his friend, but took care not to show it, and there was still the coroner's inquest to be negotiated.

He put a hand briefly on Berridge's shoulder and took his leave, his face sombre.

For the doctor had his own regrets in the matter; never again would he connive to assist an illicit liaison.

On Sunday morning Phyllis and Jenny took the children to the morning service at St Matthias' Church. Heads turned as they entered and curious stares followed them to the Berridge family pew. Phyllis found it impossible to concentrate on praying as she would have liked to do, so just kneeled down and named her parents, the two children now in her care, Mrs Williams and Jenny – and Teddy Ling. Would he hold her in his arms and kiss her again one day? Or would she never see him again? She was quite thankful to have Claud fidgeting beside her, as he gave her something else to think about. She noticed that Dr Godley was not in church; was he visiting at the Berridges? Or catching up on his sleep.

And then when they returned to 3 Travis Walk, there was Mrs Williams calling to her from the top of the kitchen stairs, her face unusually broadened in a wide smile.

'Phyllis! Phyllis, there's a gen'leman waitin' for yer in the master's study! I fink 'e's the one from Twick'nam!'

Phyllis felt quite faint with joy. In just one moment everything changed, and she beamed gratefully at the bringer of good news, sending up a silent prayer of thanks. He had heard the news and had come back to her. Oh, thank heaven for Teddy, her own dear young man! Leaving the children with Jenny, she rushed up to the first floor and knocked on the study door.

134

'Come in,' said Berridge, and in she went. There beside the playwright, smoking one of his cigars, stood Denver Towers.

'Oh!' Phyllis's gasp of surprise and disappointment was evidently interpreted as one of delight by the actor, who stepped forward with a charming smile.

'Why, Miss Bird, good morning!' he greeted her in his lazy drawl. 'Mr Berridge here has just been saying what a wonderful help you've been to his family at a difficult time.'

'Hello, er, Phyllis,' said Berridge awkwardly. 'It seems that our friend Maud Ling wants to see you, and Mr, er, Towers has come to take you over there for an hour or two.'

'But I've got to see to Claud. He'll be wanting his dinner –' began Phyllis, but Berridge broke in, remembering what Godley had said about the work of the nursery staff. And about Claud.

'But we can't disobey a command from Miss Ling, can we?' he said with an attempt at jokiness. 'Williams can surely take over Claud for a couple of hours, so if you'd like to . . .'

'I must change out of uniform first,' she apologised, and Towers waved the cigar in an expansive gesture.

'Just take all the time you need, Miss Bird. Whenever you're ready, I've got an automobile waiting outside.'

He was all courtesy and consideration, opening the door of the chauffeur-driven car for her, and then seating himself beside her.

'Maud has talked of nothing else but the recent sad event in the newspapers,' he told her as they descended the hill. 'She's been kinda worried about you, and this morning I knew I just had to do something about it. I figured that Berridge could hardly refuse to let you off the leash for a coupla hours.' He smiled at her as he spoke.

'It's very kind of you, Mr Towers, and you're right, I'm just longing to see . . .' Her voice broke, and she swallowed, unable to continue. A large white handkerchief was discreetly pressed into her hand, and Towers maintained a tactful silence until they arrived at Florizel, where he helped her out of the car and stood back to let her go on ahead to greet Maud, who came towards her with arms outstretched.

'Oh, Phyllis, yer poor little duck, what a fing to 'appen – I bin that worried abaht yer!'

'Maud – and Belle – I'm so glad to see you again!' They embraced as the tears flowed.

'Come an' sit dahn an' tell us all abaht it – that's if yer want to, o' course.' Maud put her arms around Phyllis as they sat together on the chaise longue, and at this point Towers made his apologies and withdrew.

'I won't intrude on a private conversation between ladies,' he said pleasantly. 'I'll drop by later, say about three, to collect Miss Bird and take her back, if that's OK with her.' He glanced at Maud, who nodded over the top of Phyllis's head, and then left them, closing the door behind him.

''E's bin really good, 'specially as I ain't seen much o' Teddy. Nah then, 'ow's everyfing at Travis Walk? 'Ow's 'Arold bearin' up?'

Phyllis wiped her eyes on Towers' handkerchief, and cleared the huskiness from her throat. 'Oh, *he's* all taken up with his wife and the new baby. He thought he was going to lose them both, you see, early on Friday morning, and he said to Dr Godley,

"Save her for me if you can, for God's sake" – and poor Faith Wiseman must have heard everything.'

Maud Ling took a sharp breath in and let it out on a long 'Aaaah' of understanding.

'O' course, o' course, I should've guessed,' she said, shaking her head. 'Did *you* know they was 'avin' an *affaire*, Phyllis?'

Phyllis nodded. 'I found out before Christmas, but what was the good of saying anything? She was so sure that he loved her and needed her, I believed it myself – at first.'

'The poor gal must've been in a pretty bad way to do that to 'erself.' Maud leaned closer as Belle came in with a tray of tea. 'D'yer fink she was expectin', Phyllis?'

'No, she said they used – er – birth control,' Phyllis whispered, and Maud looked quite shocked.

'Blimey, did she really tell yer that? Well, I never 'eard anyfing like it. Oh, my Gawd!'

'And I'm sure that she really *wanted* to have his child, Maud. It was an awful shock to her when we heard that Mrs Berridge was expecting another baby – in fact, that's when things started to get worse. He'd told her that he and his wife didn't – oh, it was terrible, he just didn't love Faith in the way she loved him, and he was afraid his wife would find out.'

'Hm, an' she still could,' Maud said significantly. 'I mean, we ain't the only ones to put two an' two togevver. An' what's goin' to 'appen abaht Claud now she's gorn? You ain't goin' to struggle wiv 'im all on yer own, are yer?'

'Oh, no, he's going into a special home in a few days' time, a place called Tall Pines near Epsom. And Dr Godley's got me a nursing assistant's job at a private maternity home, because he says I can't stay at the Berridges' after this.'

'An' 'e's right, yer can't. An' 'e'll do 'is best to get 'Arold out o' the firin' line, 'cause there could still be a lot o' gossip.' Maud was thoughtful. The doctor seemed to be in a hurry to remove Phyllis from the house. Was he trying to save her from the same fate as the nanny? 'Poor Nanny Wiseman, eh? An' now she'll be forgotten an' 'e'll be forgiven. That's the way o' the world, duck.'

'Which is just what Dr Godley said.' Phyllis's mouth was tight.

'But there's nuffin' yer could've done for 'er, duck. She made 'er own bed, an' she ain't the only poor, lonely, left-over woman to go that way. It's a tragedy all rahnd. C'mon, let's 'ave a cup o' tea wiv a drop of oh-be-joyful in it. Pass us the Napoleon, Belle.'

As the talk took another direction, they naturally spoke of films and filming. Phyllis longed to ask about Teddy, but thought it best to wait until Maud mentioned him.

'How are you getting on with *The Virgin Queen*?' she enquired.

'Oh, we finished that. Just abaht wore me aht, an' all.' Maud gave a reminiscent groan.

'But – Mr Towers is still here.' Phyllis could not bring herself to name Georgia Kift.

'Yeah, well, 'e's got this bee in 'is bonnet abaht 'istoricals, y'see, an' wants to make anuvver one while 'e's over 'ere, an' we're startin' on it this week. *The Court Musician*, it's called, to be made at Isleworf 'cause o' Worton 'All. It's just the right settin', so they all tell me.'

There was a certain absence of enthusiasm in Maud's voice that prompted Phyllis to look more closely at the actress. Her face was as lovely as ever, but her eyes lacked sparkle, and she looked tired.

'Are you really recovered now, Maud, after that horrid pneumonia?' Phyllis asked.

'Yeah, fit as a flea. It's just that I don't fancy anuvver 'istorical, straight on top o' the ovver one. An' Reggie Thane won't be in it, in fact 'e's talkin' abaht goin' back to the featre. It makes sense really, 'cause 'e's got such a lovely speakin' voice, an' it's a pity to waste it on films where nobody can 'ear 'im.'

'It is a big pity that you and Reginald do not make a picture again together like *On Wings of Love, cara mia*,' interposed Belle. 'So romantic and beautiful, much better than the other one.'

Maud rolled up her eyes. 'Fact is, Reggie an' Denver don't get on, and neiver wants to work wiv the ovver.'

'Is it not surprising Reginald does not want to play a bad man again? But he was most of all angry to see you as that old, sad queen left all alone at the end after the Rosamund woman sailed away to America with that other one!' Belle almost shouted. 'And she will make herself again the heroine of this *Court Musician*, and pretend to be better than you!'

'Oh, do shut up, Belle, it ain't like that at all,' sighed Maud. 'We're bofe supposed to be beautiful women after the same man, that's all!'

'And *she* will get him, though he is not worth half of Signor Thane!' Belle snapped back. 'Your public will not like this, *cara mia*. They want you in films of romance with Reginald holding you close against his chest, yes?'

Maud's eyes were sad. 'I ain't so sure abaht that any more, Belle dear. Reggie ain't the same these days. 'E's inclined to 'it the bottle an' say fings what're best kept quiet.'

Phyllis thought this might be a good moment to ask about Teddy. 'And – is your brother involved with this film about the court musician?'

Maud gave her a pitying look. ''Course 'e is, duck, wiv Miss Yankee Doodle in it. Gorn completely orf 'is chump over 'er. There's no talkin' sense to 'im since she's come on the scene. All I can say is, 'e's in for a shock when she gets bored an' finds somefin' older an' richer. She'll be orf like greased lightnin' – whisssht!'

'And the better it will be for all of us,' muttered Belle sourly. 'Teddy is a fool.'

'Steady on, Belle. Teddy's a kid, an' got to learn the 'ard way, like we all 'ad to.' Maud glanced at Phyllis, who quickly averted her eyes. 'Anyway, duck, I'm glad Charles 'as taken yer under 'is wing. Did yer say a maternity 'ome?'

'Yes, a place called Oakleigh House.'

'Oh, very nice. That's where women go to show that their 'usbands can afford ten guineas for a bed an' a doctor for the delivery. Not as posh as a monthly nurse in yer 'ouse, but better 'n a midwife on a bicycle. Charles sends quite a lot of 'is muvvers in there.'

This sounded promising, and Phyllis smiled. She ventured no more questions about Teddy, but wondered if the atmosphere at the studios was as bad as Belle Capogna made it sound. She concluded that the signora was just resentful of the way Georgia Kift had upstaged Maud Ling in one film, and looked likely to do so in another. And she, Phyllis, could understand only too well, except that she felt a different kind of resentment against the actress.

Promptly on the dot of three o'clock Denver Towers presented himself and his hired chauffeur-driven car at Miss Bird's disposal; and ten minutes later he deposited her at Number 3 Travis Walk.

'Thank you, Mr Towers, you've been most kind,' Phyllis said again, wishing with all her heart that he was Teddy.

He seemed in no hurry to return to the car. 'Quite a place Berridge has here,' he remarked, glancing up at the handsome façade of the house. 'I must bone up on his plays some time – they could be good plot material. Though maybe not as dramatic as his own life,' he added slyly. 'A houseful of women, a little governess in love with the master – and a birth and a death within an hour – wow.'

Phyllis stiffened. 'That's not a matter I wish to discuss, Mr Towers,' she said coldly. 'If you'll excuse me, I must get back to my duties.'

'Oh, no offence meant, Miss Bird. It's just that I can't help overhearing what everybody else is saying. I do beg your pardon, please forgive me. And remember, any time you need an automobile and a driver, just get in touch and it will be my pleasure.'

'Thank you. Good afternoon, Mr Towers.' Fortunately she had the key she used when with the children, so opened the front door and closed it firmly behind her.

Towers smiled to himself as he descended the steps. A typically English girl, he thought, cool and reserved, yet he was fairly sure that a passionate heart beat beneath that prim exterior. British himself by birth, Towers' upbringing in a Birmingham backstreet was a closely guarded secret, but he liked English women and considered himself a good judge of their latent sensuality. He enjoyed a challenge – and he also had a taste for virgins.

The time had come to leave Travis Walk, just nine months after Phyllis had first arrived there, full of hopes of finding a better life than the one she had left behind at North Camp. At least she had learned more about herself, and hoped she had benefited by her experiences. There had been bitter disappointments in addition to the shock of Faith Wiseman's suicide. She had fallen in love twice, first with Harold Berridge and then with Teddy Ling, both dreams had come to nothing, and she also felt she had failed with Claud; even though she now knew that he could never be a normal child, it still troubled her. When on the Tuesday she had to pack his clothes and few belongings, including the building bricks, she was as saddened by his lack of emotion towards her as she was by the fact he was leaving his home and family, possibly for life. Gannon was to drive him to Tall Pines, and Phyllis wondered if she was expected to accompany him there, but Harold Berridge told her that he would travel with his son and see him admitted as a resident. Mrs Berridge had still not been informed of the decision.

Edith was transferred for the time being to a little dressing room adjacent to her parents' bedroom, and had the freedom of the dining and drawing rooms, though was not yet allowed to see her mother, for fear of what she might let slip about Claud and Nanny Wiseman.

Mrs Chaney departed, and a new nurse took her place in the guest room, which she shared with baby Michael. Phyllis was no longer needed.

On the Wednesday, the last day of May, she said

goodbye to Mrs Williams, Cook, Gannon and Jenny. Mr Berridge handed her an envelope containing double the amount of wages due to her, and shook her hand in genuine gratitude, though she found it difficult to return his smile. Gannon carried her trunk down the stairs, and she left the third floor for the last time, its rooms empty and silent, the stair-gate unlocked.

Part II

The Road to Ruin

A pity beyond all telling
Is hid in the heart of love:

– 'The Pity of Love' by W. B. Yeats

Chapter 10

The inquest on the death of Faith Wiseman was held at Kingston-upon-Thames, and made headlines in the *Richmond & Twickenham Times*, as well as being reported in the London *Evening Standard*, because she had been nanny to the Berridge children. No recorded connection was made between her position in the playwright's household and her lamentable suicide by drowning, about which Mr Berridge spoke of his deep distress and that of his wife. Dr Charles Godley's evidence made the reason for it all too clear: Miss Wiseman had been suffering from a form of acute melancholia affecting young women, a condition which he said had sadly increased in recent years, since the war had taken the lives of so many young men. The coroner had nodded gravely at the implication.

It was not considered necessary for Mrs Berridge to be called, and it was noted that she was recovering from the recent delivery of a premature infant. The only other person called upon to make a statement was the deceased woman's married sister, who told the coroner through her tears that Miss Wiseman had been misunderstood and undervalued by her employers, adding bitterly that one of the children she'd had to care for was an imbecile, which had greatly added to her anxieties. This statement was later removed from the report on the inquest, and the coroner brought in a verdict of suicide while the balance of mind was disturbed. He expressed sympathy for Miss Wiseman's sister and for Mr and Mrs Berridge and their children. No mention was made of their son's recent admission to Tall Pines, although this fact had quickly become common knowledge and various unofficial opinions had been expressed.

Phyllis read the report in the local paper delivered to Oakleigh House, and noted that Dr Godley had exonerated Harold Berridge from all blame, though rumours continued to circulate for a while, until displaced by the next nine-day wonder, provided by a group of vociferous local churchmen who publicly denounced the latest craze for jazz music on gramophone records, which they said reflected a downward trend in morals, especially among the new generation of young women who dressed immodestly, smoked cigarettes, drank cocktails and painted their lips bright red. Arguments raged and households were divided for and against the thundering clerics and, as Maud Ling had predicted, Faith Wiseman was forgotten and Harold Berridge forgiven. Phyllis was thankful not to have to see him or his wife again.

The kind of women who chose to have their babies in Oakleigh House, an imposing three-storey edifice on Ormond Road, were wives of men who could afford the high fees that guaranteed the presence of a doctor at delivery and the prestige that a modern, well-equipped maternity home conferred on its clients. Their husbands were professional men – bank managers, local solicitors, officers of the armed forces – but they also included members of the emerging class of self-made men whose business enterprises had prospered sufficiently for them to buy a detached house in Richmond and the recognition of their new neighbours. The war had changed many things, and the old class barriers were gradually beginning to crumble.

When Phyllis was interviewed by Matron Groves, she felt that the woman's observant grey eyes assessed her in an instant; she was told that Dr Godley had given her an excellent testimonial, on the strength of which Matron was happy to offer her the resident position of nurserymaid for a month's trial period.

'You will have to be flexible, Miss Bird. Your basic duties will be the care of the babies and the cleanliness of the nursery, but you will be asked to assist the maternity staff by sitting-in with mothers during the early stages of labour, allowing the midwife – myself in most cases – to rest or get on with other duties until the birth becomes imminent. This can be tiring, especially at night. Otherwise you will help when necessary with the serving of meals and toilet rounds, and take the babies to their mothers for feeds. We have eight maternity beds, two bays with three beds in each, and two single rooms.'

Phyllis nodded politely. 'Yes, Matron, I understand.'

She was lent two dark blue dresses and six large bibbed aprons, also three little white caps similar to the ones she had worn at the Berridges'. She was told to buy black shoes and stockings, which she already had, and at the end of the month's trial she would be expected to purchase her own uniform.

From the start Phyllis felt that she had made the right decision, or rather that Dr Godley had made it for her. Her experience of life in domestic service stood her in good stead with the patients; she was quietly respectful, quick to fetch and carry for them as required. She soon became valued as a 'sitter' with women in labour when pain followed pain with no apparent progress. She learned to be patient and encouraging, especially with those having their first baby, giving them the emotional support they needed to calm their fears. She plumped up pillows, offered sips of sweetened barley water and rubbed their backs as they sighed and writhed with increasingly strong contractions, massaging firmly up and down with a powdered hand. Under Matron's instruction she got to know the signs of approaching delivery and, when the midwife, who was invariably Matron herself, took over, Phyllis remained available to assist at delivery if she had no pressing duties in the nursery. On an occasion when the baby was born before the arrival of a doctor, Matron conducted the delivery with calm efficiency, tactfully complimenting the mother on a quick and easy birth. Phyllis watched her tie and cut the umbilical cord, and had a warm cot ready. Tea for the new mother and her attendants had to be brewed when the afterbirth had been expelled, and then she helped to wash the mother and transfer her to a clean bed in one of the three-bedded bays.

Babies were fed four-hourly, and it was Phyllis's duty to change their napkins and carry them one at a time from the nursery to their mothers' beds and back again. Breast-feeding was encouraged, but not all mothers wished to do it and, having paid the fees charged at Oakleigh House, the decision was theirs. When a baby was fed by bottle – or as Matron said, artificially fed, the general rule was to give a half-and-half mixture of cow's milk and water with a level teaspoon of sugar added to every four ounces, which was then 'scalded' in a special milk saucepan by being brought to the boil and allowed to cool. It was given in a boat-shaped bottle with a rubber teat at one end and a valve at the other to allow air in and ensure a steady flow. The bottles were cleaned with a special brush and sterilised with the teats in boiling water.

Apart from Matron there was only one other trained midwife at Oakleigh House, the pale, fair-complexioned, middle-aged Mrs Draycott, who suffered from a mysterious condition that gave her nervous palpitations. She had apparently trained Matron Groves during the war, and now spent much of her time in a little room adjacent to the matron's office, sewing and embroidering; she could make a pair of name-bracelets for a baby in ten minutes, using red thread on white tape which was then put round the wrist and ankle of each new arrival. The rest of the staff were untrained maternity nurses with varying degrees of experience, who knew the different doctors' likes and dislikes. Most of these were non-resident, as were the cook, the handyman who stoked the boiler, and the domestic staff or 'orderlies', one of whom was on permanent night duty. Matron had a flat at the top of Oakleigh House, and other resident staff had rooms on the second floor.

Quite a lot of staff time was spent 'on call', and Matron never seemed to be away from the place; she was always on hand to assist a doctor with a birth or to deliver a baby herself in the absence of a medical attendant, though a doctor's personal supervision was what the patients had paid for and expected. Her attitude towards them was deferential, but with enough authority to assure them that they were in good hands. Most of them were used to giving orders and being waited on, though when faced with the ordeal of childbirth they were as fearful as any other woman, and enquired anxiously about pain relief in labour. The current new vogue was something called 'twilight sleep', much talked about by women who could afford a doctor's attendance.

Matron explained to Phyllis that 'twilight sleep' was induced by carefully calculated injections of morphia and scopolamine, which brought about a semi-conscious and almost pain-free state during which the muscles relaxed and labour proceeded naturally and smoothly.

'That's the theory, anyway, Nurse Bird, but in practice it wears off in a couple of hours and can't be repeated too soon or too close to the birth, because it makes for sleepy babies, and that's not good. A doctor has to be present the whole time.' She smiled. 'Dr Godley has his own method of avoiding twilight sleep, by putting off the injection for as long as possible, and giving the usual "mother's mixture" of potassium bromide and choral hydrate until labour is well advanced, and then he tells them it's too late for an injection, and promises them chloroform for the actual birth. And they all think he's wonderful!'

Phyllis had left the Berridges, but she now saw a good deal more of their GP, who was a frequent caller at Oakleigh House. Not only did he attend the confinements of his own patients, but also those of GPs with no taste for the dangers of obstetrics, who were thankful to hand over to him their awesome responsibilities in this field, in exchange for a cash payment in addition to the basic fee he was paid by the patients' husbands.

During her very first week at Oakleigh House

Phyllis was called upon to assist at a delivery where Godley was in charge of the actual birth while Matron sprayed a light shower of liquid chloroform on to a square of gauze held in a metal frame about three inches above the patient's nose and mouth. It was not enough to cause complete loss of consciousness, and the mother clung desperately to Phyllis's arm during the last few agonising expulsive contractions. But then came the miracle of birth, and the pains of labour were immediately forgotten in the rejoicing of the mother – and the doctor and midwife and Phyllis – over the new life that had just come into the world. Phyllis was jubilant: this was so different from her life at Travis Walk, for here she was no mere servant at the beck and call of a *madam*. The general exclamations of thanksgiving for the birth were music in her ears.

And she suddenly thought of Teddy Ling, and how she had dreamed of being married to him one day, and bearing his children: a dream that was very unlikely to come true now.

But Teddy's sister had not forgotten her, and sent word to her through Dr Godley.

'Our mutual friend Miss Ling is asking about you, Nurse Bird,' he said. 'She wants to know how you like it here, and when can you go over to Florizel?'

'Oh, Dr Godley, I'm sorry,' Phyllis apologised, embarrassed that the doctor should be used as a messenger.

'Don't worry, I've got a very soft spot for Maud,' he smiled. 'Actually she's looking rather tired, and the signora's not very happy about all this filming at Isleworth. It would do her good to spend some time with a friend who's not talking films morning, noon and night – so shall I tell her that you'll come over soon? Weekends are best.'

'I'll send her a note, Dr Godley. Thank you very much.' Phyllis had mixed feelings about Florizel and the possibility of seeing Teddy there, with or without the irresistible Miss Kift. But if Maud was asking for her . . .

The upshot was that Matron told Nurse Bird that she need not be on call between midday and ten o'clock the following Sunday, the third in June.

Looking at her small collection of frocks, two to be exact, Phyllis decided on the daisy-patterned one in thin cotton; the neckline plunged at the back in a low V that showed her shoulder blades. A pretty straw hat, white gloves and her little Louis-heeled shoes completed the outfit, and she looked in the mirror with satisfaction; her skin was clear, and her newly washed hair swept forward on to her cheeks. It was a fine afternoon, and she decided to walk, knowing herself to be as attractive as any of the fashionable ladies parading on the riverside walk. Oh, would Teddy be there to see how nice she looked?

They were all in the garden at Florizel. A large parasol had been put up over a table on the paved area at the back, and Maud sat in state beneath it, against a background of climbing roses and the creamy Madonna lilies that filled the air with their heavenly scent, a perfect setting for the actress and her visitors. Phyllis quickly noted Belle, Reginald, the Stott boy and another young man; neither Teddy nor Georgia Kift was to be seen.

'Phyllis! Cor, don't yer look a treat – come an' join us. Yer know ev'rybody – oh, this is Dickie Seddon-Pike, a real live lordship – yeah, honest! An' Georgie's arahnd somewhere.'

Phyllis stiffened. So the Kift girl *was* there. And was Teddy also somewhere around?

Reginald Thane appeared at her side, offering iced tea from a crystal jug.

'You look a perfect picture, my dear,' he said, and her heart warmed to him because he so obviously meant it. 'I'm so glad to see that your new employment suits you.'

'It's nice to see you too, Mr Thane,' she said. 'Are you going to make another film with Maud?'

'Gladly, if I'm asked, dear,' he answered with what she thought was a touch of wistfulness, and at that moment she caught sight of Sonny Stott's pale eyes roving over her, a half-mocking grin on his face. She instinctively recoiled from the boy – though of course he wasn't a boy, he was the same age as herself – twenty-six. She wondered why Maud tolerated him at Florizel, for he made no effort to be pleasant to her guests.

Young Dickie Seddon-Pike, however, more than compensated for Stott's lack of charm. He was another devoted young admirer of the lovely Miss Ling, and he really was a lordship, having inherited the title when his father fell at Passchendaele. In other words, he belonged to Teddy's generation, those who had missed the war, though they remembered it well enough – the grim news, the ever-lengthening casualty lists, the dreaded telegram . . .

'I was frightfully lucky to be invited over here,' he confessed to Phyllis eagerly. 'A friend of mine on the *Daily Chronicle* who knows Maud's brother got me an introduction to her. Isn't she just the most adorable creature in the world?'

Phyllis smiled, and agreed that Maud was as sweet and kind as she was beautiful.

'Ah, here comes my useful friend,' he said. 'I say, George, have you met Miss – er – I'm frightfully sorry, but I didn't quite catch . . .'

Phyllis breathed an inward sigh of relief to discover that 'Georgie' was not Miss Kift but Mr George Steynes, who stared uncertainly, not sure whether he had seen her before.

She attempted to put him at his ease. 'We've met only briefly before, Mr Steynes. I'm another of Maud's friends,' she said lightly. 'Isn't this a perfect afternoon?'

At that moment Maud called to her, 'C'mon over 'ere, duck, sit dahn an' tell us all abaht Oakleigh 'Ouse,' she commanded. 'D'yer like it there? Is it better 'n Travis Walk?'

Phyllis settled herself down for a session of women's talk over tea and cucumber sandwiches, cut wafer-thin. Maud was in a chatty mood, and confided that she loved entertaining her friends, but only at Florizel.

'They 'as to come to me, duck, I don't go to them. Reggie calls these young ones "Maudie's Boys", an' I don't see why I shouldn't be nice to 'em. Does a woman good, 'avin' a few star-struck kids arahnd!' She laughed her hearty peal, but her face clouded as she continued. 'Yer don't catch me openin' fêtes an' stuff like that, Phyllis, 'cause I don't really trust the poshies. They didn't bovver wiv me when I was an 'alf-starved kid beggin' on the streets an' pinchin' a bit o' bread an' bacon for me an' Teddy. Got caught an' sent to a Waifs an' Strays' 'ome. That's where me little bruvver was brought up, though 'e wouldn't fank me for tellin' yer.'

Phyllis smiled into the shadowed hazel eyes. 'I already know that, Maud dear,' she said gently. 'He told me himself when you were so ill. I admire you all the more, both of you – the way you've risen above all that – that background.'

'Cor, did 'e tell yer that, gal? You can bet 'e'd never tell '*er*! Ah, I don't mind *you* knowin' – yer're a proper friend – but if I was to lose all me money an' turn into a nobody agin, most o' the people I know 'ud say I was as common as dirt an' look dahn on the way I talk. Oh, yeah, Phyllis, I don't flatter meself!'

By which Maud Ling meant that she did not deceive herself, and would never forget her origins. Phyllis was touched, and felt a small satisfaction that Teddy had told her what he would never tell his new love.

Other members of the crew arrived, including a bevvy of pretty, giggling girls who had small parts in *The Court Musician* and were waiting for Denver Towers to appear. Belle went off to supervise the serving of a lavish cold supper, and as Thane was pouring cocktails they heard the front gate clang. There was a general stir as Towers strode through the house and out through the open casement door, followed by Teddy and Georgia. Phyllis shrank back behind Maud's chair, but Towers made his way straight towards her.

'Maud, you're looking gorgeous tonight – oh, and is that really Phyllis I see at last? I'd have come earlier if I'd known you were here.'

And to Phyllis's utter amazement he stepped forward and kissed her in front of the company. She was aware of envious looks from the young girls, and conscious that Teddy must be watching and taking note. Denver planted himself at her side after loading a plate with cold beef and salad.

'A glass of wine, Phyllis my dear?' said Thane, at

her elbow, adding quietly, 'They finish at Isleworth next week, so with any luck that pair will be off and away.'

Denver Towers clapped his hands together and gestured for silence.

'Ladies and gentlemen, I have an important announcement to make!' he declared, every inch the actor. 'As we know, that wonderful film *The Court Musician* is almost completed, another great historical picture. We've all enjoyed filming at the magnificent Worton Hall, and I've struck a deal with Mr Samuelson that we'll celebrate with a weekend house party there before we all take leave of each other and go our separate ways!'

This caused some cheers, though as Phyllis took a glass from Thane's hand he gave her a weary smile of resignation. Sonny Stott, standing behind him, visibly brightened and gave a thumbs-up sign. Maud turned to say something to Phyllis just as Belle came bustling out of the house with a shawl.

'It is getting cooler, *cara mia*. You must take guard against the damp evening dews.'

Maud rolled her eyes, but submitted to having the shawl wrapped round her. ''E's right, Phyllis, it's beautiful dahn by the river there, wiv tennis courts an' lots o' trees an' places to walk. Be nice if yer could come for an hour or two, duck.'

'Cocktails on the terrace and dancing till dawn,' added Towers, laughing down on Phyllis's some-what bewildered expression. 'You *will* be able to come to the party, won't you? It's the second weekend of July, but I'd change it to suit you if you asked me.'

Ah, she thought, what heaven it would be, if only Teddy and I were still in love and enjoying it together! She made herself look directly towards him: their eyes met and he gave her a hesitant smile, which might have been one of apology, even regret; but then he turned back to Georgia Kift, who was holding up a forkful of meat to his mouth, and laughing. So Phyllis gave her attention to Denver Towers, who was waiting for an answer.

'I honestly don't know if I can get away, Mr Towers, but I'll try. And when we've finished supper I'd better be getting back to Oakleigh House.'

'I'll take you in the automobile. It's just outside.'

She thanked him, and was not entirely sorry when Teddy watched them leaving together. When they were settled in the back seat of the car behind the driver, Towers gave a short, deprecating laugh.

'To be honest, I'm not sorry to get away from that little gathering for a while. What with the signora standing guard over Maud, and poor old Reggie and that ghastly boy – oh, my God!'

'Oh, do you mean Sonny Stott?' asked Phyllis, without understanding his implication. 'I don't like him either – in fact, I don't know why Maud puts up with him.'

Towers kept his face straight. This girl was so innocent. The truth was that he had become bored. Georgia's predictable fling with Maud's kid brother had gone on for too long, and was getting on his nerves. She'd come back to him as soon as their liner left Southampton, though he wasn't sure that he still wanted her. He'd planned an affair with Maud Ling while he was over here, but that hadn't worked out, and he was exasperated by that big, soft Italian woman, who was always around and fussing and fidgeting with wraps, medicines and murmured endearments – it *was* quite sickening. And, in any

159

case, Maud wasn't exactly in the first flush of youth; in fact she sometimes looked downright haggard. There were plenty of young girls in the cast as extras, more than willing to succumb, but Towers did not care for easy victories. Now, *this* prim and proper little thing was something really different, and it had been amusing to see Georgia's face when he'd left with her. Hah! Serve the silly bitch right.

Yes! There would be a rich reward for whoever awoke the slumbering passions beneath this girl's chaste summer frock, but he'd need to play his cards right. She was a lady, and he'd have to act the perfect English gentleman.

So when he escorted her to the staff door of Oakleigh House and thanked her for a delightful evening, he made no attempt to kiss her again, but held her hand for a brief moment.

Phyllis had to admit to herself that his manners were impeccable.

Back in the daily and nightly routine of the maternity home, Phyllis put all thoughts of the proposed party at Worton Hall to the back of her mind; there was more than enough to occupy her in this place where she was so obviously appreciated.

'Can you work overnight for me on Friday, Nurse Bird?' Matron asked her later that week. 'The nurse on the rota has had to go to see her mother, who's been taken ill.'

'Of course, Matron. Er – will anybody be on with me?'

'There'll only be Sibley, but she's very good. And it might be a quiet night, you never know. I shall, of course, be on call as usual if there's an admission or if you run into any problems.'

On Friday Phyllis was expected to work until lunch time at one o'clock, and then took to her bed, drawing the curtains against the bright June sunshine. She dozed fitfully, but was unable to get any real sleep before presenting herself in Matron's office at half-past eight, just as the last visitors were leaving. Maud told her that there were five delivered mothers and their babies, which she knew from the morning – and Mrs Freda Lancaster, who had been admitted during the afternoon in labour with her first baby at thirty-one.

'She could still be waiting for me in the morning, Nurse Bird. The head's high, and I think it's a posterior position, which always makes for a long labour, especially when it's the first. Anyway, Dr Godley will be up to see her and leave instructions. Call me if you're worried about anything.'

'Yes, Matron. Thank you.' This at least was reassuring, for the doctor always inspired confidence in his mothers and their attendants, and Phyllis was anxious to show him that his recommendation of her had not been misplaced. She introduced herself to Mrs Lancaster and listened to the baby's heartbeat as she had been shown, using a little stethoscope rather like an ear-trumpet placed on the abdomen: pit-a-pat-pit-a-pat-a! She thought it a thrilling sound, and assured Mrs Lancaster that all was well.

Just before ten the orderly came looking for her. 'Fe docduh fin de offid, Nurf Bird!'

Poor Sibley, who had been brought up in a children's home, had a badly repaired hare lip and cleft palate. She was on permanent night duty to keep her out of sight of the mothers who might be upset by her contorted mouth and indistinct speech. At first Phyllis had been surprised that such an unfortunate person should be employed at a place like Oakleigh House, but she soon discovered that Sibby, as most of the others called her, was reliable and conscientious, expertly changing the babies and giving them bottle-feeds during the night. She seldom spoke to the mothers, and some of them thought she was of low mentality, but this was not true; she loved babies and had an instinctive flair for knowing if they were thriving or not, whether they were hungry or crying with colic or some other discomfort. Phyllis never once heard Sibby complaining of tiredness or aching feet as the other orderlies did, nor did she appear to have any grievances about her lot in life. With no education to speak of, and no relatives that she knew about, she simply got on with her work, and Phyllis learned not to dismiss her but to value her.

'Fe docduh fin de offid, Nurf Bird!' meant that Dr Godley had arrived and was in Matron's office. When he saw Phyllis his grey eyes softened behind his horn-rimmed glasses.

'Well, now, Nurse Bird, how's our Mrs Lancaster doing?'

'Matron thinks it could be a long labour, Dr Godley, because the head's high. She said something about a – a posterior position.'

'Did she now? And she's probably right too; she usually is. It means we'll have to be patient and wait for Nature to take her course – keep Mrs Lancaster sedated with pot. brom. et chor., keep the bowel and bladder empty, and don't whatever we do let her bear down on a cervix that isn't fully dilated. That means not until we can see the top of the baby's head. Right, let's go and have a look at her.'

His cheery manner and measured sympathy had a

good effect on Mrs Lancaster's spirits, and he told her that she was in safe hands with Nurse Bird. 'And I won't be far away, my dear. We'll get through it together.'

Eleven o'clock. The mothers were tucked down and the babies were in the nursery.

'Any tea or coffee going, Miss Sibley?' asked the doctor, and the orderly at once put down in its cot the baby she was holding, and hurried to the kitchen. Soon a tray with freshly brewed coffee and biscuits was placed on the desk in the office, where Phyllis joined him but did not sit. He poured out three cups.

'So – it could be an all-night vigil, Nurse Bird?'

She shrugged and replied rather lamely, 'We don't know, do we, Doctor?'

'Ah, I see you've learned the first lesson in midwifery. If I could answer the eternal question, "How much longer is it going to be, Doctor?", I'd charge five guineas a time and be able to run a three-seater Citroën on that alone!'

Phyllis smiled. 'Shouldn't you go home and rest for a few hours, Dr Godley? Matron's on call, and she'd telephone you if Mrs Lancaster –'

He grimaced. 'I don't know, Nurse Bird. I've got a touch of the heebie-jeebies about our Mrs Lancaster. Might even consider the dreaded twilight sleep in her case, seeing that she's got a long way to go – and if I give her that stuff, I'll have to stay around. Is there an empty single?'

'Yes. I'll ask Sibley to fetch you a blanket.'

'Good, let's give her a first – a one and only injection, then. Are you all right about listening to the foetal heart? . . . Good girl!'

Midnight. Having sent Mrs Lancaster into blissful semi-oblivion, Godley went into the single room, removed his shoes and tie, hung his jacket over a chair, undid his top shirt button and stretched himself out on the bed. Sibby had spread a sheet over the green and white counterpane, and she now entered and reverently covered him with a blanket.

'Thank you, Miss Sibley my dear.'

'It all right, docduh.' She closed the door noiselessly, and went to the nursery. Phyllis sat down beside Mrs Lancaster on a small armchair with a very hard seat.

One o'clock. Two o'clock. Three. The hours of the warm summer night ticked by, and Mrs Lancaster stirred. Phyllis helped her on to a commode chair and gave her a dose of the bitter 'mother's mixture', following it with a fruit-drop to suck. The woman groaned.

'How much longer do you think I'm going to be, Nurse Bird?'

'You're making progress all the time, Mrs Lancaster. Every pain pushes your baby a little further along.' Phyllis held her hand, rubbed her back and gave her sips of chilled barley water from the rumbling refrigerator in the kitchen. Her footsteps roused Godley from sleep, and he sat up, shaking his head to dispel a fading dream. He got off the bed and padded in his socked feet to the labour room, his hair wild.

'Ugh, Phyllis, what's the time? How's the foetal heart?'

'It's steady at a hundred and thirty, doctor. She's resting quite well at present.'

Sibby was at his side, whispering, 'Vall I put fe kettle on aga', docduh?'

'Oh, yes, please, dear, thanks – let's have tea this

time. Only I must go to the jakes first. And I can't find my glasses anywhere.'

'Oo've god dem od, docduh.'

'Oh, yes, so I have. Thank goodness you're here to point out such things to me.'

All three of them sat in the kitchen, and Sibby poured out tea. Doctors' needs came before all other considerations with her, and she was never happier than when waiting upon Dr Godley. She idolised him.

'This is the worst part of midwifery, the long night vigils,' he remarked with an enormous unconcealed yawn. 'No wonder the old-time midwives had a reputation for the gin bottle to help them through a long labour.'

'It must be much worse for the mother, surely,' said Phyllis.

'Uh-huh. It isn't just the staying awake, it's the worry about how it's going to turn out. Nags at you. Makes you wonder why we do it.' He set down his cup. 'Thanks, Miss Sibley. I'd better go and have a word with poor Mrs Lancaster.'

'I'm so sorry to keep you up so late, doctor,' sighed the mother, whose contractions were now stronger and more frequent. 'How much longer do you think it will be?'

He laid a hand on her abdomen. 'You're doing very well, my dear. More than halfway there, I'd say.'

By four o'clock he had dozed off on a kitchen chair, and just after five Freda Lancaster sat up, calling for the bedpan. 'I think I want to open my bowels, Nurse!'

Phyllis had been warned by Matron that this was often a sign that the cervix was fully dilated, the downward pressure of the baby's head giving a sensation of fullness in the back passage. She helped the woman on to the bedside commode, but only a little wind passed. Mrs Lancaster groaned and strained. 'I still feel I want to go, Nurse.'

'Don't push, don't push, dear,' Phyllis said hastily. 'I'll tell Dr Godley I think you're getting on.'

Sibby came to help get the patient back on to the bed, and Dr Godley's gentle examination proved that the cervix was indeed fully dilated and the head visible as a little dark circle of hair at the height of a contraction.

'Mm. She's got a lot of pushing to do, and I've got a feeling it's going to need helping out,' murmured Godley. 'You'd better send for Gladys.'

'I beg your pardon, Doctor?'

'Oh, sorry, Gladys Groves – Matron. Send Miss Sibley to ask if she'll come down. I think we'll need the tongs for this one. Is the steriliser on?'

Matron was duly called, and was down in five minutes, in full uniform. An hour passed in preparation, with the doctor and Phyllis encouraging Mrs Lancaster to push down with each contraction, while Matron set a large trolley with the usual bowls, swabs, cord ligatures and scissors, plus the addition of the obstetric forceps, steaming from the bubbling steriliser. Every quarter of an hour Phyllis or Godley listened to the foetal heartbeat, which gradually slowed to below a hundred. At six fifteen it was down to ninety.

'Right, here we go,' said Godley, aproned and with hands soapy from washing. 'Got the Schimmel-Busch mask handy, Matron? Get her legs up into the stirrups. Urethral catheter – episiotomy – and now for the big heave-ho.'

Phyllis held her breath as he passed first one

forceps blade and then the other up on each side of the baby's head: they clicked together, forming a protective cage around it. And then came the pull.

The hefty leather-bound Register of Births at Oakleigh House that day recorded that Mrs Freda Lancaster had been delivered of a living male infant at six forty a.m. by Dr C. Godley, using Kielland's forceps, under chloroform administered by Matron G. Groves.

After being thus dragged into the world, the baby's head was temporarily elongated due to the pressure of his hard journey; he also had a livid purple bruise on the left side of his face from the forceps blade. Nevertheless he gasped at birth and made a grunting sound.

'By God, we've landed the fish,' panted Dr Godley, holding the child up and dropping the forceps into the bucket at his feet. He quickly tied and cut the dangling umbilical cord.

'Thank heaven,' whispered Matron Groves, setting aside the corked bottle and mask. She took the baby and cleared his air passages by sucking through a thin rubber tube placed in his mouth and each nostril in turn. Wrapping him in a warm towel she put him down in a cot where he continued to give little grunts, his colour changing from bluish-white to pink as the air entered his lungs.

'You've got a little boy, Mrs Lancaster,' she said softly, and a dreamy smile lit up the face of the exhausted woman. 'My James will be so pleased,' she murmured.

'And it's thanks to you three angels,' muttered Godley, breathless from his exertions. 'I couldn't have done it without you, Matron – and Nurse Bird and Miss Sibley. You know how necessary you are.'

'Team work, Dr Godley,' smiled Matron. 'Has the placenta separated?'

Having expelled the fleshy afterbirth, so vital to the baby in the womb but now just rubbish to be disposed of, Godley contemplated the long cut he had made in the mother's tender living flesh to widen the outlet.

'And now I've got to sew her up,' he said in a low voice. 'Her husband will say that I tore her to pieces. Poor girl. Poor women.'

And yet as Phyllis cleared the delivery trolley and rinsed bloodstained linen in the sluice, she reflected that Freda Lancaster was surely to be envied when compared to the three women who had attended at the birth of her son. The pangs of labour were hard, but they ceased at the moment she became a mother. She had a husband, 'my James', who would be pleased and grateful; she had a comfortable home and financial security. Matron Groves and Sibby – poor Sibby who gazed upon Godley with such adoration – would almost certainly never experience the natural fulfilment of motherhood, but would live out their lives attending on women more fortunate than themselves.

And with sudden sharpened perception Phyllis realised that these women had to be grateful for what they were allowed of the likeable, jaunty, middle-aged doctor with his thinning hair, his bow tie and his ready compliments – the crumbs that fell from the rich man's table, in a world where there was not enough love to go round.

How many lonely single women secretly dreamed about Dr Charles Godley, she wondered, perhaps even shamefully fantasising about him as she had once fantasised over a remote film actor? At least she herself would not fall into that trap, she thought, for she had seen at close quarters the folly of loving a married man, the daily frustrations and humiliations – and how it could lead all the way down to the grave. Poor women. Yes, poor women indeed!

But she, Phyllis Bird, had been invited to a party by *Denver Towers*, incredible as it seemed . . .

Chapter 11

Matron Groves heard about the weekend house party at Worton Hall from Dr Godley; she knew of his friendship with Maud Ling, and even though she never went to the pictures herself, some of her staff were fascinated by what they saw as the glamorous lives of the actress and her circle. Mrs Draycott in particular loved gossip about the world of the cinema, regarded by the other nurses and orderlies with mixed admiration, envy and downright disapproval. When they heard that Nurse Bird actually visited Maud Ling's Twickenham home, it gave her a certain dubious status in the staff sitting room, and when the forthcoming party was mentioned in the local paper under the heading 'Farewell to USA Actors', everybody wondered if Nurse Bird had been invited.

And she had. A typewritten note on headed paper from Twickenham Film Studios requested the pleasure of her company at Worton Hall on Saturday, 8 July 1922, for as long as she was able to stay and join the celebrations. Maud's indecipherable signature was scrawled at the bottom. Phyllis hesitated to show the invitation to Matron as a reason for asking for the evening off on that day. There had been a lot of condemnation recently of modern music and dancing, the drinking and smoking that went on in certain circles, and Phyllis wondered if she should decline rather than lose her place in Miss Groves' good books.

It was Mrs Draycott who paved the way and made it right with Matron. One of this lady's duties was to give out the mail that arrived at Oakleigh House, and she had watched as Nurse Bird opened the envelope at coffee-time.

'That looks intriguing, Nurse Bird! Is it an invitation to something?'

Phyllis had blushed and put the envelope in her pocket, but later Mrs Draycott found an opportunity to waylay her and mention the newspaper report of the house party; she actually asked point-blank about the invitation, and Phyllis had no choice but to admit that yes, she *had* been invited, but was unsure whether she should accept.

The next thing was that Matron herself mentioned it in the little milk kitchen, quite casually.

'I believe you've been invited to a party at the film studios, Nurse Bird. Mrs Draycott is quite envious!'

Phyllis coloured as she brushed out feeding-bottles, rinsing them in bicarbonate of soda.

'Yes, Matron, Miss Ling has kindly asked me.'

'How did you meet her?'

'Through the Berridges, Matron, the family I was with before I came here.'

'Oh, yes, of course, that poor nanny – such a shocking business. Dr Godley was most upset by it. But – is it this Miss Ling who's giving the party, then?'

'Er, yes, it's to celebrate the end of – the completion of her latest film, Matron.'

'Well, Nurse Bird, I always try to avoid showing favouritism towards any member of my staff, but I don't see any reason why you can't have a half-day on – Saturday, isn't it? Just so long as you are back at

Oakleigh House at a reasonable time, and ready to go on duty at eight on Sunday morning.'

'Thank you very much, Matron.'

'And Mrs Draycott will want to hear all about it, I'm sure!' added Miss Groves, who had in fact discussed the matter with Dr Godley and taken his advice.

Phyllis was cautiously grateful, not being quite sure whether she wanted to go or not.

The first problem was what to wear. She had seen some beautiful dresses in Gosling's window, but even with the generous cheque her father had sent her for her birthday, they were out of her price range. One in particular had caught her eye, in silky buttercup-yellow, cut on the cross, sleeveless, low-waisted and flaring out from below the hips – oh, imagine dancing in Teddy's arms, the skirt whirling around her legs! She went away and thought about it, and decided to go back and ask if she might see it – and to her delight, it had been reduced in the summer sale. She tried it on, and it was a perfect fit. It was hers! The salesgirl also sold her a matching headband that fastened at the side with a glittering clip, the two long ends hanging fashionably down on to her bare shoulders. She took the outfit back to Oakleigh House in its cardboard box, and it gave her a new confidence: she was now looking forward to the party, and rivalling Georgia's looks . . .

The next problem was how to get to Worton Hall, a fair distance and too far to walk. She knew she would feel self-conscious travelling on buses in such a glamorous outfit, but to hire a taxi-cab would be much too expensive. Once again Mrs Draycott stepped in and persuaded one of the maternity nurses, a Miss Trigg, to lend Phyllis a long pale green cardigan.

'Wear it over your dress, Nurse Bird, and put the headband in your handbag. That nice little straw hat of yours will look all right with the dress, and we'll just have to hope it doesn't rain!'

The day was fine and warm, and Phyllis's heart beat a little faster as she changed out of uniform and put on the dress, adding her long green necklace – but Mrs Draycott stared, and so did Miss Trigg and the rest of the staff when just before three o'clock a taxi-cab drew up outside Oakleigh House and the driver announced that he had come for Miss Bird. Could Maud have arranged it – or Teddy? No, Phyllis knew that if it wasn't Maud who sent the cab, it must have been Denver Towers.

She smiled in shy acknowledgement of the curious stares and envious smiles as she got in, knowing that she looked good in the dress and accessories; she carried Miss Trigg's cardigan over her arm in case it grew chilly later.

When the cab drew up at the entrance to Worton Hall, it was like arriving at a fine stately home with spacious grounds. A wide terrace swept down to a lawn where a game of croquet was in progress, and Phyllis immediately saw Teddy Ling and Georgia Kift awkwardly attempting to knock little wooden balls through iron hoops set in the grass. Judging by their faces, they did not seem to be enjoying themselves much – not like the tennis players in the nearby courts, whacking the balls back and forth to shouts and applause from a circle of spectators. 'Oh, well played! Some volley!'

'Look, there she is – c'mon, duck, we're over 'ere!' Maud called out, and Phyllis thankfully made her

173

way to the garden bench where the actress sat with the watchful signora. She had not been with them two minutes before the tennis match ended and Denver Towers came straight towards them, his white shirt and trousers emphasising his tan. His light blue eyes lit up at the sight of Phyllis.

'Ah, you *have* come,' he said, smiling down at her. 'I was afraid you wouldn't, that's why I sent the – my God, you look lovely, Phyllis. I like that dress – wow!'

'Finished yer game, then, you an' them ovvers?' asked Maud.

'Sure, there's nobody else can hit a ball. Georgia's hopeless, and the guys are otherwise occupied. Say, Phyllis, do you play?'

Of course she did, she'd played every weekend with Rosie Lansdowne on the grass courts at North Camp. 'But I'm not exactly dressed for –' she began.

'Oh, come on, just one set, to show me what you can do!' he challenged her, laughing.

'That dress'll be fine, duck, it's nice an' loose,' Maud reassured her. 'Take orf yer 'eadband an' fetch a pair o' tennis shoes an' a racquet from the games room at the back. Denver can find anuvver couple to make up doubles – what abaht that electrician 'oo was playin' this mornin'?'

Tennis – and in her new dress! It would get stained with perspiration, and pick up dusty marks, but how could she refuse? Towers was already taking her arm to lead her on to the court, and the racquet-wielding electrician was happy to partner one of the young bit-part actresses to play against them. Phyllis stepped nervously forward with a heavy racquet, praying that she would not make a fool of herself.

She need not have worried. From the moment she returned the first serve, all her former skill and

174

enthusiasm seemed to come back to her, and she continued to return the balls back across the net, running across the court and jumping up to whack a volley, the yellow skirt flying out above her knees. The opposing pair were not bad, but Phyllis was more than equal to them, and Towers was genuinely amazed.

'You never told me you were a champion,' he said, breathless after smashing the ball back and forth and finally missing it – but Phyllis dashed across the court and returned it, robbing the opponents of their advantage point.

'Deuce!' cheered the spectators. 'Advantage server!' They went quiet as Towers served again, and within half a minute it was over: game and set to Mr Towers and the girl in yellow. He threw down his racquet and embraced her on the court, just as Mr Ling and Miss Kift returned from the croquet lawn. Teddy looked glum, and Georgia furious; they'd lost all their spectators to the tennis match just played, and the actress had also lost her temper.

'That has to be the *stoopidest* English game I ever heard of!' she declared, shrugging off Teddy's arm.

'C'mon, it's time for cocktails,' soothed Maud as the guests congregated on the terrace, standing in groups or lounging in deck chairs, listening to the gramophone music. Phyllis combed her hair and put the headband back in place, replacing the rubber-soled shoes with her own dainty Louis-heeled pair. Her face was flushed from the game, and she was conscious of admiring glances in her direction. She was especially aware of Teddy Ling's eyes upon her, and deliberately turned to look him full in the face. Georgia had left his side and was dancing to the tune of 'I Wish I Could Shimmy Like my Sister Kate', waggling her slim hips and calling on the others to join in. But Teddy and Phyllis simply gazed at each other across the terrace.

If only he would walk over towards me now, she thought, and take my hand and say that he's sorry; if he would only tell me that he's not in love with Georgia any more and wants to come back to me – and still thinks me the sweetest girl in the world – would I forgive him?

Oh, of *course* I would, my own dearest Teddy! I'd take you back in front of all these people, and hold you close and kiss you and forget all about Georgia Kift. Oh, Teddy, Teddy, can't you see who loves you the most?

Her soft brown eyes were full of silent appeal: surely he could read their message! Was he about to cross the terrace towards her? For a moment she thought he hesitated.

But he did not. He lowered his eyes and turned away, holding out a hand to Georgia, who seized it and shimmied around him. The moment had passed.

Phyllis found Denver Towers at her side, holding two tall glasses. 'A highball for a beautiful champion,' he said, handing one to her. 'There are a lot of guys with their eyes on you, but I'm not gonna take any risks. You're staying with me, kid.'

She took one last look at Teddy and Georgia shimmying for all they were worth, and told herself to face facts. She knew that she looked lovely and had a handsome film actor as her open admirer – so why not enjoy herself?

'Thank you, Denver,' she said, raising the glass to her lips and smiling.

The afternoon and early evening passed in a variety of entertainments, and Phyllis joined in a riotous

176

game of hide-and-seek in the grounds, chatted with Maud and her circle and was introduced to Mr Samuelson and the actor-director Fred Paul, who told her she was pretty enough to be in pictures. Supper was served out of doors and Towers was constantly at her side, helping her to game pie and salmon mousse; he saw that she always had a drink at hand. She caught sight of a determinedly high-spirited Teddy from time to time, and after supper he offered to put on a film show with discarded bits from *The Court Musician* to entertain them. Maud and Reginald Thane agreed to this, but Towers loudly dismissed the idea as a helluva bore, and Georgia just wanted to go on dancing. Towers slid his arms around Phyllis and led her in a slow foxtrot as a saxophone wailed 'After You've Gone'. She let her head fall on to his shoulder and gave herself up to the sensuous music and his whispers in her ear.

'Little dancing buttercup – mm-mm, so sweet, so soft – don't you feel the same as I do, kid? Just wanna be alone with you someplace.'

For Denver Towers was getting impatient; he had seen the silent exchange between Phyllis and young Ling, and was tired of these damnfool rituals. It was time to go in for the kill.

Phyllis's head was spinning, and her thoughts broke up into fragments that floated away in the summer dusk. She felt the response of her body to his closeness, the body of a lonely woman that longed for its natural fulfilment. The record came to an end and was replaced by a quick and lively one, 'Toot Toot Tootsie Goodbye'. Georgia grabbed hold of Teddy, but Towers had had enough. He threw an arm around Phyllis and led her off the terrace.

*

177

'You are tired, *cara mia*. We should go home so that you can rest.'

'Yeah, maybe we will, Belle.' Maud sounded weary. 'Though I don't really like leavin' little Phyllis Bird be'ind.'

'She will not want to leave, she is enjoying herself far too much,' said Belle impatiently. 'That girl can look after herself, there is no need for you to worry about her.'

'I ain't so sure, Belle. She's such an innocent little fing for 'er age.'

Belle Capogna frowned, arranging a shawl around Maud's thin shoulders. 'She is not a child. She will not thank you for taking her home early.'

Maud closed her eyes, and tried to dispel her uneasiness. If only Teddy hadn't been such a fool over the American girl. It served him right that Denver Towers was now flirting openly with Phyllis, who looked every bit as good as that sulky hussy Kift, and was ever so much nicer. Maybe Belle was right, and she wouldn't thank Maud for dragging her away too early.

'All right, then, Belle. Only I'd just better tell Phyllis we're goin'. I can't see 'er anywhere, can you? An' I've got 'er green cardigan an' 'andbag.'

'There's Reginald, you can tell him – and give him her things. And then I take you home.'

Maud smiled and sighed. Dear old Belle could be irritating, but her love was real, and there wasn't too much of it about in the world of today. Not since the war that had taken the love of her life. And the son she had borne him in pain.

It was dark under the trees, a whirling warm darkness laced with gin-based cocktails, a heady mixture on a magic summer night. He was leading her down a woodland path between towering rhododendron bushes, and when she stumbled over a root, he lifted her up in his arms. She clung helplessly to him, her arms around his neck as he carried her towards a grassy space between the sheltering bushes where he set her down and at once started to smother her with kisses.

'It – it's a midsummer night's dream,' she heard herself whisper in reply to his murmured endearments, his boldly roving hands.

'It's all of that, honey. God, at last I've got you alone, all to myself.'

It was as if she was melting, dissolving in his arms, all else forgotten in a tremendous longing to yield to her body's desire. What a relief it would be if – and yet there was a little bell ringing at the back of her mind, warning her of danger.

He was pulling aside the shoulder-straps of the dress. 'Darling, let me kiss you here – and here – mm-mm – let me kiss these,' he said thickly, pushing her down on to the dry, uneven ground where every ounce of energy seemed to drain from her limbs. He was breathing heavily between kisses, but Phyllis seemed to have no words, no resistance. He had uncovered her breasts, cupping them in his hands: his lips and tongue were on her nipples, an incredible sensation. The rough grass pricked the skin of her back, and a slight fullness in her stomach was suddenly relieved by a loud belch – oh, what manners! But Towers didn't seem to notice, he was intent on pulling the yellow dress down over her body, none too gently.

'Here, darling, here,' he was muttering, and something firm and hot and fleshy was thrust against her belly. He took her hand and made her hold it, closing her fingers round its length. Oh, heavens, it was his – she gasped at the thought of the rude word for it. He laughed softly.

'That's right, sweetheart, it's me.' His hand was pushing down between her thighs, and she instinctively let go of his – thing – and made a feeble attempt to draw away.

'No – no,' she mumbled, but he was climbing on top of her, pressing her down.

'Come on, kid, you've played around with me long enough. You know what we both want. Come on, open up.'

'No!' She clamped her thighs together, crossing one knee over the other.

'Hey, Phyllis, I'm good and ready, don't play the fool. Come on, get 'em apart, will ya?'

There was no tenderness in the words or in his movements as he spread himself over her, crushing her under his bulk. She realised that she had no control whatever over what was about to happen; she could not move an inch under his weight, let alone wriggle free.

Now he was roughly prising her legs apart.

'No, Denver, no! Please, please!' Her voice rose in fear, and the next thing she knew was a hand clamped over her mouth. She could neither speak nor cry out. She could scarcely breathe as the yellow dress, so eagerly purchased, was ripped off and with it her white underslip. Almost immediately a searing pain stabbed the delicate flesh of her most secret part. Tears spurted from her eyes as she felt herself being torn apart, or so it seemed. She was totally defenceless.

Help! Help! Mother! Father! O Lord God, come and help me – help me!

But the screams were all inside her head, and made no sound. No help was forthcoming. Having forced himself inside her, he now began to thump and jerk her up and down as if he were riding a horse. Up and down, up and down he battered her against the ground, his gasps and grunts sounding in her ears as he came to a climax.

'Now – *now*! Uh – uh – I'm coming, I'm coming – Christ, I'm coming up good – wow! Wowee! Here it comes, wow, wow, wow –' and on and on it went, words giving way to animal sounds that might have been pleasure or pain, anger or satisfaction – and ending on a victory shout.

'Aaaah – aaah – tha's it, tha's all. Dear li'l Georgie – that was – uh – some fireworks, eh?'

It was over. He rolled off her, still panting, still muttering between grunting breaths. He was bathed in perspiration, but she was cold and shivering, too numb to move, too shocked to speak. She farted, and he giggled, nuzzling against her neck.

'Whoops! Was that nice, darling? You sure sent me off on a ride – wow! Best I've ever had.'

The best he'd ever had. Phyllis had been taken by a man under the stars of a summer night. She had dreamed of such an experience in the past – with Reginald Thane – with Harold Berridge – above all with Teddy Ling. But who was this man who had forced her, leaving her sore and bruised, bleeding and nauseated? Nobody she knew. Nobody she could ever love.

'Hey, we'd better get going. Put your dress on, sweetheart.' He buttoned his shirt and trousers, neither of which he had removed. Phyllis was unable to stir, and when he helped her to sit up, she leaned limply against him. He fumbled with her dress in the darkness, and tried to pull up the shoulder-straps. Her head lolled, and he cursed under his breath as he picked her up in his arms again. He had to carry her all the way back to the house, and thought it best to go in by the kitchen entrance, where he ran straight into a couple who were kissing at the foot of the servants' stairs. They turned to stare at him as he stood panting with his burden, and he gave them a knowing wink.

'A little bit of overindulgence here, I'm afraid. I'm taking her out of harm's way.' He plunged on up the stairs to the first landing where he practically dropped her down on the floor.

'Come on, kid, you can find your way from here, can't you?' he gasped. 'Just go and find your room, don't speak to anybody, just get to your room and lock the door, OK? Come on, *come on*, for God's sake, they mustn't find you here on the floor. Wake *up*, Phyllis!'

He slapped her face, first on one side and then the other. God dammit, he hadn't realised she'd got this plastered – she was out cold. And what a helluva mess she was in. There was blood and stuff on her dress, and the skirt was torn. *Hell!*

What was he to do? He didn't know where Maud's room was. *Maud!* God, what might this girl tell her? Things wouldn't look too good, and the sooner he got out of it, the better. He tried a door, and found it opened into a small room with a single bed, a chair and not much else. A man's shirt hung from a coat-hanger on a hook. It was somebody's temporary room for the weekend, probably one of the film crew. At any rate, it would do. There was nobody about, so Towers stooped down and picked up the dead-weight of her body again; he took her into the room,

182

laid her on the bed, closed the door and made his escape.

The darkness is broken by flickers of light that shoot behind her eyes and turn into needles of pain. Every nerve quivers, every muscle aches. Far away in the distance there's music, and close at hand there are lowered voices: men's voices in some kind of disagreement.

'Should've locked the door.'

'No, it was a mercy you left it open, Timbo. At least we've found her. She'll be able to sleep it off here overnight.'

'Oh, charming – and I sleep on the floor!'

'Of course not, you can have my room. I'll stay here with her.'

'Whoo, yer dirty ol' devil! Yer fancy 'er, don't yer? I've seen yer lookin' at 'er.'

'You know I don't, Timbo. But she's a decent, respectable girl, and I can't just leave her in this state. And I'll swear she never came in here on her own. Somebody's dumped her.'

'Yeah. Cor, look 'ere, she's in a bit of a mess, i'n't she? D'yer reckon –'

'Not much doubt of it. The bastard. And I'll bet he's flown. But it's up to me to get her sobered up and out of here before morning. I'm sorry, Timbo. I really am.'

'Yeah. So'm I.'

The voices recede into darkness, and she drifts away again, giddily floating in space.

Dead of night. The silence is broken by whispers, the same two voices. Hands are touching her, making her sit up. A man's dressing gown is wrapped around her, and arms support her on each side.

'Come on, Phyllis, you've got to walk downstairs. We'll help you. Come on, my dear.'

She groans aloud and belches. Another groan.

'Ssh-ssh, we must keep quiet. Don't worry, you're safe with us – only you must keep going. My car's down on the drive, I couldn't bring it up to the door.'

'Drink . . . water,' she says. Her throat is dry and tastes sour, like vomit.

'Later, my dear. We must get you away from here first.'

She stumbles along between them, and is helped into the back seat of a car. Then there is a long drive through dark streets, the noise of the engine throbbing in her head. Every change of direction makes her stomach heave.

'Easy on the pace, chum. If we get stopped by a bobby an' they find 'er, we'll be dead men.'

'Shut up, Timbo. We're nearly there.'

When they stop she is helped out of the car and held upright while her two companions walk her into a tall building and then she's in a tiny space with a door that clatters shut and then – ugh, she is carried up on a wave of nausea. A sudden jolt, another clatter, and she is out in a corridor. More walking, another door, and then another – and then there is another bed for her to lie on. She sinks on to it with a groan.

'You can have that drink of water now, Phyllis,' says the deeper of the two voices. 'And I'll dissolve a couple of tablets for you to take with it.'

'Give her the ol' mornin'-after cure,' says the other voice. 'Never fails.'

'No, just water for now,' says Reginald Thane, for

she has recognised his voice. He holds a glass of ice-cold water to her lips.

'Try to drink it all, my dear. It'll help you feel better.'

Somehow she manages to swallow half a glass of the cloudy liquid.

'Mr Thane,' she whispers.

'Yes, Miss Bird, it's me, and I've brought you to my flat at Parsons Green. When you've had a rest and – and perhaps a bath, I'll take you back to where you live. Only we'll have to make up a story to tell Miss – er, what's her name, the lady you work for now?'

'Matron!' Phyllis moans as consciousness returns. 'Oh, Matron Groves, I told her I'd be back on duty for Sunday morning.' She stares in horror as she remembers setting off for the party in a taxi-cab, wearing her new yellow dress. How long ago was that?

'It's Sunday morning now, dear, just gone half-past three. Don't worry, you're safe here until you feel well enough to go back to Miss – er, Matron. It's a nursing home, isn't it?'

'Oakleigh House in Ormond Road. I must be there for eight o'clock, Mr Thane. I promised that I would be, and – oh, I feel so *ill*!' She clasps her head between her hands.

'Look, my dear, have a rest now, and later I shall go and see this lady and tell her you've been taken ill with, er, food poisoning. It was the salmon mousse in all this heat. I'll say you've been seen by a doctor, and he's ordered twenty-four hours in bed on fluids only. Trust me to convince her, Phyllis. I'm no mean actor, as you know.'

'Oh – oh, no, Mr Thane!' Tears spill from her eyes. 'I *must* be on duty at eight.'

'She'll never do it,' says the other voice, which Phyllis now identifies as belonging to Sonny Stott. What is *he* doing here? What is *she* doing here? Nothing can surprise her now.

'You'll never do it, Phyllis dear,' she hears Thane echo sadly.

But although she felt worse than she could ever remember feeling in her life, Phyllis had resolved to get back to Oakleigh House, and somehow she summoned up the strength to stagger into Thane's bathroom. Here she discovered the full extent of the bruises on her thighs and woman's parts; her nipples were sore and her back was scratched and itching from contact with rough grass. But worst of all was the stickiness between her legs, the smears of blood and the smell of – oh, the terrible memory, too hideous to contemplate, too shocking to have really happened, surely? But there was conclusive evidence that it *had* happened, and when she took off her torn dress and underwear, soiled with dirt and blood, she was ready to die with shame. How much did Thane – and Sonny Stott – know what had happened to her? How much had they guessed?

Emerging from the bathroom in Thane's dressing gown, she begged him for some paper to wrap up her clothes, and asked if he could lend her something to wear. He offered her a pair of men's underpants and a maid's overall, apologising for having no other women's clothing in the flat, and produced a couple of sheets of brown paper and string. He returned her handbag and Miss Trigg's cardigan, which she put on, but her green necklace was nowhere to be found, and neither was the headband.

By now the time was half-past five and the sky

was light. Sonny had gone to bed, and she begged Thane to drive her to Oakleigh House, insisting that she felt better. When he realised that she had made up her mind, he agreed, though against his better judgement.

They spoke very little on the journey, though he took the opportunity to say that as far as he knew nobody had seen her after her disappearance from the terrace, and neither he nor Sonny would say a word to Maud – or anybody else – about her reappearance in Sonny's room at Worton Hall. As far as they were concerned, she had left the party at a fairly early hour.

'That's very good of you, Mr Thane,' she said weakly, and when they arrived at Ormond Road he stopped the car about a hundred yards from Oakleigh House.

'Good luck, Phyllis dear. I'll drive off straight away, before you go in,' he told her, and she nodded, unable to think of adequate words to thank him.

She prayed that the side door would be open, but it was locked. She tapped upon it, and again prayed that it would be answered by Sibby and not the maternity nurse on night duty. She tentatively called out, 'Sibby!' a couple of times, not wanting to ring the bell. There was no reply, and she tapped again. A face appeared at a window, and when she saw it was Sibby, she put a finger to her lips and beckoned the orderly to come and open the door.

'Nurf Bird! I thaw you were afleep id your room!'

'Ssh, Sibby, don't say anything to anybody, please.' Phyllis honestly thought that she was going to faint as she stepped into the corridor, but took a deep breath and managed to stay on her feet. 'Don't tell anybody, Sibby.'

187

'No, Nurf Bird, I won' fay anyhing. D'yer wan' a cup o' dee?'

'No, Sibby. No, thank you.'

And she crept away up the stairs to her room where she collapsed on to the bed. She had two hours to prepare herself before going on duty; before she had to look after mothers and babies, and face curious questions about the party at Worton Hall.

'Oh God,' she prayed, 'Oh Lord God, forgive me my sins, and help me to get through the day without anybody finding out. Help me to keep going, Lord.'

Suddenly her stomach heaved, and she only just managed to reach the lavatory in time before vomiting copiously into the toilet bowl. She kneeled on the tiled floor and retched over and over again, until there was nothing left in her stomach. Suppressing her groans she pulled the chain and checked that there were no traces of vomit on any surface before making her way back to her room; surely she would now feel a little better?

Possibly – just possibly, she told herself, she felt slightly less ill. She had *got* to feel better.

Chapter 12

The congregation of St Matthias' Church poured out into the morning sunshine at the end of matins, to be greeted by the Reverend Mr Kendall who stood outside the west door. He shook hands with his friend Dr Godley, whose daughter was with him this morning.

'How's life at St George's, Pamela?' asked the vicar, noting the smiles exchanged between her and the father she so much resembled.

'Oh, I'm enjoying my training very much, but it's nice to be home for the weekend with Mother and Dad,' replied the girl, a slim nineteen-year-old in a summery linen suit and matching hat.

'And I'm sure they're very happy to see you,' the vicar smiled, and then turned to the doctor. 'How is Mrs Godley today?'

'Feeling the heat a little, I'm afraid, but of course the sight of this young lady is the best tonic she could have.'

'Better than anything you could prescribe, eh, Doctor?'

'I can't argue with that, Vicar.' The two men would have used first names if they had not been in a public place where the formalities had to be observed.

As the vicar turned to greet the next group of parishioners, Godley too exchanged pleasantries with a number of people, remembering all their names, making judicious enquiries where he knew

189

they would be welcome and receiving compliments on his daughter's excellent looks.

She called out to him, 'Oh, come along, Dad, you'd stand and talk all day! Mother will be waiting dinner for us.'

'Yes, my dear – though it's all your fault that we've got held up. Everybody's agog to see the old doctor's daughter!'

She laughed. 'I think you underestimate yourself, Dad. I saw quite a few pairs of female eyes gazing at you, and not all of them were old! Are they patients of yours?'

He took her arm as they fell into step along Friars Stile Road. 'One of the occupational hazards of the medical and clerical professions, Pamela. For some reason our lives and our families are always of abiding interest, though most of the stories told about us have no foundation in fact, and could furnish the plots of half a dozen novels. So you'd better not say anything round here about your lovelorn Irish student, or they'll have you married to a Catholic and living in a remote stone cottage a mile from the nearest well and boiling potatoes over a turf fire – to say nothing of half a dozen little bog-trotters hanging round your skirts!'

Pamela stopped in her tracks. '*Dad*! Don't *ever* talk such nonsense again!'

But her father saw the light in her eye and knew that his dire prediction had struck a sensitive chord. 'Not as long as you complete your training and don't go giving your heart away, my dear. You're much too young.'

'And Patrick's well aware of it, Dad. He's got his degree course to finish, and at least a year of walking the boards before he . . .' She hesitated, unsure of how

190

much she should show of her own feelings.

'Good, let's leave it there, then.' He gave her arm a squeeze. 'I've got every faith in your own good sense, my dear, and so has your mother. And your leave's much too short to waste on speculation about what might happen at some future time. How's that sister you were telling me about, the one who starts every day with a hymn on the ward?'

'Oh, it's easy to scoff at her, Dad, but Patrick thinks she's the best ward sister at St George's. He says that if there were only more like her . . .'

Godley sighed and resigned himself to silently listening. There was to be no escaping from Mr Paddy O'Thingummybob this weekend, that much was obvious.

Mrs Victoria Godley was sitting out on the veranda at the back of Tudor House, and told them that dinner was ready to serve. 'There was a telephone call from Matron Groves, Charles. She wants you to go over to Oakleigh House some time this afternoon if you can.'

'Oh? I didn't think any of my mothers were in at present. She must have had an admission.'

'It's not a patient, it's a nurse who's gone down with food poisoning, she says.'

'Really? Well, Matron never calls me without a good reason. I'd better go and see what's up. We have to think about the babies.'

As soon as he had finished dinner he folded his linen napkin and said he'd be off. 'It'll give you two a chance to have a cosy little chat,' he said, wondering if Pamela would confide in her mother about this fourth-year medical student and their feelings towards each other. He could only hope that it would blow over like a summer storm.

'Remember me to Miss Groves,' said his wife. 'Don't let her keep you too long.'

'Not if I can help it, Vicky. I'll be back within the hour.'

As he drove out into the Petersham Road, Charles Godley reflected that life on the whole was good. As the busiest and best-liked GP in the area, with a one-fifth stake in Oakleigh House – he was chairman of the Management Board – he was able to play Robin Hood with his wide circle of devoted patients. Those who could afford his substantial fees for home attendance and mostly simple remedies also paid for the less fortunate, the families facing hardship due to unemployment, the war widows with children to bring up; he regularly forgot to send in their bills, and sometimes quietly put his hand in his own pocket when special medication was required. He enjoyed his popularity with families and children, and carefully maintained his reputation as a genial, easy-going family doctor. He knew the benefit of a little teasing, a bit of banter to cheer up the old, the sad and the lonely – but he knew exactly how far he could go, especially with women. In a world short of eligible men, doctors were often the focus of secret passions, and on his current reckoning Godley knew of at least seven women, mainly patients, both married and single, who would gladly have responded to a glance, a touch or one word of encouragement from him. And there were at least seven more who would be seriously troubled by any recognition on his part of their silent adoration. Women as different as Gladys Groves and poor, downtrodden Sibley fell into this group – dear Sibby, whose favourite occupation in life was brewing coffee or tea for him in the dark hours of the night.

Then there were women like the actress Maud Ling and her tiresome bodyguard the signora, who did not fall into either category; Maud was a friend with whom he could relax and enjoy a joke, but again only up to a point. A doctor had always to be careful, hearing much and saying little: he had to be as safe as a priest of the Church in preserving family secrets and medical histories. And he must never allow himself to be tempted, to take the slightest risk of putting his career in jeopardy, of doing anything that would hurt poor Victoria, who had so nearly lost her life in bearing him his only child, his darling Pamela, the apple of his eye. He smiled to himself again at the thought of her; yes, he had a good life, all things considered. Much too good to take any foolish chances.

'I'm sorry to bother you, Dr Godley, especially with your daughter at home, but I'm really quite concerned about our Nurse Bird,' Matron apologised. 'She went to Miss Ling's party yesterday, and she thinks it may have been something she ate there. It was a cold buffet, and there was a salmon mousse, which may not have been quite fresh. She tried her best to struggle through her duties this morning, but fainted in the laundry room, and looks very poorly, so I've ordered her to bed. Her temperature's slightly raised – ninety-nine point four – and her pulse is around a hundred. She says she's been sick, but it doesn't seem to have made her feel any better.'

'Oh, poor Nurse Bird, what a pity. I wonder if anybody else was struck down by the salmon. I'll have to ask Maud. They'll still be indulging in riotous living at Worton Hall, because the party goes on for the whole weekend. Anyway, let's go and see the invalid.'

Phyllis was lying in bed with the curtains drawn. She had put on her long cotton nightdress under which she wore knickers and a sanitary cloth, although her period was not due. She had been too weak to protest when Matron said she would send for the doctor, and was desperate to conceal the bruises from him.

She hardly knew how she had got through the two hours following reporting for duty at eight o'clock. The ward was quiet, with nobody in labour. Matron was having a rare Sunday morning rest, and the nurse in charge was a solid type who got on with the routine work and was not a chatterer. A couple of the mothers asked Phyllis if she had enjoyed the party, and she said it had been 'very nice but rather hot', and tried to blot out the sight and smell of their breakfast eggs and toast.

'Yes, you do look rather pale, nurse,' remarked one of the enquirers. 'Was Maud Ling there? Is she as beautiful in reality as she is in her films?'

Somehow Phyllis had swallowed, smiled and given an answer of sorts as she cleared away the breakfasts. I must get through this hour by hour, she told herself. One hour at a time, eight until nine, and then nine until ten. Don't look any further ahead.

After breakfasts came the bedpan round, fresh sanitary pads were given out and washing bowls. Wooden-framed screens had to be pulled around each bed before intimate attention, and Phyllis prayed to stay on her feet. *Please, God, don't let me faint. Or be sick. Help me, I pray.*

Nine o'clock. She had reached the end of the first

hour. The toilet round was nearly completed, and then bedpans had to be emptied and rinsed, and the ward tidied.

'You'd better go to the nursery, Bird,' said the nurse in charge. 'Some of the babies are crying and need changing. The two bottle-feeds are in the fridge, so they'll need warming up.'

The sound of six crying babies was torture, but Phyllis tied on her nursery apron, washed her hands and sat down to change napkins, cleaning little pink bottoms and applying Vaseline. Every so often another wave of nausea swept over her, and she tried to suppress her stomach's heavings by breathing deeply in through her nose and out through her mouth, as mothers in labour were told to do when they felt queasy after a dose of 'mother's mixture'.

Keep me going, Lord. Just until ten.

Ten minutes to ten. The maternity nurse bustled in. 'Are they ready to go to their mothers yet? I'll see to them now, while you go and start sluicing napkins.'

Phyllis picked up the bucket of soiled napkins and carried it down to the laundry room in the basement. The bulk of Oakleigh House's linen went out to the town laundry in Station Road, but the napkins were washed on the premises, being boiled daily in a gas-heated tub. Phyllis leaned over the large porcelain sink to begin sluicing through the napkins under cold running water. She held a sink-cloth under the tap and then pressed it to her forehead, but she felt her head reeling and gripped the side of the sink. I must sit down, she thought. I must sit down but I haven't got a chair. I must hang on to this sink. I must hang on. I must . . .

Coming in search of her, the maternity nurse

found her assistant lying on the stone floor of the laundry room.

'Now, then, Nurse Bird, what's this that Matron's been telling me about you? How are you feeling now, my dear?'

Dr Godley was sitting on the side of her bed and holding her hand. Matron's tall figure stood behind him, a navy-blue blur. Tears oozed from under Phyllis's closed eyelids at the sound of the familiar kindly voice, but she could not speak.

'So how was the party, Phyllis? And was our friend Maud allowed to enjoy herself, or did the signora stand guard over her the whole time?' While he spoke he felt her pulse and laid a hand on her forehead. 'Can you open your mouth for me, my dear, and say the traditional "aah"?'

'Aah,' groaned Phyllis, and turned her head aside. She mustn't cry. And he mustn't try to examine her, please God.

'Good girl. Now just lie still on your back.' He gently pulled back the sheet and placed a cool hand on her abdomen, covered by her nightdress. Matron made a movement as if to pull it up, but he waved her hand away.

'So, my dear, Matron says that you think it may have been a vengeful salmon mousse that's caused the trouble. When did you first start feeling bad? Have you been sick? Just a little? Any diarrhoea or pain in your tummy? Does it hurt when I press *here*? No? Good.'

He covered her over again. 'All right, Phyllis, I think your diagnosis is probably correct. Fish and hot weather aren't a very good combination. All right, all right, my dear, don't upset yourself, all you need is

196

twenty-four hours in bed with nothing but water to drink. Have we got any soda water, Matron? That might help do the trick.'

He stood up. 'Thank you for letting me know, Matron, and I'll look in again tomorrow morning. I'll enquire of Maud whether there were any other casualties of the demon salmon at Worton Hall. Meanwhile, just let her rest. Let's leave her in peace with her thoughts.'

Miss Groves was surprised by the cursory nature of his examination; Dr Godley was usually so thorough, and she thought that Nurse Bird looked absolutely dreadful, but he had not even listened to her chest or palpated her abdomen, apart from checking McBurney's point for possible appendicitis.

'Shall I send a specimen of stool to the laboratory at the Royal Richmond Hospital, Dr Godley?' she asked.

'I don't think so, Gladys m'dear – not unless she's still no better tomorrow or has diarrhoea. Talking of the Royal, I believe that poor Matron Watt is bracing herself for another royal visit. At least that's something you don't have to put up with!'

He steered the conversation away from Nurse Bird's distressing symptoms, and waved aside Matron's apologies for calling him away from his family on a Sunday afternoon.

'You were quite right, Gladys, I needed to see her and now that I have I'm pretty sure that she'll be better by this time tomorrow.'

For Charles Godley knew a hangover when he saw one, and this poor girl was clearly the victim of overindulgence in alcohol. He wondered how she had got back to Oakleigh House in the state she must have been in, but seeing that she had, the less said the better. He only hoped no worse fate had befallen her: she was such an innocent child for her age.

And he suddenly thought of his daughter Pamela, in love with this bloody Irish fellow.

Left to her thoughts, Phyllis had plenty to meditate on during the next twenty-four hours of bed-rest and soda water. No visitors were allowed apart from the orderly, who changed her water jug, and a couple of quick calls from Matron. With newborn babies under the same roof, strict precautions had to be taken, for the spectre of gastroenteritis was an ever-present threat. Even so, dear Sibby had silently come to her room in the night with a blessedly welcome cup of tea and an arrowroot biscuit.

As her body recovered from the effects of intoxication and physical assault, her memory began to clear, revealing the nightmare in all its horror. It would not be shaken off, though her mind reeled away from it, afraid of what she might remember; but as the hours passed she found herself reliving what had happened. It was like being forced to watch a film sequence being run through a projector again and again, shadowy and flickering on a screen.

First there was sunshine and gaiety: she had played tennis in her yellow dress, and people had clapped and cheered every time she returned the ball. There was talk and laughter, food and drink with Maud Ling and friends, the fun of playing hide-and-seek like children in the grounds of Worton Hall. And there was a moment when Teddy Ling had been about to come back to her, she was sure of it. They had gazed into each other's eyes . . . but the moment had passed and that was when the sky began to darken. She recalled seeing him and Georgia dancing madly together, their bodies frantically shaking, their arms and legs flailing grotesquely – while *she* had danced slowly with somebody else, and the music had played 'After You've Gone'. And that was where the nightmare began.

It had been all right at first – hadn't it? She'd enjoyed dancing with him, the man who had whispered to her and called her a little dancing buttercup; the other girls had envied her, but – oh, no, here was the nightmare looming, and Phyllis moaned on her bed, turning her head from side to side to get away from it, not to think about it, not to remember it. She simply could not *believe* that something so horrible had happened to her. *How* had it happened? How could she have *let* it happen? And the shocking answer was that she hadn't stopped it because – oh, God help her – she had been *drunk*, for the first and only time in her life. And it would be the last time, for she would never touch drink again. And she knew in her secret heart that she had actually wanted to do it, the unnameable act between a man and a woman, that union of bodies that she had learned about from books and the whispered confidences of friends, for her mother had never spoken of it. Adam and Eve. The King and Queen. Her own parents. Mr Berridge and Nanny Wiseman. And was *that* what they did? Something so painful, so brutal, so degrading? Was *that* the secret referred to in the Song of Solomon and in *Jane Eyre* and in the pages of *Family Doctor* magazine? If so, she was cured of romantic dreams for ever, completely and finally cured. *Never* would she have anything to do with it again, not ever. She would accept her lot as a single woman, one of a generation of women made spinsters by the war. She would turn her thoughts towards duty and service, those ideals of Christian womanhood throughout the ages. She would model herself on Matron Groves, and devote her life to –

But these noble thoughts were interrupted by the latter part of the nightmare, the rest of the film that she had to watch and relive. She cringed anew with shame and embarrassment as she recalled that somehow, heaven knew how, she had been discovered and rescued by Mr Thane. Reginald Thane, the screen idol over whom she had dreamed and fantasised before she left North Camp, not so long ago, only last year. He had been a true friend to her – he and that odd young man Sonny Stott – but although she was grateful beyond words for the way they had saved her from the shame of discovery, she felt she never wanted to see either of them again, or Maud Ling, or any of that circle. She would put that part of her life behind her, and try to forget that she had ever known it.

Suppose – oh, just *suppose* that her parents should ever find out what had happened to their daughter: there was a word used to describe a woman that yielded to a man without being married, and it would be just too awful to contemplate. Her one consolation was that they never *would* know, and neither would Matron Groves or Mrs Draycott – or Dr Godley who had believed her story about the salmon mousse.

Phyllis Bird heaved herself out of the bed and kneeled down beside it.

'Lord, I thank Thee that Thou hast rescued me from the pit,' she whispered, using the comforting archaic words of the Bible and Prayer Book. 'From now on I vow to Thee that I shall turn away from temptation and the vanities of this world's pleasures and – and with Thy help I intend to lead a godly, righteous and – and sober life. And to follow Thee as Thy faithful maidservant. In the name of Thy Son, my Saviour Jesus Christ – Amen.'

Phyllis rose from her knees, thankful that no one but her Saviour – and Mr Thane and the Stott boy and the *other one* – oh God! – knew her dreadful secret.

But it was not that easy to dismiss the recent past. When Dr Godley visited on Monday morning and pronounced Nurse Bird fit to return to duty the following day, she felt ready to have a bath, get dressed and eat something more substantial than water gruel and dry toast. On Tuesday she reported for duty at eight a.m., and was told she could take two hours off in the afternoon. It was heaven to feel well and she would have gladly worked all day, but after lunch she went into the staff sitting room and there faced a barrage of questions. Mrs Draycott and others on the staff of Oakleigh House were impatient to hear about the party at Worton Hall, and what had happened before Nurse Bird had succumbed to the tainted salmon.

'Who was there, Nurse Bird?' – 'What did Maud Ling wear?' – 'Is she really in love with Reginald Thane, or is it all on his side?' – 'But he's married, isn't he?' – 'Is that American actor as handsome as they say?' – 'Did you meet him to speak to?' – 'When will we be able to see these two new historical films at the cinema?'

'Oh, and Nurse Bird, is it true that Maud Ling has got a brother who charms everybody he meets?' – 'Is it true that women fall for him all the time, even that beautiful American actress who came over with Mr Towers?'

'Is it true, Nurse Bird? Is it true?'

She was surrounded by them, a flock of inquisitive birds, clamouring, demanding answers. She couldn't bear it, she couldn't cope with it – and to everybody's astonishment she burst into tears and ran from the sitting room, up the stairs to her own room where she locked the door and sat sobbing on the bed.

This gave rise, of course, to endless speculation.

'Poor girl, she must have had a disappointment. D'you think it was over Reginald Thane?'

'More likely that American actor, the one who's just gone back to Hollywood. I expect that's why she was so upset.'

'She must be daft to think that a famous actor could possibly be serious about a nobody like her, when he's got all those actresses to choose from!'

'No, you're all wrong,' said one of the orderlies. 'I know a girl called Jenny who's a maid at the Berridges', where Bird used to work – you know, where that poor nanny drowned herself – and well, Jenny told me for a fact that Bird was *walking out* with Maud Ling's brother at one time.'

'Really? Well, I never! Are you sure?'

'Sure as I can be. Jenny said they used to meet at the tea-room at the bottom of Hill Rise, and he used to walk her back from Maud Ling's home in Twickenham, and kiss her good night down by the basement steps. She actually saw them, she said.'

'Well, did you ever! And now he's jilted her, is that it, d'you think?'

'Now, now, everybody, that's enough idle gossip for one afternoon,' Mrs Draycott told them severely. 'The poor girl has obviously been very upset, and you are not to worry her with any more questions. I absolutely forbid it. Is that quite clear?'

Having silenced them and made her authority felt, Mrs Draycott could hardly wait to share this revelation with Gladys and discuss its implications, for to her the truth was all too painfully clear. Poor Nurse Bird's indisposition was less to do with anything she had eaten, and all to do with the physical effects of a *broken heart*, which would have to be left to mend in its own good time. Mrs Draycott sighed. Nobody knew better than herself about the distress and discomfort brought on by nervous indigestion.

Phyllis took refuge in her work, and found it her best consolation. Her trial period at Oakleigh House was completed without even being remarked upon, so absorbed had she become in the daily life of the place. There was no time to brood when she had to look after two women in noisy labour, and assist at their two deliveries, and when she started to receive personal notes of thanks from grateful patients, and even presents, she began to feel that life could still be good. Even the horrific experience at Worton Hall grew fainter in retrospect, and with time would become just a dark stain on her memory, like Faith Wiseman's death – though the shock to her system still took its toll: her August period was only very slight, a brownish loss that lasted scarcely a day, though accompanied by cramps and a bad headache.

At least she was not plagued by further questions about the party. Mrs Draycott's rebuke to the gossips had put a stop to that, though Phyllis was aware of sympathetic curiosity from the filmgoers and scornful looks from those who disapproved. Interest waned, however, especially when they noted that she made no more visits to Twickenham.

'Our friend Maud has been asking me about you, Nurse Bird,' said Dr Godley in the Matron's office one August morning. 'She wants to know when you are going over to Florizel again.'

Phyllis was silent for a moment and then answered quietly, 'I find that I have very little free time here, Dr Godley, as we all spend so much of our off-duty time on call. I appreciate Miss Ling's kindness, of course, but – but I haven't really very much in common with – well, with the world of films and that kind of life.'

'Oh. Oh, yes, I see.' Godley looked thoughtful. Maud had been anxious about what had happened to Phyllis after she and Belle had left the party without seeing her – a move she was later to regret bitterly. Reginald Thane assured her that he had driven Phyllis back to Oakleigh House with her belongings, but there had been a mocking look in Sonny Stott's pale eyes that bothered her.

'I shouldn't've left wivaht seein' 'er, Charles. Are yer *sure* she's awright?'

'A little affected by the heat, and a bit of a tummy upset, nothing serious,' he had said lightly.

'Omigawd, she never 'ad an 'angover, did she?'

He'd reminded her that Phyllis was not used to cocktails, and maybe there had been a little over-indulgence, but said he was sure there was nothing to worry about.

Yet here was Phyllis telling him that she was giving up the Twickenham circle, and he could only assume that it was a direct result of her bad experience at Worton Hall.

'Just as you think best, my dear. I'll tell Maud that you're kept very busy here.'

'Thank you, Doctor. Please give her my regards.'

'And no other message?'

'No, thank you, Doctor.'

'Very well. By the way, I haven't seen you at church for several weeks.'

'No, I've been attending St Mary Magdalene's down in the town. It's nearer to Ormond Road, and we sometimes don't have much time.'

'Ah, yes, a beautiful place. And a good mixed congregation.' And you don't have to see the Berridges there, he added to himself as she left the office.

Poor Maudie, he thought. He'd have to think of a story to tell her about Phyllis's defection without raising her suspicions. The two Hollywood actors had decamped to Southampton and their liner home as soon as the house party ended, and Teddy was mooning around with a dejected air. Perhaps it was just as well that Phyllis had decided to break with the Lings; he knew that she had been let down by young Ling, and although he hadn't been surprised by that, he didn't care to watch it happening all over again.

Late one Sunday afternoon in mid-August Miss Groves called Phyllis to her office.

'I'd very much like to attend evensong at St Mary's, Nurse Bird, because my young niece is being confirmed by the bishop. Now, the ward is quiet apart from just one patient in early labour, Mrs Granger, but it is just possible that she might deliver as it's her second baby and she was quick with her first. Mrs Draycott is available to act as midwife, and Dr Rawnsley is the GP and knows that she's in, so I think I can safely go down to the church. And I might add that knowing *you're* around is reassuring.'

She smiled as she spoke, and Phyllis glowed. Had she known what the next two hours were to bring, she might not have been as sanguine, for hardly had Matron left the building than Mrs Granger, who had been resting quietly, suddenly let out a blood-curdling scream. Phyllis rushed to the labour room, where a squirming baby girl had just been born, a precipitate delivery for which they were all totally unprepared. Phyllis at once wiped the baby's face and wrapped her in a towel, silently thanking heaven that she was yelling her head off. She rang the call bell, and Martha, the orderly, looked round the door.

'What's up, Nurse Bird? Oooh, I say! Mrs Draycott said she wouldn't deliver before night.'

'Just fetch Mrs Draycott, will you? Now!' Phyllis demanded, holding the baby between the mother's legs, for the umbilical cord was still attached and not very long. 'All right, Mrs Granger, you've got a beautiful little daughter. What a lovely surprise for your husband when he calls to see you!'

Mrs Draycott took some time to come to the labour room, and Phyllis proceeded to tie and cut the cord. She sat Mrs Granger up and gave her the baby to hold.

'Don't pull on the cord, nurse, don't pull on the cord, whatever you do!' panted Mrs Draycott.

Phyllis would not have dreamed of doing so, and simply replied, 'I think it's ready to come.' A lengthening of the cord and a slight gush of blood indicated that the afterbirth had separated, and Phyllis told Mrs Granger to give another little push.

'Ah, there we are, that's it – well done!' Phyllis was triumphant at the outcome, but she also considered herself very lucky that there had been no frightening complications like a sudden haemorrhage or a limp, blue-faced baby. She was also fortunate in her patient, who was overwhelmingly grateful and did not complain that there had been no doctor or even a midwife present when her baby was born. It was hardly in keeping with the high reputation of Oakleigh House.

'Well, I'll take over here now, Nurse Bird, and somebody had better let Dr Rawnsley know.' Mrs Draycott seemed short of breath and Phyllis wondered if she was about to have one of her attacks of fluttering heart palpitations.

'Shall I ask Martha to telephone him, and I'll stay here and help tidy up?' she suggested, not wanting to leave the mother and baby with a midwife who might collapse. There were a whole series of tasks to be carried out: the weighing and labelling of the baby, who had to have a binder put round her tummy and needed a nappy and nightie; the mother had to be washed and changed, and there was the placenta to be examined, not to mention the longed-for pot of tea to be brewed.

'Martha doesn't like the telephone, so you'd better go,' said Mrs Draycott, and at that moment the doorbell rang. Phyllis's heart sank at the thought of an admission – oh, don't let her be too far on, O Lord! – but she closed her eyes with a sigh of relief when Dr Godley strolled into the labour room. He assessed the situation in an instant.

'My dear Mrs Granger, what a wonderfully quick, smooth delivery!' he beamed, while giving Phyllis a surreptitious wink. 'What have we got here, then? Oh, what a little peach – and just like her mother. She's going to be a beauty!'

To Phyllis his arrival was nothing short of a miracle. It turned out that he had been talking to Dr Rawnsley earlier, and the other GP had mentioned that his patient Mrs Granger had been admitted that day, but that he was due to attend the confirmation service at St Mary's. Godley had offered to look in and check on her progress before going home.

'All's well that ends well, Nurse Bird,' he said, but Phyllis felt that she had learned something from the incident about the awesome responsibility that a midwife carried. She had a new awareness of the need for calm efficiency and good judgement such as Matron Groves always showed. All might *not* have ended well, and she hoped she would not be left alone with Mrs Draycott again when a delivery was imminent.

Matron's return was greeted with the good news, but she immediately reproached herself at not being there for Mrs Granger. Dr Godley assured her that Nurse Bird had done an excellent job, and poor Mrs Draycott was given six drops of tincture of opium and sent to bed.

At nine o'clock, when the night staff were on duty, Matron and Dr Godley stood on the iron balcony overlooking the garden at the back of Oakleigh House. It was a lovely clear evening, and Phyllis sensed the happiness that radiated from Gladys Grove as she savoured this brief, innocent interval with the man she loved.

'Is there any tea going, Nurse Bird?' he called to her, and when she carried two cups out to them on a tray, he detained her.

'Miss Groves and I have been talking about you, Nurse Bird. You have a natural talent for midwifery, and you ought to take your training to qualify for the Central Midwives' Board. And I know just the place for you, the Booth Street Infirmary in Lambeth – used to be a Poor Law infirmary, but it's been upgraded. There's a new separate maternity department with the best consultant obstetrician I know in charge, a man called Poole, who taught me all I know of the mechanics of childbirth. I'll personally recommend you if you apply there.'

'It's a very poor area, Dr Godley,' remarked Miss Groves, looking askance at Phyllis. 'And I shan't thank you for sending Nurse Bird away just when we've all come to value her so much.'

'Well, let's keep her here until next year, then; let her have about a year to learn what she can from you and then she'll be halfway trained by the time she gets to Lambeth.' He turned to Phyllis and smiled. 'It's what you need, my dear – to do something for poor women worn out by childbearing in very different conditions from what we have here. You're worth something better than Oakleigh House, Phyllis, waiting on all these pampered madams!'

'Oh, so that's what you think of us, is it, Dr Godley?' said Matron in mock indignation. 'Well, thank you. Thank you very much!'

The doctor laughed. 'Come, now, Gladys, you know what I mean. How would I manage without you? And by the way, we're halfway through the year – isn't it time you came over to dinner at Tudor House? I'll speak to Victoria about it, and we'll arrange a date and get some champagne in.'

'Please don't put Mrs Godley to any inconvenience,' said Matron quickly, but she looked pleased by the invitation. Suddenly Phyllis thought of Faith Wiseman and the contrast between two women who were both in love with married men. Miss Groves accepted what she was allowed, and was grateful; she asked for no more. Miss Wiseman *had* demanded more, and that had been her tragedy.

The following day Matron spoke to Phyllis again

about midwifery training. 'It's all very well for Dr Godley to tell you what to do with your life, Nurse Bird,' she said with a smile. 'Personally I think you should pay a visit to your parents and discuss it with them before you make an application.'

Phyllis nodded. It had been some time since she had visited North Camp, and her conscience now reminded her that she ought to see how her mother was managing after a year without her daughter. It also made sense to discuss her future plans with her father.

'You probably won't get home for Christmas, Nurse Bird, but I could spare you for a few days in early September while the weather's still good. See how things are at home before you embark on a six-month course with no break – and probably another six months' service as a qualified midwife at the infirmary or on the surrounding district. Heaven knows, I don't want to lose you, but Dr Godley's right, you ought to be registered, if your parents agree.'

It seemed incredible to Phyllis that it was only a year since she had left home. So much had happened during that time, and she had gained a whole world of experience, both good and bad.

Her father remarked favourably on her more mature appearance and attitudes.

'I'm happier about you working at this – er – maternity home, Phyllis, rather than at that playwright's house,' he said with a certain awkwardness at even mentioning the words 'maternity' or 'midwife' to his daughter, a single woman. 'This matron sounds a sensible woman, and I suppose you ought to take the proper training if you're going in for – for that sort of work. Who knows, you might end up as a district nurse here in North Camp, working from home! That would be ideal, because you'd have your independence and be able to keep an eye on your mother at the same time.'

'I suppose that could happen one day, Dad,' replied Phyllis cautiously. 'How do you think Mum's doing these days – I mean, how is she really?'

'You can see for yourself, Phyllis. I think she misses you – well, we both do, but at least I get out to the shop, whereas she – well, she's crawled even further into her shell, and there could come a time when she'll never go out at all.'

'Oh, Dad, that's so awful, so sad – and so sad for you too,' said Phyllis helplessly.

'I know. We're not the only ones, we know that only too well, but it doesn't make it any easier.' He turned away to hide his face from her. 'The fact is, Ethel's never going to get over the loss.'

As always, Phyllis could think of nothing to say that would be of any use. Perhaps he was right, and she might one day return to live at home as the district midwife for North Camp. It would be one way of putting a single life to good use, and it wasn't as if she was the only one; a whole generation of women was in the same position: Matron Groves, Sibby, Miss Trigg, Rosie Lansdowne, Betty Goddard, Mrs Williams – and Faith Wiseman, who had not survived. May the Lord help *her*, Phyllis Bird, to make the right decision . . .

Ethel Bird seemed to brighten up during her daughter's visit, and they went out shopping together and took a walk in the old woods that bordered the river boundary of the two counties.

'Do you hear any news of that poor little boy Claud Berridge, Phyllis?'

'I see the family doctor at Oakleigh House, and he says that Claud's settled in at Tall Pines,' Phyllis replied. 'And sometimes I run into Mrs Williams or Jenny in the town, and they say Mr and Mrs Berridge go to visit him – but I really don't know how long he's likely to stay there.'

'And you haven't been to see him yourself?'

'No, Mum, it's a part of my life that's over now. And he's quite incapable of showing any affection, which makes it so much more difficult.'

Mrs Bird sighed. 'My heart aches for his mother.' She paused, and then seemed to make a determined effort to say something more cheerful. 'It's nice to see that you're making a life for yourself, Phyllis. Your dad seems to think that you'll be the North Camp district midwife one of these days. You're definitely better at looking after mothers and babies than trying to teach in an infant school, aren't you?'

And Phyllis agreed that yes, she preferred nursing to teaching.

On the morning that she was due to return to Richmond, her mother called her with a cup of tea and the promise of a special treat.

'Guess what's for breakfast, Phyllis! Do you remember how you and the boys used to love having kippers for tea? We used to get them from that man who had the Saturday stall on the Parade, and we ate them with lots of bread and butter and gallons of tea – remember? Well, what do you think I've got for you today?'

But Phyllis already knew. The smell of frying kippers floated up the stairs from the kitchen and wafted on the landing outside her room. And the aroma that she had once sniffed with such eager anticipation now gave her a queasy sensation in her throat, as if her stomach was rising up in revolt. She knew that she could not touch a kipper or anything else, not even a cup of tea.

And that was the moment when poor Phyllis first began to suspect the trouble she was in – the sorrow and shame that she would not be able to hide.

Chapter 13

It was the end of Phyllis's peace of mind and her new confidence in the future.

'But when did you start feeling queer, Phyllis? You were all right last night, weren't you?' Mrs Bird's face was creased with bewilderment as her white-faced daughter boarded the Waterloo train.

'Oh, don't worry, Mum, it's just a passing tummy upset. Something must have disagreed with me.'

'But you haven't eaten anything that your dad and I haven't had too. I thought you'd really enjoy a kipper – you always have done before.'

The train started to move off, and Phyllis pulled down the window at the door. 'Don't worry, Mum, it's nothing – but I'm really sorry about the kipper. Goodbye! Take care of yourself now.'

'And you too, Phyllis. Make sure you see your doctor if it hasn't settled by tomorrow. Goodbye!'

Mrs Bird waved and Phyllis waved back, but she knew she had no hope of feeling better until she saw the blood of her September period. She wasn't sure when it was due, for as she didn't keep a diary, she could not remember when the August one had been. She tried to recall events at Oakleigh House that might give her a clue. Yes! It was on that busy day when they'd had two women in labour, and she'd had to divide her attention between them; they had delivered within an hour of each other. She remembered having tummy cramps and a headache, but there hadn't been time to stop and worry about herself, and she'd put a maternity pad inside her knickers. Later she had found only a slight reddish-brown stain on it, not like a proper period. *Had it been a proper period at all?* As far as she could think back, she hadn't had one in July, but she'd put that down to shock. She'd missed periods before, as at those terrible times in 1916 and 1918 when she'd been in her early twenties and the news had come through about her brothers, first Tom and then Ted, killed in action. Sorrow had descended on the house in Rectory Road, and that was the way it had affected her.

She made a tremendous effort to force herself to remember and relive the horror of the evening of 8 July. What exactly had Denver Towers done that had hurt so much and made her bleed? That long, fleshy *thing* had been thrust into her woman's passage, and pushed and pushed again and again; there had been a lot of moisture, as if she or he had wet themselves. When he had at last taken it out, it had left a stickiness between her thighs and smears of blood – *her* blood – from where he had torn into her tender flesh.

So, what exactly had *happened* then? She now had to face the truth, that they had had 'conjugal relations', even though they weren't married. *Family Doctor* also called it 'conjugal union', and the purpose of it was to conceive a child.

Oh, merciful God, had *she* conceived a child on that terrible night? Was she now expecting a baby as a result of that shameful ordeal? Oh, no, no, no, no, *no*, Lord, let it not be, please God, *please*, not that!

She frantically thought back over all that she knew about the subject – scraps of knowledge gleaned from medical books and dictionaries, the Bible and some romantic novels. *Woman's Weekly*, like *Family Doctor*, had a readers' letters page where a lady doctor gave advice about periods and pregnancy and how to calculate when babies would be born: 'You count nine calendar months from the first day of the last period.' And there had been the exchanged confidences between friends, both at school and later: stories like what had happened to Clara Hemmings, who had been sent away from North Camp by her parents – to have a baby, so it was said, though when she came back there was no baby, so what had happened to it?

And of course there had been Faith Wiseman, who'd defiantly admitted that she and Harold Berridge had conjugal union on a regular basis, only they had used *birth control* – something that men used to prevent conceiving babies. But Denver Towers wouldn't have used one of those, would he? And it would be too late to use birth control after it had happened, wouldn't it?

This idea led her to remember other dark, sinister whispers about women who had 'got rid of it'. There was that answer to a reader in *Family Doctor* which had said, 'What you are suggesting is a criminal offence.' There were terms like 'out of wedlock' and 'fallen women' – there had been a home for fallen women at Aldershot, set back behind a row of sycamore trees, providing refuge for girls who had taken the road to ruin . . .

Phyllis shivered inwardly. *Surely* it couldn't have happened, not on that one and only time, could it? If only there was somebody she could confide in, but there was no one, because no one must know. Oh, how would she endure the agony of waiting for her

September period? She would pray morning, noon and night for it to appear.

Dr Godley was coming to the end of afternoon surgery, held at the front of Tudor House. He provided two waiting rooms, one for his private patients and a larger one for those on the panel, though it was not a hard and fast distinction; when patients particularly needed privacy, they were allowed to use the quieter, smaller room. The consulting room was common to both, and was comfortable and well-furnished with an examination couch and a large roll-top desk. An array of diagnostic instruments was laid out on a side table, and the room, like Dr Godley himself, smelled pleasantly of good soap and mild disinfectant.

He glanced at the clock. Five to five. It had been a busy afternoon, and there was only one more patient to see, a young man who had been sitting in a corner of the larger room with mothers and fidgeting children; he had let everybody else go in front of him, so that he would be the last in. Dr Godley tapped the bell on his desk to signal that he was free, and the young man rose and entered, closing the door behind him.

Godley did not recognise this man wearing a brown tweed suit, white shirt and highly polished brown shoes. He wore a necktie with some sort of emblem, like a school or a club tie, and his complexion was ruddy, with reddish-brown hair and wide-set blue eyes. He had what Godley thought a countryfied air, and as he gave a tentative smile, the doctor caught a whiff of fresh perspiration, the sort of smell he associated with anxiety rather than lack of hygiene.

Here's a young fellow with an intimate problem that he doesn't want his family doctor to know, thought Godley; so he's come to consult a stranger.

'Well, you look healthy enough, young man!' he said with a smile. 'Take a chair. Are you a newcomer to Richmond?'

'Er, yes, Dr Godley, but it isn't for me health that I'm here to see ye.'

The soft West of Ireland accent at once alerted the doctor. 'Go on,' he said, the smile fading.

'Me name's Patrick Browne, and I'm from County Kerry. I'm about to start me fifth year o' medical studies at St George's Hospital, Hyde Park Corner.'

Godley waited. He wasn't going to make it easy for this fellow – he only looked a boy – who had barged into his consulting room with God only knew what kind of story. He felt his heart rate increasing, and an ominous prickling at the back of his neck. What was he going to hear?

'It's like this, y'see, sir – Dr Godley,' Browne continued. 'To come to the point, I'm here to tell ye that I love your daughter, Pamela, she's the dearest girl in the world to me – and – and I'm askin' your blessin' on our marriage.'

Charles Godley sat stock-still. What dire news was this? What madness had befallen his little girl? He realised that his mouth was dry, and moistened his lips with his tongue.

'I've a good mind to show you the door,' he said with deadly quietness. 'The dearest girl in the world, as you have the audacity to call my daughter, is nineteen years old and has just completed her first year of training to be a nurse – so has another two years ahead of her, after which I hope that she will practise as a staff nurse for a further year or so. You have the most crucial part of your medical degree course still to come, which has to be paid for, and no prospect of earning a penny before 1924 at the very earliest. So what are you talking about?'

Mr Browne's face flushed, and he ran a finger round the edge of his collar.

'I'm desperately sorry to cause ye – to bring unwelcome news, sir. I can only say again that I love her with all my heart, she's the only girl for me, and if ye don't believe me, well, that's unfortunate for her and for me. But – I have to marry Pamela, y'see.'

The words fell heavily on the air. The window was ajar, and Godley could hear a chaffinch on a branch, sounding a persistent *pink-pink-pink-pink*, like a warning, followed by a questioning *weet? weet?*. On the Petersham Road a horse and cart trundled by. Time held its breath, and Charles Godley was to remember the moment all his life.

'Where is my daughter now?' His voice was a thin croak.

'She's not come with me, sir. I've left her back in London.' Browne rose from the chair, clasping his hands in agitation. 'She – she wanted to come with me, but I thought it better if I faced ye meself, so that ye could take out your anger on me and not on her. I'm mortally sorry, Dr Godley, but I'll do me best for her, so I will, as God sees an' hears me.'

Godley took a breath. His hands were clenched and he looked away as he asked the question to which he already knew the answer.

'Is my daughter expecting a child?'

'She is, Dr Godley, sir, next March. It's three months now, an' we want to get married before the end o' next month.'

'It'll kill her mother.'

'Please don't blame her, sir. I accept all the blame for what's been done. And I love the air she breathes, Dr Godley. Me first thought is to take care o' her and look after me child.'

Dr Godley knew that it took two to make the mistake for which this boy said he accepted all responsibility, but furious anger rose up in his throat. He had to make a conscious effort to stay in his chair and not leap up and throttle this young dog with his bare hands.

'And what will you live on?' he demanded. 'What about your medical degree? And where will my daughter live?'

'Me father will help us out. He's a pig farmer in Kerry, y'see, an' doin' very well. He'll tide me over until the child's born an' we can start lookin' ahead again.'

'And is my daughter to live on this – this pig farm while she's waiting for –'

'No, no, Dr Godley, though me mother an' sisters would be glad to look after her – no, we'll look for a little place in London, an' I'll carry on with me studies.'

'And may I enquire who is going to pay for this little place in London and the rest of your course – always supposing that you pass your final examinations after this slight interruption?'

'Me father, Dr Godley. He'll tide me over, as I said, and I'll pay him back in the course o' time. I won't always be a student, y'see.'

'Oh, God help her, my poor child. My little Pamela.' The words burst out of Godley in his grief and rage, though he did not raise his voice. 'You'd better go back and fetch her here to me. Let me see her and speak to her.'

Patrick Browne now stood over him. 'Can ye believe me, Dr Godley, that I *love* her? I loved her from the first moment I saw her, and made up me mind I'd marry her. It's only just that it's happened earlier rather than later, y'see. It won't make any difference in the long run –'

Godley wanted to say, Shut up, shut up, you Irish bastard, you bloody pig farmer who has dared to lay your filthy hands on my precious darling. I wish you to hell.

But all he actually said was, 'All right, all right, just go and fetch her. I must see her and speak to her myself.'

'I'll bring her to ye for sure, Dr Godley – but don't ye be upsettin' her now, will ye? Because if ye do, I'll take her away again.'

And hearing this, spoken pleasantly enough, Charles Godley truly understood the change in his life. He had lost Pamela to another man, and nothing would ever be the same again.

'If you ask me, Gladys, I think you let Dr Godley have too much say in matters that don't concern him,' Mrs Draycott remarked. 'He may be good at midwifery, but he shouldn't interfere with your nurses' lives. That poor girl Bird had hardly got over being jilted at that party, but he must start talking about sending her to some horrid slum where she'll be among the lowest of the low. I know about these infirmaries: they're just glorified workhouses, and it's a shame to send a nice girl like Bird to a place like that.'

'She's not being forced to go, Mrs Draycott,' replied Gladys Groves patiently. 'And it's absolutely right that she should train for the Midwives' Register. She'll be here for a year, and heaven knows

I don't want to lose her. She's become one of my best maternity nurses in the time she's been with us – and *that* was Dr Godley's doing, if you remember.'

She smiled indulgently at the older woman, who had trained her as a midwife during the war on a busy district where most of the trained staff had gone to nurse the wounded. She always addressed her old teacher as 'Mrs Draycott' in deference to her twenty years' seniority, for the woman had been like a mother to her at a time of great loneliness and loss; and now that her skills had declined with failing health, she still occupied a position of authority at Oakleigh House, as a sort of housekeeper on her good days.

And Matron did listen to her, and agreed that Nurse Bird certainly looked peaky these days, and seemed hardly able to concentrate on her work. Had anything happened during September that might have upset her? Was she missing the Twickenham circle? She seemed to have no other close friends.

'I might take an opportunity to have a word with Nurse Bird myself, Mrs Draycott, but we must remember that she's not a girl; she's in her twenty-seventh year.'

'But with precious little experience of the world, Gladys,' replied the older woman, shaking her bottle of milk of magnesia and pouring herself a generous dose. Her stomach was playing up again, and that usually meant another attack of palpitations was on the way.

All her worst fears were confirmed by *A Handbook for Midwives*, surreptitiously taken from the shelf in Matron's office. It gave a detailed list of the early signs of pregnancy. Cessation of menstruation;

nausea, especially on waking; frequency of passing urine; a feeling of fullness and possibly tingling of the breasts – and Phyllis had them all. The September period had not appeared, and her body felt different in an indefinable way: it had started on a natural process which would take nine months to complete. She was *pregnant*, she was *in a certain condition*, she was *expecting a baby* and, dating from 8 July, she must be just ten weeks and four days into the inexorable progress of it. Her impassioned prayers had not been answered.

What was she to do? Where in God's name could she turn for help? The very thought of her parents knowing filled her with dread, and to think of telling Matron Groves was, well, unthinkable. She knew that the advice page in *Woman's Weekly* would say that she should consult a doctor, but just *imagine* going to Dr Godley, a man she respected and who liked her, a man who worked with her in the labour room and took an interest in her career, and telling him that – no, she could *not* imagine it. The shock, the surprise, the disappointment in her – it didn't bear thinking about.

And there would be some at Oakleigh House who would gloat over her downfall, the one or two maternity nurses who resented her quick promotion to Matron's trusted assistant and obvious favourite of Dr Godley – ah, yes, they would enjoy Nurse Bird's unexpected fall from grace!

What to do, where to go? In her present utter despair, there was only one way out: the one Faith Wiseman had taken.

'Is anything the matter, Charles? You seem pre-occupied this evening, and you hardly touched the

223

salad.' Victoria Godley was concerned about her husband's unusual silence, the more so as he seldom brought his work home with him. He never discussed cases with her, and even when a tragedy occurred, as when he failed to save a patient he felt should not have died, he never burdened her with his afterthoughts.

He had not answered, so she tried again. 'How was the surgery this afternoon? It seemed to go on and on. Were there many children? They always –'

'Vicky, my dear,' he suddenly burst out, 'what did Pamela tell you about this student fellow, this Patrick Browne who's stuck on her?'

'Ah.' His wife smiled knowingly, almost coyly. 'Now, Charles, you wouldn't expect me to repeat confidences meant for a mother's ears only, would you? We ladies must have our own little secrets, you know!'

'So she *did* talk about it. Did she say she's – does she imagine herself in love with him?'

'Oh, Charles, how strange that sounds, coming from you! Haven't you noticed that our daughter has grown up? Some girls of her age are married and have children. Why should our Pamela be any different?'

'Because she's training to be a nurse and ought not to be thinking of – Vicky, my dear, what did she say to you? Please tell me. It's important that I know.'

Mrs Godley's pale face flushed. 'Why, what did she say to *you*, Charles? Why are you in such an extraordinary mood this evening? Something must have happened. What is it?'

'Look, my dear, we both might have to take another look at the situation. Suppose that Pamela was determined to marry this – this boy, and give up her training to do so? She'd give us a grandchild within a year, and we'd have to accept it, wouldn't we?'

'Charles! What nonsense you talk sometimes! A beautiful girl like Pamela is bound to have admirers, and be in and out of love several times in the course of her training. What do you expect with young nurses and medical students? Cast your mind back to *your* student days!'

'You haven't answered my question.' Godley's voice was oddly stern for a man who was always gentle with a semi-invalid wife. 'Suppose she *did* marry this paddy and gave us a grandchild next year, how would *you* feel about it?'

'I'm simply not prepared to discuss such a thing, Charles – and I'm very sorry that you have no better opinion of Pamela's good sense and moral judgement. Something must be troubling you – you're tired or – don't say any more, you're upsetting me.'

It was no good. She wouldn't listen, and he couldn't tell her. But she'd have to be told, and as soon as possible. He would ask her sister over from Putney and let her break the unwelcome news. Only it would have to be soon – like the arrangements for Pamela's wedding.

Late at night on Saturday, the last day of September: darkness and chill, with a fine drizzle falling as she descends the grassy slope to the clump of trees where the two Pen Ponds are separated by a wide bank. It is the very same spot where the Ascension Day picnic was held – how long ago now? Only four months, but it seems like a different era. And little had any of them known then that it was Nanny Wiseman's last few hours of life. Early the next morning her body

225

had been found here, floating at the edge of the Great Pond. Tomorrow morning somebody will find *hers*, and then everything will be known: her father and mother will be told, and her friends at North Camp and all their neighbours; Matron Groves and Dr Godley will be informed, and all the staff at Oakleigh House, the Berridges and the whole of Richmond will hear that another young woman's body has been discovered in Pen Pond; the post-mortem examination will show the reason for suicide. Dr Godley will again be giving evidence at a coroner's inquest.

And I shall know nothing of it, she thinks as she goes towards the waiting water. I shall be finished with the shame and sorrow of the world. Where will my spirit go? Will the Lord have mercy upon my soul?

No answer comes out of the darkness and silence: she is utterly alone.

The grass is wet at the edge of the pond. Shall I take off my coat and the little cloche hat? And my shoes? No, I'll go in as I am, fully dressed. How deep is the water at the edge, a foot? Two feet? Here I go, then – *oh*! it's so cold. Go forward, wade in quickly – ugh, so *cold*! It's up to my thighs – go on – my waist – go on, go further in, oh! the water's swirling round me, and – *oh*! I can't touch the bottom, I'll soon be under – I must let my head go beneath the surface, let the water close over me. It will soon be done. I shall soon be at peace. Soon, soon! Let me sink now, Lord . . .

And she *would* have sunk beneath the water; it would have poured into her lungs and stomach, and she would have lost consciousness, but for one important fact that Phyllis Bird in her desperation had not taken into account: her body – her strong, healthy woman's body that had so longed for fulfilment and which now carried another budding human being deep within it. Whatever her mind had decided, this body had strong instincts of its own, and would not accept a death sentence. It began to fight for life. Her head lifted itself above the surface of the water and coughed and spluttered. Her arms flailed and joined forces with her legs to struggle with the encircling water and swim towards the bank. Swoosh and splash and gasp and spit – and there she was at the water's edge again, clinging to a tussock of grass, her chest heaving, her heart pounding, her breath sobbing as the truth dawned on her. She had been rescued, not by another person but by her own body: it had intervened to bring her back from death.

She crawled up out of the water and lay on the bank in her drenched clothes; her hat and shoes were gone. She heaved herself up to a standing position and took a few steps in her stockinged feet, wincing as she trod on a stone. One foot in front of the other, left, right, left, right – and off she went in the dark, back to Sawyer's Hill, back to Richmond Gate where the Star and Garter Hotel was being rebuilt as a home for ex-servicemen. A man's figure stood near to the site, possibly a watchman on patrol, and Phyllis quickly vanished into Queen's Road, stumbling as she went but making quite good progress in her dripping clothes and bare feet, for her stockings had been torn to shreds. Her brain told her to make her way back to Ormond Road by the quiet residential streets behind Richmond Hill: she reached Friars Stile Road, where most of the houses were in darkness; an occasional night light burned here and there in an upstairs window. A long walk down Onslow Road brought her to The Vineyard, and by now she was limping badly, for both feet were sore and bleeding. The shops were shuttered and silent, though a few midnight strollers were abroad, and Phyllis shrank back into the shadows; if she could just get down through the Hermitage she would come out almost opposite Oakleigh House. Not much further, and then Sibby would let her in at the side door. Nearly there . . . She limped round the corner into the alley.

But then a heavy hand fell upon her shoulder, and a helmeted policeman towered above her.

'Now then, young woman, what're yer doin'? Where d'yer think ye're goin' at this time o' night? Gawd, ye're soakin' wet! What's yer name?'

Having come so far without being accosted, this sudden encounter seemed to emphasise her plight, and she realised how she must appear. She swayed under his grasp, feeling as if she was about to collapse in the street.

'Steady there, miss. Just tell me yer name.'

She opened her mouth and gave a belch that turned into a retch. A trickle of fluid escaped her lips.

'All right, spit it out, that's the way,' he said more gently, but still gripping her shoulder. 'Is yer name Phyllis Bird, by any chance?'

She moaned and nodded. 'Yes.' It was the first word she had spoken since crawling out of the pond, and was a hoarse whisper.

'Thank Gawd for that. Mrs Draycott's waitin' for yer at Oakleigh House. Worried out of 'er mind, she is. They looked in yer room an' found yer wasn't there. Gawd, look at the state o' yer! You're comin' along with me, Miss Bird!'

*

Another admission just after eleven brought Matron down from her room, and as there was another patient already in advanced labour she foresaw a busy night, especially as the maternity nurse on night duty was inclined to panic. Gladys Groves suppressed a sigh, for she was tired after a demanding day; she had not even the consoling prospect of seeing Dr Godley, for neither of these patients was under his care. Old Dr Stokes had been notified that his patient was likely to deliver soon, and the new admission was one of Dr Rawnsley's. She too was making good progress, and as Matron thought it likely that the two would probably deliver at more or less the same time, she sent Sibley up to Nurse Bird's room to warn her that her services might be needed.

'What's the matter, Sibley? What do you mean by charging up and down this corridor and waking everybody up?' demanded Mrs Draycott, appearing at the door of her room in a long flannelette nightdress with collar and cuffs.

'Matro' want Nurf Bird in the labour roo'!' cried Sibley distractedly. 'But he iffen in her roo' – an' he iffen in fe toile' or humbody elfif roo'!'

'Not in her room or the toilet or somebody else's room? Where is she, then?' Mrs Draycott was immediately alarmed. 'Oh dear, I'd better go down and see what's happening.'

Hastily changing into her uniform, she arrived in the labour room to find Matron and Dr Stokes delivering the first patient.

'Send Nurse Trigg to look after the other lady until we're free,' Matron told her quietly. 'And do everything you can to find Nurse Bird. If she hasn't turned up by – in another quarter of an hour, let the police know.'

The search proved in vain. Every member of the resident staff was woken and questioned by an increasingly worried Mrs Draycott. Nurse Bird had not been at supper, and one of the orderlies said she thought she had seen her leaving Oakleigh House at about ten and walking down Ormond Road towards the town centre.

Which could also mean the river. Mrs Draycott's alarm turned to heart-stopping fear. The girl had been looking more unhappy than ever lately, yet nobody had taken her aside to ask her what was the matter; they had all been too discreet, too shy to intrude on a delicate private grief. And now heaven only knew what poor Nurse Bird's broken heart had led her to do . . .

At half-past eleven Mrs Draycott put through a call to the police station in Red Lion Street, and within a few minutes a uniformed police sergeant arrived at Oakleigh House to ask for a description of the missing woman and details about when and where she was last seen. All the staff were up drinking tea and discussing her disappearance, and Mrs Draycott grew more frightened by the minute. There had been that awful case of the Berridges' nanny, hadn't there, which Nurse Bird had always refused to talk about. Mrs Draycott knew that she would never forgive herself if Nurse Bird had done the same thing.

In the labour room Dr Stokes' patient was safely delivered, and he was preparing to leave. Dr Rawnsley's patient was nearly ready to deliver, and Matron sent word to Mrs Draycott to keep her informed about Nurse Bird. Matron Groves' thoughts were much the same as the housekeeper's, and she prayed from her heart that the girl would be found safe and well.

Oh, how I wish I had spoken to the poor girl and given her some comfort! she agonised. How shall I live with myself if . . .

It was twenty minutes after midnight when the police constable rang the front doorbell, and Mrs Draycott trembled as she answered it. When she saw the dripping, limping figure leaning on his arm, she burst into thankful tears. Two or three other staff members helped to get the girl upstairs to her room where they removed her soaked clothes, exclaimed over the state of her feet, and dressed her in one of Mrs Draycott's thick nightdresses. Her feet were bathed and bandaged, and she was put into bed with three hot-water bottles.

Matron Groves offered up a silent, heartfelt prayer of thanks as soon as she heard the news, but as she was engaged in the second delivery with Dr Rawnsley, she asked Dr Stokes if he would kindly see Nurse Bird before he left the building.

'Well, well, my girl, you've caused a lot of trouble, and given poor Matron the fright of her life,' he said sternly to the white-faced invalid being fussed over by Mrs Draycott. 'Can you give me any idea of what happened to you?'

'I fell in the water,' she whispered. 'But – I got out again.'

'Well, thanks be for that, my girl. But how did you come to fall in the Thames?'

'I was – out walking. I – I wanted to – to be by myself. And I fell in,' she replied weakly, briefly opening her eyes and closing them again.

'Were you with anybody else when this happened?'

'No, I was on my own. Nobody else.'

'And I believe that a police constable found you

231

and brought you back here, safe but very wet – is that right?'

She nodded.

'Thanks be to God for that man!' said Mrs Draycott fervently, wiping her eyes on a corner of her large apron.

'Well, I hope you realise that you're a very lucky young woman, Nurse Bird,' said the doctor, a little less severely. 'You are getting the very best possible treatment from these good ladies here, and I'll mix a sedative draught for you to take with hot milk.' He glanced meaningly at Mrs Draycott. 'Seeing that the incident has ended well, perhaps the less said about it, the better. We don't want any more scandals. Is the constable still here? I'll have a word with him.'

And so Phyllis fell asleep in a warm bed, her life spared and her story hushed up. At some point during that night a change took place in her: she found hope again, and with it a different attitude towards the new life growing within her. Its life had been saved with hers, and she now had to face the fact of its existence and her duty to it. Her action – or inaction – had brought it into being, and it was hers to protect, not to destroy. She resolved to put her trust in the Almighty, her Saviour, who alone had the power to forgive sins and look after His own. He would help her to do the right thing for herself and her unborn child.

But first the world had to be told, not of her suicide, but of her *ruin*.

After the two delivered mothers were put to bed, Matron went back to her room, first looking in on Nurse Bird and finding her asleep. Their interview could wait till morning, when they were both rested, she decided.

'My dear Nurse Bird – Phyllis – my first thought this Sunday morning was to give thanks for your safe return to us! But how are you feeling now? What happened to you, my dear? Did you really fall in the river while out walking late at night?'

Phyllis heaved herself up in the bed as Matron drew up the one little chair in the room and sat beside her. 'No, Matron. It was in the greater Pen Pond in the park.'

Miss Groves gave an involuntary gasp at this echo of the Berridge nanny's tragic end. 'Oh, my dear – go on. What were you doing there?'

'I went to – I walked into it to drown myself. But I couldn't.'

This was in fact what Gladys Groves had thought she might hear, but she was still shocked. She put a hand to her mouth. 'Oh, my dear – you poor dear girl – why didn't you come to me with your trouble? Why didn't you confide in me? I blame myself. I should have sent for you and made you tell me.' She took Phyllis's hand in both of hers. 'Will you tell me now?'

She expected a tale of disappointment in love, what Mrs Draycott had called 'a broken heart'. What she heard took her breath away.

'Matron – I'm going to have a baby.'

Gladys Groves' face went blank. 'What? Oh, *Phyllis*! Are you *sure*?'

'Yes, Matron. I think – I think it will be about the beginning of April.'

For a moment Miss Groves could think of nothing to say. Of all the women and girls she knew, this one was the last she'd have thought likely to fall victim to such a calamity.

233

'Can you tell me – who is the father?'

'It was at Worton Hall.'

'Oh, that time. Oh, my God. So – is there any hope of – of marriage, Phyllis?'

'No, Matron. He's gone.'

'Oh, good grief, and we never once thought – never suspected – and after all our hopes for you. Oh dear!' For a moment Gladys Groves was close to tears.

But then she rebuked herself sharply: for heaven's sake stop this useless wailing and think of the tragedy that has just been averted!

'Well, my dear, the first thing we must do is to be practical. We shall have to call Dr Godley to see you and advise about what to do next. Do your parents know?'

'No, Matron. Nobody knows – yet.' Phyllis's tone was dull and flat.

'No, of course not. But they'll have to be told. Oh, Phyllis, I'm so sorry – more sorry than I can say.' Gladys was again at a loss for words, at the thought of what this young woman would have to face: shock, grief, anger, contempt – a great deal of gossip and very little sympathy.

Dr Godley arrived at nine thirty. Matron had telephoned him and asked him to call that afternoon, but he had come at once.

'What is it, Gladys? You said it was Phyllis Bird again. What's happened this time?'

'Come into my office, Dr Godley.'

He followed her into the room with a sinking heart. What now? She closed the door.

'Prepare yourself for a shock, Dr Godley. Phyllis tried to drown herself in Pen Pond last night.'

'Jesus wept! Why wasn't I called? Is she all right now?'

'Dr Stokes was here, and he saw her. Yes, Dr Godley, she's all right, if you can call it all right for a single girl in her position to be three months pregnant.'

His mouth literally dropped open. 'What? *What* did you say, Gladys? Phyllis Bird?'

'Yes, I'm afraid so, Doctor. Some actor or such like at that party at Worton Hall. There's no possible hope of marriage. She's . . . ruined, that's what people will say. I've told her that her parents will have to be – why, Dr Godley! Dr Godley, whatever is the matter?'

For he had sat himself down at the office desk and let his head fall upon his crossed arms. And he was crying.

'Oh, poor girl – oh, the poor, dear girl. My poor little girl! Oh God, if there be a God, have mercy on me! My little girl!'

He sobbed uncontrollably while Gladys Groves looked on in absolute incredulity, unable to believe her eyes and ears. If this was Godley's reaction, what on earth were people going to say! What would they *think*? She hardly dared face her own thoughts. She simply stood beside him, watching helplessly.

After a minute he raised his head and looked up at her with tear-filled eyes. 'Forgive me. And help me, please, Gladys, my dear friend. Help me to do what's best for everybody.'

She did not hesitate. She laid a hand on his shoulder and spoke with measured calm. 'You know I'm always here for you, Charles.'

'Thank you, my dear.' He took out a large

235

handkerchief and wiped his eyes. 'And now we'd better go and see what we can do for poor Phyllis. Oh, my God. My God . . .'

Chapter 14

Phyllis lay back on her pillows and closed her eyes. A sensation of deep peace filled every part of her: it was like being immersed in a warm, soothing bath. She had not imagined such kindness as this.

'Things won't be easy for you, Phyllis my dear,' Dr Godley had said. 'But take heart, you're among friends and I shall be personally responsible for your care. You'll stay here with us at Oakleigh House and continue your duties as soon as you feel well enough. Matron Groves will look after you, to see that you don't get overtired, and there'll be no nonsense about refusing to eat – that's right, isn't it, Matron?'

'Certainly, Dr Godley,' Miss Groves had replied promptly.

'Very well, then. We'll let you rest for a day or two, Phyllis, to make sure there are no ill effects from – oh, my dear girl, how could you attempt such a terrible thing? Why didn't you come to me?' His voice shook on the last word, and Miss Groves had quickly intervened.

'Let's be thankful that she had second thoughts, Dr Godley, and we'd better leave her now. She needs to rest, as you say.'

They had left her room, but she no longer felt alone.

Gladys Groves was still trying to adjust her thoughts to this extraordinary situation. Any other unmarried member of staff found to be pregnant would have been instantly dismissed, but as Dr Godley was Chairman of the Management Board that governed Oakleigh House, he was able to allow Nurse Bird to remain on the staff.

'She could be put on night duty when she begins to show, Gladys. We'll hide her away like poor Miss Sibley. If all goes well, she should be able to stay here until the start of February, when she'll be seven months, but we'll have to see. I'll find a suitable mother-and-baby home where she can go to be delivered – some are a good deal better than others.' He sighed heavily. 'What the poor girl can't realise now is the heartbreak she's going to have to face when the child goes for adoption – or to some ghastly babies' home. Oh, that a girl like her should have come to this!'

Looking at his drawn and haggard features, Miss Groves knew that she had to face up to her own emotional dilemma. Looking back over the past three years since she had been appointed Matron, she considered her relationship with this man. On the surface it was entirely platonic: they worked together in the labour room, shared moments of high drama, triumph and occasional tragedy; they understood each other's techniques and read each other's thoughts. And she had grown to love him, quietly and selflessly, respecting his status as a married man, content to be a woman in the background of his life, demanding nothing more than their excellent professional partnership and his easy, jovial friendship.

And now *this*. Her first stunned reaction to his display of emotion over 'his little girl' was that he was actually Nurse Bird's natural father, which would explain his interest in her career; but the girl had spoken of her parents at North Camp and the loss of her two brothers in the war, so unless she had been unknowingly adopted by the Birds it seemed most unlikely that she was the illegitimate daughter of a man who would have been barely twenty when she was born; and why should he run the risk of bringing her into the vicinity of his wife and daughter, where her true identity might be discovered?

The other explanation was scarcely more believable. Could it be possible that in a moment of madness he had fathered a child upon Nurse Bird? When and where would it have happened? And yet his behaviour seemed to suggest that this might be the case. Had he told Phyllis to pretend that it had been an actor, now conveniently returned to America? It seemed so incredibly out of character – and yet he was doing what he could for the girl, and she, Gladys Groves, had to follow his lead.

She was disappointed in him – and yes, she was hurt, of course, how could she not be? But she couldn't just stop loving him because of this. She would have to show kindness and tolerance towards Phyllis Bird, and defend her from deprecating remarks from the other staff. She was in for a testing time: they both were.

'I've got an enormous favour to ask of you, Gladys.'

'Yes, Dr Godley?' They were alone in her office. 'If it's in my power, you know I'll do what I can.' What on earth was coming now, she wondered.

'Can you take a half-day off on Thursday, October the nineteenth, and come down to St Elizabeth's, that Roman Catholic Church in The Vineyard? I need you to help me through an ordeal.'

She nodded and waited for an explanation, but he hesitated.

'What do you want me to do, Charles?'

'There'll be a wedding there at three o'clock – my daughter Pamela's marrying a medical student from St George's. It'll be a hole-in-corner affair, and Victoria's taking it badly. Her sister will be there to support her, but I – I'll be giving the bride away, and – oh, will you be there for me, Gladys?'

And in a moment of revelation Gladys Groves saw and understood everything. An enormous burden was lifted from her shoulders as she realised that his concern for Nurse Bird was simply a reflection of the sorrow he felt for his *daughter*. Oh, thank God, thank heaven! Gladys could have danced and sung for sheer relief, but she kept herself entirely under control for his sake. In fact she felt guilty for rejoicing, because he was so clearly suffering.

'Of course I'll be there, Charles.'

'Thank you, my dear. I probably won't be able to speak to you because I'll be otherwise occupied, but I'll know that you're there. We're having a very small reception back at Tudor House afterwards – just a few close relations, Victoria's sister and mine – I lost my brother in France, as you know – and a few friends, Dr Bell and Matron Watt from the Royal – she knows Victoria from the Ladies' Linen League. And yourself, of course.'

'And the bridegroom's family?' prompted Miss Groves gently.

'They're all over in Ireland, pig farmers. I don't know if the parents are coming or not.'

'They'll surely come to their son's wedding, so maybe I could make myself useful by talking with them – making them feel that they're part of the day,' she said carefully.

'Yes, maybe you could do that, Gladys, maybe you could. Victoria won't and I can't – so thank you.'

There was a pause, and then he added in a low tone, 'She must be due about the same time as poor Phyllis.'

'I see. You know, Charles, it's not so terrible. It's happened before.'

'Yes, but it's very different when it's your own.'

'Your daughter is at least getting married, unlike Nurse Bird. She'll be able to keep *her* baby. And you know, Charles, everything will be all right when you see your grandchild.'

'I don't know, Gladys. It'll be a nine-day wonder in Richmond.'

'Until the next one comes along – you know what you always say.' She looked at him, and her features softened. 'By the way, Phyllis is looking a lot better. She's eating again, and the colour's come back to her cheeks.'

'Good. Are the other nurses treating her decently?'

'If there was any unkindness, any mockery, it would be severely reprimanded. And they all know it.'

'How's Mrs Draycott taking it?'

Gladys smiled. 'She hasn't stopped fussing over Phyllis since the night she was brought back to us. And not a single attack of palpitations! It's given her a whole new lease of life.'

'Well, I suppose that's good – as long as Phyllis doesn't get killed with kindness.'

And they both chuckled quietly, old friends sharing a little joke.

*

The wedding of Miss Pamela Godley to Mr Patrick Browne at the church of St Elizabeth of Portugal took place without prior announcement in the local newspaper, and by the time it had exploded into a nine-day wonder the newly married couple had returned to London where a tiny flat had been rented for them above a confectioner's in Brick Street. Here the new Mrs Browne spent many hours alone, as her husband's studies demanded his presence at the hospital for lectures and long hours of ward experience. Her sudden departure from St George's School of Nursing was a separate wonder among her tutors and the friends who had been fellow probationers. One or two of them visited her and shook their heads over her reduced circumstances, as they saw it, discovering that Mr Browne's father paid the rent for the flat and Mrs Browne's father supplied her with an allowance for their daily needs. Her pregnancy began to show as the days darkened and London turned grey and foggy.

Similarly, by the start of November Nurse Bird's waist had noticeably thickened, and by the end of the month she had a definite bulge under her apron, so she was assigned to night duty, eight p.m. till eight a.m., with three nights off in a fortnight. With eight beds, not all of them occupied for much of the time, the work was not particularly hard, and both she and Sibby usually managed to rest for an hour or two in the night, but a patient in labour could take up all of Phyllis's time and attention. A delivery meant that Matron had to be called and the appropriate GP summoned; by the end of such a night she was exhausted and fell thankfully into bed. Sleeping in the daytime became easier as winter set in, though she usually woke a couple of times to visit the lavatory, and Mrs Draycott would heat milk for her, just as Sibby hovered over her at night with tea and coffee. It was a tolerable routine, and Phyllis had a curious sensation of detachment, as if time was suspended and she could not see where the future might lead; neither did she care to.

Against the advice of Matron Groves, she did not tell her parents. There was no need for them to know, she pleaded, and Dr Godley supported her. She planned to visit them as soon as possible after she had been delivered and the baby taken for adoption. Some excuse would have to be made for such a long absence after her September visit – but she was determined to spare her mother and father this calamity – and to spare herself the shame of their knowing. Miss Groves thought it a mistake, but Dr Godley told her to leave it to Phyllis to decide.

'Wait and see,' he said. 'Leave well alone, and see how things turn out.'

Matron did not argue, though she was of the opinion that most secrets came out eventually. Godley was looking older, she noticed: there were new lines around his eyes, and his mouth tended to droop at the corners. It was as if he had lost the bouncy resilience that had been his outstanding feature; even his bow tie seemed less jaunty than formerly.

Others noticed the change, among them Maud Ling and the signora.

'Prop'ly knocked the stuffin' aht of 'im, this 'ow-d'ye-do wiv Pamela,' said Maud gloomily. 'What wiv Teddy clearin' orf to 'Ollywood, an' little Phyllis Bird desertin' us, an' poor ol' Charles wiv a face like a week o' wet Sundays, there ain't much to laugh abaht these days.'

'I do not understand this Phyllis, to be so cold when you are so kind. She is much ungrateful,' grumbled Belle.

'I dunno. Must be *some* reason for droppin' us all of a sudden. Charles is a bit cagey, an' I reckon Sonny Stott knows somefing. I got a good mind to go rahnd there an' ask 'er straight aht what I done wrong.'

'What, to this maternity home? Everybody will see you go in, and there will be many rumours!'

Maud guffawed. *'That'd* give the buggers summat to talk abaht, eh, Belle? They'd be takin' bets on 'oo's the farver! Ha, ha, ha! Yeah, that's what I'll do, I'll get a cab an' go rahnd there tomorrer aft'noon!'

And she did. The orderly who opened the front door to her gasped and ran to tell Mrs Draycott that *Miss Ling* was at the door, saying she'd come to see Nurse Bird.

'What? *Miss Ling*? Good heavens, girl, show her in, show her in! I'll take her to my own sitting room,' said the housekeeper, all of a flutter.

Maud was duly ushered in. 'On night duty, is she? I s'pose I'd better not disturb 'er, then, if she's sleepin'.'

'No, wait, Miss Ling, while I go up to her room and see. She sometimes wakes around this time, and I make her a cup of tea.'

Phyllis was indeed awake and sat up in bed with a start when she heard about the visitor.

'Oh, Mrs Draycott, will you please tell her that . . . oh, no, I'd better see her. She might as well know. Will you tell her I'll be down straight away?'

'Yes, Phyllis. Just put your dressing gown and slippers on. She's in my sitting room.'

As soon as Maud saw Phyllis, she gasped, burst

into tears and opened her arms. Phyllis shed tears too in the perfumed warmth of her friend's embrace. Mrs Draycott stared and then reluctantly withdrew, though she hung around outside the door.

'Oh, yer poor little duck! 'Ooever would've fought it? You're the very last one I'd've – yer should've tol' me! 'Ere, 'oo was it? Not Teddy, was it, 'cos if it was, I'll 'ave 'is guts for garters!'

'No, no, Maud, not Teddy, not your brother. Don't think such a thing of him.'

'Then 'oo dunnit? Oh, no, not that – was it that bastard Denver Towers?'

Phyllis lowered her face and nodded.

'Christ! Don't tell me it was at Worton 'All, that night Belle an' me left yer there?'

Phyllis nodded again, without raising her head.

And now Maud Ling wept in earnest, with bitter regret. 'I blame meself, I blame me bleedin' self for this, yer poor little fing. I *said* we should've stayed or taken yer wiv us. Oh, Phyllis, I let yer dahn good an' proper!'

'No, no, Maud, you can't blame yourself. You didn't do it, *he* did it, and I let him do it. I'd had too much to drink. It was . . .'

She could say no more, and Maud howled so loudly that Mrs Draycott decided to re-enter her sitting room.

'Is there anything I can do for you, Miss Ling? Perhaps a pot of tea and maybe a drop of brandy in it? I can't allow Phyllis to be upset, you see, not in her –'

'I'm ever so sorry, I – I . . .' Maud wiped her eyes and made an effort to calm herself. 'An' to fink I didn't know nuffin' abaht it all these monfs – yer must've gorn frough 'ell, Phyllis.'

'We very nearly lost her, Miss Ling,' said Mrs Draycott grimly, and when this was explained to Maud, she went white with shock.

'Fank Gawd yer got good friends 'ere, Phyllis, but when I fink – oh, it brings it all back to me, yer see, duck – I bin frough it all meself.'

And Phyllis heard for the first time a story that few knew about the famous film actress: that she had borne a son in 1918 to an officer in the Royal Flying Corps who had been shot down before the child was born, without even knowing that he had fathered a child.

'I very nearly died 'avin' 'im, duck, an' it was touch an' go for weeks arterwards – but oh, 'e was a lovely baby, 'is name was Alexander after 'is farver. I've never loved anyfing so much in all me life.'

'But – what happened to him, Miss Ling?' Mrs Draycott's own eyes were full of tears.

''E's bein' brought up by Alex's parents in St John's Wood. Ever so posh, they are, lovely 'ouse, an' 'e gets the best of everyfing – but I don't see 'im. I did at first, but it broke me 'eart. They 'ardly let me touch 'im – 'e just wasn't mine any more, even though I was 'is muvver.'

Again Maud dissolved into sobs as her memories flooded back for the first time in years. ''E'll be four years old – five in March, bless 'im. Yer get used to it, Phyllis, but yer never get over it. Ye'll 'ave it all to face, duck. I'm sorry, I really am, but like I said, it's brought it all back. Anyway, I'll stay in touch now I've seen yer again.'

'Oh, Maudie, if only I'd known . . .' Phyllis put her arms around the actress's thin shoulders.

'Not many know, duck, only Teddy an' Belle an' dear ol' Charles, o' course – 'e's upset abaht 'is daughter, but at least she'll be able to keep 'er baby.'

'You loved your baby's father, Maudie, so it must have been terrible to part with him – but it won't be the same for me, because I've got no feelings at all, only shame at what happened. But thank you so much for coming, and for telling me. God bless you, Maudie – and yes, we'll stay in touch now.'

They parted with a kiss, and Phyllis returned to her bed. Mrs Draycott saw Miss Ling out, and thought what a fine tale she'd have to tell Gladys that evening.

Christmas came and went; cards and gifts were exchanged by post between Phyllis and her parents, and she explained that life at Oakleigh House was busy but satisfying, with very little time off. She wrote that she would probably not visit North Camp again until the spring, and wished them a Happy New Year as 1923 came in.

At the cinemas there were queues to see *The Virgin Queen* and *The Court Musician*, while at the Richmond Theatre Harold Berridge's new play, *Full Circle*, was presented in time for Christmas, *Key to Tomorrow* having been transferred to the West End. Phyllis saw none of them, because she practically never went out; she was now quite large and ungainly, and spent all her time when not on duty sleeping. The patients began to make comments to each other as she attended to them and their babies, assisted by the faithful Sibby, and it was one such remark that shook Phyllis out of any complacency that she might have had about the attitude of the general public towards women in her situation.

'This is supposed to be such a superior place to have a baby, yet at night all we have to look after us and our babies is a shameless hussy who waddles around as bold as brass.' The woman's voice was just loud enough to be heard by the other mothers in the bay. 'She's not fit to be seen! And her only assistant is a mental defective. It isn't right, and my husband is sending a letter of complaint to the Chairman of the Management Board.'

Phyllis stayed silent, pretending not to hear, and Sibby gave no sign of having heard; but the words lingered in Phyllis's head and she was not surprised when Dr Godley told her that he thought the time had come for her to leave Oakleigh House.

'I think I've found the right place for you, Phyllis,' he said. 'It's near Epsom and it's got a rather strange name, Lahai-Roi.' He wrote it down for her, and repeated the pronunciation – La-Hay-Roy. 'It's run by a Miss Bishop with two trained midwives, and a local GP attends if a doctor is needed. I think we'd better send you there in February. I wish you could stay and have your baby here, but unfortunately we can't do that.'

Phyllis too wished that she could stay, but knew that it was out of the question: she would not be welcomed by the respectable married women whose husbands paid a substantial fee for delivery in a private maternity home.

'Thank you very much, Dr Godley. I'll do whatever you say.'

'I'll forward your letters from North Camp, and if you'd like me to send yours off by post from Richmond, just send them to me at Tudor House in a larger envelope, and I'll see that they go.'

She thanked him again, marvelling at his endless kindness; she knew about his daughter's hasty wedding, and guessed that it was this that prompted him to assist another girl who had got herself into trouble.

She left Oakleigh House on a cold morning in early February after an emotional leave-taking from Matron, Mrs Draycott and a heartbroken Sibby. Dr Godley himself drove her to Lahai-Roi.

'Courage, my dear – not much longer to go. Another eight weeks, I reckon.'

About the same as his daughter.

Chapter 15

Lahai-Roi was quite difficult to find, being three miles out of Epsom, well off the beaten track and hidden among trees; it was approached by an unpaved lane, and the early Victorian building had at one time been a family home. Phyllis was personally greeted by the proprietress, a lady in her middle forties with a good figure, neatly and becomingly dressed. She invited Dr Godley to stay for a cup of tea, but he declined, saying that he had to get back to his practice; in fact he felt that Phyllis would be better facing this new experience alone and speaking for herself.

'Good-day to you, Phyllis. I'm Miss Bishop, Lahai-Roi is my home and its residents are all in my safe-keeping. You will find that we try to be as much like a family as possible. Let me first take you up to your dormitory – there are two of them, and you're in Restfulness.'

In restfulness? Phyllis did not understand until they reached the two four-bedded rooms on the first floor, one with the name 'Peacefulness' on the door, while the other was 'Restfulness'.

'This is your bed, Phyllis – you'll share the room with Madeline and Dora. The fourth place is unoccupied at present.'

Each bed had a small locker beside it, on which was a Bible. There was a large communal wardrobe, and a row of hooks along one wall. Phyllis only hoped that her bedroom companions would be congenial; she had got used to having a room of her own.

'It looks very nice,' she said, feeling that some reaction was expected.

'Right, I'll take you down to meet some of the other residents,' said Miss Bishop, smiling. 'You can hang your coat on a hook there – and there's a shelf for hats and gloves. Ready?'

She led Phyllis down to a large, rather old-fashioned sitting room where a welcoming coal fire was burning, and two young women sat in uphol-stered chairs; one was sewing, the other struggling with some crochet-work. They were both obviously pregnant, and looked up curiously at the newcomer.

'This is Phyllis, who has come to join us,' said Miss Bishop. 'I'm sure that Elizabeth and Dora will soon make you feel at home. We also have Madeline, who's around somewhere, and Daphne, Grace and Mary, who are attending to their babies in the nursery. We use Christian names for the residents, and Nurse Boyd and Nurse Cunningham are available to help and advise you with any problems, as well as being in charge of the nursery and what we call our little hospital, where the babies are actually born. You are all expected to do some light house-work, sweeping and dusting the dormitories and living rooms – and I also like every one of you to make a little garment for your baby – something that will go with the child to its new home. How are you two getting on with yours?'

She examined the work they were engaged on. 'Oh, yes, Elizabeth, very nice, you're such a good needlewoman – you really must teach some of the others how to sew a straight seam! Oh dear, Dora,

251

your crocheting needs to be tighter. You haven't got the tension quite right, have you? Perhaps you should unpick it and start again. If at first you don't succeed – you remember what we were all taught at school – try, try, try again!'

She smiled brightly. 'I'd better go and see what Cook's preparing for us in the kitchen. Take a seat, Phyllis, and have a little chat with Elizabeth and Dora.'

Phyllis sat down, unable to think of anything to say. She felt apprehensive, and the baby was kicking violently after the journey.

'So when's yours due?' asked the girl called Dora, picking up her crocheting and eyeing it doubtfully.

'About the beginning of April,' answered Phyllis, adding after a pause, 'Miss Bishop's very nice, isn't she? I like the way we use Christian names.'

'Well, if we called each other "Miss" So-and-so, it would be a constant reminder of our unmarried state, wouldn't it?' said Elizabeth with a shrug.

'Miss Bishop's all right,' said Dora, 'but watch your step with Nurse Boyd. She's a real nasty piece of work. God help you if you get *her* when your pains start!'

'Yes, we heard poor old Grace screaming for hours,' added Elizabeth.

'*And* we heard Nurse Boyd shouting at her and smacking her, didn't we, Liz? None of us got a wink of sleep that night.'

This was hardly reassuring, and Phyllis was about to say that a woman in labour tended to make a lot of noise when the pains were very severe, but then she decided to keep quiet about her experience of midwifery in case they asked her too many questions.

'Does – er – Miss Bishop deliver most of the

babies?' she enquired, thinking of Matron Groves.

'Good Lord, no, she's not a midwife. She leaves all that to Nurse Boyd and Nurse Cunningham! Miss Bishop's job is to save souls.'

Both girls rolled their eyes and giggled briefly. 'We get marched off to the Primitive Methodist Chapel on Sundays, and we have prayers every morning after breakfast,' said Dora. 'And because you're a new girl, it means we'll all have to hear the story of Lahai-Roi again.'

'Yes, what exactly does it mean?' asked Phyllis with interest.

'Well, if you know the story of Abraham and Sarah who were both very old and had no children –' began Elizabeth, but she was interrupted by a tall, handsome, enormously pregnant girl who had just entered the room.

'You're not telling the new girl about how that dirty old man crept into Hagar's tent holding his joey aloft and saying that God had told him to get a son by fair means or foul?' she asked in the most aristocratic accent Phyllis had ever heard: Maud would have called it cut-glass.

'Sssh, *sssh*, Madeline! For goodness' sake, you'll shock poor Phyllis!' cried Elizabeth.

'Rubbish, nobody's shocked here. We've all been poked, except for the three old maids. So what's *your* story?' she asked, sprawling in an armchair and squinting towards Phyllis, who felt immediately on the defensive.

'It's probably similar to everybody else's here,' she said, wanting to lower her eyes but feeling that she should stare straight back at this girl. 'I'm expecting a baby in April.'

'What do your parents think?' demanded Madeline.

'They don't know.'

'Ha! What rot. Everybody knows everything. My stupid parents think that just because they've sent me away to be buried in this dump for months, nobody among their friends will know that I'm having a bastard. Of course they know! The whole county knows. "I say, have you heard that Lady Madeline Courtney had disgraced the family name?" – "Good God, we've all known that since it happened! Tell us something new!"'

The other two girls exchanged glances and looked at Phyllis.

'Put another record on, Maddie,' sighed Elizabeth. 'Why don't you start making something for your baby? Surely you could knit a pair of bootees!'

'Can't sew, can't knit. And I'm damned if I'm going to be press-ganged into it – nor am I going round with a broom and a mop like some wretched servant girl,' retorted Madeline. 'Holy Saint Bishop gets paid jolly well for our board – in fact she must make a fortune out of us, more than enough to employ domestic staff to do the cleaning jobs.' She turned to Phyllis again. 'How old are you?'

To Phyllis this was a question that ladies did not ask. And was Madeline really a Lady?

'I'm twenty-six. How old are *you*?' she countered.

'Good God, that makes you the oldest one here. We're all naughty girls of seventeen and eighteen. One went out last week who was only sixteen.' She yawned. 'God, I'm bored out of my mind. Nothing to do. Nothing to read. No gramophone, no cigarettes. What a life!'

'Oh, shut up, Madeline!' exclaimed Dora. 'If you only made an effort to learn something useful –'

'No, *you* shut up, you common little nobody! Don't

254

you *dare* start lecturing me. You'd be in the kitchen scrubbing out pans if you were at Osborough Place.'

'But you're not at Osborough Place now, Madeline,' Elizabeth reminded her sharply. 'You're at Lahai-Roi, and so are we all – all in the same boat, so there's no point in putting on airs and graces with *us*.'

Phyllis held her breath, wondering what Madeline's reaction would be. She looked as if about to make a sharp retort, but changed her mind, heaved her heavy bulk up out of the chair and left the room without another word.

'You mustn't mind her, Phyllis,' said Elizabeth, pushing the needle in and out of the seam on the little nightgown she was making. 'It must be *awful* to belong to an old landed family and be in trouble. I suppose she's just as ashamed as we are, really.'

Phyllis could think of no reply, but Madeline had raised a question in her mind: who was paying *her* fees at Lahai-Roi? Either Matron Groves or Dr Godley – or perhaps they were sharing the cost. However could she repay them?

At prayers next morning Miss Bishop invited the other six residents to tell Phyllis how Lahai-Roi got its name. The Bible was opened at the book of Genesis, chapter 16.

'Will you read this chapter aloud to us, Phyllis?' she asked, and Phyllis obediently read it through.

'"Now Sarai Abram's wife bare him no children: and she had an handmaid, an Egyptian, whose name was Hagar . . ."'

She continued to read the story of how Abram at Sarai's suggestion 'went in unto Hagar', and she conceived – and how this led to trouble between the

255

two women. A quarrel ensued, and Hagar fled into the wilderness where she was found by an angel of the Lord beside a fountain, or well of water. He told her that she would bear a son, but in the meanwhile she must return to her mistress and submit herself to Sarai's authority.

'"Wherefore the well was called Beer-lahai-Roi . . . And Hagar bare Abram a son: and Abram called his son's name, which Hagar bare, Ishmael."'

'Thank you, Phyllis. The "Beer" simply refers to the location of the well Lahai-Roi, which is mentioned again two more times in Genesis, and you'll see from the margin note that the name means "the well of Him that liveth and seeth me". So the Lord showed pity on Hagar, who, like yourselves, was an unmarried mother who would have died in the wilderness with her baby, had not the Lord sent her to this beautiful well, Lahai-Roi, where she could drink and be refreshed, and where an angel appeared to counsel her. You can read the rest of Hagar's story in Genesis, chapter twenty-one, where she was again driven out into the wilderness by Abraham and Sarah – who by then had new names and a son of their own, Isaac. You will read how once again the Lord came to the rescue of her and her son. It's such an inspiring story of the Lord's mercy, and it doesn't gloss over the fact of human frailty. And that's why I changed the name of this house from Hunter's Moon to Lahai-Roi, a place of refuge for women and girls in Hagar's situation.'

She smiled at the six young women seated round the breakfast table, and Phyllis thought what a good woman she was to make this her life's work.

'And now we shall bow our heads and offer up a prayer of thanks to the Lord who showed His loving kindness to Hagar so long ago, and still shows it to us today.'

Half a mile from Lahai-Roi was a tiny hamlet with a few cottages, a combined post office and general store, and a place of worship in the form of the Primitive Methodist Chapel Dora had mentioned, built more than a hundred years before. It was surprisingly well attended, considering its isolation: farmers' families came on foot or by farm-cart or bicycle, and some of the congregation walked all the way from Epsom and back on a Sunday morning or evening to hear the word of God proclaimed through the ringing tones of the minister, Mr Pond. It was he who had inspired Miss Bishop, the sole inheritor of her family home, to rename it Lahai-Roi as a haven for fallen women from families 'of the better sort', who could afford to pay the necessary fees for their errant daughters, rather than send them to one of the many harsh and punitive institutions where the inmates had to work very hard for their board, usually at laundry work, housework and finger-chafing needlework. While most of Miss Bishop's residents were sent by their parents, some were paid for by their employers as a matter of conscience, where the father of the child was known to be a son of the house in which the girl worked, or some other relative. Miss Bishop knew, for example, that if Dora's child was a healthy boy he would go to a foster home where the family could keep in touch with their grandchild, though a girl was to go for adoption and a boy with any obvious deformity such as club foot or hare lip would probably languish in a children's home.

Phyllis, being older than the average resident, soon

made a good impression on Miss Bishop, who found her a likeable young woman with a submissive manner, a willing worker and someone who might be a good influence on the disruptive Lady Madeline Courtney of Osborough Place in Staffordshire. Miss Bishop sighed. That girl was the most difficult she had ever had to deal with – unresponsive to kindness or reason, resistant to gentle religious instruction and defiantly opposed to any form of discipline. Nurse Boyd had been heard to mutter on more than one occasion that Lady High-and-Mighty should be shut in the broom cupboard for twenty-four hours on a diet of bread and water, 'to bring her down to size', but Miss Bishop's Christian beliefs forbade any kind of physical restraint – 'This is not a reformatory,' she said. To send Madeline back to her distracted parents, however, would be an admission of failure, and Miss Bishop was pinning her hopes on Phyllis, a sensible girl whose background was something of a mystery; her fees were paid by a Richmond solicitor on behalf of a client, probably a married man who at least acknowledged his duty, or so thought Miss Bishop.

On Sunday mornings the residents accompanied the proprietress to the Primitive Methodist Chapel, whatever their persuasion; the nearest Anglican church was at Epsom, and there was no transport at Lahai-Roi. Even Madeline consented to go, as it was a chance of fresh air and exercise during the dreary winter months. They walked between leafless trees and splashed through puddles in the rutted lane, with Miss Bishop constantly warning them to be careful. On the Sunday after her arrival Phyllis was walking with the expectant mothers, while Daphne, Grace and Mary walked in front of them with Nurse

Boyd; Nurse Cunningham stayed at the house to look after the babies, and attended chapel in the evening with the cook. Phyllis heard Nurse Boyd telling Grace to 'put on a better face', and when she stole a glance at the girl she saw such utter misery in her eyes that she decided to have a word with her when they reached the chapel.

However, there was an embarrassing distraction. As they filed in through the single door, a little girl of about seven called out to her mother and brother, 'Oh, look, there's the balloon ladies coming in!'

'Yes, and three of them have gone down!' added the little boy.

'Hush, don't be so *rude*!' their mother hissed, but it was all too obvious that the children had heard the expression 'balloon ladies' used about the residents of Lahai-Roi, and Phyllis's cheeks burned.

That's what they really think of us, she thought, and imagined that everybody in the chapel must have heard.

'Horrid little brats, need their ears boxed,' said Madeline in a loud whisper that also carried round the white-plastered walls.

'Be quiet!' ordered Nurse Boyd, but the damage was done, and Mr Pond's kind smile as he greeted them could not undo it. Phyllis tried hard to concentrate on the scripture readings and sermon, but the image of the 'balloon ladies' lingered disconcertingly.

That same afternoon, when the three mothers had given their babies the two o'clock breast-feeds, for bottle-feeding was not an option at Lahai-Roi, Phyllis invited Grace into 'the Quiet Room', once the book-lined study of Miss Bishop's late father.

Remembering all the kindness she herself had received at Oakleigh House, she closed the door and sat down beside Grace.

'Would you like to tell me what's the matter, Grace dear?' she asked quietly, and it was as if flood-gates were opened.

'My little girl's going to her new parents on Tuesday, and I'll never see her again!' the girl cried out in anguish. 'I love her so much, but I'll never, never see her again!'

And she began to cry bitterly and brokenly, a girl of barely eighteen who had got into trouble and turned her parents' lives upside down; but she was also a mother weeping for the child of her womb, about to be taken away from her for ever. 'It's worse than the pain of having her, Phyllis, much worse – and it'll never go away.'

Holding the girl in her arms, Phyllis began to understand the sadness at the heart of Lahai-Roi. How would she feel if it was Teddy's child she was carrying? How could she give it up?

Yer get used to it, Phyllis, but yer never get over it. Maud's words came back to her as she tried to think of what comfort she could offer.

'She'll go to a good home, Grace, to parents who'll love her and do their best for her.'

'Yes, but she'll never know her *real* mother. Nobody'll ever love her more than I do. I'll never know what happens to her, whether they'll tell her she's not theirs. I'll never stop thinking about her, wondering about her – not if I live to be a hundred. My baby, oh my little baby!'

And she went on crying while Phyllis rocked her in her arms. It was not the last time Phyllis was to encounter this agony at Lahai-Roi, and she learned

260

that there were no words to ease the pain: sometimes the only way to comfort those who weep is to weep with them.

One wet February day followed another, but the mornings and evenings gradually began to draw out, and the first snowdrops appeared beside the front pathway. Grace went home to her parents looking tired and hollow-eyed, and two more girls arrived, one due in April, the other in May. Elizabeth was the next due to be delivered, and as her time approached she began to get backache and tightening of her abdomen that made her wince and hang on to furniture, which alarmed her companions, who thought the delivery was imminent. After several such scares, the nurses assured her that it was 'just the head going down', and Nurse Boyd told her to stop whining and get on with her work; the baby would come in its own good time.

'Bitch!' said Madeline, who was also gritting her teeth from time to time with the discomforts of late pregnancy. She was an enormous size, and being a tall girl with strong muscles due to horse-riding, she was seldom comfortable and slept badly, tossing and turning in the dormitory, frequently getting out of bed to use the chamber pot. 'Restfulness' was hardly an appropriate name for the room in which the four occupants were disturbed at all hours of the night.

Elizabeth finally went into labour in the last week of February, when her waters broke and made a pool on the floor of the dining room during post-breakfast prayers. Off she went to the strictly separated rooms at the back of the second floor, called 'the hospital', and all that day the residents listened for sounds of pain and news of progress. Even Madeline was quiet

261

and showed her anxiety by pacing up and down the living room and the passage that linked the kitchen and dining room. At five o'clock that afternoon there were a few noises from the hospital when Elizabeth gave two long-drawn-out groans and Nurse Cunningham's voice could be heard saying something like, 'Push again! Push again!' – and then they all gave a sigh of relief on hearing the unmistakable cry of a newborn baby. They relaxed and looked at each other: it was over! A message was sent down that Elizabeth's baby was a girl.

Apparently Elizabeth needed stitches, and half an hour later the residents saw Dr Renshaw's car draw up at the front door. He was the GP who most often attended the residents, and on this occasion he was not alone; there was a young woman with him. Miss Bishop met them at the door and escorted them to the hospital, and when the business was done the doctor and his companion went to Miss Bishop's private sitting room for refreshments – after which they suddenly appeared with her in the residents' room.

'You all know Dr Renshaw, and today he has brought his niece with him to meet you all,' said Miss Bishop with her usual pleasant smile. 'Miss Vaughan is training to be a doctor, and we're very happy to welcome her to Lahai-Roi today.'

'Are we? Do animals in the zoo like being gawped at?' muttered Madeline with a scowl at the dark-haired, lively-looking young woman. Phyllis hastily shushed her.

'That's right, and I'm so pleased to meet you,' smiled the visitor. 'I hope to specialise in obstetrics when I'm qualified, so I begged my uncle to let me come with him today.'

A rather awkward silence followed. 'What hospital are you at, Miss Vaughan?' asked Phyllis, simply to show some interest.

'The London Hospital in Whitechapel Road,' came the eager reply. 'They're taking more women students now, after the loss of – so many men.' Miss Vaughan looked grave and momentarily lowered her voice. 'But I'm hoping to get post-graduate experience at an infirmary in Lambeth, because there's a very good man there, a splendid teacher.'

A memory was stirred. 'Isn't that a very poor area, Miss Vaughan?' Phyllis ventured.

'Yes, but so's the district around Whitechapel Road – I mean, London's full of poor areas as well as very rich ones. I particularly want to work with poor women who – er . . .' She hesitated and tailed off, suddenly remembering that these pregnant girls were also poor women in a different sense. She flushed slightly and continued, 'I just want to be a *women's* doctor, and –'

Dr Renshaw cut her short. 'I think we'd better be getting back now, Mildred. I'll be late for my evening surgery. Thank you, Miss Bishop and, er, ladies. I'll see you again soon, I'm sure.'

Miss Bishop saw them to the door, and Phyllis was left with the impression of an intelligent young woman who was ambitious but not for herself. Miss Vaughan really wanted to do some good with her life, and Phyllis sighed when she thought of the collapse of her own ideals, inspired by Dr Godley and Miss Groves – and destroyed in one black hour.

February gave way to March, and on a wild and windy night Madeline's pains gripped her with an intensity that took her breath away. Phyllis, Dora and another girl, Penny, sat up in their beds and heard the agonised screams that penetrated down to their dormitory.

And that wasn't all they heard.

'Yes, well, now you've got to face it, you insolent slut. Squeal away, squeal your proud head off – you're no different from any other woman now.'

'Oh, help me, Nurse Boyd, I'm sorry, I'm sorry – I never knew it would be as bad as this!' Madeline's cut-glass voice was shrill with fear, cracked with sheer physical agony.

'Didn't you? Well, I've got news for you, Lady High-and-Mighty. It's going to get worse than this – a whole *lot* worse, and serve you right, you stuck-up bitch. You've done nothing but make trouble here, you're the worst of the lot. But I'll tell you something, madam – before this night's out, you're going to beg for mercy. Oh, yes, you most certainly are!'

Phyllis and the other two listeners could not hear every word, but the gloating relish in Nurse Boyd's voice, now that she had a hated resident in her power, sent shudders down their spines.

'Miss Bishop! Can I see Miss Bishop?' pleaded Madeline between shrieks of pain.

'No, you can't fool that poor woman tonight, your ladyship! She's been much too soft with you, but she's not here now, and you're going to get the workhouse treatment. That's where you should've been sent in the first place – to the workhouse, where the poorest girls have to go!'

'Nurse Boyd, please, please – give me something for the pain – something for the backache, for God's sake!'

'Yes, I'll give you something, my lady. Throw off the sheet – pull up your nightgown – turn over and

264

show me your great fat backside – and *there* you are
– take *that*!'

And they heard the sound of an enormous smack
as a large, hard hand landed on an expanse of
buttock. Scarcely had the ensuing yell died down
when the other buttock caught a second whack.

'And shut up, or you'll get another. Shut *up*, I said!'

By now Dora and Penny were whimpering. 'She's
killing her,' whispered Dora.

Phyllis got out of bed, knowing that she had to do
something – but what? She could not call Nurse
Cunningham, who was away for the weekend. She
had two choices: either to call Miss Bishop from her
room on the other side of the house, or go up to the
hospital herself and tell Nurse Boyd to stop torturing
a helpless woman in labour.

Miss Bishop was not a midwife, or even a trained
nurse, and as a middle-aged spinster she kept away
from the hospital, leaving that aspect of the residents'
needs to two trained midwives. They had full
authority to oversee women in labour as they saw fit,
sending for a doctor when they thought it necessary,
but usually managing without one. The proprietress
had become aware that the residents greatly preferred Nurse Cunningham, and had heard whispers
about Nurse Boyd's harsh treatment of girls in
labour; but when on occasion she had tentatively
mentioned this, the nurse had immediately replied
that the girl in question had been uncooperative and
had needed a firm hand. It was her word against the
girls', and Miss Bishop had let it pass.

So what was Phyllis to do? Get dressed, for a start.
She hastily pulled off her nightdress and put on her
clothes, gave her hair a quick brush and set off for the
hospital. She had never been to this part of the house

265

before, but the sound of screams and angry words led her straight to it. She opened the door and saw Madeline cowering on a narrow bed which had a red rubber sheet spread over a horsehair mattress, and Nurse Boyd stood over her with an arm upraised. As they turned to look at Phyllis standing in the open doorway, they both froze into stillness, like a tableau. Nurse Boyd's jaw dropped.

'What's up, Phyllis? Somebody else started?' she asked, lowering her arm and wiping her hands on a towel. 'You're not supposed to be up here, you know.'

Madeline groaned, 'Phyllis! Oh, Phyllis, help me, do!'

'Be quiet, you. Come on, Phyllis, out with it. What's happened? Somebody's waters broke?'

'No, Nurse Boyd,' said Phyllis with quiet strength, entering the room and closing the door behind her. 'I've come to be with Madeline in labour. I'll stay beside her, I won't interfere – but I'm staying here, in this room.'

'Thank God, Phyllis, oh, thank God for sending you,' gasped Madeline. 'Don't go.'

'What? Oh, no, you're not! You're getting out o' here *now*!' retorted Nurse Boyd. 'Out! Go on, out you go!'

'No, Nurse Boyd, I'm staying.'

'Listen to me, young woman, I'll take hold o' you and heave you out o' that door in five seconds flat. So are you going or do you want to be chucked out?'

'If you throw me bodily out of this room I'll go straight to Miss Bishop and bring her here.'

'No, you won't. She never comes over here, she leaves all this bit to us midwives. She'll be fast asleep,' replied Nurse Boyd, a little taken aback by Phyllis's calm self-assurance.

'I shall wake her up and tell her that you are ill-treating Madeline. I shall tell her what I've heard, and bring her here to see for herself.'

'Look here, I'm not taking threats from the likes o' *you*,' shouted the woman. 'If you want to stay here, you can bloody well stay, and I'll go and leave you on your own to cope with this slut who got herself pregnant by a groom in her father's stables – did you know that?'

'How any of us became pregnant is nothing to do with how we should be treated in labour,' replied Phyllis with conviction. 'And you're free to leave me with Madeline if you wish. I've seen a great many births and assisted midwives and doctors at Oakleigh House in Richmond. I'm well able to cope with a delivery.'

'Maybe, but you're not registered, and not supposed to deliver without a doctor present. There'd be a big row if you delivered her and she bled to death,' said the nurse vindictively.

'Then stay and deliver her yourself, the choice is yours,' said Phyllis, while Madeline gripped her fingers so hard that they felt half crushed. 'But I am not leaving.'

Nurse Boyd was beaten. This polite, usually submissive young woman, now nearly twenty-seven and a favourite of everybody at Lahai-Roi, had revealed a will of steel, and the midwife had to yield. If she withdrew, the story of her cruelty would come out, and this time there would be two witnesses against her instead of one helpless girl, half-crazed with pain. She had no choice but to put a good face on it and give no cause for complaint.

Phyllis stood beside the bed, for there was only one small chair, and the nurse used it. Without interfering in any way, she whispered words of encouragement to Madeline from time to time, and the girl calmed down, managing to relax between contractions and gritting her teeth when she felt her abdominal muscles hardening again. Every five minutes, then every three minutes, and by five o'clock every minute, which was when Phyllis thankfully heard the characteristic grunting, straining sound in Madeline's throat that meant that the cervix was fully dilated and the baby was on its way through, helped by the mother's own voluntary efforts.

'Come on, then, let's get pushing,' said Nurse Boyd sullenly, and Phyllis prayed that there would be no delay at this crucial stage. She whispered her own instructions to a panting, grimacing Madeline.

'Take a big breath in, Maddie, hold it and *push*, that's right. You might find it a bit easier if you draw your knees up and put your hands behind them, like this – that's better.'

'I thought you said you weren't going to interfere,' grumbled the midwife, concealing her surprise at Phyllis's cool management of the situation. Another twenty minutes passed, and Phyllis's prayer was answered: a large baby girl emerged at a quarter to six, and her lusty cries were the sweetest sound that Phyllis had ever heard. While the midwife attended to the infant Phyllis waited beside Madeline for the separation of the placenta, which was expelled within another seven minutes. Still she did not desert her post, for she did not want to leave Madeline to Nurse Boyd's tender mercies. She washed her friend and helped her put on a clean nightdress and maternity pads, then eased her into the wheelchair used for transferring mothers from the hospital to their bed in the dormitory. Tired but triumphant, she wheeled Madeline down to 'Restfulness', to be greeted by a rejoicing Dora and Penny, who were quite overwhelmed by what she had achieved.

Madeline's delivery of a nine and a half pound baby daughter was in many ways a turning-point for Phyllis. It gave her a new understanding of her own potential, the reserves of strength on which she could draw when circumstances demanded it. After careful thought she decided not to make a complaint to Miss Bishop about Nurse Boyd. The woman had been given a salutary warning, and Phyllis thought it was unlikely that she would indulge again in the kind of sadistic cruelty that had brought Phyllis to Madeline's side. Rather than cause an uproar at Lahai-Roi that might spread beyond its walls and damage its reputation as a safe haven, it seemed more expedient to give the woman a second chance and to take no action for the present.

Although nothing official was said, however, the unofficial reaction among the residents was considerable. Phyllis's rescue of Madeline was endlessly recounted, and timid newcomers like Penny took new heart. Miss Bishop could not help noting the lightening of the atmosphere, and put it down to Madeline's complete change of attitude from rebelliousness to quiet submission, surely a sign of repentance. In fact, the change was brought about by love for the baby fathered upon her by a stable groom. When the innocent little creature nestled up to Madeline's flowing breasts, it was not only nourishment that she drank; Madeline's heart yearned over her, and like Grace and countless others she dreaded the day of parting from her for ever. In vain she wrote impassioned letters home, begging her parents to let her arrange for long-term foster care in the vicinity of Osborough Place, but Lord Courtney dismissed all her appeals, saying that the family had already been put through enough trouble and expense to keep her shameful secret, and she was not going to cause a scandal now.

'And I haven't got any money of my own, only what I'm allowed, so I can't afford to live anywhere else with my poor baby, Phyllis,' she said mournfully. 'Father's right, I've caused nothing but trouble to everybody. She'll probably be better off with a decent couple than with somebody like me – but oh, how I shall miss her. I'll never get over missing her.'

Tears filled her eyes, and once again Phyllis was unable to offer any real words of comfort, only the helpless pity of a friend.

The March days brought daffodils and crocuses, and Phyllis mentioned these signs of spring in her letters to her parents, as if they were blooming in the garden at the back of Oakleigh House. Each week she took her stamped letter placed in a larger envelope addressed to Tudor House, and put it in the pillarbox outside the post office and general store near to the Primitive Methodist Chapel. And each week a letter arrived from North Camp, via Oakleigh House, where Dr Godley had collected it and redirected it to Lahai-Roi. By the end of April Phyllis expected to be delivered and discharged from Miss Bishop's haven for fallen women – and she planned to visit her parents straight away, before recommencing her duties at the maternity home for more fortunate mothers. It was a goal towards which she strived as her body grew wearier and more cumbersome, but she sometimes felt that the pregnancy would never end.

Yet it did. On 26 March, a Monday, Phyllis woke with a dull, persistent backache, which gradually became stronger. Miss Bishop saw her struggling with the morning sweeping and dusting of 'Restfulness', and told her to leave the cleaning and rest on her bed until dinner time at one o'clock. Phyllis thankfully did as she was told, but the pain continued, accompanied by a regular tightening of her dome-like tummy. She had no appetite for dinner, and when she tried to get off the bed she could scarcely straighten up. Was it possible that she could be starting in labour already? Or was it just the baby's head going down, as the midwives so often said about early pains? She winced as another tightening began, and made herself take deep breaths in and out, as Matron Groves taught the mothers in early labour at Oakleigh House, but it was no use; when the next wave of contraction gripped her abdomen she cried out in pain.

'Phyllis! Phyllis, where are you? Miss Bishop says are you coming down to dinner?' called Penny.

'I – I'm sorry, Penny, but I can hardly move. I think I must be starting – in labour,' she gasped, but her heart was filled with fear: now that her own time had come, had she the strength to endure the pain, the courage to face the peril of childbirth?

In fact Phyllis's labour was relatively short, though the pain took her almost to the limits of endurance during the hours of that afternoon. She did her best to use the intervals between contractions to rest and give her mind and body time to prepare for the next searing onslaught of teeth-gritting, fist-clenching agony when it seemed as if her back was about to break. With no other relief than the bitter-tasting mixture of potassium bromide and chloral hydrate, she thought of Oakleigh House and imagined Matron Groves at her side; she heard her voice and saw her face more clearly than the moving shapes of the two Lahai-Roi midwives attending her. Nurse Boyd was carefully taciturn, and Nurse Cunningham, a solidly built, plain-featured woman, was kindly enough and drank quantities of tea while Phyllis writhed and moaned.

'All right, Phyllis, you're getting there, no labour lasts for ever. Are you getting any feeling like wanting to open your bowels?'

'Not yet, Nurse – not yet,' groaned Phyllis, though by five o'clock there was the beginning of a sensation of pushing.

'There you are, I told you she was getting on,' said Nurse Boyd, looking down between Phyllis's outspread legs. 'There's the top o' the head, see, when she gets a pain.'

Nurse Cunningham pressed the little ear-trumpet stethoscope on Phyllis's abdomen, and nodded. 'That's ticking away all right. Come on, Phyllis, it's time to do some work.'

And work she did, for the next forty-five minutes, pushing and resting, pushing again and resting, over and over again. The pain during pushing was terrible, but in a way it was easier to bear than the earlier pains had been, for now she was adding her own effort to the process, and felt the descent of the baby's head to the pelvic floor, exactly the same sensation as when straining on the lavatory seat to empty her bowels. Soon, soon she would be rid of this burden, this unwanted bastard planted so brutally, so heartlessly in her body by Denver

Towers, whose face she could no longer envisage, nor did she want to remember him.

'She's nearly there. Come on, Phyllis, another push, another push!'

'Come on, you can do better than that – push harder!'

And with one last enormous effort she felt a splitting sensation between her legs, as something hard and round came through.

'There's the head! Stop pushing, Phyllis, and pant in and out!'

She would have panted anyway, in breathless exhaustion. The body slithered through, and the midwives exclaimed, 'There it is, and it's a boy! Got the scissors and string?'

Phyllis heard their voices as if from a long way off. The pain was over. The child was born. She was free again.

'Here, come on, sit up and take hold o' your baby. You can put him to the breast straight away. It'll help the afterbirth out.'

Phyllis heaved herself up as a bundle was thrust into her arms. She looked down at the baby, wrapped in a towel. He had given a good loud cry as soon as he was born, but now his little face was calm and unwrinkled. His dark blue eyes were bright, his nose a little button, his mouth round and rosy, open already to take the nipple. A tiny hand pushed out of the towel, as if searching for something to hold. Phyllis put her forefinger on his palm, and his fingers immediately curled round it: it was their introduction. He was hers, flesh of her flesh, and he was the most beautiful thing she had ever seen.

'I'll call you Paul,' she whispered. 'After St Paul the apostle.'

'No, call him by the name Paul was born with,' said Nurse Boyd. 'Before he was Paul he was Saul. And this one hasn't had much of a start either, so call him Saul – and in any case his new parents'll call him something else.'

So it was Nurse Boyd, of all people, that named Phyllis's son. And as she looked down at him love welled up within her like a fountain, a love such as she had never known before, filling her lonely heart to overflowing. All she wanted to do was gaze upon her baby son in adoration.

Chapter 16

Dear Miss Groves,

After careful consideration I have decided to write to you, and I apologise for any inconvenience caused by so doing. My wife and I have become increasingly concerned about the health of our daughter, Miss Phyllis Bird, who is employed as a nursing assistant at Oakleigh House. We have not had a visit from her since September, when she told us of her plans to take midwifery training, and we were happy about this; however, she never mentions it now, and pleads that she is too busy to get away to visit her parents, not even for a day.

In recent weeks her letters have become less frequent, and convey very little information. She has twice referred to yourself as 'Miss Bishop', and I have the impression that something is troubling her, and that she is not being entirely open with us. I therefore beg for an assurance from you that Phyllis is in good health, or that if not, you will inform me to the best of your knowledge regarding any difficulty she may be experiencing.

My wife is of a nervous disposition, and I have not told her about this enquiry. Please find enclosed a stamped envelope addressed to myself at Bird's Outfitters of North Camp,

Hants, and I shall be greatly obliged to you for an early reply.

Yours respectfully,

Ernest J. Bird, Esq.

4 April 1923

Dear Mr Bird,

Thank you for your letter of 2 April. To the best of my knowledge your daughter Phyllis Bird is in good health, but I understand your anxiety, and so I have passed on your letter to Dr C. Godley, her medical attendant, so that he may answer your enquiry.

I send my good wishes to you, and hope that Mrs Bird is well.

Yours sincerely,

(Miss) G. Groves, Matron, Oakleigh House

For the first week after delivery, Phyllis lived for the babies' feeding times: six, ten, two, six and ten were the most wonderful hours of each day, for then she held her baby in her arms and opened her nightdress to give him the breast-milk on which he thrived. From the start he was a good feeder, nuzzling his face against her soft warmth, clutching with his starfish hands, suckling contentedly and bringing up wind as soon as she held him up against her shoulder and patted his back. At night she was only too glad to be woken up to give one or two night feeds, as was the routine at Lahai-Roi, for Saul was the joy of her life; gone was the emptiness of years, for he filled every corner of her heart.

'My little Saul,' she would whisper to him as he was put in her arms. 'My own dear, darling little boy.' And she resolutely closed her mind against the unthinkable: that in six weeks' time or thereabouts he and she would be – but no. *No!* Never.

After seven days of bed-rest she was told to get up and dress, which meant that she could go to the nursery and attend to Saul herself before and after feeds, changing his soiled nappies for clean ones. She was now virtually his sole carer, and the spring days passed in a haze of love and happiness. She was expected to do light housework again, and rest from three to four in the afternoon, but time and again she would creep into the nursery between feeds, just to gaze upon his little face in repose, one arm flung up beside his head – or awake and stirring, his little legs thrashing up and down, his mouth stretching in a whimper of discomfort if his nappy was wet. Phyllis was his handmaid and devoted slave: she was his mother, and he was her son. There was no past or future, only the blessed present.

'There's a visitor for you, Phyllis.' Miss Bishop gave a slight frown when she saw Phyllis reluctantly putting her baby down in his cot after the two o'clock feed, having managed to extend the time until nearly three.

'A visitor, Miss Bishop?' Phyllis felt a sudden stab of alarm as a vision of some official with a briefcase flashed across her mind's eye, together with the dreaded word 'adoption'. No, let it not be anything like that . . .

'Yes, a Miss Ling. I've put her in the Quiet Room, and you may talk with her in there. And before you ask, Phyllis, I'm afraid that you may *not* take her to the nursery. It's not our policy at Lahai-Roi to show the babies to any visitors except in very exceptional circumstances.'

Phyllis's face fell. 'Oh, Miss Bishop, I –'

'You may spend an hour in the Quiet Room with your visitor, Phyllis.'

'Thank you, Miss Bishop.'

There was nothing formal about Maud's greeting, though Phyllis felt an odd constraint at the sight of this particular friend; Maud had been through it all, and her story was not a happy one.

'Phyllis, me little duck! Come on, give us a big 'ug!'

'Oh, Maudie, I've got the most beautiful little boy, I've called him Saul and he was born on March the twenty-sixth. Oh, he's such a darling.'

'I know, duck, I 'eard from Charles that ye'd 'ad the baby. 'Ow did it go? Was it an 'ard time?'

'Oh, it hurt, Maudie, but not that bad, and as soon as I saw my baby I forgot all about the pain. And he's so *good*, Maudie, he hardly ever cries, and when I feed him I feel such love –'

She broke off, because Maud's face was blank and unsmiling.

'Why, Maudie, what's the matter?'

Maud Ling could have wept at what lay ahead for her friend, but she had not the words to warn her, nor the heart to mar her happiness during this brief period of motherhood; so she veered away from the subject.

'Nuffin', duck. Charles sends 'is best regards an' ev'ryfing, only 'e can't come to see yer, 'e's gorn orf to London to see Pamela. She went into labour this mornin', so she's probably got it by now.'

'Oh, yes, poor Dr Godley. I knew his daughter was due about the same time as me. And that reminds me, Maudie, there's something I want to ask you about him. He's always been so kind to me, even sending on my parents' letters here, and posting mine to them. Is *he* paying the fees for me here? He recommended the place, and brought me here. I mean, who else could it be?'

Maud looked rather embarrassed. ''E *would've* paid for yer, Phyllis, 'cause 'e's got a soft spot for yer, but I told 'im I would.'

'*Maud!*'

'No, duck, it was the least I could do, bein' responsible for what 'appened. I let yer dahn, leavin' yer to the mercy o' that rat. No, Phyllis, don't argue, I'll never forgive meself for it.'

'But, Maudie –'

'No, duck, I don't want to talk abaht it. 'Ere's some o' Belle's I-talian stuff for yer tea, 'alfway between bread an' cake. She done it specially for yer.'

'Oh, that's very kind of her.' Phyllis was not sorry to change the subject, and asked, 'How is Signora Capogna?'

Maud, who had been strictly forbidden by Belle to return with the mother and baby, answered with another pieces of news. 'She's missin' Teddy, o' course, same as me, an' 'e don't write much from 'Ollywood, but we know that Miss Yankee Doodle soon fahnd somebody else. I fink 'e's stayin' aht there for a bit, just to save 'is face.'

Phyllis's cheeks burned crimson. 'Does he – does he know about me, Maudie?'

'Nah, no need. By the time 'e comes back ye'll be back too, at Oakleigh 'Ouse, an' it'll be as if yer never went away.'

Just to mention Teddy was like talking about somebody from another life, and Phyllis lowered her eyes. Then she brightened, and her eyes lit up. 'Maudie dear, Miss Bishop says I can't show you Saul, but I *do* want you to see how beautiful he is – so

279

I'll ask her if Nurse Cunningham or Nurse Boyd may take you up to the nursery and –'

But Maud raised her hand and shook her head. 'No fanks, Phyllis. It'd make me fink o' my Alex, 'cause 'e was a lovely baby an' all. It'd break me 'eart to see yer little boy an' know that – oh, Phyllis, what a wicked shame.' And Maud could not hide her tears. Phyllis hastened to apologise.

'Dear Maudie, I'm sorry, I should've thought . . .' she began, but then realisation dawned: Maud's tears were for *her*, Phyllis. And in that moment the terrible dread that she had so far managed to suppress reared up to the surface of her consciousness, a monster from the deep.

'I shall find some way to keep him, Maud,' she said in a voice sharpened by fear. 'I can't part with him, not my precious son.'

Maud's face was bleak as she put her arms around Phyllis's rigid body and said quietly, 'Yer'll 'ave to, duck, same as all the ovver poor girls 'ere. There's no work for a gal wiv a new baby to look after, an' no 'ome an' no money to pay for fosterin'. There's only one kind o' job for the likes o' them, an' you ain't that sort. I know 'cause I bin frough it all – nobody wants yer. What I 'ave to tell meself is that my Alex is bein' brought up in 'is grandparents' 'ome wiv ev'ryfing money can buy, an' your little chap'll be better orf in a proper 'ome wiv two parents – that's what yer got to tell yerself.'

'But Maud, I can't, I *can't*, I'd rather die!'

'Yer tried that before, gal, an' it didn't work,' Maud reminded her, though her big hazel eyes were full of pity. 'I better go nah, Phyllis, or your Miss Bishop'll be arter me. Oh, my Gawd, it's a sad world, an' I'm that sorry I can't do nuffin' abaht it for yer, duck.'

They kissed goodbye, but Phyllis's cheek was white and cold. She could not thank Maud for coming, because her visit had marked the end of her rejoicing over Saul. All she could think of now was the agony of parting that awaited her in another four or five weeks. How would she *bear* it, seeing him go, not knowing what his future would be? Who would love him half as much as she did? What would happen when he woke up and cried for his mother's gentle hands, her soft, full breasts, her loving whispers of his name? A stranger's hands would hold him, and a hard rubber teat would be thrust into his mouth – oh, God! For the first time since his birth she gazed into the abyss, the blank emptiness, a loneliness worst than anything she had known before. She flung herself down on her knees and called out like Hagar of old:

'O Lord, have mercy on me! Help me! Help my innocent son and me!'

But no comfort came.

It was a girl. After an eight-hour labour the twenty-year-old mother was delivered of an eight-pound baby daughter on 6 April just before eleven at night, in the little flat in Brick Street. She was attended by a district midwife, and her husband only just got home from a long day at St George's Hospital in time to hear the baby's first cry. Charles Godley was at his daughter's side, for as soon as he received the telephone call from his son-in-law to say that Pamela was in labour at last, he had left everything to board the Waterloo train and get in a taxi-cab to Brick Street, arriving at six on a fine spring evening. The midwife had looked askance at him, not too pleased to be overlooked by a doctor, but he made no attempt to interfere with her ministrations, and at the time of delivery she was glad of his unobtrusive assistance.

'All right, my darling, I'm here with you,' he assured Pamela from time to time, and as the new baby made her appearance, he put his hand to his mouth to suppress a cry of wonder.

'Oh, Pamela, it's a little girl, a sweet little thing – oh, bless her!'

'Thank you, Dad, it's been a help having you here,' the new mother replied dutifully, but then her eyes brightened. 'Oh, I can hear Patrick coming up the stairs – Patrick! Oh, Patrick my love, look, we've got a little girl!'

'Heart of my heart,' whispered the young husband, leaning over the bed and enfolding her in his arms. 'It's the happiest day I ever did live, surely.'

Their tears of joy mingled, and Dr Godley wistfully caught the midwife's eye. 'Let's have a look at this pretty little girl, then,' he said, and she handed him the yelling bundle.

'We're goin' to call her Roisin,' said Patrick fondly. 'That's a rose in Irish, y'see.'

'Roisin – pronounced Rosheen,' mused Godley, looking down at the little screwed-up face. She was going to have red hair like her father. Silently he added to himself, You were right, Gladys my good friend. It doesn't matter now that the baby's born, and I'm a grandfather.

'I suppose this calls for tea all round?' he suggested. 'No, no, Nurse, you get on with your work, and I'll put the kettle on. I'm just the odd-job man around here now.'

'That's very good o' you, Dr Godley,' the midwife answered as the after-birth slithered out into a bowl held ready for it. What a nice man he was, she thought, and hoped that his daughter appreciated him as she ought.

After he had poured out cups of tea for the four of them, he said, 'I'll stay overnight in the armchair, so's to be on hand. But now I must go out to that call-box on the corner and telephone your mother.'

Ernest Bird was by now both mystified and alarmed. He had written to this Matron on 2 April, and received her rather evasive reply on the 5th, since when there had been nothing more. The doctor had not got in touch, and the last letter from Phyllis had been dated 16 March; yet Miss Groves had said that Phyllis was 'to the best of her knowledge' in good health. What had she meant by that? Mr Bird began to suspect that his daughter was no longer at Oakleigh House. Was she at those film studios, getting involved with the sort of people she knew her parents disapproved of? He actually waylaid Rosie Lansdowne when he met her in North Camp, to ask if she had heard from Phyllis lately, but she said she hadn't, and neither had Betty Goddard. When he tentatively asked if she had any thoughts about Phyllis's life in Richmond, she confessed that she and Betty believed Phyllis to be in love with Maud Ling's brother, Teddy, though this was just supposition; they were in fact as mystified as he was by her silence. Following this brief exchange, wild rumours spread throughout North Camp: some said that Phyllis Bird had become a small-part actress in films, meaning that she had turned her back on her sorrowing parents and gone to the bad, as many had prophesied she would.

On Monday, 9 April, when there was still no word from this Dr Godley, Mr Bird could wait no longer and decided to travel up to Richmond on the Tuesday. It meant closing the shop and giving his apprentice tailor a free day. He did not tell Ethel of his plans, but left the house at the usual time, saying that he might be late back that evening as he had to see his auditor at the end of the financial year.

He travelled on the train to Waterloo, and then down to Richmond, his apprehension growing with every mile. Outside the station he took a taxi-cab to Ormond Road, and was set down at Oakleigh House.

He rang the doorbell, and a maid answered. When he asked if he might speak to the matron, she led him to a small study where a large, pale but very civil lady came and introduced herself as Mrs Draycott, Matron's deputy and housekeeper.

'I'm afraid Matron's very busy at present, sir. It's the time for her morning round of the patients, you see,' she said importantly. 'But maybe I can be of some assistance to you, if you do not mind telling me your business?'

'My name's Bird, Mrs Draycott,' he replied, and immediately saw the gleam of interest in her eyes. 'I've been in touch with the matron about my daughter, Miss Phyllis Bird, who is employed here.'

'Oh, I see, you're Mr Bird!' said the lady eagerly. 'Oh dear me – well, in that case I'd better tell Matron you're here, because I'm sure she'll want to see you straight away, sir.' And off she bustled.

It did not look good. Something was wrong. Very wrong.

Within a minute Miss Groves came into the room, firmly closing the door on Mrs Draycott and declining her offer of a tray of tea.

'Ah, good morning, Mr Bird. Do take a seat. I owe you an apology for not answering your letter more fully, but the circumstances were most unfortunate. I usually see Dr Godley almost every day, but family matters took him away to London, and he did not call at Oakleigh House for several days. He returned on Sunday, and I handed him your letter. I'm sure that he would have replied straight away – let me see, today's Tuesday – did you not hear from him today?'

'If I had, I wouldn't be here asking about my daughter, Matron,' replied Bird with a sharpness that he would not normally have used to a lady. 'And seeing that Dr Godley has not seen fit to reply, I am hoping that *you* will be able to inform me. Is my daughter here or not?'

Miss Groves hid her confusion under her customary calmness of manner. 'I am sorry, Mr Bird, but she is not.'

'I thought not, Matron. So will you kindly tell me where I might find her?'

'She's staying at a house about three miles north of Epsom, Mr Bird. She went there in February.'

'Then why wasn't I told?' demanded Bird, rising from his seat. 'Why didn't *she* tell me and her mother? What on earth is going on, Miss Groves? Is she employed at this other house?'

Gladys Groves saw that discovery was inevitable. 'Mr Bird, I'm very sorry, but Phyllis wished the matter to remain confidential. I suggest that you go to the place and see her yourself – though it will be a shock to her. She never intended that you should know.'

Ernest Bird sat down heavily, silenced by the secrecy implied in this woman's quiet voice, and by the obvious sympathy she felt for his predicament. His thoughts began to untangle in his head, and as he looked back upon the last six months, various facts took on a new significance. Phyllis's last visit had been six months ago, and Ethel had said that she looked peaky when she left without having breakfast. She had apparently left Oakleigh House for somewhere else in February, without telling her parents, and the behaviour of that other woman – what was her name? Draycott – had hinted at some sort of trouble. This matron seemed a good sort of woman, not to be trifled with, but there was no mistaking that look in her eyes – a look of regret, of pity. Who was she sorry for – himself? Phyllis? Like a mystery that at last resolves and reveals itself, Ernest Bird understood what his daughter had tried to hide. His face paled, and he put a hand up to cover his eyes.

'Is my daughter expecting a child?' The voice sounded thin and reedy, unlike his own.

'She was expecting a child, Mr Bird, and it was born on the twenty-sixth of March, a boy.'

There was a long silence. Ernest Bird took out a handkerchief and wiped his eyes and forehead. 'Thank you, Matron,' he said at last. 'I think I've known for some time that it was something like that, only I just didn't acknowledge it to myself.'

'I expect you'll want to go and see her now, Mr Bird,' she said kindly.

'Yes, I – I want to, as soon as possible. Epsom, you said?'

'Yes, Mr Bird, a very good private maternity home for – unmarried women and girls. It's called Lahai-Roi – I'll write it down for you – and it's run by a Miss Bishop. Did you come by car?'

'No, I've never learned to drive. I came up by train.'

'Ah, I see. I'm afraid there's no direct line to Epsom

from Richmond, and I think you'll have to change at Putney and go via Wimbledon. Will you take a little light refreshment before you leave?'

'No, thank you, Matron. The sooner I see my daughter . . .' She thought he looked like a man reeling from a heavy blow.

'And the baby, Mr Bird. I believe he'll be going for adoption soon, and I shall be very glad to have Phyllis back here with us again. She's one of my best maternity nurses.'

'Thank you, Matron. Thank you for everything.'

'Good morning, Mr Bird. And good luck.' She held out her hand and he shook it.

The train service turned out to be inconvenient, to say the least, and Bird seemed to spend most of the journey waiting at small railway stations. He changed at Putney for Wimbledon, but was then told he would have to go to Raynes Park. Eventually he boarded a train that got him to Epsom Station by half-past two, where he found that buses to Lahai-Roi were few and far between. Out in Epsom's broad High Street he asked passers-by if there was a taxi service, and was directed to an old coachworks in a side road.

'Is it possible to get a cab to Lahai-Roi?' he enquired at the entrance of a large, dark shed.

'Matt!' bawled a man to somebody out of sight. 'Here's a gen'leman says he want to go to Hunter's Moon!'

'Oh-ah. When's he wan' to go?'

'He looks as if he wan' to go today, Matt.'

A corpulent red-faced man appeared out of the gloom. 'Do 'ee wan' to go to Hunter's Moon today, squire?'

'I want to go to Lahai-Roi as soon as possible – now, if you can take me,' said Bird. 'I'll pay you well, of course.'

'Oh-ah. Oi'll jus' get ol' Tess out o' the yard.'

And within another quarter of an hour Bird was seated beside the man in a two-wheeled, three-seater trap drawn by a round-bellied mare who lifted her head and neighed for sheer pleasure at finding herself trotting along country lanes between fields and woodland.

'Who be 'ee goin' to see, then, squire?'

'My – my daughter,' Bird heard himself reply. What would be the use of pretending?

'Oh-ah. Some tells Oi it's the maidservant they be goin' to see. It never be the father o' the child what pays for her to stay at Hunter's Moon – Oi means Larry-Roy,' grinned the man, and the thought came to Bird that somebody must have paid for Phyllis.

The trap eventually reached a narrow, rutted lane between tall trees, and the house came into view.

'Do 'ee want Oi to wait for 'ee, squire?'

'Er – how long can you wait?' asked Bird, his heart thumping at the thought of the emotional scene ahead.

'Oi can wait an hour for 'ee, squire, only Oi'll ha' to charge 'ee for't.'

'Very well. What's the time?' He consulted his watch on its chain. 'Nearly three. Can you be here at four?'

'Oi can that, squire.'

Bird got down and approached the front door. He rang the bell, and a tall, neatly dressed lady faced him.

'Good afternoon, madam. My name is Bird. I believe my daughter Phyllis is here.'

She stepped aside and gestured for him to enter. 'Yes, Mr Bird, she is. I am Miss Bishop, the proprietress of Lahai-Roi. Is she expecting you?'

'No, she isn't, Miss Bishop.'

'Is she aware that you know she is here – and the reason for it?'

'No, Miss Bishop. I only discovered today that Phyllis has had a baby boy, and she doesn't know that I – that I know.'

'Then perhaps you'd like me to tell her that you are here, so as to prepare her for the surprise of seeing you, Mr Bird?'

'Yes, perhaps it would be best if you took me to see her, Miss Bishop, and stayed with us in case she's distressed.' Not to mention my distress, he thought, bracing himself for the meeting.

'Very well. I'll call Phyllis to the Quiet Room, and take you to her there.'

A five-minute eternity ensued, and then Miss Bishop returned and beckoned him to follow.

He entered a room and saw a tired, anxious-looking girl with heavy breasts.

She saw her father.

'Dad!' She took a step towards him, hesitated and then was caught in his arms. 'Oh, Dad, Dad, I'm sorry. I'm so sorry, Dad.' She did not even ask how he had found her out.

'All right, my girl, don't cry. Ssh, ssh. I've found you, that's all that matters.' And they both wept with a kind of relief, though Bird quickly dried his eyes and composed his face.

'I'll leave you alone for a while,' said Miss Bishop. 'And if Mr Bird wishes to see the baby, I will have him brought to you. There is no objection to grandparents seeing the child.'

289

Phyllis eagerly interposed. 'Please, Miss Bishop, *please* let my father see Saul now, if you don't mind. I do so want him to see my baby!'

'Very well, Phyllis. You stay here, and I will bring the child down to you.'

When she reappeared with the sleepy baby and placed him in his mother's arms, Ernest Bird shed more tears.

'Oh, Phyllis, my girl, when I think of what you've been through. You should have let us know.'

'I couldn't, Dad. I was so ashamed. It was – he was an American actor who went back to California, and doesn't even know about Saul. But that doesn't make any difference to the way I love my baby. Oh, Dad, did you ever see anything more *beautiful*?'

'He's certainly a fine little chap,' said the new grandfather, regarding the baby with something like awe. 'What's going to happen now, then? The matron at Oakleigh House said you were going back there.'

'Yes, that's the idea, Dad, and Saul – oh, they say he's got to be adopted, but I can't bear the thought of it, Dad. I just can't *bear* it!'

She dissolved into despairing sobs, and Ernest Bird felt that many lives depended on what he said next.

'How soon can you get yourself packed and ready to leave here – you and the baby?'

'What, *now*? Oh, no time at all. I haven't got a lot of things, just a few clothes, and I can carry Saul. Why, Dad, where are we going?'

'I've got a little two-wheeler gig waiting outside, and we could squeeze in with the driver. He could take us to Epsom Station, and then I reckon our best way would be to go up to London and come down again on the Southampton line. It's all cross-country otherwise.'

Phyllis's face was a study in joy and thankfulness, but Miss Bishop looked doubtful. 'Are you sure that this is a right decision, Mr Bird?' she asked. 'Have you discussed it with your wife?'

'No need,' he answered at once. 'I'm very grateful for all you've done for my daughter, Miss Bishop, and I'll recompense whoever has paid for her board and lodging here. Get your things together, Phyllis, and wrap up the baby well. We're going home.'

Saul was howling and Phyllis's breasts were dripping when they reached North Camp Station. No taxis waited at such a small place, and they walked the half-mile to the house in Rectory Road.

'Oh, you're home, Ernie!' called Mrs Bird from the kitchen as he entered the front door, motioning Phyllis to stay outside for a few minutes. 'I thought you'd be back later than this.'

'All right, Ethel, come into the parlour and sit down on the sofa. I've got something to show you.'

Mrs Bird wiped her hands on a tea-cloth and did as she was told. Phyllis stood out of sight while her father settled her mother on the sofa.

'Prepare for a big surprise, Ethel, and a bit of a shock – but nothing to worry about,' he said in a voice that shook slightly. Ethel looked up at him in alarm.

'What is it, Ernie? Don't play games – out with it! And there's a baby crying somewhere quite near. What's happened?'

'Just sit there, Ethel, and wait – wait! I'll show you.'

And Ernest took Saul from his mother and carried

him into the parlour where he placed him carefully into the arms of his astonished wife.

'Good heavens, Ernie, what's this? Who's is it?'

'It's your grandson, Ethel. Phyllis has had a baby, and his name's Saul, like that Israelite king in the Old Testament. He's two weeks old.'

Ethel looked down at the baby, who stopped crying and nestled in her arms. She gazed and gazed upon his face as if she was seeing a vision.

'His eyes are just like Tom's,' she said in wonder. 'And he's got Ted's nose and chin – remember how he took after my dad? Oh, Ernie, he's the living image of my boys that I lost – I can't believe it. Thanks be to God who's sent me another son!'

Ernest Bird always said it was at that moment when his wife's sorrow was healed, and she returned to the land of the living.

Chapter 17

The tremendous relief of being at home with her parents and their acceptance of her baby gave way to a curious sense of detachment on Phyllis's part. After the exhausting experience of childbirth and the mounting anxiety that had followed over losing Saul to strangers and never seeing him again, she found that she needed breathing space to adjust to her changed circumstances. Saul was occasionally fretful, and the greater part of her time, both by day and night, was taken up in feeding and soothing him, with her mother invariably hovering near at hand.

Mr Bird got the step-ladder from the shed and climbed up to the loft, from which he brought down the stoutly build cot used by Phyllis and her brothers as babies.

'The old highchair's up there as well,' he said to Ethel. 'We'll need that later.'

'Yes, but we need a good baby bath *now*,' she answered. 'One of those nice enamel ones with a wooden stand. Oh, I've got such a lot of things to get in for him!'

The cot was put up in Phyllis's room, and caring for her son was her constant occupation. She scarcely ventured outside before the third week in April, although Mrs Bird indulged in an orgy of shopping. A pram was ordered from Silver Cross at an Aldershot store, and there were baby clothes, new cot linen and blankets to be bought, also three dozen napkins, safety pins, Pears' soap, baby powder, cotton wool rolls and two enamel buckets with lids – plus a little blue-ribboned basket for all of Saul's necessities.

The Bird family's GP, Dr Stringer, was asked to call, and he consulted at length with Mrs Bird with scarcely a glance at Phyllis, who sat silently in her milk-stained nightdress, having woken late after a disturbed night. Then he turned to her abruptly.

'Well, well, well, Phyllis, my girl, you are extremely fortunate in your parents, and I only hope that you are grateful to them for their goodness, after behaving as you have done.'

'I do appreciate them, Dr Stringer, I really do,' she replied in a low tone, eyes downcast.

'Don't forget that the child must be registered by the parent – and you are the sole parent – within six weeks of birth. You'll have to go to Epsom, the place of his birth, for that.'

'I'll see that it's done, Dr Stringer.'

'Good. You've got plenty of milk, I take it?'

'Oh, yes – and Saul feeds very well.'

'Hm. Well, I hope that you're not just going to sit about and do nothing. Your mother needs help with all the extra work she's taken on. And you'll have to start thinking about earning your keep, young woman. How old are you? Twenty-seven? Good heavens, at your age – ah, well.' He sighed deeply and shook his head.

The doctor's words and general attitude towards the prodigal daughter proved to be typical of the reaction of friends and neighbours in North Camp, as Phyllis discovered on her very first walk out with her mother. Mrs Bird pushed the fine new pram with her grandson installed in it, and Phyllis thankfully inhaled the fresh air of spring. Trees were in leaf-bud, and the front gardens were full of daffodils and early tulips. Phyllis could have skipped along the pavement for sheer delight – until they met old Miss Jarvis, a pillar of the parish church, in conversation with Mrs Allingham, the vicar's wife.

'Good afternoon, ladies!' said Ethel Bird with a brightness they had not seen or heard in her for years. 'Who wants to take a peep at my new grandson?'

Phyllis could see at once that they were torn between conventional admiration and tight-lipped disapproval, and knew that if she had not been there they would have given way to cooing and sighing over Saul to please his doting grandmother. As it was, they glanced under the hood of the pram and nodded at the little face framed by a blue woollen hat.

'Oh, very nice – yes, Mrs Bird, he's, er – yes, certainly,' murmured Mrs Allingham.

'I can see that you look after him very well, Mrs Bird,' sniffed Miss Jarvis.

Both women nodded towards Phyllis but avoided her eyes, nor did they address her directly. Before they were out of earshot she heard mutters of, 'You wouldn't believe she'd have the face to come back here and brazen it out, would you?' and, 'That poor couple, when you think what they've been through . . .' She was not sure whether her mother heard, or how much she would have minded if she had; all her smiling attention was on Saul.

Mr Bird offered to accompany Phyllis to Epsom to register her baby's birth, but she declined.

'You can't afford to shut the shop for another

whole day, Dad. It's my responsibility, and I'll go on my own.'

After a day of train journeys and changes, she returned with a birth certificate that showed her son's Christian names as Saul Peter and his surname as Bird, born to Phyllis Mary Bird, spinster, father unknown. She felt that everybody she met could see the hateful piece of paper burning a hole in her handbag, just like the shame burning in her heart. What a life-long burden to lay upon her son, her baby who would grow into a boy and then a man. When he sought employment or wished to marry, he would have to produce this evidence of his origins; what would he think of his mother? Would he ever ask her about his father, and what would she tell him?

Speculation was rife in North Camp on this very subject and, when Phyllis stood by the font of the parish church on a blowy Sunday afternoon and watched the Reverend Mr Allingham pour water over Saul's downy head and pronounce him baptised in the name of the Father and of the Son and of the Holy Ghost, she was sure she heard whispers as his names were repeated: was he named for his unknown father Saul (an odd choice) or Peter? His grandparents were also his godparents, there being nobody else the family felt they could ask, and a Sunday tea of tinned salmon, bread-and-butter and home-baked fruit cake was all the celebration held to mark the occasion.

Without telling his wife and daughter, Mr Bird wrote to Miss Bishop enquiring about who had paid Phyllis's fees at Lahai-Roi. Phyllis had told him that it was Miss Maud Ling, the film actress, and while he did not disbelieve his daughter he wondered if the child's father had used Miss Ling's name to cloak his own identity. Miss Bishop replied that a firm of Richmond solicitors had paid on behalf of a client, and when he wrote to them offering to reimburse the money, they replied in long-winded legal language that their client would neither accept his offer nor reveal his or her identity. He decided not to pursue the matter further.

However, word travelled from Epsom via Nurse Boyd to a midwife acquaintance in Richmond and so to a maternity nurse at Oakleigh House that enquiries had been made about the matter, and Mrs Draycott pricked up her ears. Whispers were exchanged and incidents remembered, like Dr Godley's interest in the girl who had worked for the Berridge family, his especial kindness to her and their mutual friendship with Maud Ling. Whispers turned to rumours and began to fly around Richmond like a swarm of buzzing bees, adding to the stories of the doctor's daughter and her hasty marriage, and now the news of a baby born indecently early. Like father, like daughter, some said . . .

In North Camp Phyllis now found herself subjected to the full blast of moral indignation such as only a small town can show towards trans-gressors. Overheard muttered remarks were one thing, but rejection from those she had looked upon as friends was much more wounding. When she encountered Betty Goddard in the Parade, her greeting was met with embarrassed blushes and clumsy excuses.

'I've joined a cycling club now, Phyllis, so I'm afraid I can't go out with you at weekends,' Betty said, and then added, 'I just couldn't believe it when

I heard. I mean, to think we used to talk about what happened to that Clara Hemmings, and now *you* of all people. My parents blame the cinema, and it's upset them so much that I don't go any more. I'm sorry, Phyllis, I really am, but you'll have to excuse me now – my mother's waiting over there. 'Bye.'

No invitation to tea, or even to speak to Mrs Goddard, whose averted face was more eloquent than words.

An even worse blow awaited Phyllis when she called upon Miss Daniells. In response to Dr Stringer's admonition that she should think about earning a living, her first idea was to offer her services as assistant teacher again at the Infants' School. She met with a blank wall.

'I'm very sorry, Miss Bird, but I'm surprised that you should even think of such a thing. How could I possibly take you back in the circumstances? This is a Church school, and the Reverend Mr Allingham visits regularly to make sure that the children are not only taught their letters and numbers, but to have basic standards of right behaviour instilled into them.'

'But, Miss Daniells, I thought you'd be willing to help me – to have me back just for a while!' protested Phyllis, staring at the ageing schoolmistress in unconcealed dismay.

'My dear Miss Bird, it's not a question of what I'*d* be willing to do, it's the parents who would object,' came the reply. 'It so happens that I have an assistant teacher who is not as good as you were, and can't even play the piano – but to take on a young woman in your situation would be quite out of the question. I suggest that you look for domestic work to tide you over while the – er – child is very young, but if you take my advice you'll get away from North Camp, because I can assure you that people here will never forget. Never.'

Go away from North Camp? Leave her son? Miss Daniells had always been candid, but Phyllis was quite unprepared for this implacable reaction, and she walked slowly and dispiritedly back to Rectory Road, longing to hold Saul in her arms again. With his warm body pressed against her heart, and his first windy smiles turning up the corners of his rosebud mouth, she knew she would be comforted.

'No, Phyllis, *no*! He's only just settled down after crying half the morning – ever since you fed him. I won't have him disturbed now, do you hear?'

Phyllis did not answer her mother, but walked up to her room where she shed the first tears since coming home.

April passed into May. Phyllis's next step to find suitable work was an application to Aldershot Hospital as a nursing assistant. It was a small place with two wards, one for men and one for women; children were put in the women's ward. The matron seemed a pleasant enough woman, and sympathetic towards Phyllis's position, but she said she could only offer her domestic work.

Phyllis's face fell. To take a bus journey each day to work long hours sweeping, dusting and sluicing was hardly what she had in mind; she might as well apply for domestic service in North Camp. The matron smiled and offered another suggestion.

'There is a Moral Welfare Home for mothers and babies run by the Church Army not far from here, Miss Bird, and perhaps you could do useful work there among these, er, unfortunate girls, seeing that you – er – share their experience. What do you think?'

Phyllis brightened at once. 'Oh, yes, Matron, that

299

would suit me very well. I could do some good there,' she said eagerly. 'I'll apply to the Church Army for –'

'No, leave it to me, Miss Bird. I will write on your behalf, and say that I think you would be suitable. It might be better that way, don't you agree?'

'Yes – oh, thank you, Matron! Thank you very much,' said Phyllis, and waited a week for news of the outcome.

Which was unfavourable. The matron wrote regretfully to say that there were no vacancies at the Moral Welfare Home, and in any case the staff were expected to live in; she had not the heart to say that her recommendation of an unmarried mother had been thrown back in her face. The women were there to be *reformed*, she was told, not to be subjected to the bad influence of a girl with such a history. Phyllis swallowed her bitter disappointment and decided to settle for a cleaning job; she would work for whoever needed somebody to scrub floors and wash down walls – the butcher's, maybe, or the fishmonger's. It was time to throw away whatever remained of her pride.

It was her old friend Rosie Lansdowne who gave her the first encouragement, the first bit of luck. Having heard the local gossip in her father's dairy shop, she called on Phyllis and without preamble offered her work in the dairy sheds behind the shop, where milk-churns arrived early each morning from local farms and had to be got ready for distribution on horse-drawn milk-carts, some in bottles, some ladled out directly into jugs brought by housewives to be filled.

'You'd be in the "clean" dairy, Phyllis, where the milk gets measured out into bottles and small churns for the floats; once they're out o' the way, you'd spend the morning scalding-out and scrubbing – everything has to be as clean as a whistle.'

'And your parents don't mind having me there?' asked Phyllis cautiously.

'My dad says all he wants is a good girl who'll do the job properly, and it's up to you to take it or leave it,' replied Rosie cheerfully. 'If you'd like to give it a try, come round and see him.' She did not add that she had exchanged sharp words with Betty Goddard, and finally silenced that young lady by reminding her that Betty's brother, Sidney, had married Mary Cooper in a hurry because he'd got her into trouble.

'I'll come and see Mr Lansdowne, then, Rosie, and thank you so much.' Phyllis's eyes filled with tears, and Rosie winked and gave her a pat on the shoulder. 'Now then, now then – when am I going to see this beautiful baby boy o' yours?' she asked, and although Mrs Bird was not too happy about showing off Saul when he'd just been changed and put down to sleep, Rosie promised not to utter a word, and was allowed to gaze down upon his peaceful little face.

'He's gorgeous, isn't he?' she breathed, and when Phyllis was showing her out, she asked in a whisper, 'Was it Maud Ling's brother? You can tell me, Phyllis, I won't spread it round.'

'No, Rosie, it wasn't Mr Ling. It was a film actor who's gone back to America.'

'Oh, what a shame, Phyllis. Half the old busybodies round here think it was somebody in films, and the other half think it was that playwright, you know – Harold Berridge.'

Phyllis stared in horror. Suppose – just *suppose* – that the Berridges ever got to hear such a dreadful lie? Little did she realise that in Richmond the story of the poor drowned nanny was being talked of again, and Berridge's reputation as a womaniser; his name ranked equally with Dr Godley's in the speculation over Saul's paternity.

Work in the dairy began very early, and Phyllis was glad that it was summertime as she rose before five. The work was hard, and her hands became roughened with constant immersion in hot water and washing soda, but there was a friendly, easy-going camaraderie between the dairymen and the brisk female workers. Phyllis got used to the all-pervasive smell of milk, and felt comfortably hidden away from the public gaze, but the saddest consequence of going out to work was the loss of her own milk. She did her best to preserve it by squeezing it into a clean pudding-basin so that Mrs Bird could transfer it to a bottle and feed it to Saul while his mother was absent, but in the absence of regular stimulation the supply dwindled within a couple of weeks and was insufficient. Mrs Bird wanted to put him on Allenbury's Food, an expensive powdered preparation, but Dr Stringer advised boiled cow's milk as being the next best thing to breast-milk. Phyllis's own suggestion that the milk be diluted and sweetened as at Oakleigh House was disregarded, and she mourned the passing of that special closeness with her baby, the intimacy of nourishing him directly from her body with the very best of food. Those precious moments could never come again, and for her it was a foreshadowing of further and greater separation to come.

By mid-June life at 31 Rectory Road had more or less settled into a routine, and Phyllis began to relax a little. She usually finished at the dairy by four o'clock, so was able to spend the rest of the day at home with Saul. Mrs Bird had started attending church again, and renewed her membership of the Mothers' Union, now busily occupied with preparations for the summer fête in July. Under Mrs Allingham's leadership the MU was to have two stalls: home baking and handcrafts, and Mrs Bird was helping with the latter.

'You're nimble with your needle, Phyllis, so could you make some little items for the stall?' she asked. 'Pincushions, spectacle cases, little purses for small change, that sort of thing. They always sell well.'

Phyllis willingly got out her workbox. She was making a patchwork quilt cot-cover, and had plenty of odd scraps of material. She was pleased that her mother had regained her interest in church activities, and had no resentment against the Mothers' Union for barring membership to the unmarried; on the contrary, she looked forward to her mother's meetings on Tuesday evenings, for it meant she had Saul all to herself for two precious hours. At ten weeks he was holding up his head and reaching out with uncertain hands towards the blue rattle that his mother or grandparents held above him. He focused his big blue eyes on their faces and gurgled happily at the sound of their voices, basking contentedly in a golden world that knew nothing but love. Ernest Bird called him 'the little monarch of all he surveys', and was thankful for the change that Saul had made to his wife's life, though he was rather more sensitive to local attitudes than Ethel. At Bird's Outfitters he firmly defended Phyllis.

'Her greatest mistake was to trust a man who deceived and deserted her,' he would reply to officious enquiries accompanied by significant looks, and he emphasised that it was always the woman who suffered in these cases, far more than the man who took advantage of her. People learned not to criticise Phyllis in his hearing, especially because, as a churchwarden and member of the Parochial Church Council, he was a respected member of the community.

Out of his hearing there were plenty of wagging tongues. 'It was those film studios that were her downfall. That's where she got in with the wrong sort,' they tut-tutted. 'She's lucky that her poor old parents have taken her back home with the baby – just fancy, at their age! It's a crying shame after all they've been through, losing both their sons in the war.' Few commented on the improvement in Ethel Bird's looks, the new light in her eyes, the spring in her step; they found it easier to deplore the event that had brought her beloved grandson into being.

Yet below the surface of the Birds' lives there were constant tensions. Every so often a sharp disagreement arose between mother and daughter over their 'little monarch', quite often in the middle of the night when he woke up and both of them came to his cot.

'Leave him to me, Phyllis. I think he's got a touch of colic. You gave him that last bottle too quickly, and his poor little tum-tum's full of wind – isn't it, my precious?'

'I don't think it *is* wind, Mum. I made sure he brought it all up,' protested Phyllis. 'He just needs his nappy changing, that's all.'

'Oh, do go back to bed and leave him to me, Phyllis! You've got to be up early – no, leave him to *me*, I said!'

'He's my baby, and I want to see him –'

'He's my grandson, and I know a lot more than you do about babies. Now, will you go back to bed?'

Phyllis literally clenched her teeth to stop herself from answering back, and did as she was told. She tried to be grateful, reminding herself that she had not had to part with her baby, but she was beginning to feel that he was no longer hers.

Ernest Bird saw and sympathised with her difficulties, but advised her to defer to her mother.

'She brought up the three of you, after all, Phyllis, so it stands to reason she knows best. Try to be patient with her. She likes to do everything for him, and it's made a new woman of her.'

Tell that to some of the gossips who are always saying how sorry they are for her, Phyllis thought bitterly, but held her peace.

Things came to breaking point on the day of the summer fête, the second Saturday in July. The stall-holders gathered in the morning on the vicarage lawn to put the finishing touches to their displays, and Phyllis had a day off from the dairy; she was helping her mother to set out the little knick-knacks she had made, along with larger items like aprons, tea-cosies and some pretty rag dolls. Under an oak tree a few yards away Saul lay sleeping in his pram. Something about this sunny scene and the Bird girl's calm complacency, as she saw it, infuriated Mrs Allingham, and she felt an overwhelming urge to disturb it.

'Wasn't that a splendid speaker we had last Tuesday at our Mothers' Union meeting?' she enthused to the group of ladies in their summery dresses, and there were nods of agreement, though one or two glanced quickly at Phyllis and her mother.

'Oh, yes, she was very good – so inspiring,' echoed a lady in turquoise silk with a fringed hem. 'What did she say they were called – the Ladies' Christian League of Friends, wasn't it?'

'The Ladies' League of Christian Befrienders,' Mrs Allingham corrected her. 'Wonderful women who give up their time to befriend girls who, well, who have fallen by the wayside and have to depend on charitable institutions to take them in and care for them – and the unfortunate babies they bring into the world.'

There was a very uneasy silence. Mrs Bird busied herself with writing price tickets, but Phyllis raised her head and looked straight at the vicar's wife.

'The Befrienders' main aim is to do just that, Mrs Allingham,' she said quietly but clearly. 'They *befriend* young girls who've been brought up in orphanages, without families to support them when they go out into the world as domestic servants. *Some* of the Befrienders visit girls in mother-and-baby homes, but their first object is to prevent such tragedies in the first place.'

A subdued murmur of agreement followed her words, and Mrs Allingham flushed. 'Oh, no doubt you would know more about their work than I do, Miss Bird,' she said nastily. 'I suppose you benefited from their visits yourself.'

One or two gasps were heard, and Phyllis replied in the same cool tone. 'No, the Befrienders visit girls in the sort of charitable institutions you spoke of, Mrs Allingham, girls with no family or friends. I was in a private maternity home.'

'I wonder that you care to admit as much, Miss Bird! And I wonder who paid for you to stay at this *private home*, because I happen to know that it was not your own poor father – your good, forgiving parents who have been so patient and generous, and taken on responsibilities that are rightly yours.'

'Right, I think I'd better leave now,' said Phyllis, feeling that her self-control was about to desert her. 'I'll see you later, Mother. I shan't be coming back for the fête.' And dropping the items she had made for the stall, she walked over to Saul's pram and began to push it away.

'Have you no shame at all?' Mrs Allingham shouted after her. 'Don't you care *at all* for the way you have disgraced your mother in the eyes of all her neighbours?'

'No more than you have disgraced your husband and the Church with your spiteful tongue – a busybody in other people's matters,' retorted Phyllis over her shoulder, the condemnation from St Peter's epistle coming appropriately to her mind. 'You won't ever see me in church again.'

There was a flurry among the ladies, one or two of whom thought that the vicar's wife had gone too far and got what she deserved, though nobody said as much.

Mrs Bird also said nothing, but adjusted her hat, pulled on her gloves, picked up her bag and hurried after her daughter, more concerned for Saul than for Phyllis.

That evening, after a summer fête humming with the aftermath of what had happened in the morning, the vicar sent for his churchwarden, and told him gravely that Mrs Allingham had been deeply insulted and offended. Unless a full and unreserved apology was received from Miss Bird, he said, the family would not be welcome at the parish church.

Ernest Bird said that he could not force his daughter to apologise, but he offered to write an apology on her behalf; he added that in his opinion she had been excessively provoked. This did not go down at all well with the Reverend Mr Allingham, who replied that Mr Bird's position as churchwarden would be discussed at the next meeting of the Parochial Church Council. Mr Bird nodded, rose and left the vicar's study, saying that he had nothing further to add.

At Rectory Road Phyllis stood by what she had said, and reproached her mother for not putting in a word on her behalf at the public clash with Mrs Allingham.

'Everybody says that you're a different woman – a *new* woman, Mum – since you got your grandchild. At least my disgrace has had its good results as well as all the shame I've had to endure in North Camp.'

There was a bitterness in her tone and in her eyes that she had not shown before, and Mrs Bird shrugged, not denying the truth of what she said. She made Phyllis a cup of tea and told her to take things easy for the rest of the day.

'It'll all blow over,' she said, but this was small comfort to Phyllis, who would have given anything for a motherly hug. Up in her room she made a decision. She wrote a letter to Matron Groves saying that she felt ready to return to Oakleigh House to take up her duties there, leaving Saul in the care of his loving grandparents. On the Monday morning she posted it off, and waited in hope and fear for a reply. How often would she be able to visit Saul? Would he grow away from her and turn to his grandmother? If so, how would she manage to bear with his divided heart?

The Reverend Mr Allingham was forced to accept Mr Bird's formal written apology for his daughter's outburst on the morning of the summer fête, because it was clear that an apology from the girl herself would not be forthcoming, and the vicar had no wish to lose a reliable churchwarden. However, Mrs Allingham absolutely refused to speak to Bird, and her sympathy for his wife appeared to have evaporated.

'She'll spoil that boy in the same way that she has spoiled that wretched daughter,' she predicted, but got little response from the Mothers' Union members; perhaps they agreed with Mr Bird that she had provoked Phyllis beyond endurance.

Oakleigh House, Richmond

Dear Nurse Bird

Thank you for your letter. I am glad to hear that Saul is making good progress, and that your parents are so attached to him. That is very good news.

Regarding your application to resume your former position as maternity nurse at Oakleigh House, however, I very much regret that this will not be possible, due to various circumstances that have arisen since you left us in February. It has nothing to do with your character or your skill and conscientiousness as a nurse, and I will be very happy to supply you with a reference for any other application you may make, away from the Richmond area.

May I make the following suggestion? Now would be a good time for you to take up your idea of training for the Midwives' Register; it would give you a valuable qualification and the chance to make a new start in your life. I recommend that you apply to the Booth Street Infirmary in Lambeth, where the new maternity department is in a separate building, Theodora House; there is an excellent obstetrician in charge, a Mr Poole, who gives lectures and is known for his teaching abilities. If you decide to apply, I will ask Dr C. Godley to write a personal letter of recommendation to Mr Poole.

May I say how very sorry I am, Phyllis, to decline your application, but for you to return to Richmond would be unwise. I am sure that your best way forward would be to become a qualified midwife.

With my very best wishes,

Yours sincerely,

    (Miss) Gladys Groves, Matron

Another rejection, and so unexpected: Miss Groves was kind, sympathetic, regretful – and evasive. *Why* would it be 'unwise' for Phyllis to return to Richmond when she had received nothing but kindness at Oakleigh House, and an assurance that she would be welcomed back there after her discharge from Lahai-Roi? She read the letter through several times, seeking for clues as to why the situation had changed, but all that struck her was the initial C placed before Dr Godley's name; it made him sound more distant, more formal than the kindly doctor she remembered. Had the business of his daughter Pamela changed his attitude? If North Camp could be so harsh in its condemnation of an unmarried mother, perhaps Richmond would be the same? Phyllis speculated until her head ached, but could come to no definite conclusion, and after further painful reflection on the question of long separations from Saul, she decided to follow Matron Groves' advice and apply to the Booth Street Infirmary. In her letter she said nothing about the son she loved more than anything else in the world, nor did she tell her parents until the day in mid-August when she was officially informed by letter that she had been accepted for midwifery training, to commence a six-month course on Monday, 3 September.

'Well, Mum and Dad, I've got news for you,' she announced tentatively that evening after tea. 'I'm going away again.'

'You're never taking Saul away with you?' asked her mother sharply, while her father looked alarmed.

'What do you mean, Phyllis?' he demanded.

'No, I'm not taking Saul, that's just it – I'm leaving him here with you for six months while I take midwifery training in London. I've been accepted at the Booth Street Infirmary in Lambeth.'

They still stared at her in bewilderment.

'When are you going, Phyllis?' asked her father.

'At the beginning of next month. I'll be living in staff quarters and working long hours at first, but when I'm qualified and settled somewhere in a place of my own, then I'll be able to take my son and look after him myself. I can't tell you how grateful I am for everything I owe you –'

She got no further, for Ethel Bird interrupted sharply, her eyes full of fear, '*No*, Phyllis, he's staying here with your dad and me, whatever you do, wherever you go. He's our grandson, our own blood, the same as my two boys that I lost. You can leave North Camp if you want to, but Saul stays here with me – with us.'

Ernest Bird rose from his chair with a worried look at his wife's set face, and gestured to her to be quiet. 'Come, now, there's no reason why you've got to leave us again, Phyllis. We like having you here, and people are coming round to the idea of you having a – a baby. Please, Phyllis, don't leave us, girl. We want you to stay.'

But Phyllis was suddenly shaking from head to foot with the suppressed rage and grief of months. 'No, you don't! My mother doesn't, anyway. You heard what she just said – she'd much rather have me out of the way, so that she can have Saul all to herself – look after him, feed him, discuss him with that pompous Dr Stringer, and keep him away from me as much as possible!' Her voice rose, and Ethel Bird jumped to her feet as if to prevent her grandson from being forcibly removed from her.

Having started to speak her feelings, Phyllis now could not stop: she shouted the accusation that had burned in her heart for so long.

'You've never loved me like you did the boys, and you've resented me just for being alive after they were killed! You've never once spoken up for me against those old crows in the Mothers' Union, that hateful Allingham woman, the whole self-righteous lot of them in North Camp! Dad has at least tried to say a word on my behalf, but you – *you* – you'd rather I was *dead* like Tom and Ted, so that you can have Saul all to yourself. Well, don't worry, I'm going – going away for good.'

'*Phyllis!*' her father broke in with tears in his eyes. 'Phyllis, don't talk like that, it isn't fair. Remember what would have happened if we hadn't taken Saul. He'd have been adopted by strangers and you'd never have seen him again. You told me that yourself when I came to see you at that home.'

Phyllis turned blazing eyes upon him. 'Oh, Dad, can't you see, my son *has* been adopted, and maybe I never *will* see him again – because I'll never come back to North Camp. *Never!*'

Part III

An Excellent Woman

Love Virtue, she alone is free;

— *Comus* by John Milton

Chapter 18

Nurse Webb was feeling out of sorts, in fact she was in a thoroughly bad mood. This time last year she would have been attending confinements in Lambeth, a familiar figure with her bag, an angel of mercy to women and a scourge of idle husbands. She'd lost her own husband in the war, and her nine-year-old son Billy was having to stay at his gran's in the New Kent Road while she slogged her guts out in this rotten hole, Theodora House – they said it meant the gift of God, for heaven's sake! – ordered around by the ward sister, a flibbertigibbet in a navy dress and folded triangular veil that hung halfway down her back.

'Have you replenished the sack of pads, Nurse Webb? Have you given a bedpan to that girl who's got to lie flat? Get Nurse Anderson to help you lift her. She's torn from stem to stern.'

She hasn't half the experience I've had, thought Ginny Webb, who had practised as a district handy-woman respected by local doctors for over ten years – until the Central Midwives' Board caught up with her and threatened to stop her practising on pain of prosecution unless she took this ridiculous training for the Register – six months in Theodora House, which included enduring old man Poole's lectures – huh! she could teach *him* a thing or two about mid-wifery in the real world – and then another six months out on the district she already knew so well, being 'supervised' by a so-called trained midwife breathing down her neck and forever telling her to wash her hands. Mrs Starling wasn't so bad. She was a big, forthright cockney you could have a laugh with, who called the coarse brown cotton-wool maternity pads man-hole covers. But that streak of single blessedness Miss Bird was a pain in the arse. She'd better not try teaching *me* anything, thought Ginny Webb, or I'll turn round and tell her a few home truths.

'Shall I start changing the babies, Nurse Webb?' asked fellow pupil-midwife Anderson, who was on with her this afternoon.

'Yeah, Nurse, I'll be with yer in a tick,' she replied, glancing at the ward clock. A quarter to two. Another three and a half hours before she could escape from the pong of women's leaking privates and breathe the fresh March air . . . and she'd see her Billy again, poor little chap. She usually took him to the pictures on a Saturday afternoon, but it would be too late by the time she got to her mother's.

But then came a surprise: just after three Nurse Webb was summoned to Sister's office and told there was an emergency on the district. A Mrs Simmons of Old Paradise Street was in labour, and pupil-midwife Lamb had gone to attend her; it was a notoriously bad area and Nurse Lamb had only just started on the district, but Mrs Starling was out on another case, and had asked if Nurse Webb could be spared from the ward to go to Nurse Lamb's assistance. Could she not! She dashed to the cloakroom for her coat, and was off like a shot. This was more like it! Let me see, she thought, which one was Nurse Lamb? Oh, blimey, it was that holy one who thought she'd been 'saved', and drove them all crazy on night duty singing hymns as soon as the morning rush began. Old Paradise Street would soon put paid to *that* caper!

Nurse Barbara Lamb had been having an afternoon nap in her room on the second floor of Theodora House, having been up most of the night with the wife of a local grocer in Pitt Street. Mrs Starling had left her with the woman, and she had delivered her alone and unaided, apart from the help of the Lord in whom she trusted. With thankfulness she had recorded in her own personal Case Register the details of the birth, after the mother's name, age and address.

Normal delivery of living female infant at 6.05 a.m. on Saturday, 26 March 1927. Weight 6¾ lbs, no abnormalities seen, cried well at birth. Placenta and membranes expelled complete at 6.15 a.m. Blood loss 8 ozs. Condition of mother and child satisfactory on completion of labour.

I thank Thee, dear Lord, for using my hands in Thy service, Nurse Lamb said silently as the cry of the newborn baby filled the room, and when Mrs Starling dashed in at half-past six she was full of praise for her pupil.

But now Nurse Lamb was awakened from her nap at half-past two in the afternoon, and told to go at once to 17 Old Paradise Street, where Mrs Cath Simmons was in labour and likely to deliver soon, it being her fourth child.

'Mrs Starling'll be with you as soon as she can, Nurse Lamb,' said the orderly who had brought the message. 'She's just gone out to a case in South Street.'

Barbara Lamb sent up a quick prayer as she pulled on her clothes, picked up her bag and clattered down the stairs. The bicycle shed was next to the boiler room, and she hastily got out the old bone-shaker she had used in the night. She then had to hurry back to the District Room to consult the map on the wall: ah, yes, Old Paradise Street was off Lambeth Walk, and her best way would be to go down Kennington Road and then turn right.

Many, if not the majority of the mothers having their babies at home in the area, were hard-working wives of tradesmen and shopkeepers, or the cheerfully struggling stall-holders who sold everything from block salt to second-hand clothes in the Lower Marsh street-market known as The Cut, where braces and stays hung from makeshift crossbeams. Yet not all of them managed to keep up a front of respectability: there were mean streets behind the main thoroughfares where families lived in damp, rat-infested basements unfit for human habitation, haunted by ill-health and chronic poverty.

Nurse Lamb arrived at just such a dwelling on this chilly afternoon, and was stunned by what she saw as she entered. To her horror, Mrs Simmons lay helplessly drunk on the floor in a spreading warm puddle; her waters had broken, and two tipsy women were hoarsely telling her to push down. A dirty-faced little boy and girl cowered in a corner, and another child, not yet walking, crawled alongside them.

'Is – is there any hot water? Or clean towels?' faltered Nurse Lamb, staring helplessly at the three women and then at the three children. The two attendant neighbours muttered something and hiccuped. There was a bed of sorts, covered with coats and smelly blankets, but there seemed no way of lifting Mrs Simmons off the floor. Nurse Lamb kneeled down to try to examine the woman, but when she managed to pull down the soaking wet knickers it was clear that the cervix was fully dilated and the baby's arrival imminent. What on earth was she to do?

Panic rose in her throat, and no words of prayer would come to her in this horrible place. With trembling hands she opened her bag. The children whimpered, and she tried to calm herself by talking to them, for words of any kind were lost on Cath Simmons and her friends.

'I'm Auntie Barbara, and I've come to help your mummy,' she whispered. 'We – we must all put our trust in the Lord Jesus. He – He loves all little children – and everybody.' And I must trust in Him to show me what to do, she added desperately to herself.

And it seemed that her silent prayer was answered, because to her inexpressible relief the door opened and in strode a purposeful lady carrying a large cardboard box: not Mrs Starling but Nurse Webb, who was in fact a fellow pupil-midwife. She looked as if she was prepared to do battle.

'Mrs Starling's out on another case, an' she's sent me 'cause I know me way around this area. How's she doin'? Good God, what a sight! Have yer had a look down below?'

'I – I think she's pushing, Nurse Webb, b-but I can't move her, you see.'

'Well, for a start, get rid o' these two good-for-nothin' old soaks – out yer go, the pair o' yer – *out*!' And with more than a little help from Nurse Webb's brawny elbows the two women were hustled out of the door. When one of them resisted, she got Ginny's stout lace-up shoe at her backside, and the door was firmly closed behind her.

'Cath Simmons may be drunk as a skunk, but she's havin' a baby. Come on, Lamb, get yer scissors an' string ready, this is goin' to be a quick 'un!'

And sure enough, during the next three minutes a baby boy was born, just as a policeman arrived at the door, summoned by another neighbour who took the three children to her own poor dwelling.

''Allo, Nurse Webb,' grinned the constable. ''Avin' trouble?'

''Ere, go an' fetch the 'usband, will yer? Down at the King Alfred, most likely. This is a case for takin' the baby away overnight for safe-keepin'. Nobody here's in a fit state to look after it. Can yer get a van round in about half an hour, to take it to Theodora House? Thanks!'

'An' we'd better get the sanitary inspector round next week,' she muttered, looking round the room. 'An' the cruelty people – they might find a few sticks o' furniture an' some beddin'. Did yer ever see anythin' like it? Cath Simmons, if yer wasn't out like a light, I'd say yer ought to be bloody ashamed o' yerself –' She stopped in mid-sentence as the figure of a woman appeared in the doorway. She was slim and upright, wearing a long navy gabardine and matching hat with a badge pinned to the upturned brim.

'Good afternoon, Nurse Webb – and Nurse Lamb. She's delivered, I see. Were you here?'

'Yeah, an' just as well I was, Miss Bird. Mrs Starling's had to go out on another case, so she sent me in her place, an' –'

'She'd no business to do so,' said the newcomer,

entering the room and assessing the situation at a glance. 'Is the placenta out?'

'I think it's just coming, Miss Bird,' said Nurse Lamb, holding an enamel bowl ready to receive it, and gently rubbing the patient's abdomen, which tightened up under her hand.

'Good! I think our next job will be to get her up off the floor, Nurse Lamb. I'll hold her under her shoulders, you support her legs. Thank you very much for your help, Nurse Webb, but I'll take over now. Good afternoon.'

'Oh, very sorry to interfere, I'm sure! *You* wasn't here for the delivery, so it's just as well I was!' retorted Ginny Webb. '*And* I've made arrangements with the constable to take the baby to Theodora House overnight an' get the husband out o' the pub.'

'Thank you, Nurse Webb, that will be all. And if you go now, you'll be with Billy an hour earlier than you expected, won't you?'

The mention of her son's name had the effect of defusing much of Ginny's indignation, for it was true, she *would* be at her mother's by half-past four. 'Right, I'm off, then,' she said, and disappeared forthwith. Miss Bird smiled at the harassed pupil.

'Now, Nurse Lamb, we've got a busy time ahead of us. Dear me,' she murmured, looking at Mrs Simmons' pale, blotchy face, her lank hair already thinning, her mouth open as she snored, showing gaps among her decayed teeth. And not as old as I am, thought the midwife.

'We'll give her a wash, Nurse, and see how she feels when she wakes up. I don't care to take the baby away from a new mother if it can be avoided. For one thing, this is the child's home where he will be living, and it will make her feel even more inadequate. We'll

323

see what the husband has to say, and I might be able to arrange for a neighbour to sit in, just for tonight.'

'What about feeding the baby, Miss Bird?'

'I keep a few bottles and a tin of Trufood at home, and I'll make up a couple of feeds to bring here – but first we've got some tidying-up to do, haven't we?'

And hanging her coat and hat on a hook behind the door, she rolled up her sleeves and filled a kettle to heat water on a gas-ring for washing Mrs Simmons. She worked in a smooth, unhurried way, and Nurse Lamb began to feel that here was a model to follow.

Mr Simmons, surly and smelling of drink, arrived home, having been brought from the King Alfred by the constable.

'I keeps aht o' the way for this sort o' caper,' he muttered. 'Any bread an' cheese goin'?'

'I really don't know, Mr Simmons, and don't you want to see your new son?' asked Miss Bird. 'Your other children are with a neighbour.'

'Oh, yeah, the woman over the road usu'ly 'as 'em.' He eyed his wife doubtfully. 'Cor! She's aht for the count, ain't she? Won't get much sense aht of 'er till termorrer, and there's nuffin' for me to do 'ere, so I might as well clear orf agin.'

Barbara Lamb shuddered at the thought of what had happened between Mr and Mrs Simmons which produced these poor children; she tried not to think about it, but the horrid image persisted in her mind's eye, and made it difficult for her to concentrate her thoughts on the love of the Lord Jesus.

Having made the sleeping woman reasonably clean and comfortable, Miss Bird went off on her well-maintained Raleigh bicycle, which had carriers at the front and back, and Nurse Lamb took the baby on her lap and dressed his umbilical stump, winding a bandage round his tummy. Mrs Simmons moaned, fluttered her eyelids and grimaced.

'Ugh, what a taste in me marf!' Two tears squeezed out and trickled down into the lumpy pillow, and she turned unfocused eyes on Nurse Lamb. 'Nurse – 'ave I 'ad the baby, then?'

'Yes, Mrs Simmons, you've got a lovely little boy,' said the pupil, wiping the woman's eyes and forehead with a face-flannel wrung out in cold water from the one and only tap.

Whey-faced, Cath Simmons attempted to apologise. 'I'm ever so sorry, Nurse. It was me friends, yer see – they shoved the stuff dahn me froat, said it'd ease the pain,' she muttered shakily. 'I ain't a reg'lar drinker, and ain't 'ad nuffin' to eat all day, that's why it knocked me aht. An' what wiv 'im laid orf from 'Ay's Wharf wiv 'is back, it's all got me dahn. Sorry, Nurse.'

'Don't cry, Mrs Simmons, it's all over now,' said Barbara, finding pity in her heart for the woman in spite of her revulsion. 'Miss Bird's coming back soon with some milk for your baby.'

And within twenty minutes the midwife had returned.

'Good girl,' she said with a smile and a nod. 'Ah, I see you're awake, Mrs Simmons. How're you feeling now?'

'Ashamed o' meself, Nurse. An' ever so sorry.'

'All right, my dear, we'll say no more about it. Just don't ever touch the stuff again, that's all. Remember the children depend on you, and now there's the new baby. I've got a little feed in a bottle for him, and another for later, but now we'll make you some tea – and you must drink plenty of water to make milk for you to feed him yourself.'

'Yeah, Nurse. Very good o' yer, Nurse.'

'Have you got a name for him?'

''E'll prob'ly get called Eric if 'e's a boy, that's what me ol' man said.'

While baby Eric took two ounces of the weak milk mixture from Nurse Lamb, Miss Bird told her that she was going to call at the neighbour's to ask how she felt about keeping the children overnight. She took half a crown from her purse, and as soon as the woman saw it her tired eyes lit up.

'Cor! Fanks, Nurse! I'll keep 'em safe till mornin', then,' she grinned, for this was more than enough to supply supper and breakfast for them and her own brood.

'Don't let them sleep with your children if it can be avoided, I think they may have – er – dirty heads,' warned Miss Bird.

'Blimey, all the kids rahnd 'ere are crawlin'. That's nuffin' new,' said the woman, pocketing the precious half-crown. 'Tell yer what, Nurse, we wouldn't mind if yer was to give us some advice abaht 'ow to stop 'avin' 'em!'

Seeing the grubby-faced, bare-footed children clinging to their mother's skirt, Miss Bird experienced a pang of pity and anger at the conditions these people accepted as normal.

She lowered her voice and said rather awkwardly, 'You know about the East Street Welfare Clinic up by the Elephant and Castle, don't you?'

'Go on! You ain't tellin' me to go there, are yer, Nurse?' said the woman, looking surprised, if not shocked. 'That's against the law, ain't it? Yer can get into trouble for that, can't yer?'

'No, you go there for advice, and – er –' Miss Bird was not quite sure what words to use. 'They can fit you with a device that prevents you from conceiving, you see.'

'My man wouldn't 'ave none o' that, and ye'd 'ave to pay, wouldn't yer?' said the woman doubtfully. 'I 'ad an aunt went to one o' them places, an' 'ad to be took to 'ospital after they done it. Nearly died, she did. I don't want none o' that, Nurse.'

Miss Bird took a deep breath and told herself to be patient. 'We're talking about two different things, my dear. What happened to your poor aunt sounds like a – an abortion, which is wrong and dangerous, as you say. But I'm talking about – er – what they do at the East Street Clinic, which is to *prevent* it happening in the first place.'

The woman looked confused, as well she might, thought Miss Bird, deploring her own ignorance on the subject of birth control. She repeated her advice to go along to the clinic and just have a word with a nurse there. Thanking her again for taking the Simmons children, she returned to Number 17 where Nurse Lamb was ready to leave. It was past seven and getting dark.

'I wonder, Miss Bird,' began Nurse Lamb timidly, 'I wonder, would you mind if I say a prayer before we go? For the new baby and his mother, I mean?'

'Very well, Nurse Lamb, as long as you keep it short. And don't forget Eric's father and his brother and sisters.' And I'll pray that the poor soul doesn't have another within a year, she added silently to herself.

Mrs Rawson was standing at the door of Number 35 Richmond Street when Miss Bird arrived back at her lodgings.

'There y'are at last, Phyllis! A woman's been round

'ere sayin' why aren't yer at this big meetin' at the town 'all. It's chock-full o' women, lots of 'em wiv children, an' the police are there an' all – did yer know about it?'

Phyllis Bird sighed. 'Yes, I do, and I'm sorry you've been bothered, Rose, but I've been out on a case in Old Paradise Street for Mrs Starling – and I must confess the last thing I want now is to go to a big, noisy public meeting!'

'No, yer look whacked out, Phyllis,' agreed Rose Rawson, peering at her friend and lodger in the lamplight. 'Go an' put yer bike away, an' I'll make a cup o' tea. Fancy a boiled egg?'

'To be honest, Rose, I really *ought* to go. Mr Poole asked me to look in on it, and report back to him. Tea would be lovely, thanks, but no egg – and I must nip outside to the lav before I have an accident. I couldn't face using the one in that poor woman's home!'

After quickly washing her face and hands, and brushing her conveniently short hair, Phyllis looked in the mirror on her dressing table. Tired-looking but not bad for thirty-one, especially compared with some of the worn-out women she saw every day. Today was 26 March, and she ought to be at North Camp for Saul's fourth birthday. She'd tried to get this weekend off, but it just hadn't been possible at a busy time. She knew that his doting grandparents would make it a happy day for him, and when she had her holiday in June, she would be able to spend a whole week with him, but she still felt the pain of living apart from the love of her life. Her parents were very good, and she was grateful to them, as they now admitted that they were to her, for giving them a grandson to love; but she envied Nurse Webb who could see her Billy so much more often, and acknowledge him as her son. Saul called Phyllis 'Mummy', but it was Granny to whom he always turned because he saw her every day and not just at three- or four-week intervals. Apart from Mrs Rawson, nobody at Theodora House or on the district knew that the formidable Miss Bird was the mother of a child . . .

'Here's a nice cup o' tea, Phyllis, an' some o' these arrowroot biscuits yer like,' said Rose, a short woman with legs bowed by rickets as a child. 'What's this meetin' all about, then? The woman 'oo came 'ere askin' for yer said there was this lady doctor layin' down the law – is it summat like the suffragettes?'

'No, Rose, we've had the vote for ten years now. Dr Helena Wright's a campaigner for – er – another matter.' She hesitated, for the subject of legalised, government-approved birth-control clinics was still a very thorny one, and doctors, nurses, midwives and health visitors could damage their careers by openly supporting the campaign for them. And she frowned, remembering her own futile attempt to give advice in Old Paradise Street that very afternoon.

'Oooh, is it about them clinics they're openin' more an' more of? The ones that Roman bishops got in such a state about last year?' asked Mrs Rawson, wide-eyed, and when Phyllis nodded she gave her opinion in no uncertain terms.

'Yer better keep away from them clinics, Phyllis. They get attacked. People throw bricks frough the winders, an' shout 'orrible words at the nurses. Don't yer 'ave nothin' to do wiv 'em!'

'Don't worry, Rose, I'm only going to have a look. I'll stay at the back and, come to think of it, I'll change out of uniform, and just merge in with the crowd.'

'Mind yer don't say nothin' to nobody, Phyllis.'

'I'll try to keep my mouth shut, Rose, I promise!'

Even after Rose Rawson's warning, Phyllis was unprepared for what she found both inside and outside the impressive baroque-style Lambeth Town Hall that evening. The steps up to the entrance were crowded with women and a scattering of men, from all walks of life. Some held up placards while others pressed leaflets into the hands of passers-by; some of these had been torn up and thrown on the pavement in disgust. Policemen were keeping a watchful eye on demonstrators, and Phyllis stared in astonishment at three black-coated, dog-collared clergymen in furious argument with each other, two against one.

'You're making the biggest mistake of your career!' said one of the two, while the other contemptuously added, 'You're a disgrace to the Church we serve.'

The odd one out flushed angrily, though he was determined to keep his head cool. 'I shall pray for you!' he told them in a tone more threatening than forgiving.

'Oh, my word, it's Miss Bird!' exclaimed a female voice close at hand. 'Did you see that? He's the vicar of St Martha's.'

Phyllis turned round to find one of the pupil-midwives at her side. 'Nurse Anderson! Hello, have you come to hear Dr Helena Wright?'

'Yes, Miss Bird. Mr Poole told us at our lecture today that we should attend if we're off duty. He told us to look out for Dr Norman Haire too – he's another speaker. He opened a clinic at St Pancras last year, and says that all medical students should be taught about – you know.'

'We'd better start calling it birth control, Nurse Anderson.'

'Yes, Miss Bird.' They exchanged a smile. Carrie Anderson was a pleasant girl in her late twenties who had given up an office job in order to take midwifery training.

'I say, d'you mind if I come in with you, Miss Bird? This crowd looks as if it could turn ugly.'

'I was about to suggest the same thing. And I'll call you Miss Anderson, as we're off duty.'

They literally had to push their way into the entrance hall, and elbow themselves through to the main meeting, where five representatives of the Society for the Provision of Birth Control Clinics and a chairman faced the audience from a raised platform. One lady was standing and addressing the assembly, a handsome woman in her late thirties whom Phyllis correctly assumed to be Dr Wright.

'And the gentleman on her right must be Dr Haire,' said Carrie Anderson. 'Who's the grand-looking old lady with the fox fur and all the pearls?'

'I don't know, but she looks very important, a useful person to have on committees!'

The other two members were a vivacious woman of about thirty with a smart hat over her dark hair, and a younger man who was assiduously taking notes, his head bent over his writing-pad.

Phyllis concentrated her attention on Dr Wright, a forceful and convincing speaker.

'I cannot begin to describe the wretched conditions of the wives of the unemployed in this day and age,' she stormed. 'Undernourished and anaemic, burdened with constant child-bearing, they are old before their time and simply too tired to raise themselves to a better kind of life. And those who

331

most need help are the ones least likely to apply for it. They confuse contraception with abortion, and I'm convinced that such ignorance is our real enemy.'

Phyllis realised that she was in complete agreement. She had only to think of Cath Simmons and her neighbours in Old Paradise Street. 'She's so *right*, Miss Anderson!' she whispered to her somewhat surprised companion.

'Make no mistake about it, the women of this country are waking up to new freedoms since the war,' went on the impassioned woman doctor. 'And when women have control over their own bodies, the desperate measure of abortion will be made unnecessary. Birth control is not only a benefit to women, but to children too. All children should be wanted and welcomed, because births should be *planned*.'

There were shouts of 'Rubbish!' and 'Against God and Nature!' but these were countered by orders to 'Shut up!' and 'Just *listen* to her, can't you?' Dr Wright seemed to have the general support of her hearers, but it was the next words that she uttered that caused the near-riot.

'These poor women are married to men who refuse to use the sheath obtainable from some chemists and general practitioners, yet their remedy is simple enough. At our clinics the women can be fitted with the Dutch cap or cervical cap, which is passed into the vagina and fits securely over the neck of the womb. This appliance when used with a special chemical cream, will prevent conception from taking place in most cases –'

Even Phyllis gasped at the explicitness of the words, which she had never before heard uttered in public, outside of the lecture room at Theodora

House. There was a huge uproar, with cries of 'Filth!'
– 'Shame on you, woman!' – 'Obscenity!' – and
predictions that such disgusting practices would
bring down the government, the country and the
British Empire. Police officers rushed in from outside
and only just prevented a section of the crowd from
storming the platform. Phyllis grabbed Carrie
Anderson's arm. 'Out we go,' she ordered *'Out!'*

As the police cleared the hall, Phyllis saw Dr Haire
take hold of Dr Wright and the younger woman, to
hurry them off the platform, while the younger man
took care of the old lady with the pearls. She had a
momentary glimpse of his face and was amazed to
recognise him as George Steynes, the young man
who had been infatuated with Maud Ling. So the old
lady must be his mother, reasoned Phyllis, who
could just remember seeing her at the Berridges'
dinner party when Claud had torn Maud Ling's
gown. Yes, and there had been talk of birth control
over dinner on that occasion, so Maud had reported;
she had been both amused and startled by such a
subject in mixed company. So George Steynes had
obviously kept up his interest in it, and here he was
again, accompanied by his mother – what was her
name? – oh, yes, the Honourable Mrs Agatha
Steynes, widowed by the war and now supporting
her son in his campaign. For Phyllis, stumbling out of
the hall with Miss Anderson, amidst much shouting
and argument, a flood of memories surfaced: a series
of pictures from that time in her life, of Maud Ling
and Teddy, Belle Capogna and Reginald Thane – the
whole of that Twickenham scene came again to her
mind. She had never been back to Richmond since: it
had been another time, another place . . .

It was now quite dark, and had started to rain.

'You'd better hurry back to Theodora House, Miss Anderson. Thank you for coming to the meeting with me. Good night.'

'I don't think I'd have dared to go in if you hadn't been there, Miss Bird. Good night!'

The Booth Street Workhouse dated from the mid-nineteenth century, but had been upgraded to the Booth Street Poor Law Infirmary shortly before the war. It had now lost the words 'Poor Law' from its name, and in 1920 the maternity wards had been moved to new purpose-built premises in nearby Ely Place, and named Theodora House, the old maternity ward being converted into a children's ward, which the infirmary had not previously had; children had been put into the women's wards.

Theodora House was a multi-purpose building. It had room for twenty mothers, ten in Edith Cavell Ward on the ground floor and ten in Octavia Hill Ward above it, with nurses' rooms and a small lecture room above that on the second floor. Both wards had in addition a two-bed bay for women in labour, and Octavia Hill had a Caesar theatre, which served both wards. The beds had been brought over from the infirmary, and had black iron frames, horsehair mattresses and thick rubber drawsheets. The women wore nightgowns of unbleached cotton, which fastened at the back with tapes, and once they were safely delivered considered themselves in the lap of luxury, enjoying the only rest they were ever likely to have, for those who came into Theodora House to have their babies were from the very poorest homes or lodging-houses, the sort of unhealthy hovels that no doctor wished to enter.

The two wards of Theodora House represented

only half the work carried out by midwives and pupils. Annexed to Edith Cavell Ward was a large District Room, boasting a filing cabinet bursting with case-notes, a good-sized wall map, a telephone with a list of local doctors' numbers, and a blackboard for incoming messages. These were usually delivered by personal messengers, and were nearly always urgent, asking for a midwife to go at once to a woman who was 'gettin' it very bad', and was quite often her first contact with the midwives, the type of woman who would have benefited most from the pre-confinement visits advocated by Mr Herbert Poole, consultant obstetrician not only to Theodora House but also to the large district around it. He was frequently summoned to make a domiciliary visit when the local GP was either unavailable or unable to deal with an obstetric emergency beyond the scope of the midwife. Miss Bird and Mrs Starling were in charge of the district pupils, and both lived out – Mrs Starling with her husband and almost grown-up family, and Miss Bird in nearby Richmond Street. What a relief it had been for her to escape from the nurses' quarters on the second floor! And all because of a happy chance, when Mrs Williams came up from Richmond on her day off from Number 3 Travis Walk to visit her mother, stepped off a number 37 bus, and ran straight into Phyllis Bird, who was wheeling her bicycle across St George's Road.

'Oh, my, ain't yer done well, Miss Phyllis!' Mrs Williams had said admiringly, looking at the smart uniform, the hat and badge, the shiny bicycle. 'One in the eye for them at Richmond!'

Of course Mrs Williams knew everything about what had happened. In fact she knew more than Phyllis about the rumours that had rocked the neighbourhood about the paternity of Phyllis's baby – the protestations of Harold Berridge, the reports of an angry scene at Tudor House when both wife and daughter had turned on a shocked Dr Godley, now very much more circumspect in his dealings with female patients and favourite nurses. But Mrs Williams did not elaborate on this, because Phyllis had always treated her well. She mentioned instead her worries about her mother, Rose Rawson, who was unable to go out to work, and could do with a really nice, respectable lady lodger to share her home in Richmond Street . . .

Richmond Street! It seemed like a sign. And Number 35 had been home to Phyllis Bird for the last two years. Rose was a perfect landlady, very proud of her prestigious lodger – and it meant they had a telephone too! The arrangement gave Phyllis the privacy she had lacked at Theodora House, and a genuine friendship had sprung up between the two women; she didn't have to pretend with Rose, who had, of course, heard all about Saul from her daughter.

'So 'ow did yer get on at that meetin', then, Phyllis? What're yer goin' to tell your Mr Poole?' Rose asked.

'Oh, don't ask me, Rose. I know what I *should* tell him, but I don't really want to.' She gave a wry little grimace. 'I was very impressed by Dr Helena Wright, and we ought to become involved with her campaign because it's desperately needed – but the thought of all that opposition – and working without pay – oh, the very idea of it makes my head ache.'

'Don't do it, Phyllis – yer could get killed. Tell Mr Poole yer got enough on yer plate already.'

It was Monday's edition of the *Daily Chronicle* that caused the sensation. Under a front-page heading

'Record Turn-Out at Town Hall to Hear Woman Doctor', the feature by sub-editor George Steynes, accompanied by a photograph of Dr Helena Wright, gave the impression that the meeting had been a triumph for her and her campaign. Mention was made of the increasing number of clinics opening all over the country in response to the first two in 1921.

'Dr Wright painted a heart-rending picture of the plight of women of the poorer classes in this day and age,' said the report. 'Objections from the large crowd were swiftly answered by the speaker and her supporters.'

The piece did not at any point emphasise the near-riot, and Dr Norman Haire was credited with quoting from Lord Dawson of Penn, physician-in-ordinary to the King: 'Birth control is here to stay. It is an established fact, and no denunciations will abolish it.'

'Strong stuff, eh, Miss Bird?' remarked Mr Poole in the District Room that Monday morning, a copy of the newspaper in his hand. 'So what did *you* make of it?'

'I was too late to hear Dr Haire, but Dr Helena Wright is a force to be reckoned with, sir.'

'Ah, yes. That's what I was afraid you were going to say. So what should we at Theodora House do about it? Should we start a clinic of our own, and become the target of every indignant churchman, doctor and newspaper?'

He smiled as he spoke, and she knew that he was testing her.

'We're already very busy serving the mothers and babies over a large area, Mr Poole, and frankly I'm not looking for any more work, especially unpaid work. What I *will* do in future is mention the

Walworth Centre to every mother I deliver on the district, whether I'm asked about it or not.'

'Hm, yes, that sounds fair enough, Miss Bird. I don't think you're likely to be sacked for that, like the poor health visitor in Shoreditch five years ago – or was it six? We've made some progress since then. Anyway, I'll now ask *you* for some advice. I've recently interviewed three applicants for the post of junior doctor here, to assist us in Theodora House and on the district. Two are men, one's a woman, and she's a devoted disciple of Helena Wright. Should I appoint her, do you think?'

'Are you really asking me, Mr Poole? You've probably made up your mind already.'

'No, I haven't. You know how I value the opinion of my midwives. What do you say?'

'How can I say anything, sir?' she replied with cool formality. 'I don't know her. I've never met her.'

'Ah, but you've seen her, Miss Bird. She was on the platform on Saturday evening with Doctors Wright and Haire. She's a promising young woman, trained at the London Hospital, Whitechapel Road, energetic and enthusiastic. And I think I'll appoint her. Her name's Dr Mildred Vaughan.'

Poole noticed that Miss Bird gave a little gasp, and just for a split second a look of alarm crossed her face, though it vanished almost immediately.

'You say you haven't met her, Miss Bird?'

'No, sir. Apart from seeing her at the town hall meeting, I've never met her.'

She'll never remember me, prayed Phyllis Bird.

Chapter 19

It was impossible not to like Dr Mildred Vaughan. On their first meeting, Phyllis Bird had been a little hesitant and avoided facing the other woman's bright eyes, but it was soon clear that the doctor had no recollection of the heavily pregnant girl who had spoken to her on a brief visit to a mother-and-baby home four years ago.

'Heavens above, Miss Bird!' she exclaimed after her first few days on the two wards. 'The condition of these poor women who come into Theodora House is as bad as any I've seen around Whitechapel Road – bowed legs and flattened pelves, toothless mouths, untreated squints – and to think they're here to become mothers! Mr Poole says that a high proportion of their babies will succumb to undernourishment or infections or both before their first birthdays. If ever there was a crying need for birth control, it's here.'

Phyllis assumed a bland expression and offered no comment. She knew that Mr Poole had no intention of starting a birth-control clinic in Theodora House because of the controversy it would cause, the unwelcome attention of the press and the fierce opposition from St George's Roman Catholic Cathedral, only a stone's throw away. It could even lose precious staff, for Sister Pollock in charge of Octavia Hill Ward, one of the best midwives in Theodora House and a Catholic, had already stated her firm objection to 'unnatural prevention', and said she would be put under pressure to resign if such a clinic was opened on the premises.

'Well, Miss Bird, have you no opinion at all?' Dr Vaughan challenged.

'We're already working very hard to improve standards of midwifery and infant care,' Phyllis answered slowly. 'And Mr Poole has a reputation for excellence which – er –'

'Which he doesn't want tarnished by association with "filth and obscenity". Am I right, Miss Bird?'

'I don't think that Mr Poole regards birth control in that way, Dr Vaughan, but he certainly doesn't want to hear those sort of criticisms applied to Theodora House,' Phyllis said, choosing her words carefully.

'Or applied to him personally – yes, I think you're right, Miss Bird. But let me tell you of an idea of mine. What about a mobile clinic? A clinic on wheels, a van that we could take out into the streets, away from the pure atmosphere of Theodora House?'

Phyllis considered for a moment. 'And who had you in mind to staff this – this caravan, Doctor?'

'Well, I shall be in charge of it, and I hope it will be possible to organise a rota of nurses to work with me, Miss Bird.'

'None of us has any knowledge of birth-control methods, Doctor – or how to teach it. I personally am woefully ignorant on the subject.'

'Ah, but I can soon teach any nurse who is interested. Just one session would be sufficient, because the technique of fitting and inserting a Dutch cap can be learned in minutes. The difficult part is persuading women to make use of the service. The art of explaining and advising – that is what takes time and patience, although the very fact that a woman has come to consult you shows that she understands the need for it.'

Phyllis looked sceptical. 'I can only suggest that you put up a request for volunteers on the hospital notice-board – the one in the infirmary, not Theodora House – and see what response you get.'

'And there was I, hoping that you would help me to interest the nurses and midwives in this vital work, Miss Bird! Mr Poole has given me permission to approach any member of staff, and you are my natural first choice.'

'And suppose I agreed to help you with this clinic, Dr Vaughan, and tried to recruit staff for it – who would back me up in the event of any serious opposition, such as the wrecking of your brand-new mobile clinic? Not Mr Poole! He may have given you permission to go ahead, but he doesn't yet want to commit himself. You could say that he's waiting to see how it goes.'

'Ah, I realise that you've thought it all out, Miss Bird, which is good. Thank you for your honesty.' Mildred Vaughan smiled. 'It's true that we have not got much sympathy from the medical profession, but there are exceptions. Likewise, the Church is broadly opposed to birth control, but again there are honourable exceptions like the Bishop of Durham – and the same goes for the press, with one or two enlightened individuals like George Steynes. That young man is going to go a long way,' she added with a little smile that made Phyllis wonder if there was a personal interest here. Young Steynes was of Teddy Ling's generation, the ones who had just missed the war, while Dr Vaughan was about the same age as herself, some four or five years older than he.

The doctor broke in on these reflections to ask

Phyllis if she could attend an informal meeting at the home of the Honourable Mrs Agatha Steynes in Nelson Square.

'She's calling it a tea-party, Miss Bird, but it's actually a wonderful opportunity for you to meet some of the people in the public eye who have given their support to the Society for the Provision of Birth Control Clinics. Are you free on Friday afternoon or evening?'

'The truthful answer to that, Dr Vaughan, is that I'm very seldom free, because even when I'm not actually working I'm on call. I only get to see my parents one weekend a month,' said Phyllis, thinking of her son growing up without her.

'But you could still be on call, Miss Bird, as I shall be. Mrs Steynes has a telephone! Come on, now, I'll take no denial – we're going to tea in Nelson Square on Friday!'

Phyllis was saved from answering by an orderly dashing in with an urgent message for her: she was to go at once to a Mrs Kemp in Homer Street who had started labour and was 'bleeding'.

'I must go,' said Phyllis, moving away abruptly. 'She's not due for another three or four weeks – I'd better call Nurse Wildgoose – she's next for a delivery.'

'She's already gone, Miss Bird,' said the orderly. 'It's her that's asking for yer.'

'Oh, heavens,' muttered Phyllis in sudden alarm. 'Mrs Kemp's probably just having a heavy "show", but it could be more serious.'

Oh, let it not be an ante-partum haemorrhage, she silently prayed as she cycled off. She knew Mrs Kemp, a pleasant, hard-working woman who had talked about limiting her family to three, but was now expecting her fourth child. When Phyllis arrived at the small but clean and tidy home, she found Mrs Kemp bleeding to death.

'I've sent a message to the police station to ask them to get an ambulance, Miss Bird,' said the terrified pupil-midwife Nurse Wildgoose, having followed the usual procedure, for very few homes had telephones. Phyllis stared at the chalk-white, semi-conscious woman lying in the blood-soaked double bed. It required no great diagnostic skill to recognise the dreaded placenta praevia. In a desperate effort to stem the torrent, Phyllis thrust a large maternity pad into the vagina and held it there with her closed fist in the faint hope that a clot might form and reduce further bleeding from the placental site. Her heart sank and a terrible sense of helplessness seized her while the minutes ticked by and the life-blood continued to flow out in an unstoppable haemorrhage. The husband gazed down in open-mouthed horror.

'Can't yer do nothin' to stop it, Nurse? For Gawd's sake, ain't there *nothin'* anybody can do?'

'The afterbirth has been lying directly over the neck of the womb, Mr Kemp,' Phyllis whispered to the distracted man; 'and then as soon as the womb started to contract, it began to separate – to peel off, and that's why she's bleeding. If we can get her to Theodora House Mr Poole will deliver the baby by a Caesarean operation.'

But Phyllis knew that the baby would be already dead, its vital oxygen supply cut off as the placenta separated from the thousands of tiny capillary blood-vessels that had nourished the baby up until today, but which were now just broken, bleeding ends.

When the ambulance arrived Mrs Kemp was

gently lifted on to a stretcher, with Miss Bird's hand still thrust inside her, for she dared not withdraw it. She stood beside the stretcher throughout the journey, and on arrival at Theodora House they entered the clanging lift and ascended to the first floor where they went straight into the Caesar theatre. Mr Poole, warned by a police message, was gowned and gloved in readiness, and an anaesthetist was all prepared to dispatch Mrs Kemp into merciful oblivion.

But she had already gone. As Miss Bird withdrew her hand, a great red gush flowed out on to the operating table and dripped on to the floor. The mother was dead with her child. Phyllis thought herself to be in the grip of a nightmare, and Nurse Wildgoose burst into wailing sobs; she was taken out of the theatre by the sister from Octavia Hill Ward, who had been called to assist at this dreadful emergency.

'One of these tragedies that nobody could have foreseen,' Mr Poole said with melancholy emphasis, pulling off his face-mask as he stood in a pool of congealing blood. 'If I'd *known* that the placenta was lying over the cervix I would have had her in and done a Caesar before she went into labour – but everything seemed fine and she was booked for a home confinement. I don't attach any blame to you or the pupil, Miss Bird, but God help the husband left with three young children.' He sighed heavily. 'Let it be a reminder to us all that we can never be sure of anything in this game. Never assume that a delivery's going to be normal, because we don't know that until it's safely over. The day I think I know all about obstetrics, let my patients beware.'

*

344

The death of Mrs Kemp and her baby girl (for Mr Poole opened the abdomen to extract the child), cast a shadow over Theodora House and the district around it for some time afterwards. Phyllis Bird found it particularly difficult to come to terms with the tragedy, and went over it again and again in her own mind. Should she have suspected the placenta was low? Should she have gone to the house earlier? And another question: should she have given better and clearer advice when Mrs Kemp had shyly mentioned avoiding another pregnancy? Ought she to have urged the woman to go to the East Street Clinic in Walworth? Facing the husband now was agony, with the children crying for their mummy; Mrs Kemp's married sister had come to help out for the time being, until after the funeral, leaving her own children in the care of a friend, but the long-term prospect for the motherless family was bleak. Kemp worked at Hay's Wharf, loading and unloading cargoes, and his income was spasmodic at the best of times. Phyllis could foresee that the children would probably end up in a Home. Nurse Wildgoose tried to visit them as often as she could, taking them with their battered pram to the public park surrounding Lambeth Palace, and buying muffins to toast for their tea, but the sadness in the little home was almost palpable.

When Friday afternoon came Phyllis felt tired and depressed; her head ached and she was strongly tempted to make her excuses to Dr Vaughan and rest in her room at Richmond Street, rather than go to Mrs Steynes' tea-party; but there was no way out of it.

'Life has to go on, as well we know, Miss Bird,' said the doctor gently. 'I'll meet you in the District Room

345

at half-past two, and we'll walk up to Nelson Square together. Dress yourself up, and look as nice as you can – we're going to meet some very interesting people!'

Phyllis put on a light-brown suit and a head-hugging matching hat with a single pink rose as decoration. A necklace of garnet-coloured beads completed the outfit, and as she looked at herself in the dressing-table mirror, a memory flashed back into her mind: the pretty buttercup-yellow dress she had purchased from Gosling's for another special occasion; a dress she had worn only once.

'I say, you look simply charming, Miss Bird!' exclaimed her companion, who was wearing a flower-patterned dress with a light jacket and a small-brimmed green hat. 'Look, my name's Mildred, as I'm sure you know, and yours is Phyllis, so let's call each other by our names to show that we're friends!'

She's determined to rope me into her campaign, thought Phyllis; but it was impossible not to warm towards her, and she smiled as they set out together up the Blackfriars Road.

Number 15 Nelson Square had a deceptively narrow façade of plain brick with wrought-iron balconies to the first-floor windows, and stone cherubs above the entrance; but once inside the visitors' eyes were drawn to a beautiful curving staircase rising up from the hall to the first floor, where Mrs Steynes held court in the prettiest drawing room that Phyllis had ever seen. Elegant chairs were upholstered in rose-embroidered brocade, and a stone fireplace with a marble surround was entirely in keeping with the delicate china ornaments and bowls of fresh daffodils and tulips discreetly placed on well-polished occasional tables. Tasteful without being fussy, the room made Phyllis recall her father's respect for clients with 'old money' as opposed to the newly rich; he would definitely describe this as old money!

Mrs Steynes in black lace introduced them to a tall, rather jolly woman called Lady Dacre, and to a Mr Thurtle, MP, who was accompanied by Mrs Thurtle – 'an untiring member of Shoreditch Council,' the newcomers were told by Mr George Steynes. There was also a Dr Bazley, who seemed to be a friend of Mr Steynes, and contributed articles to the *Daily Chronicle* and various other publications.

'I think we'll start with a cup of tea and some of your favourite biscuits, Anne,' said Mrs Steynes to Lady Dacre, and accordingly tea was served in silver Georgian ware and bone china. Phyllis found her mind wandering off to the bereft family in Homer Street, and felt that she would have little or nothing to contribute to this gathering. However, Mildred drew her into the conversation, and she became interested in spite of herself. Mr Thurtle had worked very hard to further their cause in Parliament, she was told, and in February of the previous year he had presented a bill to authorise local authorities to supply knowledge of birth control methods to married women who desired it – and the motion had been thrown out by a two-thirds majority vote. This bitter disappointment had nevertheless gained widespread publicity for the cause, and many well-known names had come forward in support of it, from H. G. Wells and Arnold Bennett to Bertrand Russell and Julian Huxley, plus a growing number of Anglican churchmen. The name of Dr Marie Stopes was mentioned, and when Lady Dacre said that she

347

had been called 'the Mrs Pankhurst of the birth-control movement', Phyllis noticed that Dr Bazley caught George Steynes' eye and gave a little grimace.

'Damned difficult to work with, though – can't tolerate any other point of view but her own,' he murmured. 'Got to be the Queen Bee all the time, so she loses support for her good ideas.'

'Spoken like a man!' cried Mildred Vaughan indignantly. 'I'll remind *you*, Dr Bazley, that Marie Stopes lectures to medical students who go willingly to hear her because they have no other way of finding out about birth control. It's simply not on their syllabus, and they say she's a splendid lecturer. Whatever emotional problems she may have, you can't deny that she's got initiative – and guts!'

Lady Dacre and Mrs Thurtle gave a restrained cheer, and the group dissolved into good-natured laughter.

'Now, let's get back to our mobile clinic for Lambeth,' said Mildred. 'Am I right, Mrs Steynes, in my understanding that you would be prepared to finance it?'

Mrs Steynes glanced at her son. 'I've told George that I will purchase this caravan for the SPBCC if I can be assured that it will be protected from attacks by opponents such as was seen at the Walworth Clinic, when bricks were thrown and the doors kicked in. I believe there was an attempt to set it on fire, and a caravan would be extremely vulnerable to such a thing.'

'We would need a safe place to keep the mobile van when not in use, certainly,' replied Dr Vaughan. 'I'm afraid I can't offer anywhere on the premises of Theodora House at present.'

'Ah, but I can,' replied Dr Bazley cheerfully. 'My

back yard. It isn't that far from where you'll be operating.'

'That's extremely good of you, John,' said Lady Dacre. 'And will your – er – premises be safe from attacks?'

'High fence and padlocked iron gates, milady,' he replied with a grin, to general amusement.

'And then we come to the question of staffing,' said Mrs Thurtle. 'Is Miss Bird a volunteer?'

'Not quite yet, Dorothy,' interposed Mildred. 'Miss Bird leads a very busy life as a senior midwife and tutor on the district in Lambeth – and when she's not actually working, she is still on call round the clock. We can't expect her to volunteer her services at our clinic in her present circumstances, though I feel sure she's going to be a great campaigner at some time in the future. She's come with me this afternoon to hear what we have to say, that's all.'

'Thank you, Dr Vaughan, but perhaps I can make a small contribution to the debate,' said Phyllis, who had been giving the matter some thought. 'It's true that nurses and midwives work very long hours, and aren't looking for voluntary work, but you may be able to recruit clinic staff from the ranks of hospital nurses who have left to get married. Patients would be more likely to welcome a married woman than a single one in such a delicate – er – intimate matter, and looking ahead to the day you're all anticipating, when birth-control advice will be given by paid staff in local authority clinics, you will have no shortage at all. Married part-timers will probably be your chief source of staff.'

Phyllis realised that she had raised her voice slightly, and that the other seven members of the group were all giving her their undivided attention.

She blushed. 'Meanwhile, as staff have to be voluntary, I think you will find some of the midwives at Theodora House will be willing to put in a limited number of hours, say once or twice a month. I personally intend to learn the basics of birth control from Dr Vaughan, and then offer my services on that basis.'

'Wonderful! Congratulations, Miss Bird. I can see you as a platform speaker one day soon,' said Lady Dacre with a significant glance around the circle.

'And would you have any objection to being shouted at by an ignorant mob, Miss Bird?' asked Mrs Steynes. 'Would you stand by and be pelted with rotten eggs and tomatoes? This is what worries me, quite frankly. All you idealists seem to be sacrificing yourselves for the sort of people who will never appreciate what is done for them. I'm appalled by the abysmal ignorance of women who have not the slightest interest in raising their standards, and if I purchase this caravan clinic, I only hope that it will be appreciated, though I have my doubts.'

Phyllis decided that she did not much like Mrs Steynes, and remembered something Maud had said – that the lady's interest in birth control was only because of her son's involvement in the campaign. *She's got to support 'im, ain't she, 'cause she finks the sun shines aht of 'is backside.*

Phyllis's thoughts returned to Homer Street, and suddenly her eyes were full of tears. Heavens, this would not do: while the others talked among themselves, she quietly got up and went over to a window overlooking the square, largely hidden by plane trees newly in leaf.

I must compose myself, she thought. I mustn't draw attention to myself, not with this lot.

350

'Forgive me, but is anything the matter, Miss Bird?' she heard a man's voice murmur. 'Are you finding the room too warm? Can I get you a glass of water?'

Oh, for heaven's sake, it was George Steynes who had followed her. Why couldn't he just leave her alone? No such luck; he was still talking.

'I couldn't help noticing how tired you look, Miss Bird. I know from Dr Vaughan how hard your life is as a district midwife in Lambeth. And so demanding.'

'Yes, Mr Steynes, it can be demanding, especially when . . .' But she could not continue. Her mouth trembled and tears spilled down her cheeks. He silently produced a large handkerchief.

'Let me open the casement window and let you breathe some air, Miss Bird.' It opened inwards, and they both moved out on to the little balcony.

'You know that Dr Mildred admires you very much, Miss Bird, and I can see why,' he said. 'Let me tell you something in confidence. My mother is willing to pay a small remittance to any nurse who offers some of her time to work in the mobile clinic. We can't mention this openly, of course, because it's – well, strictly speaking it's against the present law. But she is very anxious to be of service to the cause, and is generous with her money.'

'It's very good of her – and good of you too, Mr Steynes,' replied Phyllis, wiping her eyes and blowing her nose. She turned to look at him, and saw an earnest young man who gave the impression of being older than his years, not handsome but with a determined air, honest grey eyes and straight hair brushed back from his forehead and slicked with hair cream.

'May I ask again what upset you, Miss Bird? Was it anything that anybody said this afternoon?'

'No, no, Mr Steynes, it's just a particularly sad case I had this week – the death of a mother and her child with ante-partum haemorrhage. She leaves a husband and – and three poor little children, God help them.' Her voice shook, and he placed a hand lightly on her arm.

'If there's anything I can do to relieve the immediate hardship, Miss Bird, I'd be glad to help. Let me make a donation to this family today. I'll let you have it before you leave.'

'That's very kind of you, Mr Steynes. Thank you.'

'Do you know, I've got this strange feeling that we've met before, though I can't remember where or how long ago. *Have* we, Miss Bird?'

Phyllis had no wish to bring up the past in front of Mildred Vaughan, who might also suddenly recall a former meeting. Hardly able to deny it, she simply smiled and shook her head.

'It's your voice, perhaps – is that a Somerset or Dorset accent?' he asked.

'No, Hampshire. Only about thirty miles from London.' She turned away and rejoined the group. Mrs Steynes had rung for fresh tea, sandwiches and cake, and the talk became lighter, or at least not confined to the cause.

'Shocking business about Thane, isn't it, George?' remarked Dr Bazley in an undertone.

'George is such an insatiable cinemagoer, you know. It's his one form of relaxation,' said Mrs Steynes to Lady Dacre, who laughed and replied that all the young people she knew were mad about the 'flicks', and she herself was devoted to Douglas Fairbanks.

'Better not say anything – I mean not in front of the ladies,' muttered Steynes. Phyllis had pricked up her ears at hearing the name of Thane, but would not have dreamed of butting in.

'What was that about Thane?' asked Mrs Thurtle. 'Do you mean the actor Reginald Thane?'

'Well, yes, Mrs Thurtle,' replied Bazley, leaning towards her and whispering. 'Been arrested and charged with . . .' Phyllis could not hear the rest of the sentence, but Mrs Thurtle gave a little cry of incredulity.

'Oh, how dreadful. Whoever would have thought it?' She turned and whispered to her husband, who wrinkled his nose. 'He'll go to prison for at least five years if he's found guilty.'

Mildred Vaughan saw Phyllis's questioning look, and muttered to her, 'Sodomy.'

'Oh, poor Reggie!' The words burst out of her before she could check herself, and the others all turned to stare at her. George Steynes smacked his hand against his forehead.

'*Now* I remember! It was at Maud's, wasn't it? That's where I've seen you, Miss Bird!'

It was out. Phyllis lowered her eyes and admitted, 'Yes, I met you at Florizel, Mr Steynes, about five years ago.'

'Dear Maudie!' he said affectionately. 'I'm afraid I made a bit of a fool of myself at the time. Her brother and I were both office boys with the *Daily Chronicle*, and he got me an introduction. And I wasn't the only one. That unfortunate chap Thane used to call us "Maudie's boys". Tell me, Miss Bird, weren't you a friend of hers? Didn't you walk out with her brother at one time?'

'Phyllis, you dark horse!' exclaimed Mildred.

'Maud Ling – and her brother! Are you still in touch with them?'

'No, not at all, not for several years,' said Phyllis, so firmly that Mildred turned to Steynes for more information.

'Do you see Miss Ling at all these days, George?'

'No, I'm afraid not, Mildred, though I get news of her from time to time. Her health isn't so good, and I don't think she's made any films lately. Well, there's been a big influx of new talent, like this magnificent actress from Sweden, Greta Garbo – she's taken the cinema by storm, even eclipsed Mary Pickford.' He sighed and smiled reflectively. 'Ah, but Maud was wonderful in her heyday. D'you remember those two historical films she made, Miss Bird, with that glamorous pair from Hollywood? Thane was in those too, wasn't he? How I used to envy him! And to think that all the time he was one of those – er – Oscar Wilde types.'

Phyllis sat frozen to her seat, unable to take in what she had heard in the last few minutes. Of course. Sonny Stott – he had been at Reggie's flat that dreadful night – was it because of *him* that Thane had been arrested?

As if in answer to her unspoken question, she heard George telling Mr and Mrs Thurtle that some young unemployed men had complained about Reginald Thane, whose real name was Horace Lampitt, and that he was to be held in police custody until tried at a criminal court, possibly the Old Bailey because of the seriousness of the crime and his own fame.

'Well, he'll go to prison,' repeated Mr Thurtle. 'The British public won't stand for that sort of corruption. And they never will.'

354

Phyllis said nothing. What was there to say? These people were liberal-minded and progressive, not afraid to run the gauntlet of opposition to their cause, which was looked upon as filthy and obscene in many circles; and yet they had no sympathy for this man who had been a good friend to her when she needed one. He had saved her from a shameful exposure, and yet here she sat, silent and unwilling to say one word in his favour now that he was being universally condemned. She shivered as she recalled Towers' humiliation of him: *What with . . . poor old Reggie and that ghastly boy . . .*

Yes, of course. She'd never liked Stott, and now she understood why. She did not personally condemn Thane, for she now knew so much more about the world than she'd known then . . .

Walking back along Blackfriars Road with Mildred Vaughan, and with twenty pounds in cash in her handbag, entrusted to her by George Steynes for the Kemp family, Phyllis had little to say to her companion because she had so much on her mind. Mildred too was rather pensive and, to Phyllis's relief, said nothing at all about Maud Ling and her circle.

'Mr Steynes has been most kind,' Phyllis commented about his donation, and Mildred gave her a rather odd look.

'He and his mother can be very generous, but he's also very ambitious. He's taken up this birth-control campaign and I'm sure he won't rest until it's on the statute book. I think he intends to run for Parliament, and you can bet your life he'll go for the women's vote on this issue.'

'But he does *believe* in the cause, doesn't he?' asked Phyllis, rather surprised by this somewhat different angle on George Steynes.

'Oh, yes, he believes in it, and he'll use it to further his career,' answered her friend with a sidelong glance. 'And Helena Wright and the Thurtles and Lady Dacre – and I and all the rest of us – can also use him to get what *we* want.'

'Oh, Mildred! That sounds rather cynical. And you seemed to be such friends.'

'Friends, yes. But would *you* like to have the Honourable Mrs Agatha Steynes for a mother-in-law? Well, we must part here, Phyllis. I go down Lambeth Road and you go to Richmond Street. Thanks for coming!'

Chapter 20

As the days lengthened and the spring sunshine drew families to their front doors in even the humblest streets, the district midwives and their pupils found it quite enjoyable to cycle from one maternity case to the next, sometimes over quite long distances. In May Nurses Webb and Anderson came on to the district for their six months' experience, and Miss Bird gave them their instructions in no uncertain terms.

'Get on your bicycles, Nurses, and go and visit your expectant mothers in their homes,' she urged. 'Listen to the baby's heart and feel for its head. Find out if it's a breech or even possibly twins, and whether the head's well down or floating about above the brim. Assess whether she's big for her dates or smaller. And while you're examining her on her bed, look around you – discreetly, of course. Note if the house is clean, how many other children there are, and what condition they're in. Find out if the woman's mother lives near, what sort of neighbours she's got, and who's going to look after the family when she's confined. Is the husband in regular employment, and is he a drinker? Get to *know* your patient, listen to what she tells you, and you *may* be able to foresee trouble ahead, and prevent it. Get your foot in the door – and never mind saving their souls, Nurse Lamb!'

The last sentence was said kindly, and the other

pupils smiled at Barbara Lamb, who held her head up unabashed. She was known for her exuberant singing of hymns as she cycled to or from her visits:

'Great is Thy faithfulness! Great is Thy
    faithfulness!
Morning by morning new mercies I see;
All I have needed Thy hand has provided,
Great is thy faithfulness, Lord, unto me.'

'Perhaps if you could tone it down a little during the night hours, Nurse Lamb,' said Miss Bird, 'though I have to admit that there are worse sounds to be heard in the streets after dark. And Nurse Wildgoose, you missed Mr Poole's important lecture on toxaemia of pregnancy yesterday afternoon. There was nobody in labour on the district, so why weren't you there?'

Doris Wildgoose looked down at her shoes. 'I'm really sorry, Miss Bird, but little Dickie Kemp – that's the youngest, he's only nineteen months – he just wouldn't stop crying, and it was upsetting the other two. I think he may be getting more teeth, and he really ought to –'

'All right, Nurse Wildgoose, I appreciate what you do for the family, but I must stress that your training is very important and should not be neglected, even for good works.'

'Damned cheek, that's what I call it,' muttered Nurse Webb, picking up her visiting bag. 'Who does she think she is, tellin' us all that stuff we can see for ourselves? Them as knows their district knows their mothers, an' them as don't won't do any good wastin' time on visits before' and. I got summat better to do – an' so would she if she 'ad a fam'ly.'

'And one more thing before you go out, Nurses,'

added Miss Bird. 'Don't forget Dr Vaughan's lecture this evening at nine in the infirmary lecture room – *not* Theodora House, please note. The subject of birth-control methods and advice is going to be important to us *all* as midwives, whether we actually practise in clinics or simply advise our mothers to attend them.'

'Playin' with fire she is, if yer ask me,' was Ginny Webb's verdict. 'Yer won't catch *me* at no birth-control lecture, thank yer. Even ol' man Poole's got the sense to keep out of it.'

'Nurse Lamb, you can come with me this after-noon,' said Miss Bird. 'I've got two pre-confinement visits to make, both at the same place. It's quite a distance – we'll cycle together.'

On their way to 90 Riverside Gardens – a misnomer because it was some way from the river, and the only garden consisted of a few stunted shrubs – Miss Bird explained the reason for this visit.

'It's a mother-and-baby home run by the London County Council, and the resident midwife has had to go into hospital for an operation, so the matron has written to ask if confinements could be booked at Theodora House until she returns – or whether they could be delivered by a district midwife. I'm going to have a look at the place and see two girls who are nearly due.'

The home was located between a candle manufactory and a warehouse for storing various goods, including hay for the horses still used for milk- and coal-carts. It looked uninviting even on a fine spring day, and Barbara Lamb exclaimed in horror at the prominent name plate at the front: 'London County Council Home for Wayward Girls'.

'Did you ever see anything more unkind, Miss

Bird? How can any poor girl hope to regain her self-respect in a place that labels her like that?'

Phyllis Bird could think of no answer, remembering the relative comforts of Lahai-Roi. She was privately bracing herself for this encounter.

They were received by the matron, Miss Thomas, a businesslike sort of woman who explained that the home had to pay its way by taking in laundry from nursing homes and hemming new sheets and pillowcases for them. All this was done by 'the girls', as she called them, and they also did the domestic work.

'I have to be housekeeper, and I have one deputy, a cook and her deputy assistant,' she told them. 'The LCC sends us a man once a week to see to any repairs and attend to the boiler. We're expected to run the place on a shoestring, and the girls can be very difficult to deal with.'

'Where do they come from?' asked Miss Bird.

'Bad backgrounds, on the whole – some from orphanages; quite a few have been prostitutes, up for thieving and soliciting – and got sent here instead of prison because they're expecting. You'll hear plenty of complaints about how hard they have to work, but they are here to be reformed and retrained for useful work in domestic service. A thankless job for us, believe me!'

She took the visitors on a tour of the home, and they saw a dozen or so young women, mostly pregnant and a few delivered, working in a steam-filled laundry, hanging up washed and mangle-pressed linen, ironing with flat-irons and folding the clean articles. In the sewing room sat three girls more advanced in pregnancy, and Miss Thomas beckoned two of them to come to the delivery room to be examined, calling them by their surnames, Taylor and Woods.

'Taylor says she was raped, but from what I've learned about her she was probably too drunk to know what she was doing,' she sniffed as the tired-looking girl stared at them dully. Phyllis gave a sharp gasp and for a moment stood stock-still. Miss Thomas nodded, taking this to be a sign of disgust.

'Yes, it isn't easy to sympathise in such a case, is it, Miss Bird? Though I pity the babies, of course.'

Phyllis forced a smile. 'Now, Taylor dear, I need to examine your tummy and listen to your baby's heart. Lie down on the bed, legs straight, arms by your side – that's right. Good girl.'

'When d'yer fink I'm goin' to 'ave it, Nurse? I'm ever so tired,' said the girl wearily.

'I don't think you've got much longer to go, dear. Do you mind if Nurse Lamb also examines you, and says what she thinks?'

'Don't make much diff'rence. I got to put up wiv it, ain't I?'

'Don't be insolent, Taylor,' said Miss Thomas sharply.

Barbara Lamb stepped forward. 'Do you mind telling me your Christian name, dear?'

'Jane.'

'Oh, that's a nice name, Jane! Now, let me see . . .'

Phyllis watched approvingly as the pupil-midwife palpated the abdomen and listened to the foetal heart through the 'ear-trumpet'.

'About thirty-nine to forty weeks, vertex pre-senting and engaged, left occipito-anterior position, foetal heart strong and regular – wouldn't you say, Miss Bird?'

'I agree with that, Nurse Lamb. Thank you, Jane. We'll book you in for a district confinement, which means that when you start labour Miss Thomas will send for a midwife – and we think it will probably be quite soon.'

The girl sat up. 'Will it be one o' you two?'

'Be quiet, Taylor. You'll get whoever's on call and be grateful,' Miss Thomas scolded, but Barbara Lamb looked pleadingly at Phyllis and said, 'I'd be willing to come out to Jane, whether I was on call or not, Miss Bird.'

'We shall have to see, Nurse Lamb. Right, Matron, may we see the other girl?'

'This is Woods – Daisy Woods.' Miss Thomas lowered her voice and added, 'Not one of the brightest, I'm afraid.'

'Thank you. Would you like to examine Daisy first, Nurse Lamb, and I'll check your findings, all right?'

'Yes, Miss Bird. How're you feeling, Daisy? Rather tired, I expect.'

'Yeah, mum.'

'Don't say "yeah" like that, Woods. Say "yes" to the lady,' interposed the matron.

'Yas'm.'

'Can you lie quite flat on your back for me, Daisy?' asked Nurse Lamb kindly.

'Yas'm.'

'Have you felt the baby moving about a lot lately?'

'Yas'm.'

They both agreed that Daisy Woods was also due at any time. 'Are you happy to be delivered by one of our district midwives, Daisy?'

'Yas'm.'

'Good, so we'll expect a call from you some time soon, Miss Thomas.' And having checked the equipment in the delivery room, the two of them took their leave.

'What a horrible place, Miss Bird!' said Barbara as soon as they were outside the Home for Wayward Girls. 'Oh, if only I could bring the love of the Lord Jesus into their lives, it would be such a privilege. I *do* hope I can deliver at least one of them!'

Phyllis smiled at her eagerness. 'You might be able to swap with whoever's on call, Nurse, but meanwhile I shall contact the headquarters of the Ladies' League of Christian Befrienders, to see if they can send a visitor to 90 Riverside Gardens. It would be a challenge for them!'

Not many turned up for Dr Vaughan's lecture in the infirmary that evening. Phyllis Bird was joined by Carrie Anderson and two staff nurses from the general wards. Nurse Wildgoose had gone to the Kemps again, and Barbara Lamb had sped off back to 90 Riverside Gardens on getting a phone call to say that Jane Taylor was getting 'niggles'. Mrs Starling put in an unexpected appearance, though made it clear that she was on call, and in fact had to go out to supervise the delivery with Nurse Lamb. A junior doctor on Mr Poole's obstetric team came in and took a seat, clearly interested in whatever his young colleague had to say, and GP Dr Bazley joined him. They all sat in silence while Mildred Vaughan talked of the Dutch occlusion cap and how easily it fitted over the cervix, lubricated with spermicidal cream. It was a difficult subject for a mixed audience, thought Phyllis, even though they all had medical or nursing experience, but Dr Vaughan's burning enthusiasm was infectious, and overcame any initial awkwardness. She told them that Mrs Steynes had supplied the necessary payment for a good-quality mobile clinic, and enthused over the decorating scheme in tasteful blue and white; there would be two compartments, one for interviewing clients and gaining their confidence, the other for the actual fitting of cervical caps in a strictly clinical environment.

'The clinic will be kept at the back of Dr Bazley's house at St Mary's Corner, off the Kennington Road, and will be taken to two different sites each week,' she said. 'One session will be held in the afternoon, the other in the evening. I shall personally be in charge, and will need at least one assistant, preferably two. I can't wait to get started –' her dark eyes sparkled as she spoke – 'and my aim is to be open on Monday, June the twentieth. Now, can I count on any volunteers?'

Phyllis's face was a picture of dismay. 'Oh, Mild— Dr Vaughan, I can't possibly be there on any day that week. I'll be on my annual holiday, the eighteenth to the twenty-fifth. I'm terribly sorry.'

Mildred Vaughan's disappointment seemed almost equal to her own, but Phyllis was adamant. The North Camp district nurse owned a little bungalow at Hayling Island, and let it out to reliable acquaintances during the holiday season. It was Phyllis's most longed-for week of the whole year, and nothing took precedence over it.

'Is it just you and your parents who are going away, Phyllis? You couldn't possibly change the date?' Mildred pleaded.

'It's my mother and I – Dad just comes for the weekend because he's got the shop, but she needs the break, and it's been booked ever since we stayed there last summer,' Phyllis told her, feeling conscience-stricken but determined not to miss this week with her son. She had grown much more self-assured during the past four years, and her position of authority in Lambeth enabled her to stand tall and look straight at her former neighbours at North Camp on her monthly weekend visits – but her week's holiday away from them all was very special, and when 18 June arrived, her heart soared with joyful anticipation.

Hayling Island was so lovely. The little garden at the back of the bungalow continued down to the beach, and the front faced a field where a few donkeys were kept by the locals; she took Saul to gather mushrooms there as soon as they got up, for Mrs Bird to cook with bacon and tomatoes for breakfast. When the tide was out there were little rock-pools where she and Saul found tiny crabs and starfish, and the usual abundance of shells. They paddled and dug their toes into the sand, filled his little tin bucket and made turreted castles that the incoming tide washed away; it was paradise. Saul made friends with children staying at the other bungalows, and Mrs Bird nodded with satisfaction.

'It's the golf links that keep the island select,' she said. 'You get a nicer class of person staying when the menfolk play golf.'

Phyllis smiled at her mother's little pretensions to gentility, but on the second day of their holiday Mrs Bird said something that disturbed and annoyed her. Two old ladies had been showing an interest in Ethel's little grandson, and she confessed that she had told them that Phyllis was a widow.

'It seems harmless enough to let them think that, Phyllis. After all, we're not likely to meet them again,' she said half-apologetically when she saw Phyllis frown.

'But it's not *true*, Mum! Saul will be asking what a widow is, and it will confuse him.'

'My dear girl, any day now he's going to ask where his father is, and what will you say to him then?'

'Look, Mum, I wish you wouldn't –'

'Ssh, not in front of Saul, you'll upset him. Anyway, what difference does it make? And it saves people from asking awkward questions.'

Phyllis bit back a sharp retort, reminding herself once again that although Saul was her son, it was his grandparents who were bringing him up for her; she had not had to part with him for ever. Nevertheless her mother's words had been hurtful, and Saul sensed the tension in her, for during the night he woke up sobbing. She leaped out of bed to comfort him, but he called out for his granny, and Mrs Bird at once appeared at the door in her nightdress.

'I'll see to him, Phyllis. He's been upset, that's the trouble. All right, my precious, Granny's here, don't cry, don't cry . . .'

Phyllis went back to bed but could not sleep. Her thoughts turned to Lambeth and the opening of the mobile clinic: how was Mildred getting on? I ought to be there with her, giving her my support, she thought wretchedly. A grey cloud of sadness and frustration descended upon her spirits, though she made an effort to appear bright and cheerful the next day – anything to avoid upsetting her little son.

And when he fell and stubbed his toe on a jutting piece of rock, she rushed to pick him up and kiss it better. Granny was nowhere in sight, and he put his arms around Phyllis's neck, which consoled her more than anything else could have done. Even so, she was hardly prepared for what he said next.

'Are you Mummy or Phyllis?' he asked innocently.

What could she say? 'What do *you* want to call me, Saul dear?'

He thought for a moment, and then said, 'I call you Mummy.' She smiled and hugged him, but it was a significant moment. He was in no doubt about who was Granny.

Back in Lambeth, she heard that the mobile clinic had not yet opened. There had been a vociferous demonstration against it, led by an old priest, Father McTaggart of the Church of the Holy Family, which was the Roman Catholic church that Sister Pollock attended. They had formed a cordon around the mobile clinic and prevented women from entering it, while holding up banners proclaiming the Church's opposition to the unnatural gratification of lust and its support of the sanctity of marriage and family life.

'It was simply dreadful, Phyllis,' reported Mildred Vaughan, who was looking unusually dispirited. 'I was so cross with that silly Sister Pollock from Octavia Hill Ward, dressed up in her uniform and intimidating those two nurses from the general wards. One of them was in tears, and said she wouldn't come again. I felt like giving that old priest a piece of my mind, but Mr Poole stepped in and told me not to antagonise anybody and not on any account to speak to Sister Pollock. She's one of our best midwives, he said, and he doesn't want to lose her. And this Father McTaggart is a great friend of the poor in Lambeth, apparently, and all the children love him. "They run after him in the streets as if he was the Pied Piper of Hamelin," Mr Poole told me, and I was so annoyed that I answered him back – "And look what happened to *them*!"'

'Oh, Mildred, I'm so sorry. But when are you going

to try again? What about *this* Monday, the twenty-seventh? Get straight in there again and show them you're not to be put off. I'll back you up!'

'But they'll only turn out and oppose us all over again – unless . . .' Mildred Vaughan looked thoughtful. 'I wonder if I could ask Dr Bazley if we could hold it at his home? That's private property, and he's a respected GP. They couldn't stop us if we opened our clinic there.'

Dr Bazley willingly gave his consent, and the clinic was duly opened at his home off the Kennington Road, on a corner of St Mary's Square. George Steynes came to give support, and persuaded his mother to accompany him and talk with Mrs Bazley in the drawing room while outside on the corner the mobile van attracted quite a large crowd of women, some with children. Dr Vaughan, Miss Bird, Nurse Anderson and one nurse from the infirmary were there to staff the clinic while Nurse Wildgoose gave out leaflets; Phyllis recognised the vicar of St Martha's Church, who had been verbally set upon by two fellow clerics at the town hall meeting, and a Methodist minister, Mr Broome, and his wife from Pond Street Methodist Chapel with their three children; Mrs Broome was about six months pregnant with a fourth. A tea and coffee seller with an eye to business came and set up his stall nearby, selling drinks at a halfpenny a cup, and to Mildred Vaughan's delight Mr Poole put in an appearance halfway through the afternoon.

'How's it doing, ladies?'

'Very well, thank you, Mr Poole. We've had a small demonstration, but Miss Bird froze them with her icy stare, and of course we've got Dr Bazley and Mr Steynes to add a little masculine weight to the occasion,' laughed the young doctor. 'It seems that Father McTaggart has a wedding this afternoon, and Sister Pollock's on duty, so the women aren't put off by any awful slogans. The poor dears are shy enough as it is, without having to face that lot as well.'

George Steynes heard this exchange and took an opportunity to introduce himself to Mr Poole. 'I'm very pleased to meet you, sir,' he said enthusiastically. 'I have such enormous admiration for these wonderful women – Dr Vaughan and Miss Bird, to name but two! It's thanks to campaigners like them that birth-control clinics will be accepted and run by local authorities in another five years' time.'

'Hm. There's still a lot of opposition to it, and I'm not so sure about council-run clinics in five years,' answered Mr Poole drily. 'But I agree with you about our campaigners, who put in voluntary hours on top of their already long shifts. I just hope that they can keep up the pace.'

'Oh, I'm certain that Miss Bird will never falter, no matter how long it takes,' replied Steynes, turning an admiring glance in Phyllis's direction where she sat taking down the social details of each client – the name, address, age, marriage date and number of children. She returned a brief smile of acknowledgement, and George became even more lyrical in his praises.

'Dr Vaughan tells me that she's a splendid midwife, sir.'

'She is – a caring person and a good teacher – an excellent woman, in fact. And I don't want you birth-control campaigners to steal her completely away from her profession.'

Phyllis heard this exchange, and glowed with pleasure at the consultant's words. Her thoughts turned naturally to her son. Your mummy's just been called an excellent woman, Saul, she thought silently. That means you don't have to be ashamed of her!

Even so, the mobile clinic continued to meet with sporadic opposition, and on one August evening there was an ugly scene led by a group of men emboldened by drink and looking for trouble. They shouted 'Abortionists!' and 'Whores!' at the women going into the van, and at once Miss Bird rose from her seat and appeared at the door.

'Shame on you, layabouts! Don't you *dare* to threaten these women, or I'll send for the police and have you moved on!'

Some of them were taken aback, but others openly defied her, and encouraged the rest to start throwing stones at the van.

'Be careful, Phyllis. Come inside or you'll get hit,' warned Mildred, but Phyllis stood boldly confronting them. 'I mean it, you'll be arrested for disturbing the peace. Clear off!'

Another stone was thrown, and the word 'whore' was repeated, when all of a sudden two men in working overalls appeared and charged at the demonstrators, shaking their fists in their faces and threatening to punch their teeth in.

'Get aht of it! Scarper! Tha's a lady yer talkin' to – tha's Nurse Bird! Yer better leave 'er alone an' bugger orf, see?'

In the face of such counteropposition the demonstrators did not stop to argue, and having cleared the street, Nurse Bird's defenders touched their caps to her and went on their way.

'Good heavens, Phyllis, who on earth were they?' gasped Mildred Vaughan, open-mouthed.

'Oh, just a couple of husbands of patients I've had,' said Phyllis easily, hiding her own relief, and astounded to see that one of the men was Simmons from Old Paradise Street. She had never expected to count on him as an ally.

'But how do you keep so *calm*, Phyllis? The nurses from the infirmary would be frightened to death by that sort of violence,' said Mildred, secretly a little scared herself.

'I've faced worse than this, Mildred.'

'But *when*? How could you possibly have had to contend with worse than, well, what we've just seen?'

'These people are opposing our campaign, Mildred, but they have nothing against us personally, for all their insults. They don't know us, they're nobody to us, and so I can cope with them. It's when those that you know and love disappoint you.' She stopped.

'Yes, Phyllis? Go on.'

'Let's just say that sticks and stones may break my bones, but words – no, let's get on with our work, Doctor.' And Phyllis carried on with her note-taking of her client's history in a way that precluded any further questioning.

As the work of the clinic progressed, certain misunderstandings about the nature of its function became all too apparent.

'I'm 'opin' ye'll be able to do summat for me, Nurse,' whispered a tired-looking woman with the pallor of anaemia and hollow eyes of under-nourishment. 'I ain't seen nuffin' for two munfs, so I reckon I must've fallen again. Feelin' sick an' I'm that bloody tired, what wiv free ovvers 'angin' rahnd me all day. Me friend said yer could clear it aht for me.'

371

'Oh, my dear, I'm so sorry, but we can't do that, you know,' said Phyllis, her eyes full of pity and regret. 'This clinic helps women like you to *avoid* falling again, you see, to *prevent* it from happening. Once it's happened, and you're expecting another baby, we can't do anything about it, only to book you for a confinement.'

'Oh Gawd. They said ye'd 'elp me aht. I feel that sick an' bad, Nurse.'

'Look, I'll send you in to see Dr Vaughan while you're here, and she can give you some iron tablets to help you feel a little stronger, my dear.'

'Nah, I don't want them fings, they gave me them last time an' I was sicker'n ever. Oh, Nurse, I fought yer was goin' to 'elp me aht.'

Phyllis shook her head. 'No, dear. We can help you not to have another baby after this one, but we can't do anything now that you've started on it. I'm so sorry.'

'Yeah, well – 'e'll be bloody sorry an' all when I tell 'im I'm 'avin' anuvver.'

Phyllis's heart ached for the woman, probably not as old as herself; she never failed to be amazed at the way men blamed their wives for the condition they caused.

And there were clients like the powdered and lipsticked young girl who said she was from Bermondsey and gave an address in Spa Road.

'What is your husband's name and occupation?' asked Phyllis briskly.

'Albert – er – Thompson. He's at Peek Frean's.'

'How long has he been employed there?'

'Since he left school.'

'What exactly does he do there? Is he on the production line or in distribution?'

'Yer want to know a lot, don't yer?' said the girl with uneasy defiance.

'Yes, and I'll ask you another question. Are you married, Mrs – er? You're not, are you? You're Mrs Black's eldest girl who ran away from home. She needs your help, Miss Black, and I suggest you go home and help her with your brothers and sisters.'

'What d'yer think I ran away for? I want to get work away from all that.'

'But not the sort of work you're thinking of doing, my dear. You just go home to your mother, and maybe things will be easier in a year or two. No, of course I shan't tell her. Everything is strictly confidential here.'

Finding time for the clinic in addition to her long hours on call proved to be very tiring, but Mrs Steynes was as good as her word, and an unofficial payment was made to all clinic staff for each session they worked. Phyllis saved hers in a special account she had taken out for Saul.

In October the trial of Horace Lampitt, otherwise known as Reginald Thane, made scandalous headline news, and as predicted, it took place not at Kingston Criminal Court but at the Old Bailey. It lasted for four days, and the outcome was a foregone conclusion, because not only did three young men under the age of twenty-one accuse him of corrupting them by acts of sodomy in exchange for money, but a very articulate witness came forward to say how he too had been harassed over a long period of time by Lampitt. This was Timothy Stott, aged thirty-one, a film technician and part-time actor, who said he had actually moved away from a lucrative position at Twickenham Film Studios because of

Lampitt's persistent importuning, and had lost income as a result. When he had heard about the accusations made against Lampitt by minors, he had felt it his duty to come forward and give evidence, much as it pained him; he had not wanted to get Lampitt into trouble during the time he knew him at Twickenham, he said. His story stood up to cross-questioning by the counsel for the defence, and he gained a certain amount of sympathy in the press. Phyllis read the daily reports of the trial with a feeling of utter helplessness, as there was nothing she could do for Thane.

But on the third day of the trial another witness for the defence was called, and all over the country people read that the film actress Maud Ling had risen from a sick-bed to give evidence. Under oath she testified that Horace Lampitt had been a personal friend and film partner of hers for many years. She had known from the start, she said, that he and Stott were in a homosexual relationship – in fact it was common knowledge at the studios. When the actor grew older and got less leading roles, Stott had tired of him and moved to other film studios. He also had various lucrative business interests, including horse-racing. Lampitt had been heartbroken, and began to drink heavily as his career declined. It was then that he became involved with the young men who now accused him.

Miss Ling added that she had not intended to come forward to give this evidence in public, but when she had heard of Stott's 'lying to save his own skin', she had changed her mind.

Notwithstanding Miss Ling's testimony, the jury found Lampitt guilty, and he was sent to Wandsworth Prison for five years. Timothy Stott was also charged, under her evidence, but denied all her allegations and got a conditional discharge when his trial came to court. It was the great scandal of the day, and briefly took the nation's mind off the wretched conditions of the unemployed as winter set in once again, though there was an outcry when the Prime Minister, Mr Baldwin, refused even to see a deputation of two hundred coal miners who had walked a hundred and eighty miles from the Rhondda Valley to Trafalgar Square in miserable wet weather to plead that their families were starving.

'It's more important than ever that we press forward with our SPBCC campaign,' urged Mildred Vaughan, and insisted that Phyllis should not only attend a rally in a Walworth cinema taken over for an evening, but should give a speech from the platform about her personal experiences as a district midwife and what she saw at first-hand of the desperate conditions of poor women. George Steynes was also on the platform, and afterwards congratulated her on what he called her riveting address.

'I always thought that you would be one of our best campaigners, Miss Bird. They were all listening to you so intently, I was watching them! Can I take you somewhere for a spot of supper?'

'Thank you, Mr Steynes, but it's been a long day,' she replied, for her head was aching. 'All I want now is to get home and go to sleep.'

'Then I'll give you a lift. I'm the proud owner of one of these new Morris Minors, frightfully good at nipping in and out of the traffic. Have you been to Hyde Park Corner lately? It's just one huge standstill.'

He hardly gave her a chance to refuse, and she was thankful enough to accept, as Mildred had arranged to go to a friend's house. Steynes was zealous for her comfort, helping her into the passenger seat and wrapping a rug around her legs. It was nice to be fussed over for once, she thought, stifling a yawn. She hoped he wouldn't expect her to talk.

But he did. He asked her about her reaction to the trial and the Old Bailey, and she admitted that it had saddened her, especially as there had been nothing she could do to help Reginald Thane in his dark hour.

'I've got a conscience about him, too, Miss Bird – and about Maud,' George replied seriously. 'Our reporter at the trial said she looked thin and ill. She looked straight at that Stott fellow and called him a skunk, though of course it was objected to and not recorded.'

'I can just hear her, can't you?' said Phyllis, and gave a passable imitation of how Maud must have sounded in the witness box. 'Broke poor ol' Reggie's 'eart, 'e did!'

George Steynes smiled but shook his head sadly. 'Ah, that's the trouble – Maud's cockney accent, poor girl. She'll never survive if these new talking films take on, as I'm sure they will. Have you seen this new film with Al Jolson?'

'No, I never seem to have time to go to the pictures,' said Phyllis. 'Have you?'

'Yes, and it's absolutely amazing, Miss Bird. Al Jolson suddenly calls out, "You ain't heard nothin' yet," and proceeds to electrify the audience by singing. It nearly caused a riot! There's no doubt about it, *sound* has arrived, and Maud won't be the only film star with a problem. Some of them have got foreign accents or squeaky voices, and they won't be able to cope. It could be the end of Maud's career.'

'And to think that Reginald Thane always had such a beautiful voice,' sighed Phyllis.

They had arrived at Number 35 Richmond Street. 'Well, thank you very much, Mr Steynes, and good night,' she said, opening the door.

'Wait a minute, Miss Bird. Look here, after what we've been saying – do you think – would you care to come with me on a visit to Maud, to ask how she is, you know?'

'Oh, Mr Steynes, thank you, but I don't think so,' said Phyllis in some confusion. 'That's a part of my life that's all over now. I – I might write her a letter.'

'She'd much prefer a visit, Miss Bird.'

'From you, perhaps, Mr Steynes, but not from me.' Phyllis could not picture visiting Florizel in the company of Steynes; there was no telling what Maud might come out with. 'Thank you, but no, I'd rather not. If you decide to see her, please give her my regards. And now I simply must say good night and thank you again.'

'So you live here, not at Theodora House?'

'Yes. I have a very nice landlady who looks after me very well. Good night, Mr Steynes.'

'Good night, Miss Bird. I look forward to seeing you again. I say, there's a jolly good new play on in the West End, *A Break in Time*. It's the latest one from Harold Berridge –'

'Good night, Mr Steynes.'

Rose Rawson was waiting for her, and wanted to hear all about the evening, and the gentleman who had brought Phyllis home in his car.

'You'll never guess, Rose. I think Mr Steynes wants to take me to the theatre to see the latest play by Harold Berridge!'

'Ooh, Phyllis, what a lark! And are yer goin'?'

'No, Rose, it would bring back too many memories. And I don't want to encourage young Mr Steynes.'

'Why not? 'E sounds ever so nice!'

'You know perfectly well why not, Rose. I'm not what he thinks I am. I've got a son, and here in Lambeth nobody but you knows that I'm a fallen woman.'

Rose Rawson looked crestfallen, and muttered something about it being a great pity, and not fair. 'Never mind, Phyllis dear, I'll get yer a nice 'ot drink 'fore yer go to bed.'

Chapter 21

It was Father McTaggart's annual tradition to give a huge Christmas party in the parish hall of the Church of the Holy Family for all children within the parish – and quite a few beyond it, whether they were Catholics or not. Admission was free, and the ladies of the church baked cakes, biscuits and buns for days beforehand with ingredients paid for by the old priest, who also supplied balloons, sweets and a little gift for each child, giving up his tobacco in order to do so. Sister Pollock arranged to have the day off – it was 17 December, a Saturday – and worked very hard at preparing the sandwiches, sausages, brightly coloured jellies and fruit drinks for the party, which began at two and went on until five o'clock.

Nurse Wildgoose arrived early with the three Kemp children, offering her services in the makeshift kitchen set up by Father McTaggart and his team of helpers. Paper decorations were put up, and for three happy hours the children feasted, played games, sang songs to the accompaniment of a piano and tin whistle, cheered and booed at a Punch and Judy show, and gave no thought to the hardships of the world outside the hall.

'Oh, Miss Bird, you should've seen 'em. Their little eyes shinin' when Father told the story about Baby Jesus born in a poor manger,' said Nurse Wildgoose, her own plain features lit up by the children's innocent pleasure. 'And Sister Pollock was so *good*

379

with 'em. She gave the same welcome to everybody, whether they go to the Holy Family or not – I mean, mine don't.'

Phyllis smiled at the 'mine', but could only admire the dedication of the priest, and went out of her way to thank Sister Pollock for all her hard work, mentioning how much the party had meant to the motherless Kemp children.

'Thank you, Miss Bird, and I'm happy to think we can still be friends in spite of our deep divisions on certain matters,' replied Edna Pollock earnestly, though she rather spoiled her little speech by her next words.

'I believe that the women of England have too much self-respect to descend to the morals of the farmyard, Miss Bird. I know that you and Dr Vaughan mean well, but it's something that will never be accepted in a Christian country.'

Phyllis smiled and wisely stayed silent, for she had recently been approached by the vicar of St Martha's Anglican Church, who told her of the problems encountered by the Young Wives Group who met there every Wednesday afternoon, and included his own wife.

'Basically these ladies are too shy and embarrassed to make use of your mobile clinic, Miss Bird, and my wife and I wondered if you would come and give a talk to them,' he had suggested tentatively. 'Perhaps we might then arrange for a, er, a session to be held – privately, you understand – within the vicarage itself.'

After consultation with Dr Vaughan, the talk to the Young Wives was accordingly given, and the following week a clinic was held in the vicarage after the usual meeting. Phyllis was surprised at the numbers attending, and the membership of the group rose sharply. Some of them came from the Pond Street Methodist Church, shepherded by the minister's wife, now about seven months pregnant and an open supporter of the SPBCC.

'Mark my words, Phyllis, we're getting there,' said a jubilant Mildred Vaughan, though Phyllis knew what a risk the clergymen were taking, and prayed that the vicar of St Martha's would not be reported to the Bishop of Southwark. Although there had been significant changes in Anglican opinion since the last Lambeth Conference in 1920, there was no doubt that such active participation in the SPBCC campaign could damage his career, if not end it altogether.

Christmas was usually a busy time for the midwives, and 1927 was no exception, though Ginny Webb managed to spend Boxing Day with Billy, and Barbara Lamb was invited to share Christmas dinner at 90 Riverside Gardens, where she was now an enthusiastic member of the Ladies' League of Christian Befrienders. Carrie Anderson delivered a baby boy in a clean but crowded home, with Phyllis assisting rather than supervising her, Mrs Starling being at home with her own family, and both Miss Bird and the pupil returned to Theodora House for a late Christmas supper. Doris Wildgoose did not tell her friends how the festive day had ended for her: how Cyril Kemp had held up a sprig of mistletoe and kissed her beneath it – and how she had responded, not discouraging his attempts at further intimacy after the children were in bed. And she had no regrets . . .

When Miss Bird returned at last to 35 Richmond Street, there was a bulky parcel for her.

'I been lookin' at it, 'oldin' it, rattlin' it, an' I reckon it's summat to wear!' cried Rose Rawson. 'Come on, 'ere's a pair o' scissors to cut the string!'

Phyllis was mystified, for she had already received presents from her parents and Saul. Mildred Vaughan had given her a pair of cosy blue slippers, and as she unwrapped the parcel she saw a colour that matched them exactly: two shades of blue in a warm worsted material. It turned out to be a beautiful dressing gown with the initials PB embroidered on a pocket; a wide matching belt was also attached.

'Oooh, ain't that posh!' exclaimed Rose. ''Oo's it from? There's a card 'ere – what's it say?'

It said, 'With every good wish for Christmas and the New Year, from George Steynes.' And she hadn't even sent him a card.

'Cor! 'E must've asked that lady doctor,' said Rose admiringly. 'It's just the same colour as the slippers.'

'But I can't possibly accept it, can I?'

''Ow can yer refuse, gal? It won't do for nobody else, with them letters on.'

'Guess what, George Steynes is taking me to see *A Break in Time* at the Haymarket on Friday,' Dr Vaughan announced on New Year's Day, rather to Phyllis's surprise. She had gathered from one or two remarks made by Mildred that Steynes had shown an interest in her at one time, but that it was all over. Did this mean that it was starting again? Phyllis told herself that she hoped it was. It could be very difficult if he set his sights on herself, because, of course, any serious attachment would be quite out of the question.

'Oh, how nice. I believe it's very good,' she replied in a politely matter-of-fact tone.

382

Which made her reaction all the more surprising when the day came and Dr Vaughan said that she could not go: her throat ached, and she was sure that she was getting a cold.

'You'll have to go instead, Phyllis, I just couldn't face it,' she said, blowing her nose. 'Ugh!'

'Oh, *no*, I'm on call.'

'Mrs Starling can take over. Heaven knows we saw little enough of her over Christmas.'

'But he's expecting *you*, not me!'

'Don't argue, Phyllis. The ticket's been bought, and you have no possible reason for refusing. I know you'll do it as a kindness to me, otherwise I'll feel badly about letting him down.'

It was clearly going to be yet another occasion when Dr Vaughan got her own way, and there was no point in opposing her, thought Phyllis. She might as well go and enjoy the play.

It was a freezingly cold evening with a few powdery snowflakes whirling in the wind when the blue Morris Minor stopped at Mrs Rawson's door.

'I'm so sorry about this, Mr Steynes. Dr Vaughan isn't well, she's getting a cold.'

'Yes, poor Mildred. She telephoned me to say that she couldn't come, Miss Bird. Brrr! It's a cold night. Let me tuck you into your seat – there, now. Do you think you'll be warm enough?'

It was such an unfamiliar sensation to be looked after by a man, and at the theatre his solicitude continued. He led her to the cloakroom and waited while she divested herself of her cloak, and ordered coffee to be brought to them in the interval. When the lights were lowered and the curtain rose on Harold Berridge's latest play, Phyllis nestled luxuriously into her seat in the third row of the circle, and let herself be drawn into another world.

Steynes had the tact to keep silent during the play, but afterwards at a little supper club off Soho Square, he encouraged her to give her impressions of *A Break in Time*.

'It was well written and acted, Mr Steynes, but the end was rather melancholy, wasn't it?'

'Yes. For a moment I thought that the three men – the father and the two brothers – had actually come back to the girls and their mother, sitting there in the dusk by the fire. But then I realised that it was just the women imagining that they saw them.'

'Yes,' said Phyllis sombrely. 'The men were only memories from a time before the war.' She paused, putting down her fork on the plate. 'They were – ghosts.' She gave a shiver.

'My dear Miss Bird, don't let it upset you,' he said with quick concern.

'How can I not be upset?' she rejoined. 'I lost my own two brothers in the trenches. It's what separates my generation from yours. You missed the war.'

'Not quite, Miss Bird. I lost my father at Passchendaele, and had to grow up quickly to look after my widowed mother. She was grief-stricken.'

'Oh, Mr Steynes, of course, I'm sorry. Forgive me,' she muttered.

'It's all right, Miss Bird, I quite understand. But four or five years is hardly a generation,' he added with a smile. 'In fact you are just the sort of woman I most admire – a little older, more sensible, more thoughtful –'

'Like Dr Vaughan?' she interrupted, taking him by surprise, and for a moment he looked blank, though he answered quickly.

'I admire Dr Vaughan very much, of course – we all do – and it was through her that I met you, but she is absolutely devoted to her career. It's her life.'

Plus the fact that she wouldn't have you or your mother, thought Phyllis. And neither can I because I've got a secret that would shatter your illusions about me. But she smiled and after a short pause tried to change the subject.

'Did you get to visit Maud Ling?' she asked casually.

He shook his head. 'No. I telephoned Florizel, but La Belle Capogna told me in no uncertain terms that Miss Ling had been ill and was not receiving visitors. I sent her some flowers and I'll try again in the New Year. Poor Maudie.'

There was another pause, and then he asked suddenly, 'I say, couldn't you call me George? And let me call you Phyllis? It's such a pretty name – Greek, isn't it?'

'Yes, I believe that Phyllis was a shepherdess in Arcadia, but I'm Miss Bird of Lambeth, Mr Steynes,' she said firmly. 'And now I think it's time we were leaving. Mrs Rawson will be waiting up for me.'

When they stopped outside Number 35 he did not immediately get out of the car to open the passenger door. It was now snowing quite heavily, and the large, feathery flakes fell silently all around them. 'It's been a wonderful evening, Miss Bird – Phyllis – and I'm so grateful to Mildred for arranging it.'

'But she couldn't arrange to have a cold, Mr Steynes!'

'She hasn't *got* a cold, Phyllis. She assisted me in playing a little deception on you, just as she helped me to choose the dressing gown when she bought your slippers. I have to confess it, and I hope you'll forgive me,' he added as she stared back at him in the dim light of the streetlamp. 'Perhaps I shouldn't have told you. And please don't be cross with Mildred.'

Cocooned as they were in the car, she sensed the warmth of his body, the clean smell of his skin. Just for a moment she closed her eyes, and in the space of that half-second he reached out to her. She felt his lips, first softly on her cheek, and then upon her mouth. It was like her first kiss with Teddy Ling nearly seven years ago: it was electrifying, and she trembled.

'Phyllis dear, what's the matter? Are you cold? There's no need to be afraid,' he said quietly.

But she drew away as if pursued by demons from the past. A part of her wanted to tell him everything, here and now, all about Saul and how she had suffered for her weakness of one fatal night. *Tell him! Tell him before this goes any further – he has to know!* screamed the voice in her head.

But she didn't. She couldn't. Not at that moment.

'Thank you for everything, Mr Steynes, but I must go now.'

'But, Phyllis –'

'I must go. Let me go – please let me go!' Her voice rose, and the front door of Number 35 opened suddenly to reveal Rose Rawson standing like an avenging angel on the threshold.

'What's up, Phyllis? Are yer awright?'

'Yes, yes, Rose, quite all right. Good night, Mr Steynes, and thank you.'

When, the following day, Mildred asked her if she had enjoyed the play, she replied easily that it had been very good. 'And how is your cold, Dr Vaughan?'

*

January brought more misery to some of the poorest homes in the district when a sudden thaw and heavy rain caused the Thames to burst its banks, flooding many basement dwellings. College Street and Stamford Street were the worst affected, and any pregnant women due to be confined at home were admitted to Theodora House to ensure their safety. Children were given temporary accommodation wherever it could be found, and the Salvation Army provided family refuges. Father McTaggart took as many as could be fitted into the Holy Family parish hall, and went round shamelessly begging for blankets, warm clothing and anything useful that stores could supply. Gifts of money arrived at the town hall from all over London, but Phyllis could not help but compare these conscience-prompted donations with the tireless personal efforts of Father McTaggart, who was not a young man and was beginning to look somewhat dishevelled, in need of a clothes-brush and a razor. She began to understand something of the devotion he inspired, the unquestioning obedience with which his flock responded to his stern Roman Catholic teaching.

'Which Church is doing the most good at present?' she asked herself during one of the undercover clinic sessions at the vicarage. 'St Martha's? Or the Holy Family?' And could not decide upon a satisfactory answer.

The press came to report on the disaster, and George Steynes surveyed the scenes of wretchedness with both pity and anger.

'There's talk of a general election before the end of the year, and I've made up my mind to run as a candidate for Parliament,' he announced publicly. 'We need to get rid of Stanley Baldwin and a government that can only wrangle over revising the Book of Common Prayer while fellow countrymen are enduring conditions like these.'

This was well received by the birth-control campaigners. 'He's very young, but so was Pitt,' they said. 'He'll take our cause to victory when he gets into the House!'

Phyllis heard of his plans from Mildred Vaughan, and gave a secret sigh, half of relief and half of regret. His time now would be taken up with matters in which she could play no part. Yet no sooner had she come to this conclusion than he telephoned her at Richmond Street; she was out on a case, and Rose eagerly repeated his message when she got back.

''E 'opes ye're in good 'ealf, Phyllis, an' says 'e wants to visit that actor 'oo's in clink. The poor ol' sod's not very well, 'e says, so 'e wants yer to go wiv 'im 'cause yer was a friend of 'is.'

'Oh dear. Yes, I see. Poor Reggie. Did, er, Mr Steynes say he'd ring back, Rose?'

''E said will yer ring 'im back if it ain't too late, else 'e'll ring again tomorrer.'

'What time is it? Quarter past ten. I'll telephone now, then,' muttered Phyllis, her fingers shaking slightly as she lifted the speaker off its upright stand. He answered at once, and they made an arrangement to go to HM Prison at Wandsworth on the following Wednesday.

Phyllis was shocked at Thane's emaciated appearance in his prison garb, and her heart reproached her for not making contact before. She and Steynes sat opposite him at a plain deal table too wide for them to reach across and touch his hand. A watchful warder heard every word that was uttered.

388

'You're a ray of sunshine in this place, Phyllis,' said Reginald with a weak smile, though he had the look of a defeated man, betrayed by the one he most loved. 'I hope that life is treating you well these days, my dear.'

'I'm very well, thank you, Reggie,' she faltered as tears sprang to her eyes.

'Don't weep for me, dear child,' he said in that beautifully modulated voice that had once filled the auditorium of the Old Vic, but which had now become thin and weak. 'I've had a good life, better than most, and memories are a treasure that can never be taken away.'

Phyllis could not speak, and Steynes took the opportunity to fill the silence. 'Have you seen anything of Maud Ling, er, Reg?'

'Ah, yes, my dearest and best friend. Once again she defied the signora and came to visit me within these walls. Alas, her film career is over like mine, but in her case it's due to these talking pictures. It could be a death-blow to her.'

'Oh, no! Poor Maud – I must go and see her,' said Phyllis, wiping her eyes on a handkerchief handed to her by Steynes.

'Darling Maudie, she did her best for me in court, but after Timbo turned against me I really did not care what happened. A man in my position is always in danger. To love is to risk everything, and I lost, as I knew I would in the end.' He lowered his eyes. 'But I can look back on my glorious days in the theatre, and then in films with Maud and my Timbo – they were the happiest days of my life. Ah, yes, my dear young people, I've lived more than most!'

For a moment his hollow eyes shone, and his gaunt features softened into a semblance of the former good looks that had set female hearts fluttering. Phyllis remembered how she had once fantasised about Reginald Thane making love to her, and even now she blushed at the recollection.

'Oh, Reggie, I'm so sorry to see you in a place like this,' she said with a sob.

'Hush, Phyllis dear, I'm a philosopher, remember. "Stone walls do not a prison make, Nor iron bars a cage" – my thoughts can still take wing,' he intoned as if on stage, and his hearers smiled in spite of themselves, as he clearly enjoyed having an audience.

After fifteen minutes they were told that their time was up, and no handshake or kiss was allowed, though Phyllis blew one to him as they went out of the door.

'I'm very grateful to you, George,' she said simply when they were outside the grim building and he took her arm as they walked down Heathfield Road to where he had parked the car. 'And I'm glad we went today, because I feel that we may never see him again in this world.'

'I'm glad, too, Phyllis,' was all that Steynes answered, giving her arm a squeeze. They both knew that this sad visit had brought them a step closer to each other.

At the beginning of March the pupils' examination results were put up on the notice-board in Theodora House, and great was the rejoicing when it was known that all of them had passed. Nurses Anderson and Lamb did well, Nurse Wildgoose just scraped by and Nurse Webb's former experience was taken into consideration and set against her blotted, misspelled essays, which would otherwise have condemned her to failure. Miss Bird gave a little informal tea-party in the District Room, at which Mr Poole looked in to congratulate the newly qualified midwives and their teachers Miss Bird and Mrs Starling.

'I hope we can count on you all to stay on and give a year or two of service now that you are on the Register,' he told them. 'We need all the good midwives we can lay hands on!'

'Well, now, Mr Poole, I reckon I'll be able to stay around and help out on the district,' said Ginny Webb affably. 'After all, I know it like the back o' me hand.'

'Actually, I've got my eye on the position of deputy matron at a mother-and-baby home, Mr Poole,' said Barbara Lamb eagerly. 'The other deputy had to have a breast removed, poor woman, and the LLC will be wanting a replacement.'

'Is that the place at ninety Riverside Gardens?' asked the consultant with interest. 'Ah, yes, they need a good, caring sort of woman to encourage those unfortunate girls. Good luck with your application, Nurse Lamb, and I'll gladly give you a reference.'

'I'll be staying on at Theodora House, Mr Poole,' said Carrie Anderson. 'And doing what I can for the SPBCC.'

'Good girl.' He beamed at her. 'And what about Nurse Wildgoose?'

Doris blushed and muttered some non-committal reply. Miss Bird came to her rescue.

'Nurse Wildgoose is very much appreciated on the district, sir. I'm sure we can count on her to stay in Lambeth.'

And so they could, thought Doris, but not as a midwife for much longer. She was soon to be quietly married to Cyril Kemp, and take on his three children; and if her suspicions were correct there would be a fourth by next Christmas. She counted herself as very lucky, a plain spinster who a year ago had decided to take up midwifery to fill her empty life. And now everything was changed. She had yet to break the news to her parents – and what on earth would Miss Bird say? Deep down in her heart Doris Wildgoose had no qualms, for she was happier than she had ever been in her life.

'When may I see you, Phyllis? I need to talk to you. Are you free on Sunday afternoon? My mother would like you to come to tea, and perhaps we could drive up to the Heath. Please, Phyllis, when may I see you?'

George Steynes was not going to take no for an answer, and Phyllis's heart quailed. She knew that the moment of truth was fast approaching.

'Please thank your mother for her invitation, George, but I'd rather not come to tea with her yet – not before I've spoken to you,' she said steadily. 'I have a half-day on Sunday, and if you'd like to call for me at about three, we could go for a drive and perhaps walk up on the Heath, if that's what you'd like.'

Chapter 22

Phyllis hardly slept an hour on the night before her meeting with George Steynes, and would have welcomed a busy Sunday morning to take her mind off the coming ordeal, as she saw it; but the district was relatively quiet that weekend, and Mrs Starling was well able to cope with any calls that might come in. Phyllis took Sunday dinner in the dining room of the infirmary, to avoid Rose Rawson's eagle eye, though the landlady was tactfully silent while her lodger was dressing in readiness for the moment when the Morris Minor arrived on the stroke of three.

'Good luck, Phyllis – don't be too 'ard on yerself, 'cause I reckon '*e* won't be 'ard on yer, neiver,' she said with a meaning look as Phyllis put on her hat and gloves. They had not discussed Mr Steynes in any detail, yet the words seemed to indicate that Mrs Rawson understood what was in Phyllis's mind, and what she would have to confess – *if* she confessed.

Little was said on the journey, but the tension in the car was almost palpable as Steynes drove over Waterloo Bridge towards Euston, passing up through Camden Town and Kentish Town, and parking the car at Gospel Oak Station.

'It's a bracing, blowy day, Phyllis – shall we walk up to the top of Parliament Hill Fields? Will you take my arm?' he offered, but they walked at such a brisk pace, climbing breathlessly up over the green expanse, that it was inconvenient to link arms. It seemed to Phyllis that they were deliberately making it difficult to talk: they both knew that something important had to be said, but it was as if they were postponing it for as long as possible.

He's going to ask me to marry him, and I'm going to have to tell him why I can't, she thought, dreading the moment and wondering if he sensed that dread.

It had to come. As they arrived at the summit with its magnificent view over the Heath to the north and extending as far as the Surrey hills south beyond the Thames, Steynes seized Phyllis's arm and began to tell her what was in his mind and heart.

'You may have heard of my intention to stand for Parliament in the next general election, Phyllis,' he said as they walked on the windy height. 'I would like to represent a constituency as close as possible to where we are – Bermondsey, perhaps, or Walworth North. I feel that this is the best way in which I can serve the people, to improve their living conditions and of course to get council-run BC clinics on the statute book. I'm young, I'm strong, and I want to use what talent I've got to the best advantage.'

She glanced up at his face, reddened by the wind, eager and earnest. 'I'm sure that you'll do well, George.'

'And Phyllis, you must know what I'm going to say next. I feel the necessity for a wife – in fact, I've felt this for some time, but especially now that I'm hoping to be a Member of Parliament. I need a good woman, Phyllis, a woman I can love and rely upon, and there's only one that I know who could fulfil those criteria.'

It was unbearable, and Phyllis drew away from him in agitation. 'Stop, George, stop. Don't say any more, don't go any further – stop and listen to what

I've got to say!' she cried, to his total bewilderment and consternation.

'Why, Phyllis my dear, what on earth is the matter? Is it that you feel you couldn't love me in that way? Don't you see yourself as the wife of an MP? I can assure you, other people think the same as I do. Mildred Vaughan admires and respects you, and Mr Poole told me himself that he considers you an excellent midwife and caring woman –'

'Oh, stop, *stop*, never mind about other people. It's nothing to do with them and, in any case, they don't know the truth!' She was almost hysterical in denying any good spoken of her. 'For God's sake, *listen* to me!'

'Phyllis dear, come and sit down,' he said, taking her hand and leading her to a public bench seat. 'Calm yourself, dear, and tell me whatever it is that's troubling you. I'm listening.'

But she hid her face from him and he had to listen over her shoulder. 'It's so difficult, George, because I've got to tell you something that will make you change your mind about me – and yet it's about the dearest thing in life to me – my son!'

'I – I beg your pardon, Phyllis – did you say your *son*? You mean you have a child?' asked Steynes, trying to make sense of what he had just heard. 'Oh, are you a war widow? Is that what you're saying?'

'No, no, George, I'm not a widow, though I've been tempted to call myself one – to pretend that I am. But I've never been married. I'm thirty-two this year, and my little boy, Saul, will be five on the twenty-sixth of this month, that's a week tomorrow. He lives with my parents at North Camp. They're bringing him up and I'm grateful, but – but I just live for my monthly weekends off when I go to see him. I'm not really a proper mother to him, not in the way his granny is. And I love him so much.'

She turned her head and looked straight into George Steynes' grey eyes, full of baffled surprise. 'I'm sorry, George, there were times when I nearly told you, but it didn't seem to be the right moment, and I wasn't sure how interested you were in me. But I'm telling you now, I'm an unmarried mother with an illegitimate child. And now you know.'

It was a relief to have it said, though to Steynes it was clearly a blow, and he showed it.

'I really don't know what to say, Phyllis. This is so *unexpected*, the last thing I thought I'd hear from a woman who –'

'Ah, yes, George, you don't expect to hear such a tale from an excellent woman like me, do you? Fallen woman, more like!' she said with a short, bitter laugh. 'No better than those poor creatures in the Home for Wayward Girls!'

'Hush, Phyllis, I didn't mean it like that. I'm just rather shaken, that's all. Does Mildred . . .?'

'No, she doesn't. Nobody in Lambeth knows about Saul except for Mrs Rawson. It's why I never go back to Richmond where they *do* know. Maud knows. She actually paid for me to stay at a private mother-and-baby home at Epsom.'

'Did she? Did she really?' he asked, astonished.

'Yes, she's got a heart of gold, and I haven't even been to see her now that her career's over and her health's failing, by what Reg said. But now I think I *will* go, though I don't expect you to come with me.'

'Oh, Phyllis, forgive me. I'm just beginning to realise what you've been through. And you were obviously deserted by the – the father. May I ask who he was – who he is, if you don't mind telling me?'

'Oh, no, George, the less said about him the better, though of course I have to take my share of respons— of the blame. I was terribly upset about Teddy Ling at the time, you see. We were in love, or at least I was. He was so young, and – and there was this American actress who came over. He just took one look at her and that was that. He very nearly came back to me at one pint, but in the end he followed her to the States.'

'Where he's quite a name in Hollywood, I believe,' Steynes interposed. 'And he's married some actress, though I don't know who. But oh, Phyllis, my dear, I think I understand. I can see it now – yes, I can see why Maud paid your fees at the home. It was Teddy Ling, wasn't it? Oh, how could he have treated you like that? I thought better of him!'

This wrong conclusion added to Phyllis's distress. 'No, no, it wasn't Teddy. That's what Maud thought at first, but she was quite wrong. Teddy would never have behaved so dishonourably. It was an actor, and he went back to California without even knowing about Saul.'

'Are you just shielding Ling?'

'*No!* You mustn't believe it of him. I just hope that he's happy now with whoever he married. There, George, I've told you, and I'm sorry I didn't tell you earlier – but you know now and it's a relief to have it out. Do you want to go home now?'

She half-rose from the seat, but he put out an arm to draw her back.

'No, Phyllis, wait. I'm not going to let you run away. We just can't leave it there. I've had a shock, it's true, something I never ever thought to hear, but it doesn't alter what I know about you – what I've learned over the past few months about your work and your – your worth. But now I need to learn a little more about what you've told me.'

She saw that he was making a real effort to adjust to this new aspect of Miss Phyllis Bird.

'You say that this child lives at North Camp with your parents, and you visit him when you can?'

'Yes, on my weekends off each month, and for one week every year when my mother and I take him to Hayling Island. His granny worships the ground he walks on – for her he's been a replacement for my two brothers. She'd never give him up under any circumstances.'

'Do you mean that if you were to marry, your mother would not part with him?'

'No, never.' Phyllis spoke with absolute conviction, and the reply seemed to give Steynes a certain reassurance. There was silence between them for a thoughtful minute, and then he gently took hold of her gloved hand again.

'When are you planning to visit North Camp again?'

'Next weekend. His birthday's on the Monday, the twenty-sixth, and I'll be able to spend the Saturday and Sunday with him.' A look of pure love softened her pale features, and some of the tension eased. 'He'll be starting at the infants' school after Easter.'

'So, Phyllis, my dear, will you let me drive you down next weekend? And may I meet my rival for your affections? What did you say his name was – Saul?'

Phyllis turned herself round on the wooden bench and looked into Steynes' grey eyes in total incredulity: she saw nothing but tenderness in their depths.

'You want to meet Saul?' she asked, hardly daring

to believe her ears. 'Do you really want to see my son?'

'Yes, Phyllis, I do. And I also want to meet your parents and tell them how I feel about you.' He smiled at the joy dawning in her eyes. 'Do I have to ask your father's permission to marry his daughter?'

Phyllis continued to gaze back at him in disbelief, until he put his arms around her and drew her close to him on the seat. A couple passed them with a child in a pushchair, and an elderly gentleman walking his dog stopped and stared at the woman clasped in a man's arms, her face hidden against his shoulder, overcome by happiness.

Phyllis begged that nothing be said to anybody as yet, and she declined to accept Mrs Steynes' invitation to tea until after George's visit to North Camp. In her own mind she wanted to give him time and opportunity to reconsider his proposal. Her mother would need to be reassured that Saul would not be taken away from her, and Phyllis herself wanted time to plan for her future as a married woman and possibly the wife of an MP. She would have to give up her district midwifery, but she would continue her work for the SPBCC and play a more active public role in the campaign. Who should be told? Rose Rawson, of course, and Mildred Vaughan, who had been instrumental in bringing about this amazing turn of events. But both must be sworn to secrecy for the time being.

Can a romantic attachment ever be kept secret? Where do rumours start? No sooner had Mrs Webb, the registered midwife, diagnosed her colleague Miss Wildgoose's interesting condition than whispers about Miss Bird's meetings with a newspaper editor were spreading like wildfire through Theodora House and around the district.

If Phyllis's heart fluttered on the journey down to North Camp that Friday evening, it was a pleasurable tremor. Her parents had been asked to book a room for Mr Steynes at the Queen's Hotel on the Aldershot Road, but he would spend Saturday and Sunday with the Birds in Rectory Road, and drive Phyllis back to London on Sunday evening. A pre-birthday celebration was planned for Saul – a little tea-party on Saturday and a drive out into the Hampshire countryside on Sunday afternoon with Phyllis and George: it was too early in the year for a picnic, Mrs Bird decided. Saul was told that Mummy was bringing a gentleman with her, and his name was Uncle George.

'Mum, this is George – George, this is my mother and Dad. Where's Saul?'

'In bed and asleep, Phyllis. You don't expect him to be up this late, do you?' Mrs Bird held out her hand. 'I'm very pleased to meet you, Mr – er –'

'Oh, please call me George, Mrs Bird. Delighted to meet you both. I've heard so much about you from Phyllis.'

Ernest Bird shook Steynes' hand warmly. 'And it's a real pleasure to welcome you, George. Just make yourself at home.'

Phyllis slipped quietly upstairs to look upon Saul sleeping sweetly in his little room and to put her suitcase in the one she occupied next to his. Mr Bird took George's coat and showed him to the newly installed indoor WC. At seven the three of them sat down to a supper of cold ham and boiled beetroot with bread-and-butter, followed by apple tart and

400

custard; Mr Bird asked George about his work on the *Daily Chronicle*, and Phyllis eagerly heard her mother's news of Saul, soon to be starting at Miss Daniells' Infants' school. After the meal they listened to the wireless, and the men commented on the worsening unemployment figures and the growing unpopularity of Lloyd George, rejected by a large number of his own Liberal Party members, and the desirability of an early election. Steynes took his leave soon after nine and said he would see them in the morning at about ten, 'if that's convenient for you, Mrs Bird.'

'Good night, George,' said Phyllis as she saw him out of the front gate. 'It's so strange to see you here at home with Mother and Dad – and tomorrow you'll meet Saul. Oh, George, you've made such a difference to – to everything.'

'And so have you, Phyllis,' he told her, kissing her cheek, for there was indeed something different about her here in her parents' home. Miss Bird the efficient midwife had been left behind in Lambeth, and this Phyllis was a rather hesitant girl, subject to her mother's authority. And he loved them both.

Saul awoke to smiles and kisses from Mummy, who told him that he was soon going to see Uncle George. She became increasingly nervous as ten o'clock approached, and when the Morris Minor drew up outside she hurried down the garden path to greet her fiancé and bring him in to be introduced to the little boy, who stared up at him curiously.

'Are you Uncle George?'

'Yes, and what's *your* name, young fellow?' asked George, stooping down so as to be on the same level as the boy.

'Saul. What's in that parcel?'

'Ah! I wonder! Do you like trains, Saul? Steam engines?'

'Yes. Is that a toy engine in there?'

'You'd better have a look and see.' And in fact the parcel turned out to be a brightly painted wooden engine with movable wheels and a tender attached for little black wooden lumps of coal that Saul could shovel into the engine. His eyes sparkled. 'Is it for me?'

'Yes, Saul, it's for you – from me.'

'Oooh!'

'What do you say, Saul?' asked his granny.

'Thank you!'

'Thank you who?' prompted his mummy.

'Thank you, Uncle George!'

It was a good start to what was on the whole a successful visit. George adopted a friendly, avuncular attitude towards Saul without intruding on the boy's closeness to his grandparents and mother. Mrs Bird was entirely satisfied with him, especially on learning that he had no intention of taking Saul from her care.

Later that Saturday morning Phyllis took her fiancé to see the shop, and Mr Bird took the opportunity to have a private word with him while Phyllis and Saul wandered along the Parade.

'Phyllis was most unfortunate, and suffered more than she deserved,' Bird told Steynes frankly. 'She has shown a great deal of courage in making a new life for herself in London, and I am very proud of her.'

'I'm sure you are, sir,' replied Steynes, whose first favourable impression of this man was now fully confirmed. 'She's very well respected in Lambeth, I can assure you.'

'It's looked upon as a disaster, of course, when a single woman has a child, and Phyllis has had to face more humiliation than sympathy in a place like this,' Bird continued. 'But in our case, it's been our salvation, the greatest blessing we could have had. We lost both our sons in the war, as you'll know, and it almost killed my wife too. She seemed to have no interest in anything, no love for anybody – not for myself or Phyllis. She was only half alive, but the moment she saw Saul and took him in her arms . . .'

Ernest Bird blinked and swallowed, then continued in a husky tone, 'It brought her to life again, George. She worships that boy, and sometimes I feel sorry for Phyllis. Mrs Bird has suggested that Phyllis might call herself a widow – but Phyllis wouldn't have it, and besides, everybody here knows that she's single.'

'Thank you very much for telling me, sir. I shall respect your confidence,' said Steynes with real warmth. He felt drawn towards this man who was to be his father-in-law, and was more aware of the balance of relationships between these four people, soon to be five, for he would be part of the family.

Two little sisters aged six and three, and one boy of seven came to the birthday party on Saturday afternoon to partake of sandwiches, jelly, little jam tarts baked by Mrs Bird and of course the birthday cake she had made, a large Victoria sandwich filled with raspberry jam and covered with white icing on which five fat blue candles were lit at the end of tea-time. Phyllis led the singing of 'Happy Birthday', although it was two days earlier than the actual date, and then there were games to play with balloons – 'Mind you don't burst them, or he'll be frightened!' warned Granny – but the older boy and girl were more interested in leading Saul away to play on the stairs, where they climbed up and tumbled down in a shouting heap of arms and legs.

'Stop that at once! Somebody will bump their head, and then what will the parents say?' Mrs Bird marched the naughty trio back into the parlour to play 'Sticking the donkey's tail on', which involved being blindfolded, and quickly developed into a more boisterous game of blind-man's buff. Their gleeful shouts caused Granny to shake her head and say that Saul would be overexcited and wouldn't be able to sleep, but Phyllis rejoiced to see her son having such a good time with other children.

'He's really ready for school, isn't he?' she said to George, and when Granddad arrived home from the shop, he heard what a wonderful party it had been.

On Sunday morning they all went to church, and Phyllis smiled and greeted members of the congregation, including Mrs Allingham and Miss Jarvis, now used to the sight of Saul trotting in with his grandparents. She wondered what they would make of the serious-looking gentleman at her side: let them speculate, she thought – and just wait until he's an MP!

After a good roast Sunday dinner, Phyllis and George set out with Saul for a drive into rural Hampshire, now awakening to spring. It was a clear, breezy day, the daffodils were out in golden glory along the lanes, and primroses peeped from grassy banks. They had planned to stop at Beversley, a pretty village with a quaint High Street still much as it had been in the eighteenth century, its ancient church at one end and the village school at the other; but before they reached it disaster struck.

Poor Saul was not used to cars, and the twisting

and turning of country lanes was too much for his little stomach after his dinner. He turned as white as a sheet and was suddenly, violently sick. As he was sitting on his mother's lap in the passenger seat, the vomit went all over the dashboard, Phyllis's dress and George's trousers; it seemed to be everywhere.

'Oh, George, I'm so sorry!' wailed Phyllis as he stopped the car at a crossroads where other cars could pass. Saul began to cry, and Phyllis hugged him, which spread the sour-smelling mess even further. George had a large handkerchief and Phyllis a small one, but apart from a chamois leather used for wiping the car windows, there was nothing adequate to clear it up. They had no choice but to return to North Camp and face Mrs Bird's predictable reaction.

'Didn't I say you were asking for trouble, Phyllis, taking him out so soon after dinner when he's never been in a car before!' she scolded. 'Come to Granny, you poor little love. We'll have those clothes off you and get you in a nice warm bath. Ernest, put that big pan on to boil! And after that he'll need a rest. *I* don't know!'

George sponged his trousers at the kitchen sink while still wearing them, as he had no others to put on, and Phyllis changed her dress and wiped their shoes. She took a pail and floorcloth out to the car and cleaned it as well as she could, but the smell still lingered and remained with them on their journey back to London.

'Don't worry, Phyllis dear, it's been a wonderful weekend apart from that,' George told her, smiling. 'Don't blame yourself.'

'But I *do* blame myself. I should have been better prepared. I didn't even have a facecloth or a towel with me,' she sighed, and George privately considered that where Saul was concerned Phyllis was always blamed for what went wrong but never praised when things went well.

When George suggested a visit to Florizel one afternoon in the week before Easter, Phyllis had to decline because on her one and only half-day Doris Wildgoose was being quietly married to Cyril Kemp at Pond Street Methodist Chapel, and Phyllis felt bound to support her former pupil, now a registered midwife and 'beginning to show', as Ginny Webb remarked. Miss Bird took no part in the storm of gossip or the gloomy predictions of the life in store for the second Mrs Kemp in the cramped little house in Homer Street. She chatted pleasantly to bowler-hatted Mr Wildgoose, a Walworth butcher, and his anxious-looking wife; they were evidently putting a good face on the situation. Doris had confided to her that her father might offer Kemp a place in his shop with a view to a possible partnership later, as their son had not survived the war. Today was a time to look on the bright side and make the best of things.

With three young children to care for, there was to be no wedding-trip, but at the modest reception in the Methodist Hall, everybody praised the excellent cold beef and pork supplied by Mr Wildgoose and served with pickled onions, beetroot and cucumber. An unexpected surprise was the delivery of a good rich fruit cake from a local confectioner's with a card to the newlyweds signed, 'From Herbert Poole, with best wishes for your future.' Miss Bird gave them a rug for their bedroom and a couple of Witney blankets, but the new Mrs Kemp was grateful above all for her strong diplomatic presence.

*

It was on Easter Sunday, a week into April, that George Steynes took his wife-to-be to tea with his mother at the house in Nelson Square. Phyllis hid her nervousness and spoke with dignified courtesy; George had explained to Mrs Steynes that Phyllis was his choice, and the widow received her with conventional politeness but no real warmth. Mrs Steynes obviously considered that any young woman her son might choose to marry was extremely fortunate, and when she asked Phyllis about her family background and was told that Mr and Mrs Bird lived at North Camp where Mr Bird kept a tailor's shop, she managed to convey her belief that George could have done better for himself.

What she was *not* told was that Phyllis had a child. This had been decided beforehand when George had suggested that it might be easier not to tell her and, after some discussion, Phyllis had reluctantly agreed.

'These things have a way of coming out eventually, George, and I think it would be much wiser to have no secrets, right from the start,' she had said earnestly.

'But, Phyllis dear, we don't want to start off by giving her a shock,' George had reasoned gently. 'It isn't as if we're going to take on Saul. He's always going to live with your parents, isn't he?'

'They won't live for ever, George. If anything should happen to either one of them, I'd have to take him, of course I would.'

'Yes, but by then we'll have been married long enough to be – er – established, perhaps with children of our own. Please, let's not tell her yet, dear. Let's not put an obstacle in our way right at the outset.'

407

Phyllis did not want to put an obstacle in her own way by disagreeing with George at this early stage in their as yet unofficial engagement, and so she gave in; but it made her more apprehensive with Mrs Steynes, a woman she feared she could never truly like.

'Let me warn you both not to be overhasty,' said the majestic old lady. '*You* are still very young, George, to be contemplating a Parliamentary career, and I don't think you should be in too much of a hurry to make this other announcement. Next spring will be time enough.'

'But, Mother, that could be right in the middle of a general election!' protested George, laughing.

'Exactly. If you take my advice – and that of your uncles – you will wait until after the next election when you may be a new Member of Parliament.'

She's playing for time, thought Phyllis; she wants him to change his mind and choose a younger woman from a better background. But she smiled and inclined her head as the Honourable Mrs Agatha Steynes lifted the Georgian silver teapot. She would not do or say anything that might possibly make George ashamed of her.

When Phyllis arrived at 35 Richmond Street after a morning spent visiting newly delivered mothers and their babies, she found her old friend Mrs Williams sitting in the kitchen drinking tea with her mother.

'I'll pour yer a cup, Phyllis,' said Rose, getting up on her little bandy legs. 'Me daughter's brought us some o' them nice biscuits from the Berridges. The cook made an extra batch.' She winked, for this was a regular practice.

As well as the biscuits, Mrs Williams had brought

news from Richmond. 'We're all at sixes an' sevens, Phyllis,' she said gloomily. 'Claud's started 'avin' fits, an' Mr Berridge was that upset when 'e got back from Tall Pines last week, 'e just shut 'imself up in 'is study an' wouldn't speak to nobody, only Dr Godley.'

'Oh, poor Mr Berridge,' said Phyllis sadly, for she had learned to pity the man she had once so despised. 'And poor Claud. He must be eleven this year.'

'Yeah, but I can only think of 'im as the little chap 'e was when we last saw 'im,' said Mrs Williams. 'An' now 'e sounds no better 'n them poor invalid soldiers in the Star an' Garter 'Ome. They say there's some terrible sights in there, men 'oo've lorst their arms 'n legs, lorst their minds, shakin' all the time, Gawd 'elp 'em, ten years after the end o' the war.'

Phyllis shivered. 'And Mrs Berridge?' she prompted.

'Oh, *she* 'ardly ever goes to see Claud,' replied Mrs Williams contemptuously. 'Shallow, that's what she is, always showin' Edith orf in pretty dresses like 'er own, an' makin' a fuss o' Michael – not but what 'e's a dear little feller. But Claud might as well be –' She checked herself, but Phyllis knew that she was about to say 'dead', and her own thoughts turned as always to Saul, so normal and healthy. She wished she could convey her sympathy to Berridge, but of course she couldn't, and what good would it do?

Mrs Williams seemed to be thinking along the same lines, for she sighed and said, 'Poor ol' Berridge. I reckon the doctor's the only one 'e can talk to about Claud.'

'Does the doctor call very often?' asked Phyllis, as memories resurfaced of Godley's close association with the family and his kindness to herself.

''E drops in most weeks, an' they take a glass or two in the study. Mind yer, Godley's lookin' a bit glum 'imself these days. I 'eard 'e was trying' to get Maud Ling into a sanatorium, but that Italian 'ousekeeper won't let 'er go. Gallopin' consumption, they say,' she added, seeing Phyllis's shocked expression. 'Sad, innit? She was so lovely with Reginald Thane in that *Wings o' Love* film – but now 'e's in prison an' she's not goin' to see the year out, an' only thirty-six.'

'Oh, my God,' murmured Phyllis. 'Look, Rose, I'm going to ring Twickenham exchange now, and arrange to visit her.'

A distracted Belle Capogna took her call and more or less confirmed what had been said.

'But she will not go from Florizel, I tell you as I tell Dr Godley!' she said angrily, as if Phyllis was contradicting her. 'She will have no nurse but me, and I will not let her go!'

Phyllis next put through a call to the *Daily Chronicle*, and asked to speak to Mr George Steynes in Editorial.

'Let's go to see her, George, as soon as we can,' she urged. 'Can you drive me over tomorrow? Mrs Starling can cover for me.'

'Tomorrow afternoon,' he answered at once, for he too was seized by a sense of urgency after such a long time without contact.

And it was as if they had never been away. Maud was lying on the chaise longue with even more cushions and shawls than they remembered. She wore a lilac-coloured robe with wide sleeves that fell back when she opened her arms to Phyllis.

'I 'ad a feelin' ye'd be over today, duck, ever since

410

Belle told me yer rung up. Cor, don't yer look grand! An' 'oo's this? Nah! Don't tell me – it can't be – it *is*! Little Georgie Steynes, as I live an' breave! Come an' give us a kiss, bofe o' yer – omigawd!'

'Maudie, I'm sorry I haven't been in touch for so long –'

''Sall right, duck, I understand.'

'Maud, you're as exquisite as ever,' said George, and meant it, for there was a transparency about her beauty now that made her seem more ethereal; with her delicately pale skin and flushed cheeks, her huge hazel eyes and sweet mouth painted in a Cupid's bow, she was a vision of loveliness.

'I 'eard yer went an' saw poor ol' Reggie. I'm tryin' to get 'im aht o' there 'fore 'e turns 'is toes up. Nice if 'e could come 'ere, else I shan't see 'im agen. Belle's a dragon an' won't let me aht.'

'Maudie dear, we've got something to tell you,' said Phyllis, wiping her eyes and smiling. 'George and I –'

'Yeah, I reckoned there must be summat goin' on, what wiv yer bofe goin' to see Reg an' comin' 'ere togevver. 'Ooever would've fought it, eh? Yer little devils, gettin' up to tricks like this be'ind me back!'

'George has been so good and kind to me, Maudie. He's been to visit my parents and he's met my little boy.' Phyllis hesitated, glancing at George as she spoke, and Maud raised her pencilled eyebrows in a question.

'Your little boy, Phyllis?' she asked, giving an imperceptible nod in George's direction.

'It's all right, Maud dear, he knows all about my Saul and how good you were to me five years ago. My parents adopted him, you know.'

411

'An' George don't mind, then? Good on yer, George! Yer got a good one there – an' *you're* very lucky an' all, Phyllis.'

'Yes, Maud, I know.' They spoke and smiled in unison, exchanging a loving look.

''S a funny fing, but I keep rememberin' me own boy these days – 'e'll be ten nah, an' bein' brought up like a proper gent! I don't 'arf wish I could see 'im, though, just once before – y'know – but it'd upset 'im. 'E prob'ly finks 'is muvver's dead – it's the sort of fing the Redferns 'ud say – but p'raps one day 'e'll find aht she was Maud Ling o' the silver screen!'

'Oh, Maudie, it's so hard on you,' said Phyllis, while George stared in consternation, and Phyllis realised that he knew nothing about Maud's son.

'Yes, her fiancé was in the Royal Flying Corps and was shot down before the boy was born,' she whispered. 'She was very ill after his birth, and the grandparents just came and took him. She hasn't seen Alex since he was a tiny baby.'

'Oh, my God, what a tragedy. I never knew.'

'Not many do. Maud confided in me when I was expecting Saul.'

''Ere, that's enough whisperin', if yer don't mind! And don't be too dahn in the marf. I 'ad some wonderful years makin' films wiv Reggie – that's somefing to remember. I couldn't't've stayed on at the studios anyway, not wiv these bleedin' talkies. They're makin' 'em at Twickenham nah, an' it's a right how-de-do! Yer know the studios back on to the railway line – well, they 'as to put a bloke up on the roof to look aht for when a train's comin', then 'e 'as to give a signal wiv a red light to the studios to stop filmin' till the train's gorn past, then up goes a green light to show it's all clear! Ovverwise they'd 'ave the

412

train roarin' past right in the middle of a touchin' love scene!'

Maud's peals of laughter were irresistible, and her visitors joined in; but hers turned to a paroxysm of coughing, and Belle rushed in to offer cordials and cough syrup.

'This is just what Dr Godley says you must not do!' she cried. 'You are tired, you must rest and the lady and gentleman must go now!'

'Oh, shut up, Belle, for Gawd's sake – an' they ain't no lady an' gen'leman, they're Phyllis and George!' gasped Maud, swallowing a spoonful of cherry linctus and grimacing at its bitter aftertaste. 'An' never mind abaht poor ol' Charles Godley. 'E's got troubles of 'is own since Pamela married that Irish doctor an' knocks aht kids year after year. They got four already, Phyllis.'

'Good heavens! She had her first when I had Saul, so that must be nearly one a year.'

'Not quite, but she 'ad a late miscarriage last year, an' now she's in the club agen, poor gal.'

'Sounds as if she needs some of *your* advice, Phyllis,' murmured George with a half-smile.

'What? Oh, no, not if they're strict Roman Catholics,' replied Phyllis, and Maud, of course, demanded an explanation.

'Blimey! George is right, duck, she *does* need one o' them corks put in, wivout Paddy knowin',' she said. 'D'yer remember, George, we talked abaht birf control at a dinner party years ago at the Berridges'. I didn't know where to look, I was that embarrassed!'

'Yes, I do remember, Maudie. It was when I first got involved with the campaign. And to think that Phyllis was there and I never even noticed her.'

'You tend not to notice the domestic servants when

you go to dinner parties, George,' Phyllis pointed out, and they laughed again.

It seemed a good moment for Phyllis to ask about Teddy. 'How is your brother, these days, Maudie? Is he likely to stay in Hollywood?'

'I reckon so, duck. Belle's been mumblin' summat abaht askin' 'im to come over for a visit, an' 'e said 'e would, just as soon as 'e's finished work on the film 'e's shootin'. Must say I'd like to see the little blighter agen. 'E got married, y'know, but not to Georgia. She's been frough a couple of 'usbands.'

'Is he – happy?'

'Dunno, duck. Not as 'appy as 'e'd've bin wiv you, I dare say, but there y'are, 'e was too young an' unsteady. But nah ye've got yerself nicely fixed up wiv a good man 'oo'll look after yer like a man should.'

Maud suddenly drooped and lay back on her cushions as if she had used up all her energy, and made no attempt to oppose the signora when she bustled in again to tell the visitors that it was time for them to leave. George kissed the actress and promised they would send a wedding invitation in the not-too-distant future. When Phyllis leaned over to kiss her she put up a thin arm to pull her close and whisper in her ear.

'Fanks for comin', duck. I'm ever so 'appy for yer. Yer deserve it. Goodbye, Phyllis gal.'

'Isn't it the most awful shame about her son!' exclaimed George when they were seated in the car. 'Can nothing be done about it? I mean, *I* could call on these Redfern people and put it to them that Maud's very ill and longing to see the boy.'

'No, George. You heard what she said. It would be too much of a shock for him at ten years old, after believing that his mother was dead – or that she had deserted him. It could be very disturbing for him – and you never know, a disappointing reaction might be just as distressing for her. No, we mustn't interfere.'

'I suppose you're right, Phyllis my love – you usually are!' he said, and kissed her before driving off.

At Number 15 Nelson Square the Honourable Mrs Agatha Steynes was opening her letters with a silver paper-knife. The last one was typewritten and postmarked London, so she assumed it was probably concerned with the SPBCC. When she opened it and spread it out in front of her, however, she saw that it was a personal letter to herself, and there was no signature.

> With apologies for troubling your ladyship [the letter incorrectly began], it may not have come to your attention that your prospective daughter-in-law is the mother of an illegitimate child, a boy, born at Lahai-Roi Maternity Home near Epsom on 26 March 1923. The child now lives with his grandparents at North Camp, Hampshire.
>
> The existence of this child has been hushed up by his mother, who now holds a position of authority as a district midwife in Lambeth. She may have managed to persuade Mr George Steynes not to tell you her secret, but as a sincere well-wisher I think you should be told the truth.

An anonymous letter was despicable, of course, but before she threw it in the waste-paper basket Mrs

Steynes decided to confront Phyllis Bird with it. A gleam came into her cold grey eyes. This could be the very tool she needed to rescue her son from a misguided alliance.

Chapter 23

As the days lengthened, work on the district went through a busy period, and with new pupil-midwives to be supervised, Miss Bird and Mrs Starling seemed to be forever going out at all hours; the latter complained bitterly that she hardly saw her own family, and Phyllis found it hard to find the time to attend at the mobile clinic and the 'undercover' sessions at St Martha's vicarage, where sometimes Miss Anderson had to manage on her own. A night spent sitting up with a patient in labour might be followed by another busy day, and Mrs Rawson became concerned when her lodger rushed in and out looking pale with exhaustion and too tired even to eat. Phyllis tried to catch up on her sleep in the afternoons when she could.

'Ye'll be prop'ly run-down, gal, an' wear yerself to a shadder,' Rose grumbled. 'Mr George rang up this af'noon, but I told 'im yer was 'avin' a rest, or tryin' to.'

'Did he? Oh dear! I thought I heard the phone go, but I must have been fast asleep, and didn't really come to,' sighed Phyllis, stifling a yawn.

'No, I picked it up as quick as I could to shut it up. 'E said to give yer 'is love, an' can 'e come over on Fursday or Friday?'

'Oh, poor George! We want to go and see Maud again soon, but while the work's like this, I just can't get away,' Phyllis said with a frown. 'And the weekend's no good, because Mrs Starling's due to be off.'

'Why don't yer get that Mrs Webb to do a bit more?' asked Rose. 'She does enough gossipin', by what I 'ear.'

'Yes, that's the trouble with her. She's a good enough worker in her way, but . . . ah, well.'

Phyllis did not like to criticise the newly qualified midwife, now happily back to her old stamping-ground around the Elephant and Castle, but it was a fact that she and Ginny Webb had never truly got on, due to the older woman's resentment of Phyllis's senior status.

Rose nodded knowingly. 'Yeah, she's got too much to say abaht the muvvers, ain't she? Tells 'em orf when they fall for anuvver baby, an' blames the 'usbands all round the street. She finks she's the bee's knees, but they look on 'er as a joke, if she only knew it!'

'And she never gives them the right advice about preventing it from happening again. No, I don't really like asking for her help,' admitted Phyllis.

And yet the very next day she found herself doing just that.

'There's a letter for yer, Phyllis, came by second post,' said Rose when Phyllis got in after her morning visits, which included a mother delivered in the early hours.

'Just give me a cup of tea, Rose, and I'll go upstairs for a couple of hours – oh, all right, I'll have an egg on toast, but all I really want is a bit of shut-eye.'

'Aren't yer goin' to see 'oo it's from? It ain't from Norf Camp.'

It was most definitely not from North Camp. It was

a brief note from Mrs Steynes, asking Phyllis to telephone her and arrange a meeting at 15 Nelson Square 'as soon as you can find time in your busy schedule'.

She knows, thought Phyllis at once. She knows about Saul. She's going to ask me to give up George – and I will not.

'Blimey, yer gorn as white as a ghost, gal! What's up?'

'It's from George's mother.'

'Oh Gawd.'

'Yes. She wants to see me. She must have found out about Saul. I knew we should have told her straight away at the very beginning, but George didn't agree, and I didn't want an argument just as we were engaged. Now I wish I'd been firmer about it.'

'What'll yer do?'

'Ring her up and say I'll see her this afternoon. No time like the present.'

'But ye're whacked aht, Phyllis. Yer need a rest first!'

'My dear Rose, I shan't have another wink of sleep or a minute's peace of mind until I've faced George's mother. But first I'll have to get somebody to cover for me on the district. Mrs Starling's at a case off Westminster Bridge Road, so I've got no choice but to ask our friend Mrs Webb. I'll ring Theodora House to see if she's in.'

Ginny Webb had just arrived in the District Room and was munching a sandwich when the call came through; her broad face relaxed in a knowing smile as she listened to Miss high-and-mighty Bird, who sounded a bit hot under the collar.

'Only too pleased to help, I'm sure. Don't worry, I'll keep me eyes and ears open!'

419

'Thank you, Mrs Webb. I'll let you know as soon as I'm back on call.'

'No rush, take your time, Miss B. Nothin' serious, I hope?'

'I – I hope not. It's nothing to do with my work, anyway. Thank you very much, Mrs Webb. Goodbye.' Phyllis hung up the receiver.

Oho! Then it might be something to do with our great future MP, thought Ginny. What a scream if that precious pair had to get married in a hurry, like silly little Wildgoose! The midwife chuckled to herself as she scanned the list of deliveries expected in June.

'Good afternoon, Mrs Steynes. I wanted to see you as soon as I read your letter.'

'I'm obliged to you for coming so promptly, Miss Bird.' No Christian name, Phyllis noted. 'Please take a seat and I will ring for tea.'

'Thank you, Mrs Steynes, but I won't take tea. I've been up half the night and haven't slept for many hours. A colleague is having to take my calls while I'm here, and I'd be obliged to you if we may get straight to the point.'

'Oh, I see. Yes, you're obviously tired.' Mrs Steynes was slightly taken aback by Phyllis's unapologetic briskness of manner, but she maintained her own cold composure.

'I have received a letter, Miss Bird – an anonymous letter which I would have thrown away at once – except that I thought you should see it first, and comment on it.' And she handed Phyllis the crumpled sheet of paper.

'Thank you, Mrs Steynes. Yes, I see – and I think I can make a good guess at who sent this to you.'

'I have not the slightest interest in who sent it, Miss Bird. All I want is an answer to one question: is it true?'

'Yes, Mrs Steynes, it is true. I do have a son who was born five years ago at a mother-and-baby home near Epsom. I believe this was written by a midwife who worked there.'

'And does George know about this?'

'Certainly. I told him when he asked me to marry him, and thought that he would withdraw his proposal, but –' Phyllis's voice shook slightly, though she held up her head and continued speaking – 'but he still said he wanted to marry me. He has visited my parents at North Camp and he has met Saul – that's my son.'

'And you persuaded *my* son not to tell me about the child.'

'On the contrary, Mrs Steynes, I wanted to tell you right from the start of our engagement. It was George who persuaded me not to do so. You can ask him about it yourself.'

'I certainly will ask him, now that I have seen you and established the truth about your past. Who was the child's father?'

'That has got nothing to do with the present situation, Mrs Steynes.'

'I beg your pardon, Miss Bird, I think it has everything to do with the present situation. Does the man make payments for the child's upkeep? Is he likely to turn up in your life again and make a claim on the boy?'

Phyllis flushed, and her eyes, red-rimmed from lack of sleep, stared back with such mingled pain and anger in their depths that the old lady lowered her own accusing gaze.

'The answer is *no* to both questions, and I refuse to be cross-questioned any further. George knows my history, and says that he still wants to marry me, and that is our intention, Mrs Steynes – as he will tell you.'

'No doubt he will, Miss Bird, and it will therefore be my duty to point out to him that he can give up all hopes of a parliamentary career. Oh, yes, Miss Bird, you may stare if you please, but I can assure you that in the selection of a parliamentary candidate, a great deal of consideration is given to the man's personal circumstances, and a man who had a wife with a history such as yours would immediately be disqualified. Good heavens above, what do you expect? An illegitimate child! It would be discovered by the press, thanks to such people as the writer of this letter, and would become an enormous scandal, as George must surely know. I'm absolutely serious, Miss Bird. My son will have to make a choice between a parliamentary career which could one day lead him to be a Cabinet Minister, and who knows, possibly even the Premiership – or marry a woman five years older than himself who already has a child by another man. The choice will be his, Miss Bird, and I –'

But Phyllis had risen to her feet. 'I don't think so, Mrs Steynes. You've made me understand that the choice is mine. And I see that I have no choice.' She took a deep breath to steady her voice. 'You have no need to worry about George's career, which will never be in any danger from me and my son, I promise you. Good afternoon – and goodbye.'

With these words she left the room, holding her head high, and closing the door behind her. Mrs Steynes stared into space. It took her a minute or two to realise that she had won.

*

In the District Room that evening Mrs Webb and Mrs Starling were allocating work to the two pupils on duty.

'That one in Charles Street's all right – no need to traipse round there again – but somebody 'ud better look in on that delivery o' Miss Bird's last night,' said Ginny Webb. 'An' I'll take you, Nurse What's-yer-name, to this new case o' Miss Bird's, name o' Lavender, gettin' pains every ten minutes, so she reckons. All right, let's go. Oh! Hello, Miss Bird, so ye're back, then. Blimey, yer look all in.'

'Thank you, Mrs Webb, I'll take over my area now.'

'Ye'd be better goin' back to Richmond Street and havin' a good sleep, by the look o' yer. We can deal with this lot,' said Ginny, who was inclined to speak her mind more openly now that she was registered.

'Did I hear you say Mrs Lavender's getting contractions?'

'Says she is, but it's her first, an' she's not due for another fortnight, so it's prob'ly fixin' pains, the head goin' down – be delivered a week next Tuesday, I dare say. Go on, Miss B, get to yer bed. Nobody's indis— indispenserable, so they say.'

'All right, Mrs Webb, thank you, I am rather tired. But let me know if –'

'See yer tomorrow, Miss Bird.' And just bugger off, Ginny added under her breath.

When Rose Rawson saw her lodger's face, she held out her arms. 'Awright, awright, gal, whatever the ol' cat said, it ain't the end of the world. Go on up to bed and I'll bring yer tea wiv a drop of oh-be-joyful in it. Save yer cryin' till tomorrer.'

But Phyllis did not cry, either then or later. She pulled off her clothes, put on her nightdress, drank

423

the brandy-laced tea and collapsed into merciful oblivion; she slept for more than twelve hours, a deep, dreamless slumber in which her body renewed its strength and her mind its determination. She did not hear the doorbell when George Steynes called and demanded to speak to her; he got short shrift from the landlady.

'They've sent Miss Bird 'ome to me 'cause she was worn aht, an' I've put 'er to bed. Nobody ain't goin' to disturb 'er, an' that's that,' she declared, looking up at him, a defiant, stunted little figure on her bowed legs.

'When she wakes, will you tell her that I called, Mrs Rawson, and that I wish to speak to her as soon as it's convenient?'

But Mrs Rawson did not even answer; she stepped back inside her little house, and closed the door.

When Phyllis woke the next morning, she sat down to write a letter to George, freeing him from their engagement and wishing him all success in his career.

I feel that you are destined for great achieve-ments, and I have resolved not to stand in your way [she wrote]. I have been very happy during these past two months, but I cannot allow you to put your future in jeopardy by making an unwise marriage. Please do not try to make me change my mind, because I never shall. This will be my last letter to you.

God bless and guide you in all your endeavours.

Sincerely yours,
P. Bird

Having sent off the letter, Phyllis adamantly refused to answer any of his, or to speak to him on the doorstep of Number 35, or on the telephone or when he tried to approach her on her rounds. In the end he was forced to accept her decision, and to admit that their engagement was over. She was implacable, and nothing he could say – including an offer to give up his plan to stand for Parliament – would move her. When he appealed to Dr Vaughan to intercede for him, Mildred found that Phyllis would not even discuss the matter, though she did tell her friend the reason for her decision not to marry Steynes: the fact that she had a child.

'*Phyllis!* Oh, Phyllis, my dear – I just can't – I don't know what to say . . .'

'You don't remember meeting me nearly six years ago, do you, Mildred? At a mother-and-baby home at Epsom where you came to visit one day with your uncle, Dr Renshaw. You were still a student then, and I was one of those unmarried expectant mothers. We actually spoke to each other, and I remembered you when you came here.'

'Oh, heavens above, yes – a place with a most peculiar name, but I don't remember seeing you there, Phyllis. My dear, I'm so sorry.' Mildred was genuinely upset by this revelation.

'I was much more fortunate than most of those poor girls who had to part with their babies. My parents are bringing up my son, so I see him about once a month. I was a fool to think that George Steynes could marry me without harming his career – and he should have known too, really. His mother pointed it out to me, and I suppose I ought to be grateful to her.'

'He's dreadfully upset, Phyllis.'

'He'll get over it, and find somebody younger and more suitable. That's what his mother hopes.'

'But it's so hard on you, Phyllis – so unfair.'

'Oh, never mind about me, Mildred. Do you remember me telling you that I'd been through worse trouble – when those demonstrators were throwing stones at the clinic? Anyway, you must excuse me now, because I've got a lot of visits to do.'

A letter arrived from Mrs Steynes, containing the warmest words that Phyllis had ever received from that lady.

Your self-sacrifice does you great credit, Miss Bird, and I admire you for it. George will come to realise in time that you have done the right thing, even though he finds it hard at present, and may I say that –

Phyllis could read no further, but crumpled the letter up into a ball and threw it on the fire in Mrs Rawson's range oven.

As many a midwife has discovered, work is a great remedy for a broken heart. A woman in the pain of childbirth needs both expert help and emotional support, and a good midwife must rise above her own sorrows and anxieties in order to give that comfort. Phyllis's heart could still thrill to the sound of a newborn baby's cry and the wonder in a new mother's eyes; and it was good to be recognised and warmly greeted by her families wherever she went on her rounds.

And there was Saul: oh yes, there was her beloved son to welcome her at North Camp on her weekends off, and his easy acceptance when she told him that Uncle George was very busy in London and would not be coming to see them again. Her parents exchanged surprised glances, and would have asked questions, but she assured them that she had no regrets about breaking off an unofficial engagement to a future Member of Parliament.

In June it was time for the annual holiday at Hayling Island once again, and Phyllis was determined to enjoy every minute of it. Saul was getting noticeably bigger and sturdier, and talked a lot about school where he had earned Miss Daniells' praise and made friends with the other children. Phyllis noticed that he was developing a mind of his own, and was not always willing to obey his grandmother, who still tended to treat him like a toddler.

'No, Granny, I'm *not* tired. I want to go collecting shells with Mummy!' he said firmly when Mrs Bird said he should rest after his picnic lunch.

'No, Granny, I don't want you to read me a story, 'cause I can read one my own self, and Mummy likes listening to me!'

Of course Phyllis was comforted by these little marks of preference, but she told herself that she must always respect her mother and teach Saul to do so, because without her parents' willingness to adopt him, she would have lost him for ever. Mrs Bird was now in her mid-fifties, and sometimes found the lively youngster tiring, though she would never admit as much, for he remained the sun, moon and stars around which her world revolved. Phyllis could never forget the debt she owed her mother, but even so, the brief hours she spent alone with her son were very precious.

Lying on the beach in the sunshine on their last afternoon, watching Saul paddling on the edge of the shallow water with a boy he had met on the holiday, Phyllis suddenly thought of Maud, and made a promise to herself that she would visit her friend as soon as she could, perhaps one afternoon the following week. But when they got back to North Camp, her father silently pointed out to her a notice in *The Times*, which announced the death of the film actress at her home in Twickenham on 21 June, at the age of thirty-six. The funeral was to be held at St Stephen's Church, Twickenham, on the 25th, which was the following Monday. Bitterly reproaching herself for being too late to say goodbye to her good friend, Phyllis felt bound to attend the farewell service, even though she knew that George Steynes would be there.

Arriving back at Lambeth, Phyllis once again had to ask Mrs Webb to take over her district while she attended the funeral, and took the train from Waterloo down to St Margaret's Station, from where she walked to St Stephen's on the Richmond Road. She quietly entered the church and sat in a pew near the back. Guests were rapidly filling the large nave, and she could only see the backs of their heads and the occasional profile, but she recognised a few film and stage actors and directors, and studio technicians. She saw the Berridges come in with their pretty thirteen-year-old daughter Edith – and there was Dr Godley, looking older and greyer and sitting alone; and oh, heavens, there was George and his mother seated quite near to him.

Phyllis lowered her head and did not raise it again until the service began. The one person she could not see was Teddy Ling, Maud's only known relative: had he not been able to get across the Atlantic in time?

The organ began to play solemn music as the priest entered intoning, 'I am the resurrection and the life . . .' and the congregation rose to see the flower-laden coffin carried in on the shoulders of six pall-bearers. Phyllis's heart leaped at the sight of one of them, none other than Teddy Ling in sober black, performing this last duty for his sister, and behind the coffin walked a black-clad, veiled Signora Capogna leaning on the arm of a thin, ill-looking man who clutched a walking-stick in his other hand and seemed hardly able to get up the aisle. Phyllis realised he was Reginald Thane, and presumed that he had been released from prison to attend the occasion; but it was seeing Teddy again that awoke mixed emotions in her heart, and her eyes filled with tears for the first time since hearing of Maud's death. If only she had a companion with her . . . but nobody from her Lambeth life had any connection with the actress.

At the end of the service most of the congregation filed out to follow the coffin to the prepared place in the churchyard, and Phyllis stood at the edge of the crowd around the graveside, ready to leave immediately after the committal. A hand on her shoulder detained her.

'We've lost a good friend today, Phyllis Bird.'

'Dr Godley – oh, yes, and I've been a poor friend to her. I should have visited again, only –'

'You came with George Steynes, didn't you? Maud told me you were engaged.'

'Not any more. I broke it off because – because of my son.'

'Oh, my dear girl, I'm sorry. It's five years, isn't it?' he said, remembering the part he had played in Phyllis's trouble, and the gossip that had led to his wife's tearful accusations and his daughter's anger. 'Just before Pamela's first confinement. And how's the little boy?'

'He lives with my parents. He's a lovely child, and he's made such a difference to my mother.' Phyllis wiped her eyes and smiled. 'And what about your family, Dr Godley?'

'My wife keeps much the same – she has her good days and not so good. And Pamela's news is always the same, except that the number goes up. She's expecting number five at Christmas. The Lord knows what the final tally will be – a dozen at least, I should think.'

'Do they still live in London?'

'No, he's got a country practice in County Kerry. My wife and I get over to see them when we can, but travelling isn't easy for Victoria, so it's not very often. And, of course, it's even more difficult for Pamela, poor girl.' There was a weary resignation in his face and voice. 'These devout Catholics, you know – my daughter will be an old woman by the time she's forty.'

Phyllis remembered Maud's remark about Mrs Browne's need of birth-control advice, but something impelled her to take a different stance, and show another side to the picture.

'Is Pamela happy, Dr Godley?' she asked bluntly.

'She says she is, but it isn't the life I'd hoped for her.'

'So in that case, if she's content to be the mother of a large family living in the country and with a doctor's payments coming in, why shouldn't she live her life as she pleases?' Phyllis spoke earnestly, wondering what Dr Vaughan would make of this little speech, and how it would surprise Sister

Pollock. 'Your Pamela *chose* that life, Dr Godley, and – and . . .' She hesitated, trying to find the right words.

'And you think I should accept her choice with a good grace, is that what you're saying, Phyllis? You always had a way of putting me in my place.' His eyes lit up with something of his old humour. 'Well, my dear, perhaps you're right, and I'm glad things didn't turn out too badly for you. Are you going back to Florizel?'

'Well, no, actually I'm getting the next train back from –'

'*Phyllis!* Oh, Phyllis, I wanted to catch you before you ran off. Thanks for detaining her, Doctor! Oh, to see you again, Phyllis – come on back to the house!'

And her arm was grabbed by Maud's brother, Teddy, his handsome face pale and his dark eyes shadowed with sadness, yet so obviously glad to see her. He was heavier, broader in the shoulders, and had acquired a transatlantic accent: he had the look of a successful man.

'Hello, Teddy! So you got home in time to –'

'No, Phyllis, I regret to say I hung about too long with that goddamned film, and then when Belle wired me to come at once, I left in a hurry, but – I was too late. She'd gone. Poor Maudie, I've been a lousy brother after all she did for me. But Phyllis, how are you? Come on and meet everybody. There's Belle and poor old Reggie Thane – and d'you remember Georgie Steynes? He's here with his mother – looks as if he's going up in the world!'

Her eyes met Godley's and he gave her a nod, muttering quietly, 'You might as well face him, Phyllis, while there are plenty of us milling around. We're all here for Maud today.'

So Phyllis walked back to Florizel arm in arm with Teddy Ling, to greet Belle with a kiss and chat with Reginald. She smiled at the maids she knew, and gave a cool little nod to Mr Steynes and his mother, immediately turning away to talk to Reginald.

'Darling Maudie, she moved heaven and earth to get me out of that place on the grounds of bad health and good behaviour,' said Thane shakily. 'It was the last of many acts of kindness that she performed. She said I could come here to live, but within ten days of my arrival she passed from us. What will happen to me now, I neither know nor care. I wait only for death.'

'Do not be stupid, Mr Thane, when you well know that you shall stay here, as was my darling's last wish!' snapped the signora, who even in her grief was ordering the maids to carry round sandwiches and pastries. 'I shall care for you as I cared for her.'

'The best possible outcome for them both,' murmured Godley in Phyllis's ear. 'Nobody was ever more loyal to her friends.'

Phyllis would have liked to speak to the Berridges and enquire about Claud, who had played such a significant part in her life at 3 Travis Walk, but Harold Berridge did not respond to her tentative smile, and Mrs Berridge stared straight through her, so she turned back to Teddy, who was more than willing to talk.

'I believe you've made quite a name for yourself in Hollywood, Teddy.'

'Sure, things are getting hotter by the week now that we've got the talkies. No going back!'

'And I also hear that you're married,' she smiled.

'Two years, but getting divorced. It happens all the time out there. Remember Georgia? She's with her second husband now, and seems to be OK – in fact they're expecting a kid.'

'And what about –' Phyllis drew a breath before saying the name of her son's father – 'what about Denver Towers?'

'Oh, poor old D. T.'s never got back on track after that alleged rape incident in some Los Angeles hotel. Didn't the papers carry it over here? Some floozie out for dollars and notoriety. He said she was ready and willing, but she says he spiked her drink and forced her. It was all kinda sordid. Now he's hitting the bottle and his career's in a nose-dive. Shame, really. He had all the talents – looks, good voice, the lot – but a sucker for the ladies. Hey, Phyllis, are you all right? Here, sit down.' He drew up a chair and seated himself beside her.

'You know, Phyllis, I was a fool to let you go. I was too young and too full o' nutty ideas – couldn't see the wood for the trees. Maud was furious with me over it, but maybe it was all for the best – for you, anyway. You've done very well, by the looks of you – a very attractive, independent woman – and I've noticed that Georgie Steynes must think the same! Don't look now, but . . .'

Suddenly Phyllis felt an overwhelming urge to speak the truth to this older, more experienced and worldly-wise Teddy Ling. It would be her first and last opportunity to do so.

'There's somebody who's not here today, Teddy. Maud's closest relative – her son, Alex.'

'Ah. She told you about him, then. She must have thought a lot of you, Phyllis, because only a handful of people know about Alex.' Teddy spoke quietly, clearly taken aback.

'The reason she told me was because I was in the

433

same situation – I was expecting a baby myself. Did Maud never tell you that?'

'Good God, Phyllis, no, she didn't. I can't take this in. *You* had a baby?'

'Yes, I did. And when I first told her, Maud thought it was yours.'

'Oh, no!' He put his hand to his face. 'She must've gone mad.'

'Well, I told her he wasn't yours, and that you'd never have deserted me. He's a lovely little boy, his name's Saul and he was born in March nineteen twenty-three.'

'B-but Phyllis – *who* . . .?'

'You were talking about him a minute ago, Teddy. It sounds as if I had a lucky escape. It was at the Worton Hall weekend house party when you went off with Georgia Kift.'

'Oh my God. Christ! Yes, I remember now, there were rumours that D. T. was making a beeline for you, but when he cleared off the very next day to the States, I thought that was the end of it.'

'Yes, it was for him. But not for me. And if it hadn't been for the kindness, the sheer goodness of your sister, who paid for me to stay in a private maternity home, and Dr Godley who went to a lot of trouble for me – I'd have – I'd have been completely – *ruined*. Oh, Maudie!'

She stifled a groan, and Teddy put his arm around her.

'Phyllis – Phyllis, my dear girl, I had no idea.'

'It's all right now, Teddy. I've found a good life for myself in Lambeth as a midwife and a campaigner for women's rights. And I've got my son – well, my parents have got him. My mother worships him. He's brought happiness back to that house, so I *can't* say that I regret having him. And you can tell that to D. T. when you see him again, except that he won't remember me.'

Teddy was at a loss for words, but at that moment Dr Godley came forward. He had been standing near to them and had heard most of what she had said.

'Phyllis, dear, can I give you a lift to the station?'

'Thank you, Dr Godley, that's very kind. Yes, I think this is probably a good time to go. Goodbye, Teddy. I'm glad I've seen you again.'

'You've knocked me over sideways, Phyllis, but I'm glad you told me. Will I be able to see you if I come up to Lambeth?'

'No, Teddy. You've got to go back to the States and sort things out with your wife. There's nothing for us now, it's all in the past. So let's say goodbye.'

'Goodbye, Phyllis. I'll never forget you.'

Yes, you will, she thought, but kissed him before they parted.

Back on the district in Lambeth, life went on. The birth-control campaign continued to gain ground in spite of die-hard opposition, and more distinguished names rallied to its support. The plight of the unemployed and their families did not improve, and there were rumblings of unrest among men in all industries, from miners and dockers to postal workers and the navy, complaining about low pay and unemployment dole. A beleaguered government protested that with an economic crisis looming in Europe and America, there was not enough money in the Treasury, and demands for a general election grew louder.

In Phyllis's sphere of activity, however, there was one local reform that gave her great satisfaction. Miss

Barbara Lamb applied for and got the post of deputy matron and resident midwife at 90 Riverside Gardens, and immediately clamoured for the removal of the name plate on its sooty brick frontage: so the 'LCC Home for Wayward Girls' became simply 'Bethesda', which Miss Lamb explained meant 'House of Mercy'. She proved to be very popular with the residents, as she called them, rather than inmates, and encouraged the use of Christian names instead of surnames. Some of the harsher rules were relaxed, and she held evening meetings where the girls could share feelings and problems, ending with prayers led by herself. This did not go down well with Miss Thomas, who felt that her authority was being undermined, and after some sharp disagreements with Miss Lamb, the matron applied for a transfer. She was duly moved to another women's refuge, and Miss Lamb recommended that she be replaced by a widowed member of the Ladies' League of Christian Befrienders, who had some useful experience in running a guesthouse. Within a year Bethesda became a model mother-and-baby home, and in spite of its irreverent nickname of Hallelujah House, it was a genuine house of mercy and new hope to girls who had fallen from grace in a judgemental society.

Three weeks into September Phyllis was called out to Homer Street where Mrs Doris Kemp was starting in labour, a long process that continued for thirty-six hours. Her husband was almost beside himself with anxiety, remembering the tragedy of the previous year, and Phyllis found his constant questioning an additional trial to the mother's unremitting pains. Mrs Webb and a pupil came to relieve Phyllis for a few hours, but on her return Phyllis was concerned by the lack of progress and requested a domiciliary visit from Mr Poole, with a view to admission to Theodora House and a Caesarean section. At hearing this Cyril Kemp wept aloud, and even Ginny Webb, usually so hard on husbands, patted his heaving shoulders and told him he'd got to be brave for the sake of the children. In the event, Mr Poole performed a forceps delivery at home, and Doris woke from a haze of chloroform to find herself the mother of an eight-pound baby girl at half-past six in the evening.

Amidst the general rejoicing Phyllis raised her eyebrows at seeing the baby tucked in beside her exhausted mother in the matrimonial bed.

'Oh, no, Mrs Webb, the baby must go in her cot. Think of the dangers. Who knows what might happen if Mrs Kemp rolled over and –'

'Overlaid the baby? Nah, no fear o' that whilst I'm here to watch 'em. That's just what they both need, a little bit o' cuddlin' up together, like dogs an' cats when they got babies. Ye'd know that well enough, Miss B., if ye'd ever had a baby yerself – beggin' yer pardon,' added Ginny hastily, thinking that she had possibly overstepped the mark this time.

Miss Bird did not seem to be offended, but looked rather thoughtful, and when the two of them were back in the District Room cleaning and replenishing their delivery bags, she asked casually, 'What makes you so sure that I have never had a baby, Mrs Webb?'

'What?' Ginny looked up sharply, unable to believe that she had heard right. 'Well, I mean to say, Miss B., look at yer. I mean, if ever there was a – a –'

'A spinster, a woman left over from the war that

437

took away a generation of men? Is that what you mean, Mrs Webb?'

'Well, er, yeah, I s'pose so, though I never meant no offence by it. I lost my husband, along of a lot of others, but – well, I got my Billy,' said Ginny, a little confused by this conversation.

'And I've got my son too, Mrs Webb. His name's Saul and he's five and a half and lives with my parents because I'm a single woman and have to work. And you can tell whoever you like, because I'm tired of pretending he doesn't exist, when he means more to me than anything else in the world.'

For once in her life Ginny Webb was lost for words. Her mouth literally dropped open as she stared at the other midwife, who calmly went on changing the white linen lining to her bag and adding scissors, ligatures, cord dressings and binder.

Gossip usually spreads rapidly, passing like an infection from mouth to mouth, and losing nothing in the telling; but the sudden revelation made to Mrs Webb by the senior midwife was no ordinary gossip, and Ginny took a while to assimilate it. She wondered if she had heard right, and had no wish to pass on something that might turn out to be a misunderstanding; but when Miss Bird casually mentioned 'my son Saul' while attending at a confinement, and chatted about him to the three older Kemp children, saying that he wanted to visit London and see the Tower, the new knowledge became absorbed into the collective consciousness of the nurses and mothers, and within a week it was as if the fact of her motherhood had always been known. Nevertheless, when she was summoned to attend a joint interview with Mr Poole and the Matron of Booth Street Infirmary,

438

her colleagues held their breath while waiting to hear what she had been told, and how she had responded.

They soon found out. Miss Bird had been offered the position of Supervisor of Midwives on the district, and a third district midwife/teacher was to be appointed, thus easing the heavy case-load currently shared by Miss Bird and Mrs Starling. Everybody was equally surprised and relieved by the news, and Mildred Vaughan was particularly jubilant.

'Thank heaven they've shown a bit of sense, Phyllis! They know the worth of a good all-rounder – and it'll give you more time to attend at the mobile clinic without any loss of income. You'll be able to expand your work for the campaign!'

In fact Phyllis avoided both public and private meetings where she knew Steynes would be present, and confined her efforts to clinic work and teaching birth-control methods to nurses.

Dr Vaughan was invited to a dinner party at the home of a Professor Arthur Ellis in November, a significant meeting that was to lead to the formation of the National Birth Control Council. In the course of the evening, George Steynes was warmly congratulated on his selection by the Liberal Party as parliamentary candidate for Walworth North and Bermondsey; the women's voting age had been lowered that year from thirty to twenty-one, and he was confident that he would have the support of these new voters. At one point Dr Vaughan saw Lady Dacre take him aside and ask him directly what had happened about that nice Miss Bird, and he had replied courteously that Miss Bird had broken off their engagement, to his regret, but he firmly declined to discuss the matter.

*

439

For Phyllis's last weekend off before Christmas, she decided not to spend the time at North Camp this year, but to fetch Saul up to London and let him see some of the sights he talked about so eagerly. Mrs Rawson was delighted to co-operate, but when it was put to Mrs Bird she would not hear of being separated from her grandson for a whole weekend, so she too had to be accommodated at 35 Richmond Street, and Phyllis slept on the sofa downstairs to let her mother and Saul share her room.

It was a wonderful time for the boy and his mother; he saw the Tower of London and Tower Bridge, which conveniently divided and raised its two halves to let a big ship go through. They ate in a Lyons Corner House, and gazed into the brilliantly lit windows of the big Oxford Street stores as the December dusk fell and the lights went on. Mrs Bird grew tired, her head and feet ached with so much walking, and she was horrified by the amount of traffic and the speed at which it moved; but for Saul it was all exciting, and he smiled up at his mother, holding her hand on the escalators that carried them down to the underground railway.

On the Sunday they attended the morning service at St Martha's, and after dinner Phyllis took her son on a brief visit to Theodora House where Mrs Starling and Mrs Webb were replenishing their delivery bags in the District Room; with them was a pupil and the newly appointed district midwife, Miss McNabb, a Scotswoman with her own firm ideas about how things should be done. Saul chatted away happily, and Mrs Webb remarked on his nice manners. Miss McNabb was somewhat mystified, and when the visitors had left, she asked who the little boy was.

'I presume he's a relative of Miss Bird, because he looks so much like her.'

Mrs Starling gave the others a significant look. 'Actually he's her son, Miss McNabb, up from Hampshire on a visit. Dear little chap, isn't he?'

'Her *son*?' gasped Miss McNabb. 'And her not married? Good heavens above, whatever next? How on earth did she manage to keep her job?'

Mrs Webb looked up quickly from her delivery bag. 'Maybe 'cause she's one o' the best midwives, an' all the mothers think the world of 'er.'

'Maybe so, but it's hardly a character recommendation, is it? It would surely be better if she kept him out of the way – or passed him off as a nephew.'

Ginny Webb's eyes narrowed. 'Maybe *you'd* try to make out he was yer nephew, but Miss Bird ain't one for tellin' lies. She's proud of 'er boy, an' we ain't complainin' – an' what's more, she's a *lady*, which is more 'n I can say for *some* busybodies round here!'

It was a declaration of solidarity, a recognition of Phyllis Bird as a woman who no longer had a secret to hide. While Miss McNabb was probably correct in assuming that Miss Bird would not have been appointed if her circumstances had been known at the start, five years of unblemished service now outweighed her disadvantage as an unmarried mother. And she was now free from the oppressive burden of concealment.

The New Year dawned on a further declining economy, and the plight of mining towns in the north of England was highlighted when Edward, Prince of Wales toured some of the worst areas. Photographs of him standing outside miserable dwellings talking to shabby men, care-worn women and half-starved children appeared in all the newspapers. His verdict that 'Something must be done!' was echoed all over the country and set him up as a champion of the people, notwithstanding his own vastly different lifestyle. Against a background of sporadic strikes and riots, the date for a general election was set for 31 May. Ramsay MacDonald, leader of the new Labour Party, was determined to oust Baldwin and the Tories from office, though many predicted a Liberal victory in spite of the unpopularity of Lloyd George.

All through May the campaigning was brisk. Red, blue and buff flags appeared in windows, pamphlets were distributed, meetings were held and canvassers knocked on doors. George Steynes toured his constituency to much cheering and waving, and his mother planned a special dinner party to celebrate his assured success. There was great excitement when the nation went to the polls, and Phyllis cast her vote for the Liberal representing Lambeth.

On Saturday, 1 June, the country woke up to a disappointing anti-climax. Labour had just managed to beat the Tories with a few more seats in the Commons, but with fewer actual votes overall. Baldwin was out and MacDonald was in, leaving the Liberals holding the balance of power.

But George Steynes was not one of them; he failed to get elected.

Chapter 24

Phyllis covered her bathing costume with the printed cotton beach-robe that also did duty as a dressing gown at the holiday bungalow, and stretched herself out on the warm sand. Her mother was settled in a deck chair, and Saul and his young companions were searching for the treasures to be found on the wide expanse of rippled sand left clean and shining by the outgoing tide. There were many more families on holiday this year because it was early August and the schools were out; Saul could not lose a week from his second year without a good reason.

For an only child brought up by an overanxious grandmother, Saul was a friendly and outgoing boy, thought Phyllis, as he called to the others filling their buckets with shells, coloured stones worn smooth by the tides, thick ribbons of seaweed with air-bladders that could be popped, and the feathery kind that quickly dried to brittleness.

'There goes the donkey-cart,' remarked Mrs Bird, and Phyllis sat up and looked towards the stony coastal path that ran between the shore and the row of bungalows, edged with tough grasses, thrift and sea-pinks that thrived in sandy soil and salty air. An old lady sat in an open conveyance drawn by a slow, fat female donkey, a white-faced boy of about eight or nine at her side. He looked longingly towards the sea and the knot of lively children, and Phyllis wondered if he was from Lord Mayor Treloar's hospital for crippled children on the island, being taken out by his grandmother; she smiled and waved to them, thanking heaven once more for Saul's health and normality.

She lay down again and closed her eyes. The sound of the retreating donkey-cart, the children's voices, the distant shushing of the little waves and the mournful cry of a solitary gull made a soothing background to her thoughts, and within minutes she drifted into a light doze.

Oh, the treachery of dreams, when the heart's true desires come to the surface and even our eyes and ears imagine that which is not there . . . the sound of footsteps approaching across the sand, getting nearer and causing her pulse to quicken in anticipation; the pause when the footsteps stopped and somebody sat down beside her, taking her hand, leaning over her, touching her face with his lips – the sun warm on their faces as he whispered her name.

Phyllis . . . I'm here beside you. I've come back. Oh, Phyllis, Phyllis, my love, I still want you.

'George!' She realised that she had spoken aloud, and opened her eyes; but there was nobody there. Only the sea and the sand and the sky, the coastal path – and her mother sitting in the deck chair with her straw hat over her forehead.

'Did you say something, Phyllis? There's a bit of a breeze getting up, and I don't want him to catch a chill. Saul! *Saul!* Come to your granny and let me put your cardigan on, dear!'

It had been a daydream, nothing more – but so real, so vivid that Phyllis had been raised to the very height of happiness for a moment, only to be dashed back to the reality of emptiness and disappointment. She swallowed, and her eyes filled with tears; even

444

her beloved son was not truly her own, and just for a moment she was overcome by a sensation of self-pity, though in another minute she had regained her composure and told herself not to be an ungrateful fool.

The sight of the invalid boy had made her think of Claud Berridge, whose death earlier that year at Tall Pines had been briefly reported in *The Times*; she had heard through Mrs Williams that he had gone into a prolonged fit during which his breathing had stopped, and he died shortly before his twelfth birthday. Oh, there was so much sadness in the world, and she was only one of thousands of women who had to make the best of a single life. She was far more fortunate than many, having her son and her work, good friendships and the annual week at Hayling Island, though this year she had seen more clearly than before that Saul was growing up without her and would eventually grow away from a mother he had never known intimately. With George Steynes as a husband to support her and give her a home, she could have seen more of Saul, and shown him wider horizons than North Camp, without taking him away from his grandparents, but that was not to be, and sometimes she felt as if a golden chalice of happiness had been held to her lips and then snatched away. For two months she had been cherished, looked after and adored, and now she had to fend for herself again; but as Reggie Thane would say, the memory could not be taken away.

She stood up, collected the bags and picnic basket, folded the deck chair and carried it under her arm. It was time to get back to the bungalow and start preparing tea.

*

445

An unpleasant surprise awaited Phyllis on her return to Lambeth.

'This is what I've always feared would happen sooner or later, Miss Bird,' said the vicar of St Martha's, who had called on her and been shown into Rose's little front parlour. 'I have my suspicions about who reported me – and the Young Wives – to the bishop, but I can't be sure, and I'm not prepared to discuss the matter with anybody other than the poor ladies themselves, who will doubtless have to face a certain amount of censure.'

'I'm very sorry, Vicar, after you've been so courageous over this.' Phyllis could only stare at him in dismay, picturing him being turned out of his living. 'And your wife and children – what will happen? You've built up such a good parish here, everybody likes you, and there'd be a huge outcry if . . . has the bishop said what he intends to do?'

The vicar smiled, though quickly restored his face to seriousness. 'Actually, things aren't too bad, Miss Bird. In fact I feel quite sorry for His Lordship. He gave me a fairly severe rap over the knuckles – well, he had to – and talked about misuse of the vicarage, which is Church property, but he knows perfectly well that I have a good congregation here, and I'm well supported by my churchwardens and the Parochial Church Council. The clinic sessions are to cease forthwith, needless to say, but otherwise I think he feels that the less said, the better. He doesn't want a scandal, and neither do I – nor does Mr Broome at Pond Street Methodist. So, Miss Bird, all I can say is thank you very much indeed for all the – er – help that you and Miss Anderson have given the Young Wives, and I look forward to seeing you in church as usual.'

'So there's not going to be any disciplinary action, Vicar?' asked Phyllis in relief.

'That is correct, Miss Bird. The only result of this will be an inevitable fall in the membership of the Young Wives. But doesn't this just go to show how attitudes are changing, as does the fact that we've kept this clinic going for two years? Because, let's face it, plenty of people knew about it but turned a blind eye, though once it was officially reported to the bishop, he had to take some action. Ah, well.'

Phyllis smiled ruefully. 'We shall miss the payments that the Young Wives always made for the service, Vicar. We don't charge women who are very poor, but we appreciate contributions from those who can afford it, and your ladies were always very generous.' She put her head on one side and looked thoughtful. 'You know, this might be the right time to stop, Vicar. Your ladies won't be as reluctant now to attend our other clinics, including the mobile one – and an influx of known churchgoers will make us that bit more respectable!'

'Quite so, Miss Bird. We have a duty to look on the bright side.'

Mrs Rawson, coming in at that moment with a tray of tea, was surprised to find the reverend gentleman and the senior midwife chortling quietly over a shared joke; she thought he had come to discuss a very serious matter, so it seemed rather odd.

Though his bid to enter Parliament had been unsuccessful, George Steynes' name regularly came to public notice. He continued to be a robust campaigner for birth-control provision, using the *Daily Chronicle* as a platform, and by giving lectures, one of which was made jointly with Dr Helena

Wright to doctors and medical students at St Mary's Hospital, she concentrating on the medical, he on the social issues. Another lecture was broadcast by the British Broadcasting Company, and when Mrs Rawson switched on the wireless one evening, Phyllis gasped and put her hand to her mouth on hearing Steynes' concise tones coming through a crackle of static, but still quite intelligible. She listened eagerly as he warned about the state of the economy, the rumblings from Wall Street in New York, threatening financial collapse in Europe.

'And as always, the heaviest burden is laid upon the shoulders of those least responsible for it and least able to bear it,' he declared. 'The poor and their children, the old, the unemployed – *they* are the chief victims of mismanagement by those in high office.'

Phyllis applauded every word he spoke, and Rose could not help noticing the effect his voice had on her. 'It was a great big shame yer sent 'im away, Phyllis, 'cause 'e never got into Parli'ment anyway,' she said sadly.

'I know, Rose – but at least nobody can say it was my fault that he didn't.'

'I bet 'e'd 'ave yer back tomorrer if yer was to ask 'im.'

'No, Rose, I can't do that. I made a decision, and we both had to accept it.'

But then came a further development, which looked as if George Steynes, twenty-nine at the close of the year and with far more social standing and experience, might be about to make a decision of his own. The *News of the World* published a photograph of him escorting a young lady to a charity performance of Handel's *Messiah* at the Albert Hall, in aid of the same poverty-stricken areas that the Prince of Wales had toured at the beginning of the year.

'We have been able to ascertain that Mr Steynes' charming companion is Miss Letitia Dickenson, the second daughter of Major and Mrs Neil Dickenson of The Old Lodge, near Farnham in Surrey,' the report said coyly. 'Presented at Court this year, she is known to be a young lady of many talents, an enthusiastic horsewoman and fearless car driver.'

So when Dr Vaughan tentatively mentioned the news that was being passed around Mrs Steynes' circle of friends, she found that Phyllis already knew, having seen the Sunday newspaper at the home of a patient.

'It's all right, Mildred, he has every right to escort whoever he pleases,' she said, trying to speak lightly. 'No doubt his mother will be pleased.'

'That's right, Phyllis. I hear she's happy about the – er – friendship,' Mildred replied, thankful that she had not got to break the news. 'It seems that Major Dickenson was a friend of George's father, and they fought together in the war. Neil Dickenson came out of it with wounds in his neck and thigh, but Captain Steynes –'

'Yes, we know, don't we? It sounds like a very suitable match, Mildred, and I wish him every happiness, naturally,' said poor Phyllis, whose head and heart were pulling her in different directions. On the one hand she had to admit that this girl sounded absolutely right for George, but when she thought of him transferring all his love and devotion to another woman, her heart ached with a terrible sense of rejection, and she knew herself to be jealous. Oh, let him not commit himself too soon! she prayed confusedly. Don't let him be pushed into marriage by

449

his mother or his uncles or the girl's family – or the girl herself . . .

But a week before Christmas these last hopes were shattered, for the notice of the engagement appeared in *The Times* for all to see. 'Major and Mrs Neil Dickenson are happy to announce the engagement of their daughter, Letitia Mary, to Mr George Steynes, only son of the late Captain George Steynes and the Honourable Mrs Agatha Steynes of 15 Nelson Square . . .'

The news was greeted by a shower of congratulations, and Mrs Steynes expressed herself 'happy and delighted' with her son's choice. In an unusual burst of candour she said that the wedding was planned for next June, probably at Farnham, and that after their honeymoon her son and his bride would move into the house in Nelson Square, where she would remain for the time being.

When Phyllis returned to 35 Richmond Street that evening she went upstairs to her room, wanting nothing but to weep quietly into her pillow, but when a call came in soon after ten o'clock she had to turn out into the cold, dark December night to answer it – and forget her own feelings for the sake of a woman in childbirth.

Christmas on the district was a difficult time for many that year, and the midwives encountered some very sad cases, but when another New Year dawned, Miss Bird had readjusted herself to her circumstances, and did not dwell on the preparations being made for the Wedding of the Year.

A significant breakthrough in the battle for birth-control provision occurred in 1930, though the early months brought disappointment. Much was expected of the new Labour Government, and Mr Thurtle kept the matter to the fore by questioning the new Minister of Health, Mr Arthur Greenwood, about permitting the Maternity and Child Welfare Centres to include birth-control advice in their services. Mr Greenwood protested that there were more pressing matters to be addressed, and in fact the beleaguered government was too much taken up with fighting for its own survival to have much parliamentary time to spare for the clamourings of the newly formed National Birth Control Council.

'He's dithering, just like all his predecessors!' complained Mildred Vaughan. 'But he's going to *have* to listen to the women of this country, just as Lloyd George had to listen to the suffragettes. Just wait till he sees who we've got lined up on our side, and we *won't* be put off for another year!'

These were not idle words on her part; after nearly ten years of vigorous campaigning, the various pressure groups were joining forces to demand action, from the women's section of the Labour Party to the Women's National Liberal Federation, the National Council of Women and the Workers' Birth Control Group; these were joined by progressive public health authorities and maternity and child welfare centres and other local bodies in an unstoppable tide.

'We're having a major public conference in the Central Hall, Westminster, and Greenwood will have to give us an answer,' said Mildred Vaughan excitedly. 'That'll be on the fourth of April, and you've got to be there, Miss Bird! You represent the grass roots of the movement, the actual practical application of birth control. Lady Dacre and the Thurtles and George Steynes do a wonderful job standing up there on public platforms and making the necessary noise, but it's you and Miss Anderson and all the nurses who staff the clinics who deserve the laurels. It's to be an all-day event, and I insist that you show your face for at least an hour in the afternoon – no ifs or buts!'

Phyllis had very mixed feelings. The fourth of April was a Friday, and preceded her monthly weekend at North Camp. If she could get away by about two o'clock, she could look in at the Central Hall for long enough to satisfy Dr Vaughan, and then go straight to Waterloo Station and get the train in time to see Saul before his granny sent him to bed.

The one thought that troubled her was the fact that George and his fiancée would be at the conference: would she be able to keep her composure if she had to face them and wish them well? She had hitherto avoided meetings where he was likely to be present, and had not seen him face to face since that awful time when she had refused to speak to him about their broken engagement, nearly two years ago. Surely she should be over that by now? Why did the idea of his approaching marriage cause her such pain? It was neither sensible nor rational, for after all, she had set him free . . .

The weather was perfect, a beautiful spring day, and after handing over the necessary report to Mrs Starling, Phyllis returned to Richmond Street where she changed into a simple dark blue dress with a navy jacket and a neat little matching hat with a pale blue silk bow at the front. At thirty-four she was slim and self-assured, though life experience had left its mark on her face; there was a fine network of lines around the brown eyes, and her mouth drooped a little in repose, though her mirror never showed her the moments when every feature lit up with spontaneous pleasure and satisfaction, as when a baby was safely delivered into her hands.

'Cor, yer don't 'alf look posh!' said Rose admiringly. 'Ye'll be as good as – as any Lady de la What's-'ername!' The slight hesitation meant that she had Miss Letitia Dickenson in mind, and Phyllis gave a little sigh, for that young woman had youth on her side.

She kissed Rose and picked up her overnight bag. 'The place will be absolutely packed, and everybody who is anybody will be there. Nobody'll notice me!' she said with a half-smile. 'What I'm looking forward to is seeing Saul again in about four hours from now. Goodbye, Rose dear – see you again Sunday evening.'

Dr Vaughan had not exaggerated. A substantial body of distinguished men and women had come forward to support the campaign, from literary men like H. G. Wells and Arnold Bennett to philosophers and scientists such as Bertrand Russell and Julian Huxley. The medical profession was represented by Lord Dawson and others, and the Church by Dean Inge and some of the more enlightened bishops. The Chairman, Mrs Eva Hubback, announced that the time had come to demand state birth-control facilities, and a strongly worded resolution had been drawn up to send to the Minister of Health.

Phyllis heard the roar of consent to this as she entered the hall, but her eyes went straight to George Steynes sitting on the platform; Mildred Vaughan sat near to him, but there was no sign of any other young woman, so Miss Dickenson must be somewhere in the body of the hall, Phyllis thought. She watched as Mrs Hubback finished her speech and George rose to applaud, as did the whole assembly. He stood and smiled and clapped – and then he looked down at the crowd and saw Phyllis, a slender figure dressed in blue, standing right in the middle of the cheering throng.

That was the moment when George Steynes saw his destiny, and knew what he had to do. He did not hesitate, and Phyllis watched open-mouthed as he dashed to the side of the platform, not caring who saw him as he leaped down to the floor of the hall. She could no longer see him above the heads of the standing crowd, but simply stood stock-still, waiting for him to reappear, for she somehow knew that he was elbowing his way through the packed hall towards her.

And then he was there at her side.

'Phyllis, oh, Phyllis, you're here.' He took her hand in his, and she looked up into his face. She saw the longing in his grey eyes.

'I must speak to you, Phyllis – don't run away. I have to talk to you. Let's get out of here. Give me your arm – let me carry that bag – oh, for the love of heaven, come outside and let me talk to you!'

'But, George, what about Miss Dickenson?' she gasped as he drew her along through the crowd towards the exit that led out into Storey's Gate.

'She's not here. Neither is my mother. But *you* are, Phyllis, and I'm not letting you go again.'

Had he taken leave of his senses? No! Something like hope began to stir in her heart. Did this strange behaviour on the part of a normally careful and methodical young man mean a change of mind – and a change of heart? This was no wish-fulfilling daydream on a beach, this was a very real, very noisy gathering of people with a common cause in mind.

454

Outside the hall, he continued to keep a tight hold upon her. 'Come on, Phyllis, this way,' he panted, almost dragging her along Birdcage Walk and into St James's Park, green and beautiful with the trees decked in their new foliage and the sun glinting on the water of the lake. Only then did he slacken his pace and lead her across the grass to a seat beside the water.

'Oh, what it means to see you again, Phyllis! Mildred told me you were coming, or else I wouldn't have been there.'

'You wouldn't have been there?' she echoed, remembering how Mildred had made her promise to attend at some point in the afternoon.

'No. They want me to give it up. My mother has never really liked me championing such a cause, and then when the Dickensons came out and said they didn't think it a respectable issue for a man to get himself involved in, I had practically decided to withdraw from the SPBCC. I hinted as much to Mildred, and she made me promise to come to this conference before I finally bowed out – and then I saw you. Oh, Phyllis, I saw you and knew that I still need you – still love you. My dearest, darling Phyllis, I've missed you so much – oh, so much.'

And there on the park bench he took her in his arms, just as he had done on that other public seat two years ago. She put her arms up around his neck and they held each other close for a long, long minute in which their true desires were made clear to them.

'I did it for the best, George. I didn't want to hold you back in your career,' she whispered.

'I don't care about my career, not if it means losing the woman I love – and in any case, I didn't get voted in! But I've been at fault too, Phyllis, my love. I've

455

been too much influenced by my mother. She meant it for the best, but I shall have to let her know that I must make my own decisions from now on. And one of them is that I need *you*, Phyllis, not just because you're thoughtful and sensible and share an interest in the campaign we've both supported, but because I love you, and don't want to go through life without you. I've been a fool, but – but – Phyllis, may I ask you again – will you marry me?'

She could hardly speak through her tears of joy, the sheer incredibility of this April afternoon, but he had his answer in the radiant smile she gave him.

'Yes, George, yes! I've learned a lot too – but what about your engagement?'

'I'll be doing Letitia a favour, and her parents will agree when they know that I intend to continue to fight for state birth control. If she sues me for breach of promise I shall just have to weather the storm. My mother won't be pleased, but she'll come round to it eventually, and I shall tell her gently that I must marry whom I please and not a wife she's chosen for me. Oh, Phyllis my darling, tell me this isn't just a wonderful dream!'

For answer she hugged him closer and whispered, 'I love you, George, and it's no dream.'

When he heard that she was planning to get a train to North Camp for the weekend, he almost jumped off the seat in his eagerness to offer her a lift instead.

'I'll take you, Phyllis. I've got an Austin 7 now, and it's a beauty. Listen, I'll telephone the Queen's Hotel to book myself a room for tonight and tomorrow, and when I see your parents I shall humbly beg their pardon for allowing you to break off our engagement – I should have put up more of a fight! – and I'll telephone Mother to say I shan't be home until

456

Sunday. There'll be time enough to tell her the reason why.'

'Don't hurt her, George. She worships you, just as my mother worships Saul, and I do understand how she feels.' In her newly discovered happiness, Phyllis had no wish whatever to upset Mrs Steynes more than was necessary; in fact she felt deeply sorry for the old lady, sitting among the ruins of her plans for George's June wedding. 'I just hope that one day she and I may be on good terms. Perhaps when she sees that you're happy, she'll accept me.'

'Oh, Phyllis, do you think your parents will have any time for me at all?'

'They'll be very glad to see you again, George, I'm sure of it, especially when they see how happy I am! I didn't tell them much, but they know it was I who broke it off, not you.' She gave a chuckle. 'And you'll see a big change in Saul. He's seven now, and has very definite ideas of his own. I think my mother finds him rather a handful at times, but Dad's very good with him. He realises that Saul's growing up and needs a man's presence.' She suppressed a sigh, and George was at once concerned.

'Phyllis dear, if you want to have Saul to live with us, that's perfectly all right with me. I'd be happy to be the male presence in his life – in fact I'd look on him as a son.'

'George, you're too good,' she told him with a grateful look. 'But you know, I couldn't take Saul away from my mother. I honestly believe that it would kill her – or put her back to being the broken woman she was when my brothers were lost. I'd love to have my son living with us, but I can't see it happening. If we could have him to stay with us on a fairly regular basis, that would be a good compromise.'

'Then that's what we'll do, my darling, and see how we go on from there,' said George. 'As long as you know that he'll always have a home with us if he needs one. And now, when are we going to be married?' He was suddenly quite boyish, and his eyes sparkled. 'As soon as you like, as far as I'm concerned!'

'But we've got to have somewhere to live, George.' She spoke rather timidly, because she was unable to imagine sharing Number 15 Nelson Square with his mother.

'What about a flat to start with? There are some new apartments up in St John's Wood.'

'Oh, I don't know – aren't they a bit expensive?' She hesitated because she wanted to stay in Lambeth if possible. 'Dr Bazley's got a nice home off the Kennington Road, and I think there's one for sale nearby. We must take time to have a good look round, George.'

'As long as we don't take too much time. Remember, we've lost two valuable years!'

There were many causes for rejoicing during that summer. Dr Vaughan and Lady Dacre clapped their hands and shouted 'Bravo!' when they were told of the re-engagement of George and Phyllis, and although there was predictable fury at The Old Lodge and angry tears at Nelson Square, the Dickensons soon persuaded themselves that Letitia had had a lucky escape from a man who persisted in associating his name with something as disgusting as birth control for the ignorant lower orders.

The Central Hall conference had far-reaching consequences. As Mildred Vaughan had predicted, Mr Arthur Greenwood could not ignore the resolution sent to his Ministry, and just three months later a certain departmental memo was issued and began to make its way around the corridors of power. Headed 'Ministry of Health Memo 153/MCW', it conceded that local authority maternity and child welfare clinics should be allowed to give birth-control instructions to mothers whose health would suffer by further pregnancies.

'We've done it, we've done it, and without any Act of Parliament!' crowed Mildred Vaughan, literally dancing down the length of Edith Cavell Ward in Theodora House. 'Ten years of fighting hostility and prejudice, and we've won our first big breakthrough – hip, hip, hooray!'

There was a round of clapping and laughter from the women in the beds, and smiles were on every face, with a few exceptions, like Sister Pollock, who was absolutely convinced that her colleagues were making a great mistake. Mr Poole shook hands with Dr Vaughan and warned her not to expect too much too soon, but added his felicitations to her and Miss Bird.

As for Miss Bird, she walked around in a golden glow of happiness, warmed by her future husband's love and care. Their wedding date was fixed for Saturday, 26 July, and their honeymoon was booked at a small hotel on Hayling Island, so as to be in daily contact with the bungalow where Saul and his grand-parents would be staying. Ernest Bird had decided to shut the shop for a week this year, to attend his daughter's wedding and then take a holiday.

Everything seemed to be going right for Phyllis and George in this momentous year, as if fate wanted to make up for the sadness and separation of the past. A small but pretty Victorian house had come on the market in West Square, not too far from Theodora House and in the area that Phyllis had learned to love and look upon as her own. George had put a down payment on it, the contract was signed, and it would be their first home.

If the happy couple had planned a quiet wedding at St Martha's Church with only close relatives and friends present, they did not get their wish, for the church was filled to overflowing, and a loud cheer went up when the bride and groom appeared, he in a sober dark grey suit and she in a powder-blue dress with a flowery straw hat.

'Cor, ain't she a picture!' exclaimed Mrs Williams to her mother, and Phyllis's own parents could only agree, while Saul stared in surprise at his beautiful mummy. Mrs Steynes senior could not bring herself to attend. Two uncles, one on his father's side and one on his mother's, came to wish George joy in his marriage, accompanied by their wives and a sprinkling of his cousins, but the absence of his mother cast the only shadow over an otherwise perfect day. The bride's father gave her away, Dr Vaughan and Miss Anderson were bridesmaids, and Mr Poole made a very appreciative speech at the wedding reception, which was held in St Martha's Parish Hall and spilled out into the vicarage garden. As many midwives who could take time off from their duties came to the wedding, and the older Kemp children tucked into sausages and meat pies, discovering a new and interesting playmate in Saul Bird.

'Eat up, it's all been paid for,' they were told by a swaggering twelve-year-old Billy Webb, who had overheard his mother speculating on whether

George Steynes or Mr Bird had footed the bill, or whether they'd gone halves – but either way, it was as good a spread as she'd seen in a long while. In fact, everybody agreed that it was a wedding to remember.

How far should we intrude on the new husband and wife when they found themselves alone together in their Hayling Island hotel room? Only long enough to assure ourselves of their perfect happiness.

George had been feeling secretly nervous and not quite sure how he should approach his wife, knowing that her past experience had been brutal, and his own was limited; he warned himself to be both careful and patient with her, taking his time and possibly not fully consummating the marriage on the first night.

Yet when the hour came, Love showed him the way, and he was surprised by Phyllis's swift response to his tentative advances. Her ardour quickly roused him to greater passion, and they were carried up together to reach a pinnacle of shared exultation that astonished them both by its intensity: they seemed to be at one with each other in the summer night, floating far above the starlit sea.

So we shall not linger, but leave them sleeping in each other's arms . . .

Chapter 25

The Labour administration under MacDonald proved disappointing. The promises to reduce unemployment and shorten the dole queues were not fulfilled, and there were early predictions that the government would not last. George Steynes refused to join the condemnation, saying that no government would be able to withstand the disastrous economic situation in the USA and Europe – in Germany two and a half million were out of work – and with such a tiny majority it was inevitable that MacDonald's party appeared weak and ineffectual. By 1931 there was a political crisis, and with the threat of national bankruptcy looming, desperate measures had to be taken: a National Government was formed, a coalition headed jointly by MacDonald and Baldwin in an uneasy Labour-Tory alliance.

In this first year of their marriage, young Mr and Mrs Steynes lived in a world of domestic happiness, in contrast to the social unrest all around them. They both worked very hard, he as political correspondent for the *Daily Chronicle*, with the prospect of becoming the next editor, while she was much involved in establishing the birth-control services at maternity and child welfare centres, some of which were more co-operative than others. She ran classes for nurses, mostly from the ranks of those who were married and therefore unable to practise full time in hospitals. For the first few months she was available to help with midwifery on the district when the staff were hard-pressed, but at some time in the spring she realised that she and George were to be blessed with a child at Christmas; she was now thirty-five, and George would not allow her to continue working, so concerned was he for the health and welfare of his wife and child.

Saul came to stay with them on alternate week-ends, and for half of the school summer holiday, and although Mrs Bird was not happy about his visits to a capital city torn by demonstrations and riots, the boy was always thrilled by the comings and goings at the house in West Square: Mummy and Uncle George had a large circle of acquaintances.

It was Lady Dacre who first said that George ought to stand for Parliament again.

'Walworth North and Bermondsey was a practice run for you, George,' she said. 'You learned a lot from it, and now that you've got a good wife behind you –' she looked towards Phyllis and smiled – 'you should try again. What about Lambeth South? Get yourself selected and be ready for when this National Government comes to grief. It's already tottering!'

Phyllis was filled with apprehension, and all her fears returned to trouble her: that her known history would seriously hinder her husband's chances. She dreaded the thought of him losing again. Yet Lady Dacre's words had fired his enthusiasm, and when he was adopted by Lambeth South as their candidate his way seemed clear. He was determined to go for it. The fall of the coalition came sooner than expected. In September Britain went off the gold standard, and in October a general election was called, less than two and a half years after the last one.

Phyllis was seven months pregnant, and secretly

463

thankful to have this excuse for not playing a part in her husband's election campaign. In normal circumstances she would have stood on platforms beside him, addressed women's groups, given out leaflets and canvassed in the familiar streets. As it was, she could only watch from the sidelines, praying that he would not be disappointed or humiliated. George's mother now visited West Square to take tea and make rather stilted conversation with the expectant parents, and they made return visits to Nelson Square, usually on Sundays when George was most likely to be free; but the old lady never spoke of the approaching election and Phyllis suspected that both she and her mother-in-law would be heartily glad when it was all over.

When polling day arrived, and the people turned out in droves to cast their votes, a fog of doubt settled over Phyllis's spirits. George had assured her so often that she meant more to him than any career, in or out of Parliament, and yet she trembled inwardly as they set out in the car to the town hall. The polls had closed at nine, and counting began at once. Lambeth South was one of the earlier constituencies to announce results, and Phyllis waited at the back of the platform in her voluminous navy-blue maternity smock with its neat white collar and cuffs. She wore a navy hat, gloves and shoes, a contrast to the smart outfits of the other wives whose husbands waited nervously for the returning officer to appear. She caught sight of her mother-in-law in the hall, accompanied by her brother; the old lady had not been able to stay away, but kept herself apart.

It had just gone eleven o'clock when the councillor acting as returning officer came to the front of the platform to give the result of the voting, and a hush fell upon the packed assembly.

'The numbers of votes cast are as follows . . .' Phyllis felt light-headed as the figures were read out, hardly making sense in her ears. Eight thousand odd for the Labour man, eleven thousand for the Tory, and fourteen and a half thousand for the Liberal candidate.

'And so I hereby declare that George Griswold Steynes has been duly elected as Member of Parliament for Lambeth South.'

An enormous cheer went up, and Phyllis rose to her feet as George stepped forward to acknowledge the acclaim of his supporters. When the cheering had died down a little, he cleared his throat and made a short speech of appreciation.

'I want to thank all of you who have trusted me with your vote, and all who have worked so hard for this result,' he said with some emotion. 'I now pledge myself to your service, and with God's help I shall endeavour to bring about some much-needed changes.'

There were further cheers, and then George turned and held out his hand to Phyllis, who was lurking self-consciously behind the returning officer and others on the platform. He gave her an encouraging smile, knowing that she felt shy about her condition.

'And with my wife beside me, I shall be even better able to serve Lambeth South to the best of my ability,' he added, raising his voice a little. 'Come here, my dear – ladies and gentlemen, my wife, Mrs Phyllis Steynes!'

As she stepped forward to take her place beside him, nobody was prepared for what followed: the cheers, the shouts, the throwing of caps in the air, the sheer volume of noise was overwhelming.

'Miss Bird! Miss Bird! Nurse Bird!' they roared. 'Hooray for Nurse Bird!'

'Phyllis!' shrieked Rose Rawson, and some of the mothers and midwives present also cheered for Phyllis, for Phyllis Bird, for Phyllis Steynes; arms were waving, feet were stamping, voices were hooraying and hurrahing.

'Bravo!' shouted Mr Poole, beaming and clapping, and Mildred Vaughan echoed him, while Mrs Webb and Billy led the singing of 'For she's a jolly good fellow – and so say all of us!'

Tears filled Phyllis's eyes, and she held out her hand to George's mother and uncle, beckoning them to the platform. The old lady too was in tears, but Phyllis embraced her like a daughter, and George kissed his wife and his mother, which brought forth another round of cheering; it went on and on, until Phyllis thought it would never stop.

To find out more about Maggie Bennett and other fantastic Arrow authors why not read *The Inside Story* – our newsletter featuring all of our saga authors.

To join our mailing list to receive the newsletter and other information* write with your name and address to:

The Inside Story
The Marketing Department
Arrow Books
20 Vauxhall Bridge Road
London
SW1V 2SA

*Your details will be held on a database so we can send you the newsletter(s) and information on other Arrow authors that you have indicated you wish to receive. Your details will not be passed to any third party. If you would like to receive information on other Random House authors please do let us know. If at any stage you wish to be deleted from our *The Inside Story* mailing list please let us know.

If you enjoyed A Child of Her Time, *why not try further Maggie Bennett titles, all available in Arrow . . .*

A Child's Voice Calling

Young Mabel Court, child of her mother's hasty marriage to a spendthrift, becomes 'little mother' to her brothers and sisters growing up in south London at the start of the twentieth century.

With poverty never far from the door, the battle to stay respectable is finally lost when the family breaks up in tragic circumstances, and Mabel is thrown upon the dubious mercy of her grandmother, the sinister Mimi Court, who has her own dark secrets.

But faithful Harry Drover of the Salvation Army, in love with Mabel, gets an opportunity to prove his devotion when Mabel falls foul of the law and has to fight for her own survival . . .

A Child at the Door

Orphan Mabel Court's dream comes true when she enters the Booth Street Poor Law Infirmary as a probationer nurse. But it is August 1914, and her world is about to be turned upside down.

She soon meets Norah McLoughlin, another probationer, and the two girls – together with Mabel's childhood friend Maudie, now a music-hall dancer – become firm friends.

As war rages across Europe, they try to keep their spirits up but when Mabel's fiancé Harry Drover is wounded at the battle of the Somme, Mabel realises that the life she and Harry had always hoped for is now an impossibility. Then when Maudie falls pregnant by an officer, and Norah's young man is lost at sea, all three girls are forced to face the fact that life will never be the same again . . .

A Carriage for the Midwife

Born into the squalor of the Ash-Pits, young Susan Lucket is determined to raise herself above the poverty of her childhood. Discovering she has a natural talent for nursing, she forges a new life for herself – and as an independent, unmarried midwife, she is a woman far ahead of her time.

But when Edward Calthorpe, youngest son of a privileged landowner, offers her marriage, the memory of her terrible childhood returns to haunt her. And when Edward's wayward brother seduces little Polly, her beloved younger sister – and then betrays her in the most brutal of ways – Susan faces losing everything she has struggled for . . .